Dear Reader,

Before I wrote *Silence of the Wolf*, I read about how scientists were of differing opinions on whether red wolves were a separate species. Some thought Eastern gray wolves and coyotes had mixed to create red wolves, and some thought red wolves had evolved separately. *Silence of the Wolf* was born of the idea to answer the question: Who came first, red wolves or gray wolves? And that's when I dove into the research that was available a decade ago. Now, with new research available, I'm back to the books, seeing what the scientists have to say.

When Eastern wolves in Canada, thought to be red wolves, came back in numbers, they quit mating with coyotes. In coastal Texas and Louisiana, red wolves have been located with the highest red wolf DNA, at 78 percent, despite no protection from coyote hybridization.

Biologists are breeding red wolves in captivity with Eastern wolves, but they grow tamer with every generation. Purely wild red wolves that have never been in captivity are quickly facing extinction.

Hybrids are really rare—according to scientists, less than 4 percent.

When scientists found ancient DNA for Eastern wolves, the DNA was not that of gray wolves. Biologists have tried to breed Western gray wolves with coyotes in captivity without a lot of success. One report, that was later disputed, claimed that red wolves have mostly coyote DNA.

In 2019, the U.S. Fish and Wildlife Service, backed by scientific evidence, met and acknowledged the red wolf as a true distinct species, named *Canis rufus*.

There still are some hybrids of the species with coyotes.

So for all my wolf lovers out there who adore the red wolves as much as I do, faith is restored that they really do exist and are not just the hybridization of gray wolves and coyotes. It still begs the question—which came first? Red wolves or gray wolves? At least, as far as my fun-loving wolf shifters are concerned, in a teasing way.

It is said that *Canis etruscus*—a species of canine that became extinct during the early Pleistocene Age—is the ancestor of the gray wolf. It has been described as a small, wolflike dog. You might wonder then about the dire wolf, which was as big as our current largest modern gray wolves. But the two wolves actually coexisted during the Ice Age. Then the dire wolves died off and the gray wolves carried on. As for red wolves? It's a mystery.

The study of genetics is fascinating. In the past, we would have had a harder time identifying where the wolves evolved from. DNA has helped to make that more possible!

No matter where our journey leads us in the world of wolves, I hope you enjoy that I try to include real-world happenings in my stories—some unbelievable, despite being true, but that makes it all the more fun for me—and hopefully for you!

That's how the *lupus garou* came to be.

Thanks for enjoying my books over all these years!

Terry Spear

Praise for Terry Spear

"Nobody does werewolf romances like Terry Spear. The romance sizzles, the plot boils, the mystery intrigues, and the characters shine."
—*The Royal Reviews* for *Silence of the Wolf*

"With nonstop action, thrilling suspense, danger, a beautiful setting, and well-drawn characters, this story will keep readers guessing right up to the very satisfying ending."
—*Romance Junkies* for *Silence of the Wolf*

"Yet another fantastic book from the amazing Terry Spear... The writing was excellent and the plot exciting with plenty of surprises."
—*The Romance Reviews* for *Silence of the Wolf*

"Ms. Spear is one of my go-to authors when I want to escape with a book guaranteed to entertain."
—*Long and Short Reviews* for *Silence of the Wolf*

"The vulpine couple's chemistry crackles off the page, but the real strength of the book lies in Spear's depiction of pack power dynamics."
—*Publishers Weekly* for *Heart of the Wolf*

"Essential reading for werewolf-romance fans."
—*Booklist* for *Alpha Wolf Need Not Apply*

"The perfect, upbeat escape that gives you a lot of action, intrigue, sweet romance, steamy moments...will leave you sighing and fanning yourself."
—*Fresh Fiction* for *You Had Me at Wolf*

"Wolfy fun and romantic goodness."
—*Harlequin Junkie* for *Silver Wolf Christmas*

Also by Terry Spear

RED WOLF
Joy to the Wolves

WOLFF BROTHERS
You Had Me at Wolf
Jingle Bell Wolf

SEAL WOLF
A SEAL in Wolf's Clothing
A SEAL Wolf Christmas
SEAL Wolf Hunting
SEAL Wolf in Too Deep
SEAL Wolf Undercover
SEAL Wolf Surrender
SEAL Wolf Pursuit (novella)

HEART OF THE SHIFTER
You Had Me at Jaguar

BILLIONAIRE WOLF
Billionaire in Wolf's Clothing
A Billionaire Wolf for Christmas
Night of the Billionaire Wolf

HIGHLAND WOLF
Heart of the Highland Wolf
A Howl for a Highlander
A Highland Werewolf Wedding
Hero of a Highland Wolf
A Highland Wolf Christmas
The Wolf Wore Plaid

SILVER TOWN WOLF
Destiny of the Wolf
Wolf Fever
Dreaming of the Wolf
Silence of the Wolf
A Silver Wolf Christmas
Alpha Wolf Need Not Apply
Between a Wolf and a Hard Place
All's Fair in Love and Wolf
*Silver Town Wolf: Home for the
Holidays*
Tangling with the Wolf (novella)

HEART OF THE JAGUAR
Savage Hunter
Jaguar Fever
Jaguar Hunt
Jaguar Pride
A Very Jaguar Christmas

WHITE WOLF
*Dreaming of a White Wolf
Christmas*
Flight of the White Wolf

HEART OF THE WOLF
Heart of the Wolf
To Tempt the Wolf
Legend of the White Wolf
Seduced by the Wolf
Night of the Wolf (novella)
Day of the Wolf (novella)

SILENCE
OF THE WOLF

TERRY
SPEAR

sourcebooks
casablanca

Published by Sourcebooks Casablanca, an imprint of Sourcebooks
P.O. Box 4410, Naperville, Illinois 60567-4410
(630) 961-3900
sourcebooks.com

Originally published in 2014 in the United States of America by
Sourcebooks Casablanca, an imprint of Sourcebooks.

Printed and bound in Canada.
MBP 10 9 8 7 6 5 4 3 2 1

To a writer I had never met, Bonnie Gill, who asked if I'd share a room with her at RWA Fantasy, Futuristic, and Paranormal's first conference, and of course I said, "Sure!" We spent long hours talking about writing and chasing down crazy clues all over New Orleans for a game—missed seeing the man wearing the nun's habit and still won! And witnessed the bouncing truck. That was the highlight of our vampire and ghost tour. Believe me, you don't want to know about the bouncing truck. Keep looking forward and moving forward, and follow your dreams!

CHAPTER 1

WITH A SNOWSTORM THREATENING, TOM SILVER EXAMINED the tracks of the second wolf reported this week by a disgruntled farmer. The tracks circled the sheep pen and then loped off toward the woods. The farm was in the Silver Town werewolf territory—not that the human farmers had a clue they lived in an area claimed by a pack of gray *lupus garou*.

Wearing an old jacket, hip-high rubber boots, and dungarees, farmer Bill Todd scowled at Tom. "Your brother said he'd take care of these wolves. Three weeks of threats to our sheep, and nothin's been done about it."

"We're looking for them," Tom assured him, standing to his full height.

"Sheep and calves are being threatened at different farms and ranches," Bill railed. "Five. We can't be up all night patrolling for wolves all the time—and your brother said we wouldn't have to. I swear, if I see a wolf, I'm going to shoot it dead before it gets to my livestock."

"We'll get the wolves that are doing this," Tom reassured him. They had to—before a farmer or rancher shot an innocent were-wolf or a wolf that was all wolf. He glanced at the tracks the wolves had left.

"The three of them arrived before sunrise. I heard a noise, came running out here with my rifle and a camp light, and shined it right into their glowing green eyes. When I set the lantern down and aimed the rifle, they raced off. I took a shot, but the damned weapon jammed."

"We'll take care of them. Do you mind if I leave my pickup

truck here for a while?" Tom didn't wait for an answer. He immediately stalked through the snow, tracking the wolves.

Bill called after him, "Hey, a snowstorm's headed this way. You can't hunt them now."

Tom kept going. He appreciated the farmers' and ranchers' frustrations, even though Tom's oldest brother, Darien Silver, took responsibility for their losses as the owner of the land the farmers leased. The pack couldn't afford to have humans accidentally shooting werewolves or harmless wolves. Some pack members were too newly turned to have a lot of control over their shifting, particularly with the full moon approaching in another week.

Tom followed the trail, which seemed to indicate only one wolf had run this way. Tom knew better. One would precede the others, leaving what looked like one set of tracks to disguise how many were in the "pack." The trail the lead wolf left would also make it easier for the others to follow.

Flurries whipped into a thicker curtain of snow. Tom wanted desperately to shift and run the wolves down. But his brother had ordered that none of the pack shift within five miles of farms and ranches until they resolved the matter.

Tom had only managed to cover a mile and a half from Bill Todd's spread when his cell jingled. He didn't have to look at the ID to know Darien was calling him and would order him home. "Yeah, Darien?" Tom continued to watch the trees as he followed the wolf tracks.

"Bill Todd called me. Said that fool youngest brother of mine tore off, looking for wolf tracks—*unarmed*—and the snow's coming down hard, so there's barely any visibility. He said, and I quote, 'No damn sheep is worth the life of a good man.'"

Amused that Bill would say that, as much as he loved his sheep and wanted the wolves dead, Tom paused. The snowflakes grew fatter, nearly obliterating any open space between them. The snow quickly filled up each of the paw prints left behind.

Breathing heavily, Tom picked up his pace, not wanting to stop.

"Tom, we'll get them. Some other time. I want you home. The snow's coming down hard enough that you'll lose track of them soon. Visibility is worsening."

"We have to stop this, Darien."

"I know. We will. Come home." Darien sounded like he was asking, but Tom knew better. His brother was the pack leader and his word was law.

Tom stopped and smelled the air, hating that he couldn't catch any whiff of which wolves were causing the trouble. He surveyed the Colorado blue spruce trees for any movement. He felt in his bones that the wolves were watching him, waiting to see if he'd keep searching.

Wolves didn't normally attack people. But Tom and the rest of their wolf pack suspected these were not wolves but rogue werewolves—and that meant all bets were off.

"Next time, I'm not stopping for anything," Tom warned both Darien and the wolves that might be observing him.

He saw movement. A gray wolf's tail rose for a second as the wolf turned and bounded through the woods.

Tom took off running, forgetting he hadn't ended the call with his brother. Darien could hear Tom's heavy breathing and his quickened pace as he stomped over the frozen ground.

"Tom, if I have to—"

"I saw one of them, damn it."

"Who was it? Did you recognize—"

"Just the flash of a gray tail. I don't know who it was."

"You can't run him down. Not as a human. It could be a trap."

Tom stopped running, swore under his breath, and again watched the woods.

"If three of them are responsible, you won't be any match for them even if you shift."

Tom hesitated.

"Damn it, Tom."

"All right. Tomorrow, if we have fresh tracks, I'm hunting them down once and for all."

———————————

Elizabeth Wildwood had barely arrived in Silver Town before the snowstorm hit. Surprised the owner of Hastings Bed and Breakfast was a gray wolf, Elizabeth was thankful the sweet woman didn't seem to mind what Elizabeth was—or wasn't. She had four more days' leave from her job at the *Canyon Press* in Texas to write an article on skiing at a Colorado resort. But that wasn't the only reason why she was here.

She quickly retired to her room and called North Redding, a red wolf from Bruin's former pack, which was now led by another red wolf Elizabeth didn't know. Technically, her father had also belonged to the pack, but she had never been part of it. North had been the only one from the red pack to treat her without scorn. Elizabeth hoped to connect with him despite the storm, but she wouldn't go to his place to meet him. His home was too close to where her uncle lived.

"North, I just got in. We can meet tomorrow. I'll give you the time and place in the morning."

"You said you would arrive tomorrow. You were supposed to stay with me. You agreed I'd pick you up at the airport and bring you to my house."

"I never agreed to that, North. I said I'd decide when I arrived in Colorado." She didn't want to say she didn't trust him. Truth was, she didn't trust her uncle. If North let it slip that she was in the area, Uncle Quinton or her half brother, Sefton, might try to finish what they had started last time. Especially considering *why* she was here.

"You're afraid I'll tell your uncle Quinton that you're here?

Is that it? If he knew what I planned to share with you, he'd kill *me*!" North was angry that Elizabeth didn't believe in him, but she couldn't. He might not be working with her uncle and half brother, but he *was* still in their pack. It was just safer this way.

"I flew in early ahead of the snowstorm. Why won't you at least tell me what the evidence is?" she said to placate him.

"Can't."

"Fine. Talk to you tomorrow." She had hoped never to return to that part of the country. After her parents were murdered, it hadn't been home for her. It never would be. Killing her uncle wouldn't make things right, but it had to be done—for her parents, for her, and for the pack she had never belonged to.

The next morning, with eight inches of new snowfall, Tom Silver knew he wouldn't be able to track the wolves who were stalking farmers' calves and sheep. Not when the culprits left no scent.

Tom's middle triplet brother, Jake, was dealing with problems at their leather goods factory. Their eldest brother and pack leader, Darien, joined Tom at the floor-to-ceiling sunroom window as he stared out at the beauty of the snow decorating the boughs of the pine trees and making them dip to the snow-covered ground. A fire roared in the fireplace, the room as cozy as a wolf's den with its soft, wraparound brown velour chairs set around a marble coffee table. The views of the outdoors made the room feel as though it was open to the wilderness.

Tom cast a nod in his brother's direction. "Morning, Darien."

Humans often mistook them for each other because they were so similar in build and appearance. Wolves smelled the difference. None of *them* made that mistake. Darien had the darkest hair and eyes of the three, and Tom was the fairest—"of them all," Jake liked to joke.

"Hey, Tom. I know you wanted to go after the wolves again today. I doubt you'd find much of anything." Darien wore Lelandi's pink apron over a brown wool sweater and had a few splatters of oatmeal on his blue jeans. This was his usual attire, oatmeal mush and all, when he fed his triplet babies—two boys and a girl. A couple of gobs of cereal clung to strands of his dark-brown hair.

He often took care of the kids in the morning so that his mate, Lelandi, the smartest, most effective psychologist in the area, could see clients. Not to mention that she was the only *lupus garou* psychologist around.

Tom swore he would buy his brother a manlier apron when he had the time. He glanced down at a splotch of oatmeal on his brother's sheepskin slipper boot. "I'm glad to know I'm not the only one who looks that messy after feeding your brood."

Darien gave him an elusive smile, warning him that when Tom found a mate, *he* was in for the same trouble. "Two of the ski patrol are out sick today with the flu, and the resort could use you up there."

That got Tom's attention and he stiffened, alert and wary. Every time one of them got sick with flu-like symptoms, they worried about the wolf getting a virus that would prevent their shifting from wolf to human form.

"Don't worry. It's not anything like the cases of 'wolf fever' we had before," Darien said quickly. "Jake will relieve you at noon. And a couple of other things…" He cleared his throat.

Tom couldn't read his brother's expression. Wolves paid attention to slight shifts in body language, and he could usually tell what his brother was thinking. But not this time. Which meant something was up and Tom wouldn't like it.

"First, Anthony and Cody Woodcroft are on the slopes today. Their dad said that he wanted the ski patrol to kinda watch out for 'em. If they get into *any* trouble at all, he wants their passes pulled and them off the slopes. He also wants to be notified at once."

"Okay, can do." The boys had gotten into trouble before, mainly for participating in high-risk adventures, but Tom had never heard of them doing anything unsafe or against the rules on the slopes. Since it was the first item on the list Darien wanted to talk about, Tom figured it was the least problematic. "The other thing?"

"Bertha Hastings said she has a guest at the B and B doing a story on our ski resort. She missed the ski shuttle and Bertha wanted to know if you could run her up to the slopes, since you were going that way."

Tom narrowed his eyes a little. "Is she a wolf?" Bertha wasn't beyond matchmaking. He could imagine Bertha had delayed the woman on purpose so she missed the shuttle.

"She is and she isn't."

"She either *is* or she *isn't*," Tom countered.

Darien looked serious now. "Let's just say she's part wolf. We can't put the town off-limits to visitors, but a woman like that could cause trouble for the pack."

"Part wolf?" Tom echoed, frowning.

"I'm sure you can resist this woman's charms. She's up here doing a story on a ski resort. I don't trust the other bachelor wolves in the pack to leave her alone unless one of us takes her in hand to signal the others to keep their paws to themselves."

Tom understood why Darien wouldn't take care of the matter himself. Running a pack and the town and raising three toddlers kept him busy. Still, he didn't like it. "Why couldn't—"

"Jake's busy and he's mated. That leaves the situation up to you to handle. They'll listen to you and back off."

Tom had thought he would be tracking the mysterious wolves who had been sneaking around their territory—a much more suitable task for a pack subleader. Now he had to babysit a couple of male teen wolves and a woman who wasn't quite a wolf?

He took a deep breath. Still, he knew his brother's reasoning was sound. Wolf-shifter females were rarer than males in any pack—and jealously guarded too. The Silver pack had been through some trouble of that sort with female shifters from the neighboring red pack. The men in the red wolf pack felt that the gray wolves should have had no claim to the red she-wolves. Tom knew Darien would like to avoid that sort of situation again with this newcomer.

"All right. But I'll be patrolling this morning, so I won't be able to watch the teens *or* the woman all that much."

"Alert the ski patrol to watch the boys and let you know if they do anything that's unsafe. The others can be your eyes and ears. When our bachelor males see that the woman's *with* you—so to speak—the word will spread and hopefully no one will hassle her. Learn when she's leaving the area and work yourself into her schedule. If she doesn't leave the slopes until later this afternoon when you're free, you can be her ski buddy."

Tom raised a brow.

"You know what I mean. Make sure you're with her until she leaves. I don't mean you have to stay with her overnight."

"Not happening." Although one-night stands with humans were acceptable for wolf shifters, Tom didn't dare show any interest in a human around here. In this town, every wolf would hear of it. Too much of a problem with rumor control. And a part wolf? What the hell did that mean anyway? "I'm off."

Tom threw on his parka, grabbed his gloves, and headed out. He had no doubt a woman who was part she-wolf wouldn't interest him in the least.

———

Decorated in Queen Anne–style furniture, Elizabeth's bedroom at the B and B made her feel like she'd been transported to the past.

The chairs had clawed feet, and everything from the footboards to the canopy over the bed was draped in ecru lace.

Elizabeth paced across the elegant bedroom. She had called North to arrange a time and place to meet with him. He had agreed to hand over the evidence of her uncle's complicity in murdering her parents in exchange for the deed to her family horse farm, but the red wolf was *not* happy.

"What do you mean you're in *Silver Town*?" North snarled.

"I'm writing the article for my newspaper here. Bring the evidence to the ski resort. You should be able to arrive there by two. Right?"

North didn't say anything, but she could hear his highly agitated heavy breathing on the line.

"I won't meet you at your place," Elizabeth continued, disregarding how irritated he was with her. "I'll be at the Timberline Ski Lodge at two."

"You couldn't have picked a worse place for me to meet with you." North finally let out his breath. "If I have any trouble getting there—the road conditions are bad due to the snowstorm—I'll give you a ring."

"All right. See you this afternoon otherwise." She ended the call and left the room to join Bertha, the owner of the B and B, in the kitchen for breakfast.

She hadn't realized the B and B was run by a gray wolf couple, but she'd been fortunate that the husband was off on a trip somewhere and his wife was really nice to her. She thought maybe Bertha was just an oddity, but then again, maybe because Elizabeth wasn't a gray wolf, Bertha didn't care *what* she was.

"Good morning, Elizabeth," Bertha greeted her. The woman had springy silver curls and a round face and a cherub smile that reminded Elizabeth of Mrs. Claus. She wore a colorful burgundy and blue floral dress that matched the bouquets of flowers sitting on the dining-room table, kitchen bar, and tables in the common room. Ivies wound around wrought-iron plant stands, and small ficus trees were grouped next to the big windows that looked out on a tree-filled yard blanketed in snow.

"Good morning. The kitchen smells delightful." Elizabeth sat down at the table covered in white lace to have a cup of steaming-hot chocolate and a freshly baked cinnamon roll. The frosting melted over the top and dripped down the sides.

The scent of cinnamon filled the kitchen, and Elizabeth took in another deep breath. Just breathing in the sweet, sugary smell was bound to pack on the pounds.

"Are you sure the ski patroller won't be too put out about having to drop by and pick me up?" Elizabeth asked before she took a bite of the homemade cinnamon roll. If she didn't ski enough to burn up the calories on the slopes, she would *have* to run in her wolf coat in the woods tonight.

"No, Tom has to drive right by here to get to the slopes. His brother Darien said Tom works until noon and would bring you home anytime you're ready."

"He doesn't have to do that. I can take the shuttle."

The front door opened, bells jingling, and though Elizabeth couldn't see the new arrival, she assumed it was her ride. She didn't rise from the table, not wanting to appear too anxious or foolish if it wasn't Tom.

"Tom, is that you?" Bertha called out. "We're in the kitchen."

"Yeah, is the lady ready?" Tom sounded a little gruff, annoyed, put out.

Just like Elizabeth had assumed he'd be. She should have called a cab, if they even *had* cabs in Silver Town.

Tom strode into the kitchen as if he was on a mission and ready to get it over with.

He was tall, and his light-brown windswept hair and shadow of a beard gave him a rugged look. His cheeks were full of color from the cold. His eyes were the same rich shade of light brown as his hair, and they were instantly locked on hers.

He took in a deep breath, and she did too, in a wolf's way of determining how someone felt. Instantly, she knew he wasn't all human.

She got a whole lot more of a perspective than just emotions.

He was one hot-looking *gray wolf*. And that could mean trouble for her.

CHAPTER 2

TOM SILVER STARED AT THE WOMAN. SHE WAS *TOO* A WOLF. HE took another deep breath of the cinnamon-filled air, of the woman's sweet scent of red wolf…and something else. *Coyote.*

She was petite like a red wolf, but more than unusual because she wasn't all wolf. He'd never met a wolf-coyote mix before. Never heard of a coyote shifter. Now he wondered if the coyotes he'd seen that dared encroach on their territory were shifters, not just plain old coyotes.

He immediately thought of the Native American legends of Coyote, the trickster god, full of mischief, a thief, wily and sneaky. *And* a shape-shifter. Maybe that was where the tales had come from, based in part on the truth, just as werewolf tales of old were.

The lady's hair was a mass of shiny, dark-red curls. Her eyes were a clear blue-green, her skin ivory except for a pale smattering of tiny red freckles barely visible across the bridge of her nose and cheeks. She was a busty little thing. The sweater was formfitting— the style that showed off a woman's curves. And she had them in abundance.

He glanced at Bertha. She gave him one of her warmest match-making smiles.

Tom barely avoided shaking his head.

"This is Elizabeth Wildwood from Canyon, Texas. Elizabeth, meet Tom Silver."

"Thank you for taking me to the resort," Elizabeth said quickly, her expression wary, her heartbeat ratcheting up a couple of notches. She looked as astonished to learn he was a gray wolf as he was to learn what she was. She must not have known Silver Town was wolf-run.

He smelled a tangy scent on her that revealed her concern. If she worried that he intended to hit on her, she needn't bother. A woman who lived much closer to home would have appealed more.

He let out his breath and said to Elizabeth, "Are you ready to go?"

"Yes, um, let me wash my hands real quick." Elizabeth leaped to her feet. Without waiting for him to move out of her way, she brushed past him to get to the kitchen sink.

His gaze lingered on the formfitting black ski pants that revealed her shapely ass and legs. Fur-topped snow boots reached to her knees, and her aqua sweater zipped up to her chin.

The fact she was a shifter sure would be a wolf draw. At least he thought so, as pretty as she was. Bertha raised her brows at him, her smile fixed. Why hadn't Darien filled him in? Tom had thought she might be a nonshifting human who had *lupus garou* roots, and that was why Darien had said she was *part* wolf. From what Tom understood, wolves were just as attracted to those non-shifters as to full-blooded *lupus garous*. The eager males might not be put off by Elizabeth's wolf-coyote heritage.

Elizabeth grabbed a parka off her chair, pulled it on, then snatched up a backpack. He led her to the front door.

"Have fun, you two," Bertha called out in a *much* too cheerful manner.

"Thanks," Elizabeth said back sweetly.

Having fun wasn't what Tom intended. Ensuring the Woodcroft boys stayed out of trouble and that the she-wolf coyote didn't get herself into a mess would be a job, not a fun excursion.

He glanced back at Bertha and tilted his chin down to give her a disapproving look.

Bertha's smile only broadened. Tom shook his head.

He held the door open for Elizabeth and tried *not* to take in her appearance again, but it was difficult not to—being the wolf that he was. She avoided looking at him, which made him believe she was a beta.

That brought his alpha nature to the forefront, protective and in charge.

He shut the door of the B and B, escorted Elizabeth to his pickup truck, and opened the passenger-side door.

She eyed the interior of his truck. "Bertha… Well, she said…"

"Yeah?" Tom wondered just what Bertha had said.

Elizabeth cleared her throat.

He waited.

She finally let out her warm cinnamon-scented breath, which misted when it mixed with the icy air, and turned to gaze up at him, her eyes so striking that it was as if he were looking into a crystal-clear blue-green lake. "Bertha said you could hang around to bring me back to the B and B later, but I'll just take the shuttle."

Without waiting for him to respond, she got into the vehicle and looked through the windshield as if that was the end of the matter.

"I'm fine with bringing you back here." He shut the door, then hurried around to the driver's side.

He didn't know how he would manage to work ski patrol without thinking of *this* she-wolf up on the slopes by herself. He could imagine all the bachelor males in their pack hot-wolfing it down the slopes to get her attention and all the injuries that could result.

Darien was right. Tom would have to become her ski buddy if she stayed on the slopes this afternoon. He wouldn't leave her on her own until he returned her to the B and B tonight.

She didn't say anything as he took the road to the Silver Town Ski Resort. "Silver," she finally said. "Tom Silver."

"Yeah."

She eyed him curiously. "Are you the pack leader? And this is a pack-run town?"

He wasn't surprised she sounded so astonished. Wolf packs didn't normally run their own towns. He didn't even know of another like theirs. "Subleader. And yeah, our family founded the town. My eldest brother, Darien, runs it."

"Darien," Elizabeth said.

He glanced at her when she didn't say anything more.

"Bertha told me Darien was the one who said you'd pick me up and take me back to the B and B."

"Yeah."

She relaxed a little against the seat.

Maybe she thought Tom had seen her when she first arrived and was interested in her in some other way, but now that she knew he was just there on his pack leader's orders, she felt a little easier. She shouldn't. Once any of the bachelor males got wind of her being in town, she'd have a whole bunch of interest. Available she-wolves were a rare commodity.

"So you're doing a story on the ski resort?" he asked.

"Yeah, winter-sports kind of thing."

He nodded, trying to figure out how he would convince her that he had to stick close to her until she left town. "How long will you be here?"

"Four days."

An eternity. "I get off at noon if you want to get a bite of lunch."

"I might still be working."

So she wasn't buying his need to take charge of her. "Okay, I'll ski with you until you want to eat." He swore she stared holes into him as he watched the recently plowed road.

"Um, I'll be stopping a lot on the slopes to take pictures. You won't have any fun."

He glanced at her to see her expression, wondering if she was being honest with him, nervous that he would want to be with her. *Which was a total beta trait.* Except her voice wasn't modulated like a beta's. A beta would be nervous and hesitant, her voice soft and acquiescent. She had the soft, sweet beta part down, but she wasn't nervous and she wasn't hesitant.

She watched him with what looked like amusement—and a hint of challenge? He couldn't quite figure her out. At times she acted like a beta, but when she matched his gaze and didn't look away—that was alpha behavior. Wolves didn't switch back and forth between the two. Not normally. Unless being a red wolf-coyote mix was the reason. She was conflicted?

He didn't believe any such thing existed. Coyote packs had alphas and betas just like the wolves did. Was she pretending to be a beta? Or a beta trying to sound alpha? That thought intrigued him. He smiled a little at her. He would learn the truth one way or another, sooner or later.

"It'll be interesting to see what catches your attention on the slopes." He returned his gaze to the road. "My other brother, Jake, is a photographer also. He likes to take pictures of wildlife and flowers."

She didn't say anything.

"The two of you could probably compare notes," he continued.

"I probably won't meet him."

She spoke so quickly that he thought she might be afraid to meet more of the gray wolves.

"We'll have dinner at Darien's place. Jake and his mate might come, depending on what they're doing."

She didn't respond.

Tom tried not to smile. She wouldn't win. She had to know that. She was in another pack's territory, and they made the rules. Unless she was a loner and not used to pack rules.

"I'm sure your brother wouldn't want me intruding at a family gathering," she finally said.

"He will insist that you come." Darien hadn't, but Tom knew that he would require that she dine with him and Lelandi because she was a she-wolf. A male wolf just hitting the slopes or a mated couple or family, no big deal. But since she was an unmated female who planned to hang around longer than a day, Darien would want to keep tabs on the situation.

If Tom was just giving Elizabeth a lift to the resort, he would have dropped her off at the ski rentals. But he didn't want her out of his sight until he let the other wolves in the vicinity know she was under *his* protection. He thought he might enjoy his role as her protector.

As he drove past the ski-rental shop toward the parking lot, Elizabeth turned her head to look. "You could have dropped me off back there."

"Being a subleader, I can expedite the rental process," he was quick to say.

"Oh."

"Is your pack very big?" he asked, fishing for more information.

She didn't say anything for a moment, as if trying to come up with an answer. The coyote trickster myth instantly shot into Tom's mind.

"Big enough," she said evasively.

Which didn't tell him anything. Maybe she belonged to a coyote pack instead, and she didn't want to let on. He didn't have any problem with that.

He pulled into a parking space, and she was out of the pickup in a hurry. She slipped on her ski hat and gloves and hurried back to the ski-rental hut. He quickly joined her.

Maybe she was a rogue wolf-coyote, shunned by the coyotes and the wolves. He hadn't considered that before. If that was the case, he felt like a heel for bringing up her pack alliance when normally he thought of himself as the most diplomatic of the three brothers.

Not knowing what to say to rectify his faux pas, he walked alongside her in silence. She stared straight ahead at the ski-rental hut and avoided looking at anyone milling around and gawking at Tom and her.

Wolves, the lot of them. They smiled at him and several gave him the thumbs-up.

Damn it, he couldn't help but smile back. She was his obligation, not his conquest, and he had to keep that in mind. Even though Darien had told him he was supposed to treat her as though they were together.

A couple of the ski patrollers saw him with Elizabeth and trudged through the snow to join them. Of course, they were giving the lady a good once-, well, twice-over. Wolves were that way. The ski patrollers were all alphas. Had to be. In charge of life-and-death decisions on a daily basis, they had to take over in an emergency and couldn't wait for someone else to tell them what to do. Some were from other wolf packs and came to serve on the ski patrol during the season. They were all good friends.

Kemp and Radcliff Grey, twin brothers who were new to the pack, finally took their eyes off Elizabeth and greeted Tom with a nod.

Before either could introduce himself, Tom said, "I'll take the lady to the ski-rental hut and get her started and talk to you about what Darien wants afterward."

"Sure," Kemp said.

Tom stalked after Elizabeth when he saw she didn't remain meekly by his side. If she'd been a beta, she would have stayed with him until he escorted her to the rental hut. That had him rethinking what she was again.

One of the wolves working the ski rentals must have alerted the other three that Tom was approaching, or maybe they were more interested in who he escorted. "Tom," the four said in greeting. They all looked at Elizabeth, waiting to hear who she was.

She cleared her throat, then told them her shoe size.

"Put it on Darien's tab," Tom said. "I'll be back to check on you in a little while."

"No need," she said. "And thanks, but I can pay for it."

The four wolves looked at Tom to see his response. They were betas with the pack. That was the kind of reaction he expected. Eager to please, waiting to hear what the alpha decided. If Elizabeth had said he didn't have to come back *if he didn't want to* or nodded in agreement, it would have been seen as a beta response. To say she would pay and that there was no need for him to return was an alpha response.

"No problem," he said. "It'll only take me a minute." He looked at the guys with a silent command: *Take care of her until I return.*

They hurried to fit her in ski boots.

CHAPTER 3

ELIZABETH HADN'T REALIZED SILVER TOWN WAS A GRAY WOLF pack's territory, and she definitely didn't belong. That must be why North was reluctant to meet her here—because he was a red wolf. He should have said so, though it wouldn't have changed her plans. If her uncle decided he wanted to try to kill her again, the gray pack here wouldn't allow it. Most likely.

She'd dismissed the notion of going to either Telluride or Wolf Creek because both ski resorts were too well-known. She'd wanted an out-of-the-way place, far from any large cities but mostly far enough away from her father's old wolf pack.

Skis and poles in hand, pack on her back, ski boots on, she thanked the guys who helped equip her. They even got a ski pass for her—on Darien's account. She couldn't help but appreciate Tom's taking care of her like that, but she was still wary of other shifters. Granted, her past experience was mostly with red wolves and only a few grays. Coyote shifters avoided her as if she carried a genetic mutation that they might catch if they breathed in the same air as she did.

A couple of cute human girls frowned and folded their arms as they waited to be helped with ski boots while the wolves ignored them.

Elizabeth couldn't believe all the interest she had garnered here either. She wondered if this pack was just more tolerant of coyote and red wolf shifters. No shifters lived in Canyon, Texas, where even the human population was small. She didn't think any shifters even lived in the nearby city of Amarillo. At least she hadn't run into any in the year and a half she'd lived in the area. Because of her past troubles with shifters, she preferred living strictly among humans. She was way out of her comfort zone here, unsure of how to handle all the interest.

She thanked the guys again and headed out of the hut.

"Wait," one of the men said. "Tom is coming back for you." He sounded a little worried that they'd all be in trouble if he didn't remind her.

As if *she'd* forgotten.

She smiled. "He's got a job to do. And so do I." After leaving her snow boots in a locker, she headed for the ski lift as fast as her ski boots would permit.

She'd prefer to check the map and get oriented, but she didn't have time. She knew that Tom would return for her soon or that one of the ski patrollers or Tom might see her tear off, and he would be after her.

As an alpha, he couldn't let her get away with doing her own thing, especially since he'd made his intentions perfectly clear in front of some of the pack members.

One of the human girls waiting to be fitted for ski boots said, "Can't we get some service now that *she's* gone?"

Elizabeth glanced back to see all four of the wolves watching her, grinning. *Betas.* She smiled and gave them a thumbs-up. They did high fives with each other.

Tom would want to kill her, she thought in an amused way.

She had tried to pretend to be a sweet, innocent beta. She'd blown *that* image so badly with Tom that there was no sense in pretending any further. Professing to be a beta was nearly impossible for her kind. She'd wrongly assumed he would leave her to her own devices if he thought she was one—alpha that he was—which went to show she really wasn't all that knowledgeable about working wolf packs. Or at least this one.

She made her way to the ski lift and situated her boots on her skis but noticed one of the lift operators focused on her while speaking on his radio. As soon as she made eye contact with the guy, she knew. Tom had called ahead. The lift operator signaled to her to move out of the line. She closed her eyes briefly. Man, she'd never seen a wolf pack that controlled an operation like this.

The mix of humans and wolves standing in the lift line watched her, speculation written all over their faces. She had to have done something wrong.

Smiling, the lift operator approached her. "Got word Tom wants to ride up with you, if you'll just step out of line. He's coming."

She didn't bother arguing with the guy. He was only doing his job. She was certain he'd stop the lift if she ignored him and tried to get on one of the chairs.

She turned to see Tom headed for her while the lift hummed, carrying skiers up the steep incline. At first, she couldn't read his expression. He was smiling way too smugly.

More amused than annoyed, she smiled back. She just couldn't let an alpha, *any* alpha, dictate to her without showing her true colors, no matter how hard she tried to pretend she was just a cooperative beta.

He took her arm, leaned over, and, to her shock, kissed her cheek.

She couldn't help it. She chuckled. "You are so bad."

"Yeah, only because you made me do it," he said. "Come on, Elizabeth. Things are quiet for the moment. I'll ski with you until I get a call."

"*Made* you do it?"

"Hey, I'm just trying to protect you from all the interested males in my pack."

She laughed. "Right."

His mouth curved up as he looked down at her, and she thought he had the most heartwarming smile. Too bad he only behaved this way because the pack leader must have ordered him to. But Tom also had something to prove to the wolves in his pack who were waiting to see what would happen next. She noted that two of the lift chairs went up without anyone seated on them.

Two wolves motioned for Tom and Elizabeth to get in line in front of them. She'd never gotten special treatment like this, ever.

She hadn't wanted to cut in line, but everyone smiled at her, so she figured they would object if she tried to go to the back of the line. She was certain Tom would stop her.

She considered kissing him back, just to prove he wasn't in charge of her. Which was why she did what she did next, shocking him, she was certain. She grabbed his jacket and looked him in the eye. "I can't stand on my toes in ski boots, so lean down."

Dimples showed in his tanned cheeks. He hesitated only a second, as if processing her request. He leaned down and she kissed him full on the mouth. Oh God, his lips were warm and supple against hers. His gloved hands cupped her face. He must have dropped his ski poles to ensure she didn't move away from him until he finished.

She didn't want him to end this as he pressed his lips against hers, the pressure saying he wanted more, his thumbs stroking her cheeks, his tongue licking her lips and asking for an invitation.

She'd already gone this far, so why not? She loved what he was doing to her, heating her from the inside out. She opened her mouth just a little and took a breath, not a full invitation unless... he took advantage.

Which he did and she nearly fell off her skis. *Oh...my...God.* The wolf could kiss. But damn, she could kiss back too.

Nipping his lips, licking, tasting, chasing his tongue with hers, she gave one last full-contact smooch before she pulled away. She felt light-headed, her breath creating puffs of mist. *Smoking.*

He stood there and looked at her like she was a wet dream come true. The cheers went up, the woots, the whistles, and she laughed.

Grinning, the ski-lift operator handed Tom his ski poles. "Way to go, Tom."

When she was seated beside Tom on the chair and had begun the ride up, he shook his head as if he was trying to clear it after what had just happened between them.

"What?" she asked, turning to observe the breathtaking vista. Every tree was covered in white frosting, and the sky was bluebird blue.

He chuckled.

She glanced at him when he didn't answer. His mouth curved up as he studied her, though with his ski goggles now in place, she couldn't see his eyes the way she wanted to. He looked really cute and in charge in his red ski-patrol jacket, although she already knew he was a subleader and very much in charge.

"What?" she asked again, tilting her head to the side.

"You do realize everyone in the pack was already giving me a hard time. Probably about a quarter of our people are up here today enjoying the fresh powder. Those who did see what just happened will tell those who didn't. Oh, they won't say anything, *much*, to my face. Just the knowing smiles and slaps on the back. But you've sure got the pack stirred up, and the word has already spread. I didn't even have to call Darien to confirm the dinner arrangement. *He* called me."

She gaped at him and then frowned. "You said he already wanted me to come to dinner."

"I know my brother. He would have called before long if I hadn't gotten hold of him."

"So will your other brother, Jake, and his mate be there?"

"You bet. When I told Darien that you're a photographer, he said Jake wanted to meet you."

"Well, it was all *your* fault for trying to be in charge of me."

"About that. Yeah, I'd like to try that again. Someplace where we're not likely to melt all the snow off the slope."

She chuckled and looked at the vista as the chair rode up the cable, vibrating, the rattling noise filling the bitingly cold air. She didn't remember a time when she'd had such lighthearted fun.

Tom's radio came to life, and he listened as the dispatcher relayed information about an injury on one of the slopes. He answered the call. "I'll be there in just a couple of minutes."

"Duty calls?"

"Yeah, but I'm free at noon. We'll have lunch."

She smiled. *If he could find her.*

She still had to meet with North at the Timberline Ski Lodge. That put her on edge a bit. What if North didn't come alone? Or what if someone else came?

Someone who wished her dead?

CHAPTER 4

Elizabeth skied away from the chairlift but Tom followed her. "Noon," he said. "Meet you at the base lodge."

His comment wasn't an offer but a command. "You don't take *no* for an answer, do you?" She smiled when she asked.

He offered her a wolfish, sexy smile in return that had her whole body warming despite the chill in the air. "You never said no. See you later. Enjoy your day if I don't get a chance to meet up with you on the slopes. A blue trail is off to the left, expert to the right."

He skied along the connecting trail for the black-diamond slope.

You never said no, echoed in her thoughts. Yeah, if she hadn't really wanted to meet up with him, she would have been all alpha and said no. He had her figured.

Elizabeth watched him move like a pro and wished she could ski down the expert trail with confidence. She didn't get a chance to ski nearly as often as she'd like, since they had no skiing in Texas. But she loved the slopes and took every opportunity she could get to ski. She was definitely an intermediate skier.

She was about to head for the intermediate slope when two males on the chairlift got off and joined her.

"Need a ski buddy?" one asked, looking hopeful. He was a blond and reminded her of a Viking, muscled and with beautiful white teeth grinning at her.

"He's busy, but I'm free," the other said, looking like the first one's twin.

She chuckled. "I'm mostly just taking pictures. Sorry."

"Well, if you get tired of just taking pictures, I'm Cantrell."

"Robert," the other man said.

"You're brothers, I take it." And both gray wolves.

"Yeah. Kind of no mistaking it," Robert said with a wink.

"Thanks. Maybe I can take you up on it later. Nice meeting you both." She took off toward the entrance to the blue intermediate trail.

"Wait!" Cantrell said, catching up to her. "What's your name?"

She paused at the top of the trail. "Elizabeth."

"Elizabeth," Robert said. "Have you got lunch plans?"

"Yes, with Tom Silver."

Cantrell laughed. "I told you he'd already asked her."

"What about tonight?" Robert asked.

"I'm having dinner with the pack leaders."

"Uh, okay," Cantrell said as if that meant she planned to join the pack or something. "Well, we tried. See you around, Elizabeth." He headed downhill.

Robert smiled. "They always get the good ones." He followed his brother down the slope.

Elizabeth shook her head. She really couldn't believe all the interest, especially after what she'd gone through growing up— physical and emotional abuse from her father's wolf family for being part coyote. Shunned by her mother's coyote pack for having wolf DNA. And here she was totally welcome. Maybe because Tom seemed interested in her.

She stood to the side so other skiers could access the trail and pulled out her camera. She snapped shots of the two men traversing the hill, then of the vista. She breathed in the cold, crisp air, loving it, wanting to throw off her clothes, shift, and run through the woods, biting at the snow, rolling in it, having the time of her life.

Tonight she would.

She skied down to another intermediate run and across an easy trail where Tom and a patroller checked out a girl of about eight. She sat on the snow holding her knee and crying. Tom crouched next to her, talking to her as she nodded. Elizabeth hoped the girl wasn't too badly injured, but the sight of him speaking to her made Elizabeth believe he'd be good with kids. She wondered if the rest of the pack was like that. The two she had belonged to—as in had family ties to but hadn't really *belonged to*—had been. They just hadn't treated *her* that way.

She'd always thought of her parents as Romeo and Juliet—Romeo, the red wolf, and Juliet, the coyote—from two different families, both feuding. In the end, both her parents had died. Which meant she'd had to fend for herself against the wolves of her father's pack. The coyote pack hadn't wanted her either, since she was an alpha and part wolf. The pack leaders had feared she'd want to take over.

She was a pariah, worse than an omega, a wolf that was pushed from the pack, picked on, and left to grab scraps everyone else had left behind.

Except for one thing. She was an alpha. They couldn't beat that out of her, no matter how much they had tried. Alpha wolves were born with the take-charge tendency whether they were *lupus garous* or strictly wolves or even humans. Not all alphas formed their own packs. Some became loners and others subleaders of a pack, ready to take over if the pack leader died. Not that she would ever face such a situation.

After capturing Tom and the little girl with her camera, Elizabeth moved toward the lodge. She took several pictures of the building, with its steep alpine roof and log sides and a large veranda where visitors sat at tables enjoying hot drinks. The heat of the drinks mixed with the air, causing steam to rise above their cups. She captured photos of people waiting on the lift line and of some coming down the gently sloping bunny trail.

She snapped a shot of a teen wearing a gray-wolf ski hat who headed straight for her. He whipped around her, grinning, and skidded to a halt next to her. "Tom's girl, right?"

Before she could respond, he laughed and took off for the ski lift. She smiled. If *her* pack had treated her like that, she would never have left.

She snapped a couple more pictures—one of a man hitting a hill of soft powder, causing it to fly everywhere. If the day remained sunny, this afternoon she'd take a break from photographing and just ski. Well, after she got what she needed from North, she thought, wishing again that he had taken the evidence he had on her uncle straight to the red wolf pack's new leader, Hrothgar. North wouldn't, saying that it was her issue to deal with. Elizabeth didn't disagree, but she didn't want to get that close to the pack.

She thought maybe that afternoon she'd take some pictures when the sun wasn't as intense. When she was done, she'd try to contact Hrothgar and arrange to meet with him to transfer the evidence herself. Hopefully, he wouldn't mind making the seven-hour trip here.

She was still irritated with North. He had waited a long time before telling her he had solid evidence against her uncle. He could also have informed her that the red pack had a new leader who might consider the evidence and right the wrongs. Then again, Hrothgar might not do anything more with it than Bruin would have.

Shaking loose of her frustration, she proceeded toward the lift. She felt someone hurrying behind her, but he didn't pass her. She glanced at him as he got in line next to her for the double chairs. He didn't look at her, which told her he wasn't trying to meet up with the new she-wolf on the slopes. He was covered in cold-weather clothes, ski hat, and goggles, so she couldn't make out what he looked like. She tried to smell him, but the wind blew the wrong way so she couldn't tell if he was a wolf or a human.

He sat to her right as they took the lift up, and Elizabeth caught sight of a lovely vista beyond the man's head. She thought to come this way again, sit on his side of the chairlift, and have her camera ready.

Then the man turned and stared at her. Blatantly. She'd been looking in his direction—at the view, not at him. Maybe he thought she'd been staring at him. If he was a wolf, he definitely was an alpha because he didn't look away from her, trying to force her to glance away in submission.

She didn't need to prove anything to him. Not the way she'd had to with her former wolf pack. But the instinct was built in, and the repeated abuse she'd suffered for being who she was had made her toughen against such people. She *wasn't* looking away first.

She didn't want to have anything to do with him, but she finally smiled and said, "Nice day for skiing. Are you local?"

The man wore a black balaclava over his mouth and nose, but Elizabeth could tell from a glimpse of his cold eyes that he glowered before he looked away without answering her. Having won the confrontation, she smiled to herself. She snapped pictures of people skiing down the slope from the lift's bird's-eye view. She took a picture of the chairs behind her. Never knowing what shot might really look cool in a story, she would take hundreds while she was here. She tucked her camera away in her pouch before she reached the end of the ride.

This time when she got off the chair, she would head for the expert slope to take some shots of the moguls and the skiers traversing them on the way down. After she finished there, she'd ski back across the trail to the intermediate slope. She would find another lift to take her up to some other trails later.

The man got off the chair and she followed him, moving off to the side so the next passengers could leave the lift. She waited to see which trail he went on. Expert. *Super. Not.*

Then again, he'd ski down it quickly and be gone. She could even take some shots of him and see if he did a great job or was just an egomaniac and crashed and burned, nearly killing himself on the way down.

Smiling darkly with that thought in mind, she skied toward the black-diamond slope. When she reached it, she made sure she was out of any skier's way. She pulled her camera out and took a picture of the man. He'd stopped halfway down the trail, resting his skis on top of a mogul. Not such a hotshot after all.

He turned and looked up. Not expecting to be caught photographing him, Elizabeth quickly raised her camera to take a picture of the pines separating this trail from the intermediate one.

She heard a skier coming from behind her, the swoosh of skis against snow. Elizabeth's skis crunched into the semipacked powder as she inched over just a little more to get out of the way. Trees blocked her from moving over any farther.

The skier—had to be a man, as hefty as he was—slammed into her, knocking her down the steep incline.

Heart in her throat, she cried out. She lost her camera on impact. Fell. With her ski poles looped around her wrists, she threw her gloved hands out, trying to stop herself. The shove made her topple onto her side, crashing into the first of the moguls that *didn't* slow her fall.

Elizabeth continued to tumble down the slope. She feared smashing her head against the compacted snow and breaking limbs—her own, not the trees'. Briefly, she fretted about her camera, finding it, concerned it might be ruined. Even the worry about a spinal injury flashed through her mind as she continued the downward plunge.

She did not see her life flashing before her eyes. All she saw were snow and intermittent flashes of blue sky and more snow. Elizabeth felt panicked, unable to stop her forward roll.

She still held on to one pole, having lost the other and both skis. Slamming against one mogul after another, she finally hit one hard enough to stop her. She didn't remember losing consciousness.

Her breath had been knocked out of her though, and her wrist and back hurt.

"Miss, are you all right?" someone hollered down to her from the top of the trail, sounding far away. A youthful male voice.

She didn't know how far she'd rolled until she stopped. She thought she'd tumbled all the way to the bottom of the mountain where she couldn't roll any farther. But no such luck. She was still way up on the very steep incline amid all the bumps, staring up at the blue, blue sky.

Unable to catch her breath, she tried to calm her racing heart.

She wished she could have gotten up quickly on her own, somehow managed to make it the rest of the way down the slope, and none would be the wiser.

Now she was afraid that whoever had discovered her would make a big deal of this.

"Minx, you can't go down this way," the kid hollered.

"I've been skiing since I was three. I'll get her camera. You guys go see to her."

Her camera. Elizabeth tried to turn her head, but her back hurt.

"Come on, Anthony. You know Minx never listens to us. If she breaks her neck, we can say we told her so."

"Ha, ha, very funny," Minx said.

The ground vibrated slightly beneath Elizabeth as the boys' skis swished on the snow, then one stopped way above her, and the other came into view.

"I'm just getting her skis to warn others of danger down the slope, Cody." Anthony quickly joined Cody, yanked a cell phone out of a bag, and called ski patrol.

They were as tall as grown men, so Elizabeth figured they were older teens.

She closed her eyes, knowing full well Tom would soon get word of this.

"I'm okay," she said, even though she felt terribly winded. She didn't feel like she'd broken anything, but her wrist hurt. And she couldn't seem to catch her breath so she could rise to a sitting position.

She wanted to lie here, soak up the sun that the two boys now blocked, and get her bearings. Their faces wore frowns as they looked her over.

"Doesn't look like she's got any visible broken bones," Cody said.

"I secured the area," Anthony said to someone on the phone. He'd crossed her skis upright in the snow to warn skiers above that a safety issue existed below them.

The boys were gray wolves. She hadn't seen or scented the girl yet and hoped she wouldn't get hurt on the slope while looking for Elizabeth's camera. But she was glad the girl was searching for it and hoped it was all right. At least no one else was on the trail. Thank God.

"I'm all right," Elizabeth said. "I...just need a moment."

"Hot damn, she's a wolf," Anthony said.

She frowned at him. No one mentioned the wolf word. Or in her case, coyote either. Not in public.

As if he read her mind, he grinned. "No one around to hear me but us wolves."

And one part coyote.

"She's the one Tom must have brought up to the ski resort. All the guys are talking about her," Cody said. "*And the kiss.* Cantrell said he caught them on his phone video recorder, but he won't share unless you pay for it. A few other guys took shots with their cell phones too. They're sharing for free, sending emails to the pack."

Elizabeth's whole body warmed, and she suddenly felt feverish. She couldn't believe word had spread that fast. Or that anyone had bothered to catch their actions on camera. Sure, she knew that a pack shared information to protect themselves, but still... She thought Tom had been exaggerating.

"Where do you hurt?" Cody asked, crouching down in front of her.

Everywhere. She would be fine once she got off this expert slope, if trying to ski downhill didn't kill her.

"She's having trouble concentrating, unable to answer questions," Anthony said into his cell when Elizabeth didn't answer right away. "She's the one Tom brought up here." Anthony put his hand over the phone and said, "You're a celebrity. You'll have the entire ski patrol checking you out."

With mortification, she felt like she was having a hot flash, and she was sure she could melt the mogul she rested against into a puddle of water.

"I'm fine," she said, trying to sit up. "I'm not having trouble concentrating. Just breathing."

"No, just lie still," Cody said, his hand on her shoulder. "You might have a spinal injury." He turned to the other boy. "And tell them she has shortness of breath."

"I hurt my wrist a little, and I feel a little sore. I'll be fine if I can just get down the slope." Actually, at this point, if she could just get up. "I'm not having any trouble breathing," she amended. She shouldn't have said she hurt anywhere.

"Did you get all that?" Anthony asked, and she realized that as she spoke to Cody, Anthony must have held the phone nearer to her so that she would give the information directly to the ski patrol. "Okay," Anthony said to Cody. "Don't let her move an inch."

She rolled her eyes.

Cody smiled at her.

"I found her camera!" Minx called out from the woods.

Elizabeth breathed a little sigh of relief, though she still worried the camera might be damaged.

"Ski patrollers are on the way," Anthony said.

Great. She hoped they didn't include Tom.

"Yard sale!" a couple of skiers yelled out from the lift. Tom skied down the slope and saw an unfamiliar woman wipe out, losing her ski poles and skis all over the place.

He retrieved the two lost skis when pack members Cantrell and his brother, Robert, joined him, carrying the woman's ski poles.

"She's hot, man," Cantrell said to Tom. The two of them smiled at him as they skied down to the lady getting to her feet and brushing the snow off her goggles.

He raised his brows at them, asking in a silent way *who* they were referring to.

"Not the woman that just rag-dolled down the slope," Cantrell said. "You know. Elizabeth."

They reached the lady who had fallen, and Tom asked, "You all right, ma'am?" He handed her the skis, and Robert gave her the ski poles.

"Yes, thank you. I'm fine." Her cheeks were red from the weather or from embarrassment. She seated her boots on her skis and took off.

"I asked her to lunch," Robert said. He and his brother skied with Tom to the next lift. "Elizabeth. She said she would be busy."

"With me." Tom hated to sound so territorial. She wasn't really *with* him. But after that kiss, he was rethinking the scenario.

Cantrell laughed. "Yeah, she said so."

Tom smiled a little at that.

When the pack leaders invited a wolf to their home for dinner, that was usually the ultimate boost for any wolf's ego. Except Elizabeth. Tom wondered why she seemed reluctant.

"Man, you guys get all the good ones," Cantrell said.

The trouble was that fewer female werewolves were born, so there seemed to always be a shortage. Not that Tom expected to set up housekeeping anytime soon.

"How did you learn about her?" Robert asked.

As if the Silver brothers had a pipeline to learning about available females. Although he supposed Bertha was that for him this time.

Tom got a call on his radio from ski patroller Kemp. "Gotta come quick. Devil Man's Switchback."

"Whatcha got?" Tom got ahead of those waiting in the ski line and was promptly seated on a chair.

"The lady you brought to the resort?" Kemp said.

Tom's mouth went dry, and he tightened his hand around the radio. Elizabeth was probably not injured that badly, but since she had been with Tom, Kemp had most likely taken the situation more seriously than warranted.

At least Tom prayed that was so. "Yeah, what happened?"

"She says she's okay."

Tom sat on the edge of his chair, unsure whether to be concerned or not. "But?"

Kemp cleared his throat.

"Just spit it out, Kemp," Tom said. "What's happened?"

"Vitals look good, but the Woodcroft twins saw her first and called it in. They both say she was knocked out. She denies it, but she probably wouldn't remember."

That didn't sound good. "Is she answering your questions with full clarity?"

"Yeah. I've called for my brother to bring up a toboggan. She doesn't want to use one. You know... She's all alpha."

Tom smiled a little at that. Yeah, he already knew that about her.

"You know how it is. Someone can have no memory issues for hours or even days, and suddenly they have a problem. No visible injuries to her head though."

"She goes down in the toboggan. Any other possible injuries?" Tom asked.

"Wrist might be sprained—she was still holding on to one of her ski poles. She'll probably be a little bruised but otherwise fine."

"What exactly happened? Just take a spill?"

Kemp paused, then said, "She says a guy shoved her down the slope on purpose."

Tom frowned. More likely an out-of-control skier, though if the guy regularly skied the black slope, maybe not. "Did she get a look at him?"

"She gave me a get-real look, Tom, when I asked her the question. You know, because she was falling down the mountain—in an unglamorous way—her words, not mine. I couldn't imagine her ever looking unglamorous."

"Just help me up," Elizabeth said in the background, sounding totally pissed.

Tom smiled at hearing her dictatorial tone. "Just keep her *down* until I get there."

CHAPTER 5

WHEN TOM REACHED THE EXPERT SLOPE, HE SAW ELIZABETH'S skis placed in an X several yards above. All he could see down below were three male backsides as they hovered over the injured she-wolf.

Anthony, Cody, and Kemp.

Tom greeted them as he reached their location, praying all of this was overkill. Wolves were territorial by nature, and they'd staked their claim over the she-wolf, even if she was older than the teens. When he could maneuver around the others to observe the patient, he saw one annoyed-looking she-wolf scowling up at him. He frowned, still worried she might be injured worse than she claimed.

Tom moved closer to where she rested on her back against a mogul, the wind whipping the snow about. The white fake-fur-trimmed hood surrounded her face. A black half balaclava covered her mouth and nose, making her appear ninja-like. Her eyes were narrowed at him, her ski goggles pushed up onto her ski hat.

"What happened?" Tom asked, crouching down to speak with her.

She pulled the balaclava down with her right hand.

"I'll be all right," she said breathily, as if she was having a hard time breathing or the pain was affecting her.

She might be all right, but Tom's heart pumped way too fast. "Kemp said you probably have a mild wrist sprain."

"Yeah." Her breathing was shallow.

Tom thought maybe she wasn't used to the thinner air and was suffering from hypoxia, or altitude sickness. Or possibly she had a broken rib that had collapsed a lung.

"Do you need oxygen? Having trouble breathing?" Tom asked. "Ribs hurt?"

"No."

He didn't trust the patient completely. He'd seen a case a week ago where a twenty-three-year-old hotdogger had claimed he was okay, but his vitals had deteriorated rapidly. Tom had him medevaced out only to learn later that the skier had ruptured his spleen. Another was the case of a forty-five-year-old man who looked unsteady after he said a snowboarder had run him over. He swore he just had to catch his breath, but when he couldn't, Tom had the ambulance take the man down to the hospital. Tom heard later from Doc Weber that the patient had suffered a mild heart attack.

"Vital signs?" Tom asked Kemp.

"Her signs are good," Kemp said.

"Okay, good."

"I found her camera," Minx said. Tom looked that way, surprised that the teenaged girl was here too. Not that he should be, since she was friends with the boys. She must have been in the woods next to the expert trail, searching for the camera. A couple of pine needles clung to her bright-green ski hat, the pink and white pom-poms swinging from the ties as she tried to make her way down the steep incline to reach them. Snow clung to the camera.

"You were taking pictures when it happened?" Tom asked Elizabeth. When he'd learned she was on this slope, he had assumed she must be an expert skier.

"Yes." She gritted her teeth, trying to mask that she hurt.

"Was anybody with her at the time?" Tom asked.

"No, she was alone," Kemp said.

"Did anyone see what happened?"

Elizabeth gave Tom an irritated look. She must have had her back to the skier and couldn't see what had occurred.

"Two panting males saw her," Kemp said, a lighthearted tone to his voice.

Anthony and Cody chuckled.

Tom liked Kemp because he always had a sense of humor. It also meant that Elizabeth must be in good shape, no really bad injuries, or he would be ultraserious.

As a *lupus garou*, she'd heal well on her own. Unless she had spinal injuries or bleeding that couldn't be stemmed, she should be all right.

Kemp moved over to allow Tom to get closer. Kemp's twin brother, Radcliff, skied down with the toboggan. He had darker blond hair than Kemp, and his eyes were a lighter amber. Both men were in great shape because they served on the ski patrol regularly each season and had all the women swooning when they shared smiles with them.

Tom checked over Elizabeth's vital signs himself. They looked good.

"I'm *fine*," she said, still frowning at him. "Go help someone who really needs your assistance."

"It's noon and I'm off the clock. We still have that lunch date." Tom could imagine the boys taking notes on how to court a wolf. "You're going down by toboggan. We have several other patrollers at the resort, so no problem there."

"Except that you should have heard the flurry of 'I'm coming,' no matter how far away the other patrollers were stationed," Kemp said, grinning.

Tom could imagine, even if they were joking.

"Fine. Get me down to the base so that the whole slope isn't crowded with onlookers. I can't believe you're making that big a deal of this," Elizabeth groused.

She didn't know how much so until they placed a neck collar on her, strapped her to a board, and clamped an oxygen mask in place. She didn't have to say a word for Tom to know she was pissed. He wasn't taking a chance on her being injured further.

Peter Jorgenson, their local sheriff and a good friend of Tom's, skied up behind them, and Tom wondered what he was doing up here.

"Okay, guys, move back and give us some room." Tom meant Cody and Anthony, but when they didn't budge, he said a little sterner this time, "Cody, Anthony, *move*."

The wolves shuffled carefully away, avoiding sliding down the sharp embankment.

"So, Peter, what are you doing up here?" Tom asked as the sheriff motioned for the teens to shift further out of the way.

Peter seemed just as intrigued with the she-wolf and didn't move to vacate the area himself. The slope was treacherously sheer here, and they all stood on the sides of the moguls to keep from sliding down the icier sections.

"Took a breather while it's quiet in town. Deputy Sheriff Trevor's holding down the fort." Peter tilted his Stetson back, his dark sunglasses hiding his dark eyes, his forehead creased in a frown.

Kemp had pressed ice against Elizabeth's wrist. Tom brought out an elastic bandage and wrapped it around her wrist to prevent swelling. He made a sling to keep her arm close to her body, her wrist elevated and protected. "Were you holding on to your ski poles when you fell?" Kemp asked.

She nodded.

"Always let them go. More wrist injuries occur when skiers hang on to their poles during a fall."

"Your camera," Minx said, sliding on the icier sections as she tried to reach them.

Anthony grabbed her arm before she fell.

Tom and Kemp lifted Elizabeth onto the toboggan. Tom wrapped the blanket around her and strapped her in, while Radcliff went back up for her skis. Once Tom had retrieved her ski poles from Cody and the skis from Radcliff and strapped them on the toboggan, Minx set the camera on Elizabeth's stomach.

"Here," Tom said to Elizabeth. "Let me secure your camera." He hoped it hadn't been ruined in the fall. Jake might loan her one of his so she could complete her story, if she could still ski later before she had to return home, but Jake was possessive about his photographic equipment. He might offer to take pictures for her instead.

Tom turned to everyone standing there. "So tell me, what happened? Anyone know? Who reported her injury?"

Anthony poked the tips of his ski poles into the mogul. "She was taking a picture at the top of the trail, I guess. We saw someone speeding across the connecting trail in front of us. He skied really fast and sliced the turn too short. I thought maybe the guy was out of control and accidentally hit her. I figured we'd see him in a heap down the slope somewhere too. When we reached the trailhead, he had zipped down to the bottom as fast as humanly possible, and she had tumbled down the hill. Her arm flew out, and she cried out. She looked like she tried to stop her fall, but she hurt her wrist instead. She rolled until she stopped at the mogul."

"She was unconscious?" Tom asked.

"She appeared that way," Cody said. "She looked like she was asleep and didn't move. Then her arm jerked and it appeared she'd come to. Anthony called the emergency in."

"Is that what all of you saw?" Tom asked.

"Yeah, I guess." Cody dusted snow off his black ski bib. He wore his trademark rainbow-colored jester hat, the bells ringing on the four tassels every time he moved.

"You didn't really see what happened?" Tom asked.

"No, just like Anthony said. It appeared the same to me."

"What about the guy? Did you recognize him? See what he wore?"

"Who cared about him?" Anthony asked. "We were too concerned about the lady."

Tom looked at the girl. "Minx?"

She made a face, her cheeks red, her blond hair hanging half-loose from her knit hat. "Well, I mean, I guess. If that's what they saw, that's what happened."

"You don't think so?"

Their expressions skeptical, chins tilted down, eyebrows raised, the boys looked at her as though they didn't believe she had seen anything different.

She shrugged. "Yeah, sure."

Tom hated when kids caved in to peer pressure. "What do *you* think happened, Minx?"

"The guy hit her on purpose."

———————

That was what Elizabeth had thought too. At first, when she fell down the mountain, she was too shocked and too anxious about stopping her fall before she smacked into a tree and fractured her skull to focus on what had occurred.

She eyed Tom. His hair was ruffled by the wind, his cheeks red, his sunglasses too dark to reveal his eyes. Wolves liked to see a person's eyes. They could gather a wealth of information from them. He gave her a dimpled smile despite her scowling at him.

"You're sure the guy pushed you? Didn't just lose control and shove into you?" Tom asked.

"Okay, possibly, yes, he was out of control, reached his hand up, and shoved at me to get his balance. It's possible. Sure."

Tom said, "But not likely."

"No."

"Come on down to the hut so we can get your statements in writing," Tom said to the teens.

Elizabeth tried to remember what had happened right before the skier shoved her. She'd taken a picture of the man who had acted so hostile toward her on the chairlift. He'd taken off from the lift and headed for the slope. By the time she had reached it, he was already skiing down it. He'd stopped and peered up at her, as if checking to see if she was photographing him. How would he know she had followed him?

Maybe the guy in the chair behind them was this guy's friend, and the man had looked back to see if his ski buddy was joining him. That would make more sense. But if they were ski buddies, why hadn't the two men ridden the lift together?

"Let's get you to the base of the mountain and our first-aid hut," Tom said to her.

She took a deep breath, feeling warm wrapped snug in the blanket.

She had to admit that despite being annoyed they'd make such a fuss over her, the guys were all cute. The ski patrollers, the teens, the sheriff. And as wiped out as she felt, she would have had a really tough time making it down the slope on her own—and very likely would have taken another spill.

"Do you suspect that the man targeted you specifically?" Tom asked.

She frowned at him. He couldn't know anything about her uncle, could he?

Tom looked at her questioningly, then smiled a little. "All right. We'll discuss it more after we get you to the hut."

"I thought you were working until sunset," Peter said. "I can follow her to the hospital."

"I've got it covered. Jake's coming to relieve me," Tom said.

Radcliff shook his head. "You notice how the brothers stick together?"

Yeah, Elizabeth thought, and they might stick together to kick her out of the territory when Tom's brothers learned what she was.

Tom wasn't sure what to think concerning Elizabeth's allegations. Skiers and snowboarders knocked others down on the slopes all the time, and it didn't mean anything except that they were out of control and practicing unsafe skiing or snowboarding. Since she wasn't from here, he didn't think she'd have any enemies. Unless she'd annoyed someone on the slope and Tom had yet to learn of it.

He fully intended to get to the bottom of this. Peter would handle it from a police perspective, while Tom would stay on top of it from a pack-subleader point of view.

He took hold of the trace of the toboggan while Kemp took the tail rope to help guide it down the trails. The patrollers all preferred grabbing the trace rather than the tail rope to transport a patient. The lead was responsible for primary braking, choosing the best route, and any change in speed and direction. In other words, he was in charge, which was the way Tom liked it.

The tail operator usually wasn't needed much unless the trail was particularly steep, as this one was, and then he might be required for secondary braking. He might also be needed to observe the patient's status, though in this case, Elizabeth wasn't in any kind of life-threatening condition. Peter pulled that duty instead of being the tail operator, trying to stay close to the toboggan and still interested in the she-wolf, Tom suspected.

Kemp was also responsible for monitoring traffic as well as keeping the rope under proper tension and parallel to the fall line to halt the toboggan immediately if necessary.

Tom put his hand on the crossbar to brace during the steepest parts of the descent while sideslipping down the mountain. Kemp gripped the tail rope with both hands, underhanded, through the loop at the end. He matched Tom's speed.

"You okay?" Tom asked Elizabeth as he paused.

"Yeah."

Once he got them off the expert trail, he eased them onto Fox Run, an intermediate slope.

The teens skied past them, while Peter followed behind the toboggan and Radcliff skied next to it. The ski patrollers got another emergency call and Radcliff answered it. He waved at Tom and Kemp. "A guy jumped off a chair on Lift 3. Possibly broke both legs. Got to go."

Tom shook his head.

"Automatic revoking of ski pass," Kemp said cheerfully.

Tom smiled at him. "You think he'd ski the rest of the season with two broken legs?"

Kemp laughed. "As gung ho as some of these guys are? You never know."

When they finally reached Meadow Lane, one of the bunny slopes, they had to watch out for all the new skiers taking spills, running into each other, or falling without even taking a step.

"We're almost there," Tom said to Elizabeth, glancing back. She had closed her eyes, and he worried she might have passed out from a head trauma. "Elizabeth?"

"Elizabeth, are you all right?" Peter asked, getting close.

"Yes," she said, sounding annoyed. She still didn't open her eyes.

Peter smiled at Tom. "She doesn't like the attention."

She would get it whether she liked it or not, Tom vowed.

When they arrived at the first-aid hut, Tom came around to the right of the toboggan and unstrapped Elizabeth. He and Kemp lifted her onto a gurney that a couple of the staff brought out to them. The teens were waiting to give Peter their full statements.

"This is so unnecessary," Elizabeth griped, her voice still muffled by the oxygen mask.

"Are you always like this when you're a patient?" Tom asked.

She snorted. He chuckled.

Peter took her skis and poles, and Minx offered to hold her camera. Tom wheeled Elizabeth into the hut.

"I'll pick up your bag at your locker and follow the ambulance to the hospital in Silver Town." Tom winked at her.

She rolled her eyes. That earned her another smile.

Jake walked through the door to the hut, his expression dark. "I received updates about the lady as I drove over here to take your place this afternoon. Do you need me to take her to the hospital instead?" Jake sounded damned serious.

His brother had to be kidding!

CHAPTER 6

As soon as Jake Silver took a deep breath, Elizabeth knew he was sampling her scent, checking out the wolf-*coyote*.

The natural instinct to do so existed in both wolves and coyotes. She just wished she didn't feel so defensive. It didn't mean he was judging her for what she was. But based on past treatment, she automatically assumed the worst.

She didn't have any sisters, and her half brother, Sefton, had only used her as the butt of his jokes before he moved in with their uncle. Sefton had never teased her in a lighthearted way, like Jake did Tom. She could tell Jake was pulling Tom's leg, even though he sounded so serious. He smiled at Tom with a devilish glint in his eye.

"Cantrell sent me a short video of you," Jake said to Tom.

Tom looked clueless. Thinking it was the pay-per-view video of her and Tom kissing, Elizabeth felt her cheeks heat all over again.

Jake was as rugged looking as Tom, but his eyes and hair were darker brown. He was tall and commanding, equally in control. She wondered if their brother Darien appeared much the same. She could easily imagine humans getting them mixed up.

When Jake turned his full attention on her again, his expression grew wary, as if he was looking out for his brother's best interests. A warning. *Don't mess with the Silver pack unless you want to face down some angry wolves.*

Jake didn't have to worry about her intentions. Joining a gray wolf pack here or anywhere was out of the question because of what she was. She had to admit that she found it refreshing to see a pack run their own town and ski resort instead of hiding among humans and pretending to be just like them. She also liked how protective Jake was of his brother.

Long ago, she'd learned that she just didn't fit in anywhere. Men—human or otherwise—were a definite hazard to her health. Case in point: whoever had pushed her down the black-diamond slope had meant to injure her. Why? For taking a few pictures of the mountains? Of a skier in action?

What if the skier hadn't wanted her to capture him on camera in action or any other way? She frowned at that. She realized that even if her camera was broken, she had the card with the pictures of the man who had ridden the lift with her, if he was the other guy's ski buddy.

She had a flash of recall. She had taken a backward shot to capture the interesting vista from the lift, and she was certain the man on the chairlift behind her would be in the picture. Maybe blurred. She couldn't remember exactly what she'd been focusing on.

"I got pictures of them," she said.

Tom asked, "Of whom?"

"Of the man who pushed me down, if he rode the lift behind us, and the other who might have been with him. I don't know how good the photos will be."

Jake glanced at her camera, his face brightening at once. "You're a photographer." As if he suddenly recalled what she was doing up there.

She felt like laughing. Now it didn't matter who she was or what she intended. If she liked photography, she had an in with Jake. "I write for a newspaper." She took decent pictures, but she didn't want him to think she was a professional photographer.

Tom frowned. "We'll check out the pictures after Doc Weber runs some tests on you."

She hoped the pictures would reveal something useful. But now she had a new problem. She had to get hold of North and make arrangements to meet him somewhere else at a later time. She wouldn't be able to return to the ski slopes this afternoon.

———

Jake had to be kidding about taking care of Elizabeth. Jake had a mate, whom he adored, so Tom knew his brother wasn't interested in the she-wolf. It seemed more like a case of him trying to give Tom a hard time. Or maybe Jake was worried that Tom would show interest in the wrong she-wolf. He wondered what video Jake was talking about, particularly since his brother couldn't hide the hint of a smile that surfaced when he mentioned it.

Now Jake appeared every bit as interested in her camera and the pictures she'd taken, and nothing else mattered.

"I already offered to go with her," Peter said. "Tom's not budging. Although I also want to get a look at those pictures if this was foul play instead of an accident. And Cantrell's video, if anything important is on that."

"I agree about the pictures, Peter." Tom gave his brother a sideways glance, wondering about Cantrell's video. "I'll take care of your ski rentals, Elizabeth. After I get your stuff from your locker, I'll meet you down at the hospital."

"I need to get up the mountain," Jake said and slapped Tom on the back. "Keep me posted on the little lady."

Tom squeezed Elizabeth's hand with assurance. "I'll see you real soon."

He caught Jake's eye, saw the way his brother watched them, and shook his head. Tom loved his family, but he hadn't realized what it would feel like for *him* to be under the magnifying glass and not *them* when it came to interest in a woman.

Cody, Anthony, and Minx quickly took Elizabeth's ski rentals in hand and offered to turn them in. Thanking them, Tom headed for her ski locker where he could pick up whatever she'd left there. He hoped the man who had run into her had only done so because he was being a jerk instead of doing so on purpose.

─────────────

When Tom arrived at the hospital, the waiting room was empty, mostly because wolves didn't get sick often and healed quickly on their own. Humans were the only ones who needed much care, but the town had a sparse human population. The receptionist, a middle-aged widow, smiled at him. Maggie was dressed in her usual black-and-white kitty-cat scrubs. Everyone teased her about wearing cat scrubs when she was a gray wolf in a pack of mostly gray wolves.

"Hi, Tom. Thought you were on ski patrol today."

"Just this morning."

"Did you need to see the doctor?" Maggie rose from the chair.

The news would get all over town when he told her he'd come to check on Elizabeth. "I'm waiting to hear what Dr. Weber has to say about Elizabeth Wildwood."

"Elizabeth Wildwood." Maggie's tone of voice and smile said it all—she figured he had something going with the wolf-coyote. "Do you want to have a seat?"

No, he didn't. He just wanted to learn about Elizabeth's condition as soon as possible. "I'll just walk back."

Before he reached the hallway to the exam rooms, Maggie said, "She's pretty. Not from around here. Is she moving to town?"

"No." He wanted to end the discussion without another word.

"Ah. So...there's nothing to the video."

Tom paused. "*What* video?"

"The one that Cantrell took. Didn't you know about it? He's charging ten dollars a view. Everyone who's gotten word of it is paying for it. Even your brothers, I heard."

Tom said again, "What *video*?"

Maggie blushed. "Of you kissing a woman on the slopes. I'd say it was...Elizabeth Wildwood." She smiled. "Really nice kiss. If the eligible she-wolves weren't already interested, they'd be pounding on your door. And the bachelor wolves? They'll take notes."

Tom let out a disgruntled sound and headed for the exam rooms. "I'll kill Cantrell."

If Elizabeth had been one of their wolf pack, Tom could have walked back and learned the status of the patient, no questions asked. He would have informed Darien of her condition right away.

Even with her not being part of the pack, Darien would have to be told about her condition since she'd been injured in their territory. That was a pack's way of doing business. Doctor-patient privileges were not relevant here. Especially if they learned that the man who had pushed her was a wolf from their own pack and had done so with malicious intent. It was also important to protect the pack from another that might be angered that she'd been injured here.

Tom met Nurse Matthew Adams standing in the hall, typing notes on a computer. New to the pack, the tall, dark-haired man wore blue scrubs and sneakers. When he saw Tom approaching, his somber expression turned into a scowl. Matthew didn't have much of a sense of humor. The hospital needed him, although he hadn't fit in well with the other wolves.

Tom had welcomed Matthew to the pack and attempted to draw him out of his lone-wolf mindset, but he remained standoffish.

Matthew blocked Tom's path right away. "She's in with Doc."

So Matthew knew exactly why Tom was here. And he didn't like it.

"I know that." He had only assumed he could come to the exam room, but he didn't want to indulge Matthew. "I'll be in the staff lounge. Tell Doc I need to see him when he's done."

Matthew gave a reluctant nod. He had worked in a strictly

human hospital before this and had not been with a pack before. He didn't care for pack politics, but he did like to see to the care of wolves and not just humans. Darien had high hopes that the nurse would come around eventually and join in the other wolf activities in the pack. They needed his nursing skills no matter what.

Tom had pulled Elizabeth's camera out of his bag the first chance he'd had to see if it worked. He'd thought he might be able to take a look at the display, but he couldn't get the camera to turn on. Broken? Hopefully it was something easily fixed.

He poured himself a cup of coffee in the staff lounge and glanced out the window. A couple of vehicles drove by—a black pickup and a white minivan. Because of the snow accumulation, the streets were quiet.

Doc Weber walked into the lounge and poured a mug of hot tea. A red wolf from Lelandi's pack originally, he was gray-haired, shorter, and staying here to take care of Lelandi and her babies. Now Jake's wife would be having hers, and Doc Weber said he'd stick around a while longer. Tom thought he'd stay forever, considering how fond he'd grown of their pack.

"She'll be okay, if you've come to check on Elizabeth Wildwood."

As if the doc didn't know that was why Tom was here. "What's the verdict?"

"Mild wrist sprain, some bruising, and minor back strain. She doesn't really need any special treatment for it, but she might want to sleep for a while. She'll be as good as new before you know it."

"The concussion?"

"The scan showed no problems. She seems to be fine. If you see any setbacks…" Doc paused. "You'll watch her, right? I would keep her overnight at the hospital for observation unless you or one of your family members will be with her for the night."

"Um, yeah." Tom hadn't planned to stay with her for the night. But if Doc thought she needed Tom to watch over her, he would.

"She said someone pushed her on the slope. Did you see any evidence of bruising, particularly on her back or shoulder?"

Doc Weber rubbed his forehead like he always did when he was tired, then took a sip of his tea. "She has a couple of bruises, but considering all the clothes she wore and that the man most likely wore gloves, I doubt any fingerprint bruise marks would have occurred."

Footsteps sounded and Elizabeth joined Tom and the doc in the lounge. She had a wrap on her left wrist, her parka under her right arm, and a sack in her hand. She gave Tom an annoyed look. He could tell it was put on—or at least he thought it was.

"I'll live. Told you so. Dr. Weber was very thorough. You all made *way* too big of a deal of it."

"Better safe than sorry," Tom said, fighting a smile. She was a feisty little thing and ready to bite, and he was amused at her taking him to task. He pulled her snow boots out of the bag and helped her into them after she sat down on one of the chairs.

Doc Weber took another sip of his tea. "I gave her an ice pack she can use."

Tom eyed the wrap around her wrist. "Thanks, Doc. I'll be in touch if she begins to feel bad."

He helped her to stand, then draped her parka over her shoulders. Relieving her of her bag, he rested his hand at the small of her back and guided her down the hall and out through the waiting area. He hurried her past the reception desk before Maggie could say another word that might embarrass his charge. Like mentioning that damned video. He wanted to see it as soon as possible, but he didn't want Elizabeth to learn of it. And he *wasn't* paying to watch it!

Maggie was on the phone, *thank God*, or he was certain she would have said something to them on their way out.

Elizabeth asked, "Did you check my camera?"

"Yeah, I'm sorry. It's not working. I'll have Jake look at it."

"Great," she said unhappily.

As they exited the building into the biting cold, she looked so miserable, her chin pointed down as she stared at the snow-shoveled walkway to the truck, that Tom felt bad for her. He hoped a good meal would make her feel a little better.

"Do you think you can handle lunch?" he asked.

"My stomach is growling, if that's any indication that I have an appetite and can eat just fine."

"How do you feel about eating out? Or would you prefer that we get some food at your room?"

"I'll be fine. Really, Tom. I can dine out. No special treatment. Thanks though."

"All right. I'll take you to Silver Town Tavern for lunch. When we're done, we can return to your room, and I can apply the ice pack on your back. That will help keep the swelling and bruising to a minimum."

She looked at him with one of those almost smiles that said he'd pushed it in trying to get close and personal. But they'd already been close and personal, and if she hadn't been injured, he'd want to sample more of her kisses. Without an audience and especially without Cantrell around to use his phone video recorder!

He raised his brows. "It's the least I can do after not being there for you when you were hurt."

"I'm sure I can manage."

"Doc's orders. One of us has to stay with you until we're certain your condition doesn't deteriorate." Tom knew she shouldn't stay by herself in the event she had incurred some head trauma. She couldn't even turn her head without wincing and groaning.

When she didn't say anything, he glanced at her. She smiled at him.

"What?"

"That is the *best* pickup line I've ever heard. You are so bossy. Did you know that?"

He chuckled. "I'm free all afternoon. We can eat, then we'll drop by your place, and you can try to sleep while I apply the ice pack to your back."

"All right. I'm sure if I oppose any part of your plan, you'll disagree."

"What part of the plan would you object to?"

She rolled her eyes and then tried flexing her fingers, wincing a bit at the sore muscles in her wrist.

"It'll get better," he continued. "By tomorrow, some of the edge will be off, courtesy of our wolf…" He paused, wondering if she was the same as them because she had mixed coyote blood. He had no idea if coyote shifters healed faster.

"Yes, I heal quickly also." Her words were clipped.

He'd hit a nerve, and that made him want to know so much more about her. What was her history with the coyote and wolf packs? Why was she so touchy about her coyote roots?

Maybe he should have been a psychologist like Lelandi. Darien would have a fit if Tom even considered such a thing.

One psychologist in the family was more than enough.

CHAPTER 7

Elizabeth glanced around at the quaint old town with its covered wooden walkways that led from one building to the next. The town would look like a scene from an old Western movie if it weren't for the carved grizzlies and wolves guarding the businesses at strategic locations. The grizzlies stood six feet tall with their teeth bared and their long claws stretched out, while the wolves looked on with watchful eyes, their mouths clamped shut and their expressions leery.

A couple of chairs rocked in the breeze as if ghostly figures enjoyed the view of the abandoned two-story timber hotel across the street. Snow-covered mountains provided a majestic backdrop. Large dusty, dark tavern windows peered onto the street, and Elizabeth envisioned wary patrons watching her approach. A newcomer. Everyone would wonder why she was in Tom's company. Unless word had already spread through the entire town.

She looked at the hotel's dusty windows, pausing for a moment to consider a spot that someone seemed to have wiped a bit clean to peer out.

"A new family purchased the hotel," Tom said, noticing Elizabeth's focus. "They plan to renovate it."

"Wolves?"

"Yeah."

"In a similar style, based on the town as it is?" She loved seeing old places renovated but still featuring the original architecture. That gave the town character.

"You bet."

"That's nice." As spooky as it looked, she wondered about the hotel's history. "Is it haunted?"

"A little."

"Oh. What if ghost busters want to come to town to learn about the hauntings and discover something more paranormal? Like... wolf shifters running the place?"

He shook his head and guided her along the wooden walkway. "We'll keep mum about the ghostly happenings."

"But visitors might not."

"Only wolf pack members will serve on the staff. If guests say they saw ghosts, it's their word against the owners and staff who work there."

"Wow," Elizabeth said. "I like the way your wolf town works."

He smiled at her comment. "We only hire wolf shifters for key jobs. The humans are none the wiser, and it keeps them from running our town."

As they walked along the boardwalk, the boards creaked like they suffered from arthritis, announcing the wolves' arrival loud and clear. Tom opened the tavern door for Elizabeth. Her eyes adjusted to the lower lights inside. Amber glass lights dangled from brass rods hung from a ten-foot-high ceiling and cast a golden light over dark oak tables and an antique bar. Antique mirrors covering the wall behind the bar made the place appear even larger. Dark wooden ceiling fans were suspended but stationary. The tavern was comfortably cool already.

The wooden floor smelled of floor wax, but the aroma of the beef cooking in a kitchen made her stomach rumble. If the food tasted anything like it smelled, she was glad Tom had brought her here.

Five men sat at a table, eating sandwiches and talking, until they saw her and Tom walk into the tavern. They all smiled at her, then raised their brows at Tom.

"Boys," he said in greeting, though most of the "boys" were middle-aged.

"Miss, Tom," they all responded.

She smiled a little and said, "Hi." She sounded horribly shy when she wasn't like that at all.

Their smiles broadened. They had to be dying to learn who she was, especially since she was with Tom. She could smell that gray wolves frequented the place, but only a hint of human scents wafted in the air.

"Restricted membership?" she asked Tom.

"Yeah, wolves only, but to humans it looks like a private club. One day a year during our Victorian Days festival, we open it up to nonshifters. We hold the festival in the fall."

"That sounds like fun." Her attention swung to a bearded man who watched them as he dried a green glass behind the old bar, the polished wood worn in places where thirsty patrons had rested their arms for eons. She estimated he was about six four in height. Huge.

He smiled at her, then Tom, as he set the green glass he'd dried on the counter. His shoulder-length black hair and thick beard made him look like a rugged naturalist.

"That's Sam, and he owns the tavern and has been here forever." Tom guided Elizabeth to a table in the far corner where they could see the rest of the room, but their backs were protected. He pulled a chair out for her and, once she was seated, scooted it under the table for her. She'd never been treated with such civility. She rather liked the attention, she had to admit.

A woman entered the tavern dressed in tight-fitting jeans with sparkles on the back pockets and a peach turtleneck shirt. High-heeled brown leather boots reached midthigh, and she had the most beautiful curly sable hair piled on top of her head.

"Hey, Silva," one of the five men seated at the table said. "Kind of working banker's hours like old Mason here, aren't you?"

She gave him a bright smile. "I would have arrived sooner if I'd known *you* would be here today." She glanced in Tom and

Elizabeth's direction. After looking Elizabeth over, she offered a little smile.

Small towns, Elizabeth thought. She hadn't expected all the notice and was glad to be with Tom, who would deflect some of the attention...she hoped.

"Silva," Tom said in greeting as he took his seat next to Elizabeth.

"Tom," Silva said as she put her purse behind the bar. Sam had glanced in Silva's direction when she first entered the tavern, but when she went behind the bar, he ignored her completely.

Elizabeth tried to figure out the pack dynamics. If Silva worked for Sam, why was she late, and why didn't he say something to her? He was definitely interested in her, yet he scowled at her and didn't greet her. Then again, she didn't give him the time of day either.

Sheriff Peter walked into the tavern, frowning deeply. Without looking at anyone, he went straight to the most out-of-the-way table by one of the windows and took a seat.

All the other men watched him. So did Sam and Silva. Even Tom had turned to look at him, and not in a casual way. She recognized Tom's concern for a pack member, and she admired him for that.

Silva hurried to take a bottle of water to the sheriff. "What's wrong, Peter?"

"Nothing." He barely acknowledged her and drank the water.

He'd been so friendly on the slope. What had changed?

Silva walked over to Tom's table and said to Elizabeth, "You're new in town. Staying long?"

Elizabeth leaned back in the chair and looked up at Silva. "This is what I'd call a small town."

Silva pulled a phone out of her pocket, turned it on, smiled at it, then shut it off and tucked it back in her pocket. "Sure is, sugar. Everybody's business is everybody's business."

Elizabeth couldn't help but smile at Silva's comment. She liked it when people were honest with her. Still, she didn't answer Silva's question about how long she'd be staying.

In her condition, Elizabeth figured skiing was out for now, and she really didn't see any reason to stay longer except to see North and meet with Hrothgar. As soon as she could do so, she'd make plans for a return trip home earlier than originally scheduled.

———

Tom had cast the evil eye at Silva when she brought out her phone. If she had the video of him kissing Elizabeth and thought to show it to her, he was... Well, he wasn't sure what he would do. But he didn't want Elizabeth to know Cantrell was selling that moment—or couple of moments—he'd shared with Elizabeth to every member of the blasted pack!

He was glad when Silva slipped her phone back in her pocket.

Tom wondered what was up with Peter. Why hadn't he joined the other men? He never sat alone, and all of them loved to visit with him. The sheriff was usually as good-natured as they came, levelheaded, and a friend in a crisis. Tom didn't remember ever seeing Peter looking so troubled.

"Do you mind if I have a word with Peter, Elizabeth?" Tom asked.

"Not at all. Go ahead."

Tom didn't want to leave Elizabeth alone, but Silva had kind of a sixth sense about things like that, and she stuck by the she-wolf's side so she wouldn't feel abandoned. When a pack member had a problem, it was up to the pack to help the wolf out.

"Thanks." Tom turned to Silva. "Just get the lady whatever she'd like. I'll have the usual."

"I sure will, Tom. I've never seen him so down in the dumps, have you?" Silva whispered.

Tom shook his head, rose from his chair, and crossed the floor to where Peter sat. "What's up, Peter?"

"My brother's coming to town."

Tom had never met Peter's brother. Peter had joined their pack years ago, after his brother had left him for places unknown. Tom had no idea what the man was like.

Not waiting for an invite, since he knew from the way Peter stared out the window that he wouldn't give one, Tom took a seat across from him. "You always figured your brother was in some kind of trouble. And that's why he would never visit. You thought he wouldn't offer for you to come see him because he was into something illegal."

"Yeah," Peter said glumly.

"So you're the law. If he comes here and breaks any of our rules, you stick him in jail. What with us running the place, it shouldn't be any trouble." Because the jail was shifter-run, it was probably the only one in the States where a shifter could be incarcerated without that causing problems. One cell block was strictly for shifters with minor infractions and isolated the wolves from everyone else.

"He's bringing a mate," Peter said.

Tom frowned, hoping Peter's brother hadn't gotten mixed up with a human and would bring a whole bunch of grief to the pack. "Is she a wolf?"

"I have no idea. He's a loner. He's stayed away all these years, and it makes me think he's up to something less than legal. I just don't want him to stir up trouble for the pack. I know my duty, but…"

"He's still your brother." Tom patted Peter on the shoulder. "I'll let Darien know, and we'll all provide backup to help out if he causes problems."

"We loved to hunt and fish as kids before he took off and I joined your pack." Peter sounded a little more hopeful, finally making eye contact with Tom.

"So maybe you can do that again."

"I don't know what he wants."

"Don't second-guess it. Just make the most of his visit. You never know. He might be ready to settle down and want to join our pack, if he doesn't cause trouble."

Peter looked back at Elizabeth. "What about her?" Now he sounded *really* interested.

"Kind of a mystery." But *Tom's* mystery. Not any other bachelor male's in the pack. "Got to get back to her. Are you all right now?"

"Yeah, thanks."

Tom glanced at the other men. They dipped their heads a little in silent acknowledgment that they could step in now and help out. Two rose from the table and walked over to join Peter.

The banker said, "Do you mind if we join you?"

"I'd like that. Thanks, Mason."

Reassured Peter would be okay, Tom returned to his own table.

"Okay, so you want the usual and... Elizabeth?" Silva said. She brought out a pad and pen. She didn't need to use them, but it was part of her presentation.

"Roast beef sandwich sound good?" Tom asked Elizabeth, surprised she hadn't already placed an order. Then again, she'd been watching him, studying him. He hoped she liked what she saw.

"Sure," Elizabeth said.

"And to drink?" he asked.

Elizabeth gave a little snort. "Make it milk."

Silva glanced at her wrist. "Break?"

"Sprain. But I figure that milk helps to keep the bones strong if I fall down mountains in the future."

Silva smiled at her. "I'm Silva, by the way. I'm the proud owner of the Victorian Tea Shop."

Sam scowled as he watched them, then turned to dry more glasses.

"I take it Sam's not happy about this," Tom said. Silva had waitressed at the tavern forever, even though with their longevity, she was only twenty-eight in human years.

"Nope," Silva said. "It's time I had a place of my own. I'll waitress over there *and* I'll be the owner. Which means I can decorate it to my heart's content. If you hang around long enough," she said to Elizabeth, "you can come to the grand opening."

"Thanks. Maybe I can come back some other time."

Silva glanced at Tom as if he was supposed to keep Elizabeth here a while longer, if nothing else, to ensure that Elizabeth came to her grand opening.

Elizabeth cleared her throat uncomfortably and asked Silva, "Do you ski?"

Silva laughed and said, "I've only been up to the ski resort one time. I went to the ski lodge and had a hot toddy." She shrugged. "If wolves were meant to ski, they wouldn't have nonslip paw pads." She paused before she left to place their orders. "You're staying overnight at least, aren't you?"

"Yeah. I am."

Silva gave her a big smile. "You've got to meet Darien's mate, Lelandi. She'd love to visit with you."

"I think we'll see her tonight."

Silva glanced at Tom. "Good. Sounds *real* good. I'll get your food." She headed for the bar.

Sam shoved a tray on the counter, two sandwiches already on the plates, along with a beer and one glass of milk.

"Why, thank you, Sam. That was quick."

He grunted at her.

Silva whipped around and brought the tray to Tom and Elizabeth's table. "He's mad at me," she whispered to them, "because I'm leaving him to work my own place and he has to find a new waitress. I've got new horizons."

"Sometimes we have to spread our wings," Elizabeth agreed. "Sometimes it's time to take a chance and make some big changes in our lives."

"You sound like you speak from experience," Tom said.

Elizabeth looked uncomfortable, then shook her head. "Silva sounds like she's in a place where she needs to make a change."

"What do you do for a living?" Silva asked.

Tom frowned a little at Silva, wanting her to wait on the other tables and leave him alone with Elizabeth.

Mason came to Tom's rescue. "Hey, Silva, another round of drinks and sandwiches over here?"

"How will you manage our money at the bank if you're over here eating all afternoon?" Silva asked cheerfully, then took off to serve the drinks.

Peter rose from the table. "Nothing more for me. Got to get back to work." He waved in Tom and Elizabeth's direction and headed out of the tavern.

Elizabeth's phone jingled.

"Excuse me," she said to Tom and got up to answer it.

Tom frowned. Her call should be private, but he couldn't help wanting to know who called her and why. A boyfriend? Tom hoped not. She'd looked more worried than happy to hear from the caller, whoever it was.

CHAPTER 8

TOM SIPPED HIS DRINK AND KEPT HIS EYE ON ELIZABETH, WHO had her ear pressed to the cell phone. As crowded and noisy as the tavern had gotten, Tom couldn't overhear the caller's part of the conversation, no matter how much he strained to hear any of it.

"I understand. We'll have to meet later," Elizabeth said.

Tom watched the emotions play across her face as she stared at the table, eyes downcast, brow furrowed.

"I'll..." She looked up to see Tom observing her. "If you get in later, I'll be at Hastings Bed and Breakfast. If you *can't* make it, I'll call you back, and we'll work something out." Pause. "Okay. Bye." She slipped the phone into her bag. "Sorry. Just a call I had to take."

"I completely understand. You didn't tell him you were invited to dinner tonight." Tom added the "him" in there, suspecting the caller had to be a he—and Tom damn well wanted to know who *he* was.

"I doubt he'll come. Roads are bad."

So he was close by. Within driving distance.

"I'm...sorry. I hadn't taken into account that you might have had other plans while you stayed here." Tom wasn't sorry. More disappointed, but he should have realized someone would be interested in the woman.

"Don't worry about it."

But he did worry about it. And then he thought it odd. She hadn't mentioned to the caller that she'd been injured. Maybe not wanting to concern the man, since he couldn't do anything about it? Or maybe she was worried he'd be angry with the pack for allowing her to be injured, and she didn't want to stir up trouble.

"If he arrives anyway, he could have dinner with Darien and Lelandi tonight," Tom offered, as much as he hated to.

"No," she said.

Bluntly. No explanation. That made him even more curious.

"He's driving?"

This time, her gaze locked on to Tom's.

He fought to keep from smiling as he drank the rest of his beer and sat back in his chair. "Was he going to ski with you?"

She smiled. "You're cute, you know? *No*, I'm not seeing him, as in he's my favorite squeeze. *Yes*, he's a wolf. *Yes*, he's driving. *No*, he's not skiing with me."

Tom chuckled. He guessed he wasn't as subtle as he'd hoped. He frowned. "Business?"

She hesitated too long. Finally, she said, "Yeah. Business."

Coyote trickster came to mind. *Again.*

Tom desperately wanted to ask her what kind of business, but he was glad the guy wasn't courting her. Tom smiled. "You think I'm cute?"

She laughed. "Yeah. You are. Just don't let it go to your head."

"After that kiss we shared on the slope, it already has."

She shook her head slightly, but she smiled.

The door jingled and they both glanced that way.

"Don't tell me," she said. "The man with Jake is your oldest brother."

"Yeah, he is."

Being in a close-knit pack, Darien, Tom, and Jake often came to the tavern midday to hang out with other pack members and hear if anyone had trouble with anything. So when Tom saw Darien and Jake enter the tavern, he thought that was the only reason they'd come. Unless someone in the tavern had texted them that he and Elizabeth were here and they wanted to check on them. Tom waved at his brothers to join them. Darien and Jake cast each other looks as if they weren't sure if they should intrude. This was their regular table, and sitting somewhere else might signal that Tom was courting Elizabeth.

"Elizabeth, meet my brother Darien."

"Don't stand," Darien said. "We look forward to seeing you tonight. Lelandi's planning a big spread and has nannies taking care of the kids."

"Thanks. She didn't have to go to all that trouble," Elizabeth said.

"Are you kidding? She's a psychologist, which means she wants to do everything just right to make you feel at home."

Elizabeth smiled faintly.

"Come, join us," Tom offered. This was the pack leaders' table, so no one needed to offer Darien a seat, but Tom could see that Darien was waiting to determine whether his youngest brother wanted time alone with the wolf-coyote lady.

Several tables had filled due to the time of day. After Darien and Jake took their usual seats, Jake waved to Silva. "I need to get back to the slopes, so if you can just get me a water and sandwich, that'll work."

"You got it," Silva said. "You, boss?" she asked Darien.

"Same."

"Coming up," Sam said, as if he didn't need Silva to tell him what to do.

Silva walked over to the bar to get the tray.

His voice low, Darien said to Tom, "The Victorian Tea Shop?"

"Yeah, there might be trouble in paradise," Tom replied.

Silva delivered the tray of sandwiches and two bottled waters to their table. "More wolf sightings around the local farmers' live-stock, I hear."

"A farmer spotted three wolves yesterday before the snowstorm hit," Darien said.

Tom leaned back in his chair. "Every time we've investigated, we haven't smelled any of their scents."

"I checked with the couple of wolf packs that live several miles from here to see if they know of any rogue wolves or if any of their pack members have been missing," Darien said.

"And nothing, right?" Tom asked.

"Nothing. Right."

"Maybe wolves that don't belong to a pack, then. Nomads," Tom said.

"Got to be."

Silva slipped her pen into her pocket. "Rumblings are that the farmers and ranchers won't wait for you and your men to take care of it."

"We're doing the best we can," Darien said. "We'll search again in a day or so. After that, another storm will hit. We won't be able to do anything until the snow settles again."

"They're bound to take off and get caught up in the storm this time, since they're so persistent." Silva smiled at Jake. "Got the babies' booties knitted." She turned to Tom. "As long as you don't pick up a woman and get her pregnant, I'm nearly done knitting baby gifts for a while."

Elizabeth blushed and Tom was certain he suffered from the same reaction, as hot as his face felt. Everyone at the table remained silent. Silva was always outspoken, but when she made a friend, she was theirs for life. She seemed to like Elizabeth right away. Maybe she reminded Silva of Lelandi; she and Silva had become fast friends.

"Have you had any dreams, Tom?" Silva went on. "You know, like Jake and Darien had?"

He was the only one who had put any stock in dream mating and the only one of the three brothers who hadn't had any dreams. He shook his head. He cast Jake an annoyed look. Of any of the brothers, Jake was the worst for not having believed in the phenomenon.

"Well, it's probably just not your time yet," Silva said, sounding sympathetic. "Unless, of course, you don't need the extra push in the right direction." She glanced at Elizabeth.

Elizabeth might never have heard of such an occurrence, and Tom wished Silva would get off the topic.

"Hey, lady, you waiting on all the tables or just that one?" some guy shouted from across the tavern.

Every head turned in his direction.

Dressed in ski clothes, three late-twenties, early-thirties male wolves sat at a table next to one of the windows. They had probably smelled that it was a shifter-only tavern, but they must not have known that the Silver brothers and their mates ran the town. Or that the three men seated at this table *were* the Silver brothers.

Everyone looked to see what Darien would do. He eyed the men and then took a swig of his bottled water.

Silva gave the newcomers a big smile. "Coming." But she didn't.

"You want me to say something to them?" Jake asked Darien.

"No. No need," Darien said, still eyeing the men.

Darien was like that. He didn't need to use his muscle to show who was boss. Yet everyone there knew he'd take the men to task if the situation required it.

Sam's beard, height, and muscular build made him look more like a grizzly than a gray wolf, and he glared at the men as he poured drinks from the tap, casting a watchful eye on Silva.

Sam might be big, but he moved fast. Tom had seen him dive around the counter, grab an unruly wolf, and throw him out the door faster than anyone could react. Just give him a good reason. And all he needed for motivation was someone being nasty to Silva.

When Silva waited on a table near the Silver brothers', the three men's scowls hardened. Sam had already given them each a beer. Granted, their mugs were empty again, but it was a busy afternoon as the wolves in the area enjoyed a reprieve from the last snowstorm before the next hit.

Tom turned back to the table, confident Sam could handle the situation but still wary about the wolf strangers, especially considering the topic at hand. "Since we've never smelled any sign of the wolves that have been sneaking around the farms, I suspect they've got to be some of our kind." He eyed the strangers again.

Jake agreed. "Yeah, I'm inclined to think they could be from our pack, or they wouldn't disguise their scent. Otherwise, we wouldn't know who they were anyway."

"Possibly. Or they just don't want us trailing them. Which brings us to which ones they are and why they're doing this," Darien said.

"Or they could just be troublemaking wolves or wolves for hire. Or some other wolves that have a beef with us," Jake said.

"You mean like the wolves from the red pack who caused us trouble before?" Tom asked.

"Hey, lady!" one of the other outsider wolves said. "Are you working only that side of the tavern?"

Sam slammed a mug of beer on the countertop, sloshing it all over.

Tom asked Darien, "Are you sure you don't want me to speak to them?"

"No. Sam will take care of it, if necessary."

Tom knew that was Darien's way of saying that Sam was Silva's protector, and he wanted him to get off the fence about mating with her. Everyone in town knew Silva only desired Sam and vice versa. Nobody wanted to get on Sam's bad side, so even if some wolves flirted with Silva, nobody was about to court her.

Tom slid a glance Elizabeth's way. She took everything in—the discussion about the wolf-pack trouble they had, the interaction between pack members and outsiders. He took a deep breath to smell her reaction and thought maybe she would be worried or anxious. She wasn't. She was ready to tackle the men, her adrenaline running high, her fingers clenched around her milk glass, her expression feral. He smiled at her. Even though this wasn't her battle and it wasn't her pack, she appeared ready to fight on Silva's behalf.

Silva might act like she needed the pack's help, but she was good at dealing with issues herself.

"I'll be right there," she said very sweetly. She enjoyed riling people who got on her bad side.

She passed by the bar, smiled at Sam, and gave him the drink order for the men seated at the table next to Darien's. Then she continued on her way to the outsiders' table.

When she reached them, the blond man scratched his beard, his cold, dark eyes focused on her. "Hell, woman, a man could die of thirst before he got a spit of whiskey in this place."

"Silva," she said in a sugary way. She could be a real tigress when she was provoked, but she also knew how to play people. "I thought you had a beer."

Tom was ready to move if any of the men got physical with her. "I'll take the redhead on the left," he said to his brothers.

Jake smirked. "Hell, Tom, that's the smallest guy of the bunch. Okay, I'll take the scraggly black-haired guy to the right."

"You need glasses," Tom retorted. "The guy on the right is the smallest one of the three."

Elizabeth chuckled. Tom smiled.

When the dark-haired man reached for Silva's arm, virtually every male in the tavern shoved his chair aside and headed for the newcomers' table. Sam was there too, a full bottle of whiskey in his clenched hand. He looked like he was itching to use it.

The man quickly pulled back his hand.

"Time to go, boys," Darien said, his eyes glittering with menace. "Storm's coming in. You better get out of town before it's too late."

The man narrowed his eyes at Darien. "It's a free country. And the storm's not coming in for a couple of days."

"I run the town."

The men's eyes all rounded as Darien got their attention.

"Well, I'll be damned," the spokesman for the group said, rising slowly. "And you are who exactly?"

"Darien Silver, and my advice still stands."

Tom and the rest of the men were ready to back Darien up with force, if necessary. If the three strangers always acted like this, a pack didn't need them.

The other two men rose from the table.

"Seems we're not welcome here." The spokesman cast one last glance in Silva's direction, then slid his gaze Elizabeth's way.

That had Tom hot under the collar.

Without another word, the three outsiders headed out of the tavern.

Jake said, "I've got to get back to the slopes."

"See you tonight," Darien replied. He turned to three men of their pack. They all bowed their heads just a little in acknowledgment and left the tavern. They would make sure that the troublemakers headed out of town.

Darien pulled Tom aside and lowered his voice. "I want you to bring Elizabeth up to the house as soon as you get her things."

"We intend to come up later, in time for dinner."

"We don't really know what's going on with her. I'd rather she stay with us until she leaves."

"All right."

"I'll see you both in just a bit," Darien said and headed out of the tavern.

Tom returned to the table where Elizabeth was still seated. She'd finished her sandwich and drunk the last of her milk. "Are we ready to go back to the B and B?" she asked.

"Change of plans." As independent as Elizabeth appeared, Tom was afraid she wouldn't like the change of plans one bit.

CHAPTER 9

Bertha's face was scrunched up with concern as she came out of the kitchen, wiping her wet hands on a towel, and greeted Tom and Elizabeth when they arrived at her inn. "Oh my, I can't believe anyone would hurt you, Elizabeth."

Bertha's curly hair drooped a little, and she smelled of soy sauce, spicy mustard, and pork chops. If Tom hadn't already had dinner plans at Darien's house, he would have opted to eat here.

"I'm *fine*," Elizabeth reiterated, but she smiled, seemingly touched.

Bertha added, "Darien called and said you're moving her to his house."

"He just told me," Tom said, not wanting to get into it with Elizabeth again.

"I don't need to leave here," Elizabeth protested. *Again.* She'd tried to talk him out of it on the short drive from the tavern to the inn.

In a consoling voice, Bertha said, "Darien told me you might have had a run-in with someone who could be more trouble, and he doesn't want to take any chances with you staying here since my husband is out of town. Not only that, but Doc Weber insisted Tom stay the night with you. You know, to…monitor your condition."

"That's not necessary. I'll be all right here. Alone," Elizabeth said.

"All right. Come on," Tom said. "We'll proceed as planned. You can rest in your room. I'll apply ice packs for a while. I'll call Darien and tell him I'll bring you out there for dinner." He wouldn't get into the issue of tonight right now. He knew Darien wouldn't agree with him about not leaving right away, but Tom really wanted to please Elizabeth.

That was a first—going against his brother's orders to satisfy a woman.

"I really don't need to stay there after dinner. We can eat and—"

"Pack leader's orders." Tom smiled when he said it, but he was serious as he preceded her to her guest room. He would allow her to rest here, but after that, they would stay at Darien's. As he hesitated at her bedroom door, he felt a cold breeze seeping from beneath it. He glanced down at the carpeted floor and took a deep breath of the winter-chilled outdoor air. Instantly, he had a bad feeling about this.

Before he opened the door, he said, "Window's open. Did you leave it ajar?"

Elizabeth frowned at him. "In this weather? No."

Senses on high alert, Tom listened for any movement in the room and tried to discern anyone's scent, but he didn't smell anything other than Bertha's and Elizabeth's feminine scents. "Go back and stay with Bertha, if you don't mind. Ask her if she opened the window."

Elizabeth made an irritated huff under her breath but retreated down the hall toward the kitchen. "Did you open the window in my room?"

"And lose all the heat in there? I should say not," Bertha said. "What's the matter?"

"The window appears to be ajar," Elizabeth said.

Tom shoved the door open and stared at the broken glass that littered the carpeted floor next to the window and covered one corner of a bedside table. Otherwise, the room seemed untouched.

"Hell," he said under his breath. As he entered the room, he yanked his cell out of his pocket and called Darien.

"What's happened, Tom?" Elizabeth called from the hallway.

Tom peered out the window. Two men's boots had left tracks in the fresh powder. "Darien, we've got more trouble."

He heard footsteps and turned to see Elizabeth staring at the room. "I hadn't unpacked my bags. While we were gone, the airport was supposed to deliver them." Immediately, she went to the closet and opened the door. "My bags aren't here."

"What's going on, Tom?" Darien asked.

"Elizabeth's room at the B and B was broken into. We're checking to see if they stole anything."

"Bertha? Did the airport deliver my suitcases?" Elizabeth called out.

"Yes, dear. I rolled them into your room when they arrived."

"Whoever broke in took her bags," Tom relayed to Darien, studying Elizabeth. She looked so pale, her eyes tearing up, and he felt terrible for her. Talk about one hell of a horrible vacation. Or…business trip. He wanted in the worst way to make it up to her.

Elizabeth pulled open a drawer and found it empty. She got a wide-eyed look of panic and quickly reached into the breast pocket of her jacket, then took a shaky breath of relief and zipped her jacket back up. Tom looked at her quizzically, but she only gestured back at the drawer and said, "I–I'd left a few things here from my carry-on that I didn't want to take up to the slopes. Plane ticket receipts, driver's license. My laptop's gone." Her lips quivered and she looked on the verge of bursting into tears.

"I'll call you right back, Darien," Tom said quickly, the sight of Elizabeth's distress making him feel like he'd been punched in the gut. He ended the call and took her gently in his arms, trying to avoid hurting her.

She said through her tears, "I don't cry over just anything."

He didn't know what to say to make her feel better. Not wanting her to think that he saw her tears as a weakness, he leaned down, took her face in his, and very lightly kissed her mouth.

He hadn't planned to. But he wanted to stop her crying. *No, that wasn't it at all.* He'd wanted to kiss her again since the moment he'd done so on the slope. And before that. When he'd laid eyes on her in Bertha's kitchen, the cinnamon sugar sparkling on her lips. He'd wanted to lick off the spicy granules, taste the sweetness in her mouth, and feel that soft and curvy body pulled up tight against him.

He separated his lips from hers, expecting her to be horrified or shocked but certainly not smiling.

"To stop the tears," he said, clearing his throat and apologizing, although he wanted to kiss her again. More. Deeper. Longer. Like at the ski resort.

"I...think they're coming on again," she said very softly but sincerely, looking up at him from beneath her dewy lashes, her expression both wickedly appealing and sweet.

He chuckled and kissed her again. His kiss was tempered with tenderness, meant only to soothe her for what had happened. Not that he didn't want more. Kissing her led to stronger passion, desire, and need. None of which he could fulfill.

She seemed needy, the way she clung to his waist, pressed against him, and sought more. He wanted to give her the affection she seemed so desperate to have. She soaked it up, matching his pacing, her lips parting, her tongue flicking across his mouth, and she seemed to love his kisses. But she also stiffened her arm, as if fighting the pain in her wrist, and he had to stop.

"Elizabeth," he said, caressing her soft, wet cheeks. "We should go."

"Yeah." She sounded reluctant but acquiescent, the fight knocked out of her.

He led her down the hall toward the living room.

"It's okay, dear," Bertha said, looking like a sympathetic momma wolf as Elizabeth wiped her eyes.

Tom called his brother back, his hand resting on Elizabeth's shoulder, wanting the contact to reassure her. "I'm bringing her up to the house."

"I called Trevor and Peter to investigate the B and B. They're on their way."

"All right, Darien. Anything else you want me to do before we leave?"

"No, just bring her over. Carol arrived with Ryan to have dinner with us. She'll provide some nursing care until we eat dinner, if Elizabeth needs it."

"Thanks, Darien." Tom ended the call and said to Bertha, "Trevor and Peter will be here shortly to investigate the break-in. Did you hear anything at all?"

"All my guests were at the slopes. I ran to the grocery store for fresh eggs, fruit, and milk for tomorrow's breakfast, so they must have done it when I was out."

"Is that a regular routine for you?" Tom asked.

"No."

"Then someone must have been watching the B and B," Elizabeth said.

"Why would someone target you?" Tom asked.

Elizabeth looked away from him. "My ID was in that drawer. I can't fly home without it."

She had purposely avoided answering his question, but she was under enough stress already so he didn't press her. For now.

"We can take care of that for you when the time comes. We're headed to Darien's house," Tom said, but he wasn't leaving until Trevor or Peter arrived to ensure Bertha wasn't at risk if the burglar or burglars returned. He peered out the picture window. "Deputy Trevor Osgood is pulling up now."

Trevor was dark-haired, his brown eyes nearly black, his khaki police uniform perfectly pressed with a jacket hanging open over it. His Stetson shaded his eyes, giving him an even darker-tempered appearance. "What the hell's going on now?" he asked Tom as he and Elizabeth emerged from the B and B. Trevor nodded in Elizabeth's direction in greeting.

After helping Elizabeth into his truck, Tom gave Trevor a sketchy explanation of the situation. Peter could fill him in on the ski accident; Tom wanted to get Elizabeth settled at Darien's place pronto.

"All right," Trevor said. "I'll do some preliminary investigating until Peter arrives."

"Let us know if you discover anything important," Tom said.

"I will." Trevor headed for the B and B.

Tom drove them out of Silver Town to Darien and Lelandi's home in the country. Tom still lived there, but because of Darien and Lelandi's babies growing into toddlers, he planned to buy a place of his own this spring. He enjoyed helping with the toddlers so he hadn't bothered looking before this, but Darien and Lelandi would need the additional room as the toddlers grew bigger.

"Did you have anything really important on your laptop? Finances?" Tom asked.

"It's locked with a password. But if they're hackers, I suppose they can get into it. No financial documents on it. Just some photos and news articles I've written. All are backed up in emails."

"Good." Tom couldn't quit thinking of a million different scenarios. "Were you followed at the ski resort? Did you feel the men had been stalking you before they attacked you?"

He was certain now that the man who had shoved her had something to do with this. And her fall had been no accident. All this trouble for one woman in one day couldn't be a coincidence.

"No. I don't believe so. It all seemed to start when I got on the ski lift with the man. He glowered at me, acting as though he wanted me to turn away like a beta would. I wouldn't. So I said 'Hi' and asked him if he was from around here. Then *he* turned away, and that was that."

"Was he a wolf?"

"I couldn't smell him. The way the wind was blowing, he could smell *me*."

"You thought you got pictures of both men?"

"Yes."

"Maybe that's why they targeted you."

Elizabeth was silent for a moment.

"I didn't smell the men who entered my room at the B and B either. Did you?" she asked.

"No. No human smell, no wolf smell." And that concerned Tom. What if these were the same strangers who'd stalked the farmers' livestock, and they were now targeting guests in town? Or just one special guest. But why?

CHAPTER 10

WHILE TOM DROVE THEM TO DARIEN'S HOME, ELIZABETH pulled her phone out of her backpack to call North. She had to tell him she wouldn't be at Bertha's B and B tonight. She paused. What if somehow North's knowing where she stayed was the reason the burglars had broken into her room? What if they had seen her leave the B and B with Tom and had followed her to the resort?

What if they were working for her uncle?

She chewed on her lip. She hated all this second-guessing.

She called North's number, and he picked up.

"Call you back later," North said abruptly, then hung up on her.

She stared at the phone. The break-in might not have anything to do with North, but she sure didn't like him not taking her call. Was her uncle Quinton visiting North? Questioning him about her?

"Anything wrong?" Tom asked.

"Um, no." She had told the truth. There might be nothing wrong. She shoved her phone back into her pack. At least she hoped that was the truth. She didn't want Tom and his pack involved in this business with her and the red pack.

When they arrived at Darien and Lelandi's two-story log home, Elizabeth guessed it had to be about ten thousand square feet, large enough to accommodate pack gatherings. Smoke curled from two chimneys. Snow piled on the windowsills and icicles dripping off the roof made the house look like a warm place to spend the winter season.

An unwanted feeling of sadness slid through her as she thought about not having a pack to belong to or someone to watch her back as she watched his or hers. She quickly quashed that notion. She'd been perfectly happy and much safer since she'd hightailed it out of the southeastern part of Colorado and settled in Texas.

Tom escorted her into the house, stopping only to remove the parka draped over her shoulders, and then led her into the living room where he introduced Lelandi. All smiles, she greeted Elizabeth, her hand outstretched. She was gentle, as if she was afraid Elizabeth would break. Elizabeth smelled that Lelandi was a red wolf who didn't *seem* to have any animosity for her, despite the fact that Elizabeth was part coyote. That open-mindedness was so foreign to Elizabeth that she couldn't fathom it.

Her red hair secured in a bun, Lelandi had on the professional navy-blue business jacket and skirt she wore for seeing her psychology clients. Her eyes were clear green, unlike Elizabeth's more blue-green, but the two women looked similar in terms of height and hair color. Elizabeth was finer boned, probably due to her coyote ancestry.

"You really didn't have to go to all this trouble for me," Elizabeth said, feeling more like an intruder in the family business than anything.

"Nonsense. Usual fare. Think nothing of it. We're delighted to have you stay with us."

The welcome was in Lelandi's voice, though Elizabeth also heard something else—a pack leader's declaration: *You will stay with us for your protection.* Elizabeth was used to being independent and on her own, so she wasn't sure how to feel about that.

The whole home was warm and welcoming, with soft velour couches and chairs, pale-yellow painted walls, and a massive stone fireplace where a fire crackled and red-orange flames spiraled upward. An extra-cushiony beige carpet was underfoot, and dark, polished wooden beams crisscrossed a high ceiling.

But something more than its physical appearance made the home inviting.

Elizabeth could sense the feel of family here, unlike in her own home. She felt safe there from her pack, but she realized there was something to be said for having a family. Her home was isolated, singular, and if she admitted it to herself, lonely.

A blue-eyed blond came out of another room and greeted her, smiling broadly and with her hand extended. Another red wolf. Elizabeth was astounded to see two of them here. Maybe red she-wolves, in particular, appealed to this group of grays, she thought.

"I'm Carol McKinley, a nurse. I've been told you've had a rough time of it, so if you're ready, I'll take you up to your room. You can lie down for a bit until we eat dinner."

Lelandi smiled. "We'll see you a little later. Get some rest, Elizabeth."

Again, the pack leader had decided. Not that Elizabeth didn't appreciate the "offer." She was all too glad to lie down for a while.

"Thanks." Elizabeth glanced at Tom. He dipped his head, letting her know he approved of the idea.

She didn't really need his approval, but she wanted him to know she cared about his feelings. When did *that* get to be an issue?

He ran his hand over her shoulder in a tender caress. "Feel better," he said emphatically, his gaze on hers.

"I'll be a hundred percent before you know it."

He smiled a little at that, and she wasn't sure if he thought she was joking. "I will," she insisted, then headed for the stairs with Carol.

"You will," Carol said, repeating Elizabeth's words like a mantra. "Half the fight is taking a positive stance."

"The other half is having genetics that help us to heal faster," Elizabeth said.

Carol laughed as they climbed the stairs. "I have to admit that's the thing I love best about being a wolf. I'm a red wolf too. Newly turned."

"Oh." She wondered if Carol wasn't used to everyone knowing

what everyone was just by smell. She didn't know what to say to Carol about having been turned, since Elizabeth herself had turned a human—and that had worked out very badly. Taking her mind off that scenario, she tried to look at the photographs of mountain wildflowers hanging on the walls.

She didn't know all the flowers' names, but some were lavender-colored, growing at the base of an alpine grove, and others were pink. She did recognize the purple thistle and golden dandelions. "Did Jake take these?" Elizabeth asked.

"He sure did. Beautiful, aren't they?"

"They are." Maybe Elizabeth could interview him for her newspaper, even if the story was really about a wolf. One hazard of working for the paper was always trying to come up with human-interest stories.

Carol led Elizabeth to a bedroom and motioned to it. "This is your guest room while you stay here. I used it until I mated with Ryan. His full name is Chester Ryan McKinley, and he's the pack leader in Green Valley. I'm sure you're probably sore from your fall. Why don't you have a seat and I'll apply some ice."

"Okay," Elizabeth said, sitting on the mattress.

Antique tables sat on either side of the queen-sized bed, the comforter satiny gold with embroidered designs of gold and moss green. An antique armoire stood in one corner and a small dresser against one wall, making the room appear rich, elegant, and out of the past. Elizabeth liked it. Nothing of hers was older than a couple of years, and the antique furniture appealed to her. She'd had to move so often that she hadn't been able to keep any of her older treasured possessions.

Lelandi came into the room carrying a pair of jeans and white socks. "Thought you might like to get out of your ski pants for now."

"Thank you," Elizabeth said.

"I'll leave you to nap," Lelandi said and hurried out of the room.

Elizabeth did feel more comfy in the change of clothes. She tried to get comfortable on the bed, but she ached all over. She definitely needed a good night's sleep.

After she rolled onto her stomach, Carol put a soothing ice pack on her back. Elizabeth fidgeted, unused to being treated so pleasantly, and by red wolves of all people!

"You know I'm part coyote, right? A lot of wolves—well, at least in my father's wolf pack—don't like that I am," Elizabeth warned Carol.

She didn't know why she had to blurt out to Carol that she wasn't a full-blooded wolf. Maybe because she really liked Carol already, and she didn't want her to think Elizabeth was something she wasn't.

"Well, they have the nerve," Carol said.

Obviously, Carol didn't realize how much animosity there could be between coyotes and wolves. Elizabeth didn't know why, but suddenly she really wanted to talk to someone about everything she had been keeping in. "They think they're better than coyotes. My mother was a coyote and a lovely person before she was…murdered. The wolves of my father's pack were no better than my mother just because they were wolves."

Elizabeth never talked to anybody about her past. Better to bury it and move on. Until North called her and told her he had the proof she needed to show her uncle was responsible for her parents' deaths. If Bruin had still been running things, it wouldn't have mattered. He might have even ordered her parents' deaths.

She felt freer to share with Carol. Maybe that was because she was a new wolf, not one who had a lot of preconceived notions about wolf packs and was intent on climbing to the top of the heap while avoiding being the outcast of the pack like Elizabeth was.

"I'm sorry to hear that she's dead." Carol sounded like she truly meant it.

Elizabeth wondered about Carol's own past, but she didn't

want to appear too nosy by bringing it up. Carol turned a little and applied light pressure to the ice pack on Elizabeth's back.

Elizabeth shivered as the chill of the ice pack seeped into her muscles. "I know someone from my father's pack did it. My father was murdered two days later, and well, let's just say I managed to escape the same fate."

"They killed your father? And then they tried to kill you?" Carol's voice reflected her disbelief.

"Sefton, my half brother, felt my mother had taken the place of his own. My father was devoted to my mother. Even though my father was good to Sefton, he must have felt left out. Here comes a new baby girl—me. My father adored me. So Sefton felt even angrier. He resented me, but he couldn't do anything about it until he was older. The stigma of the coyote mix was also an issue."

Carol shook her head. "I'm sure that must have been horrible for you. I'm sorry. I don't have anything quite like that to compare, but…" She took a deep breath. "I was turned against my will."

Elizabeth was so surprised that it took her a minute to respond. "I'm sorry. I didn't know." She couldn't say it was horrible, because being one of their kind wasn't, in Elizabeth's opinion, but being turned against one's will… A sickening knot formed in the pit of her stomach. Had it been someone in Darien's pack? Had Darien or another champion in the pack killed the one who did it? She was afraid to ask.

"I…foresaw it would happen. It still came as a great shock. I know you were born a shifter, but can you imagine being turned and not having a clue what you can and can't do any longer?" Carol asked, sitting on the bed so she could speak to Elizabeth while the ice pack on Elizabeth's back chilled her all over.

Elizabeth wanted to remove it, but she knew that it could help. She let out her breath, afraid to mention her own mistake but wanting to comfort Carol. "I turned a guy once."

"By accident?" Carol asked, sounding surprised, maybe hopeful that Elizabeth couldn't have done that to anyone on purpose.

"No. We were dating. I…couldn't court wolves or coyotes. I wasn't welcome. So I dated humans. Anyway, this guy and I really hit it off. He loved to camp and I loved the woods, so we sort of suited each other. I was his first girlfriend who didn't mind the grunge of primitive camping. I was swimming in a lake when I heard him screaming. A mountain lion had attacked him. The only way for him to live…" Elizabeth took a deep breath.

"What happened to him?"

"He…" Elizabeth let her breath out in exasperation. "You know we mate for life, right?"

"Sure. It's a genetic anomaly. That's something I love about being a wolf. I don't have to worry about Ryan straying."

"Right. Well, even with that, I couldn't keep him."

Carol's blue eyes were round. "You're mated?"

Elizabeth heard the shock in Carol's voice. If Elizabeth was mated, so what? Unless…

She discounted that notion. No way was anything more going to develop between her and Tom.

"We were mated. Not for long. He got himself killed over wanting someone else. Maybe changing him didn't turn off the part of the human brain that wants someone new and different after a while. He made a deadly mistake. Once the she-wolf he became interested in realized that he was part coyote, newly turned, *and* mated to the wolf-coyote who had changed him, she told her brother. Her brother killed the two-timer."

"Wow. He had no family to speak of?"

"None that was close to him. No great loss to anyone much."

"You were upset about it though." Carol removed the ice pack.

"At first, sure. I saved his life, and I truly had cared for him. He loved being a wolf. He just didn't realize he was part coyote. I thought it was the perfect scenario. He was happy with what he was because he didn't know any differently. But then he caught sight of the red she-wolf and decided to dump me for her.

"When he learned I was part coyote and had made him that way—which is why the she-wolf shunned him, ignoring the fact that she wouldn't have wanted him because he was also mated—he wanted to kill me. Thankfully, her brother got to him first. I left the area after that."

Carol was quiet for a long time. "You don't think what has happened to you up here has anything to do with your family, do you? Or maybe this woman's brother?"

"I…don't believe so. The wolf who was interested in my former mate is probably mated by now," Elizabeth said, hedging on the question about her family.

She thought back to when she'd run away from her pack and settled in Oklahoma near her mother's family. That hadn't been all that far from where the red pack was. Texas wasn't either. As much as she hated to admit it, she had never been able to move very far away from her family—even as cruelly as they'd treated her. They were still family, the only blood relatives she had.

But what if Carol's suspicions were right and her family *was* causing her trouble again? What if *North* had betrayed her? And told her uncle she was here? Or he might have unwittingly revealed her whereabouts or been forced to give Uncle Quinton the information.

"Where was your pack from?" Carol asked.

Elizabeth hesitated to say.

Carol chewed on her lower lip. "Not from around here, are they?"

"Southeastern part of the state."

"About seven hours from here?"

"Yeah…so not all that close." Elizabeth had a bad feeling about this. How would Carol know how far the pack was from here?

Carol looked disconcerted, her forehead wrinkled, and she chewed on her lower lip again. "You're part of *Bruin's* old pack?"

Heart pounding, Elizabeth gaped at Carol for a second, and then she clamped her lips closed. Carol *knew* them. Elizabeth hadn't thought anyone from the gray wolf pack would know them. Then again, both Lelandi and Carol were red wolves. Dr. Weber was too, Elizabeth remembered.

As much as possible, Elizabeth had stayed clear of the red pack while living with her mother and father. Her uncle and half brother had visited her—and caused all the trouble for her. She hadn't been able to get to know the other members of the pack, except North. He had come to see her a few times, the only red wolf she knew at the time who *didn't* wish her any harm.

But she'd truly believed everyone would regard her the same way as her family, no matter where in the country she ended up. She hadn't found many wolves who treated her like Tom's pack had.

Carol paused, then said, "You and Lelandi don't seem to know each other."

"I didn't live with the pack."

"Okay. I understand. But the red wolves can't think they're any better than you. They're just like you."

"They're red wolves. Not half-coyote." Elizabeth couldn't see how Carol wouldn't know that. "What happened to the red wolf who turned you?"

"He was killed after he bit me."

"Good."

Carol sighed. "As a nurse, I try to save people. I think that's the hardest part of being a wolf for me. When wolves do really bad things, they can't go to jail and live among humans. Not for extended periods of time. They'd have to shift at some time or another, and that could be a disaster. The concept of achieving justice by killing is hard for me to live with."

Elizabeth moved to sit up and groaned, still sore.

"Just lie still. I'll leave you in a second to sleep. I just wanted to share that I read an article you might find interesting. In some parts of Canada, the wolves and coyotes are mixed. Most of the wolves actually have coyote blood," Carol said.

"Really."

"Yeah. Not as much down here. The wolves and coyotes are often enemies, and the wolves will kill the coyotes that enter their territory. But up there, some red and gray wolves mix with coyotes when they have slim pickings."

Elizabeth sighed. Of course wolves would only consider coyotes when they had no other option. "Why research it?" she asked, curious.

Carol laughed. "Some controversy exists between red and gray wolf shifters. The red wolves claim they were first and gray wolves came after them. Of course, the gray wolves assert that they came first."

"The red wolves were first," Elizabeth said. "At least that's what my father and the rest of his red wolf pack said."

"That was the thing. I was curious because one had to have come first, and I wanted to know the truth. So I did some research. According to some scientists, red wolves were *not* first."

Elizabeth contemplated this, frustrated with arbitrary pack problems. What difference did it make in the scheme of things which wolf came first?

But then Carol said, "Gray wolves were first. Some mixed with coyotes and created the red wolf."

Elizabeth rolled over on her back to look at Carol. "You're kidding."

"Nope. But since I read that article, I found one that said they were purely a separate species." Carol shrugged. "So who really knows which came first?"

"Have you told Lelandi?"

"No. It's our secret."

Elizabeth felt a tremor of excitement at this new knowledge. As soon as she did more research, she would write about it in the

Canyon Press. If any of her red wolf pack heard about gray wolves mixing with coyotes, then they would know that she wasn't the only case of a coyote-wolf mix and it was a good one on them. "How come nobody knows about it?"

"Well, like I said, some still say the gray and red wolves are sep-arate species, but some DNA evidence exists to the contrary. At least in some cases."

Elizabeth smiled. "My wolf family would *love* to hear that."

"I'm sure they'd want to keep the status quo. I'm so glad to meet you. I've been dying to tell another red wolf what I'd learned, but not Lelandi. I figure she wouldn't be happy to hear the news and have to admit to the grays that her heritage could be part coyote and that her kind didn't come first. You, on the other hand, have every reason to want to know if it were true." Carol smiled.

If some red wolves were coyote-gray wolf mixes, that had Elizabeth worried for Lelandi because of the way Elizabeth's people had treated her. "What would Darien think if he learned that his mate was part coyote?"

"She could be a pink poodle for as much as he adores her."

Elizabeth chuckled. "Pink poodle?"

Carol smiled.

Elizabeth loved Carol. As for Darien, if he truly felt that way about his mate, he had to be all right. "How did you come to be turned exactly?"

"I saw the future." Carol smiled as if that was all she cared to remember about it.

Was Carol bottling up feelings, just as Elizabeth had been, not wanting to share them with anyone?

For the first time ever, Elizabeth wanted a friend like Carol so they could talk about their pasts and maybe she could work through some of the hurt.

"What have we got, Tom?" Darien asked as he leaned down. They both were peering at pictures on Tom's computer screen in the den, the room warmed by a cheery fire, the big windows looking out on the snow-covered woodland landscape.

"She takes lots of photos. These are the last few. The guy on the lift chair behind them was blurred, the camera's focus on the trees. He wore a black balaclava, a matching ski hat, and reflective sunglasses. He has on a blue-gray ski jacket and a black ski bib. There's no telling what his face looks like, just his approximate build. The guy waiting down the slope from her is wearing a brown jacket, black ski pants, and a blue knit hat. Can't see if he's wearing goggles or some face covering since his back is to us. We can call it in and be on the lookout if they are still on the slopes," Tom said, sitting back against the leather chair.

"Yeah, but if they broke into her room at the B and B, I wouldn't imagine they're skiing right now," Darien said, straightening.

"That could be. One other thing," Tom said, glancing up at his brother.

"What's that?"

"I checked her camera. It's not working."

"I'll have Jake look at it. He's a whiz at fixing minor problems with cameras," Darien said.

"I hoped maybe he could. Her ID was stolen from the B and B, and she won't be able to get her flight out without it." Tom considered the picture of the man further, wishing he could decipher who he was.

"Peter can take care of that."

That was another thing about running their town; they lived by their own set of rules. Since wolves had extended life spans, they needed to update their IDs periodically with no questions asked. That was easier in a town where no questions would even be raised.

"It could take a while though," Darien added.

Tom shifted his attention from the skier's picture to Darien, not sure what he meant.

Darien smiled. "If you wanted it to take a while for her to get her ID replaced."

"I might want her to stay longer, but the lady has a deadline on a story and a life back in Texas." And some male friend living nearby who had planned to meet her. Tom had never heard anyone in the pack talking about a beautiful red wolf-coyote shifter, so the man couldn't be with their pack.

"All right. Just saying."

He appreciated Darien for mentioning it. With that one comment, he told Tom that he approved of the lady, and Tom thought the world of him for that.

"Thanks, Darien." Then he frowned at him. "You…didn't happen to see a certain video taken at the ski resort today, did you?"

He'd hoped Maggie, the receptionist at the hospital, had been pulling his leg that both Jake and Darien had bought the video from Cantrell. He couldn't imagine his brothers wasting their money. Though he supposed they might have demanded a copy free of charge to ensure that the video wasn't somehow damning.

Darien laughed and folded his arms across his chest. "Cantrell's quite the entrepreneur. Others took pictures and passed them along in emails for those who didn't want to pay for the video version. I told you to take care of the lady. Good job. Everyone knows to keep their paws off her now. I don't think I've ever seen anything go viral that fast in the pack. Someone even sent the video to Carol."

"Lelandi saw it," Tom guessed. He didn't think anyone else would have made Carol aware of it.

"Yeah, she did. She called me and told me to buy my own copy because it was well worth it. I figured she sent a copy to Carol. The ladies viewed it again right before you drove up."

Tom shook his head and turned his attention back to the

situation on the slope. "If these guys targeted her because she took pictures of them, why would that bother them?"

"Maybe because they are wanted men. Are they human?" Darien asked.

"The way the wind blew, she couldn't tell. The guy who sat on her chair acted like an alpha."

Darien squinted his eyes as he looked closer at the picture. "The way they're bundled up, I can't tell if they're anybody I know. Half of our males could look like these men, as far as size and build go. What did you gather about the mess they made of her room at Hastings B and B?"

"The men who broke in left no scent there. That's what made me think of the wolves in the vicinity of the livestock. They haven't left a scent either."

"You think they're wolves?"

"Possibly, but I can't be sure they're the same ones I've trailed," Tom said. "With all the clothes the guy that ran into her wore, I couldn't capture any scent on her, human or otherwise. But what if he masked his scent in the first place?"

"You think they could be using hunter's spray?" Darien asked. His face brightened at the same time that Tom had a thought.

"The last person who pulled that trick with the pack was Uncle Sheridan," Tom said.

Darien nodded. "Just what I was thinking. What if this has to do with our cousins, and they're out for revenge because of the death of their father?"

CHAPTER 11

ELIZABETH SLIPPED INTO THE SUMMER-WARMED WATER, FAR
enough from the pack, she thought, that they wouldn't bother her. She
was wrong. Uncle Quinton, her father's brother, stalked toward the
swimming hole, his face red with rage, his red hair nearly the same
color. His blue-green eyes were narrowed in contempt.

Now what had happened? After her parents had died, she'd stayed
far away from the wolf pack. They shouldn't care about her any longer.
She was no longer in their territory so they should have left her alone.

"You are an abomination!" he yelled.

He'd often used those words before. She disgusted him. She was a
disgrace to the pack. She'd heard it all before.

She feared him now and swam farther away from the bank. She'd
seen that look in his eyes right before he killed a wolf who had tried to
steal a prospective female mate from their pack.

He stalked into the water, still in jeans and shirt and sneakers, and
swam toward her. He was a powerful swimmer, and though she swam
well too, she was only sixteen and didn't have the strength behind her
strokes to keep out of his reach.

He seized her hair and jerked it back, pulling her to where he could
stand in the water. "Your brother..." he started.

Half brother, she wanted to say as she grabbed her hair to try to
keep him from yanking it out of her head. Streaks of pain radiated
through the roots all the way to her brain.

"...met a pretty wolf. You know what transpired?"

She knew what must have happened without him saying. The same
thing had happened before to her uncle, and now to her half brother.
The she-wolf her brother was interested in must have learned about

Elizabeth—that he was of her blood and she was part coyote—and rejected him because of it.

"Well, no longer," he said, and she knew then her uncle intended to kill her.

She fought Uncle Quinton with all her strength, scratched and kicked and even managed to bite his arm with her human teeth, drawing blood. He hit her in the head so hard that she nearly blacked out. She knew then the only way to survive was to play dead.

Limp and no longer fighting, she attempted to fool her uncle. Then four male teens appeared, laughing and joking loudly as they headed for the water hole. Guardian angels. Her uncle released her, waded back to shore, and ran off. She couldn't smell the teens as they slowly approached her, their previous good humor gone. She knew none of them—all dark-haired, all staring at her as if they didn't know what to do with her.

She managed to make it to the shore and collapsed, coughing and choking, vowing she'd move again before her uncle made another attempt at killing her.

"Elizabeth?" Carol said, waking her from the nightmare she hadn't had since she moved to Canyon. What had brought it back?

She stared up at Carol for a minute, trying to get her bearings.

"Time for dinner. You slept all afternoon," Carol said. "Everyone is dying to see you. How are you feeling?"

Without moving? Fine. "Much, much better. Thank you."

Elizabeth wasn't used to all the concern and would have been just as happy without it. Her wrist felt much better though.

"I'm glad you feel better," Carol said.

Elizabeth knew Carol judged the way she moved. She was certain the nurse recognized that she still felt some discomfort, but she appreciated that Carol didn't make a big deal of it.

Elizabeth *would* get better soon.

"Just a little background before we go down. Darien's a gray wolf and Lelandi a red wolf, like I mentioned. Alicia was human, turned by a gray wolf and now mated to Jake. Ryan, my mate, is a gray wolf, and you already know I'm a human turned red wolf. We're an unusual couple of wolf packs, so don't feel you won't fit in. We're all different in our own ways."

"Thanks, Carol." Elizabeth couldn't help but feel that she was more of an oddity, being a wolf-coyote mix, and she still had a hard time believing that anyone could truly accept her for what she was. She was just a novelty to them.

"Let's go down to dinner, shall we?" Carol said.

Elizabeth wished she'd had a meal with Bertha back at the B and B and could have skipped all this fanfare. Even if she had it all wrong and they would accept her, she felt like she would be the center of attention she didn't want any part of.

Tom met Elizabeth on the stairs and escorted her to the table, introducing everyone right away. He loved his family, each of them smiling and trying to make her feel welcome.

She appeared a little overwhelmed. Even though she was an alpha, meeting each of their gazes as she greeted them back, he noted that she glanced at the floor several times, and he saw the tears in her eyes when she caught his gaze.

Had no one ever treated her the way a family should? He hated to think that was the case.

He ushered her to a seat beside him. Everyone had already taken their seats at the large oak dining table and started passing around spaghetti and meatballs, Italian loaves, Parmesan cheese, and salad.

"Can I help with anything?" she asked, looking uncomfortable that she couldn't assist.

"No," he said almost too vehemently. She had been pushed

down a ski slope only hours ago, for heaven's sake. This woman didn't know when to quit.

"I'm not usually pampered like this."

He smiled at her. "Let me get you whatever you need tonight."

"Okay." She let out her breath as if the notion didn't agree with her but let him dutifully scoop up whatever she wanted. "Did you look over the photos I took?"

Everyone stopped whatever they were doing to hear what Tom had to say.

"We couldn't see any faces, but we've got a description of what the two men were wearing. Jake will look at your camera to see if he can fix it," Tom said as he returned to his seat, setting a plate piled high with spaghetti and plenty of meatballs in front of Elizabeth.

"Thank you," she said.

Jake cleared his throat. "I'll take good care of it. See what I can do."

Darien turned to Carol. "Do you see anything about what happened to Elizabeth?"

Elizabeth stared at Carol. "You actually do have psychic ability? When you told me you foresaw what would happen to you before you were turned, I hadn't thought you meant it literally."

"Yeah, I see things sometimes." Carol shook her head at Darien. "Since I've joined Ryan's pack, my focus has been there. I haven't seen anything new about members of your pack."

"Did Trevor or Peter discover anything at the B and B?" Elizabeth asked.

"The two men left a trail through the woods behind the B and B, backtracked into town, and must have driven off in a vehicle parked out front," Darien said.

"With all my stuff," Elizabeth growled. "Did nobody see them?"

Tom wanted to touch Elizabeth to calm her, but he didn't think she'd appreciate it. What the hell. He reached over and took her good hand and gave it a gentle squeeze. She glanced at him, and at first he thought she'd be annoyed with him. Instead, she looked at him with those crystal eyes as if trying to read him. He gazed back at her, wanting to take care of her. To find the bastards and beat them to within an inch of their lives.

He wanted to wrap his arm around her and hold her close, to let her know she had him to count on, but he couldn't. Not yet.

"We've put out the alert to all the pack," Darien said, studying them. "If anyone saw anything, they'll let me know. Nobody's been following you?"

"When I rode with Tom to the ski resort, I didn't pay any attention to traffic." Elizabeth glanced at Tom to see his take on it.

He shook his head. "I didn't really notice on the way to the resort." Between the snowy roads and Elizabeth, he hadn't been able to concentrate on anything else. She was a total distraction.

"Why would they take all my stuff?" she asked.

"Sounds personal to me," Lelandi said.

"Taking my ID forces me to stay here," Elizabeth pointed out.

Jake said, "More likely it's for identity theft. It doesn't necessarily mean they wanted to keep you from leaving here."

"Okay." Elizabeth seemed more relaxed about that, which Tom took as meaning she wanted to leave as soon as she was able. He stiffened.

He had hoped she'd feel comfortable with his pack and remain with them for more time than she'd planned. But with what had happened to her here, he could understand her reluctance to stay any longer than necessary. She couldn't even ski if she wanted to take more pictures for her story.

"Is there any way that I can get a replacement ID so I can travel?" she asked.

"Yeah, we can do it. You don't want to stay until we can unravel who did this to you?" Darien asked.

Tom gave Darien points for trying to convince Elizabeth to stay longer. He couldn't think of a thing to say.

"I've got a deadline on the newspaper back home. And I probably won't be able to ski again while I'm here." Elizabeth grimaced as though she were loath to admit the fact.

"Do you want me to take some pictures for you?" Jake asked, looking like he was ready to go, not just to help her out but because he loved taking nature photos. The sideways glance he cast Tom said he was attempting to keep the lady here longer too.

Why couldn't Tom come up with something to say?

"I'll have to look at the photos, but I might already have what I need for the article. Thanks for the offer though."

The conversation then shifted to other topics, some about Jake and Alicia's upcoming babies and about Darien and Lelandi's toddlers, and then everyone looked at Carol and Ryan to see if they were in the family way.

Carol smiled, shaking her head. "We're waiting for a while. I'm not ready to raise babies who can turn into wolves yet."

Tom had talked to Ryan about Carol's progress. She was doing fairly well with shifting only when she wanted to and not at awkward times. He could understand her reluctance to have children until she had the ability fully under control. Wolf-shifter mothers usually had multiple births—like a she-wolf and her litter. The babies all shifted when their mother did until they became aware of their own ability. But if a mother couldn't even control her own shifting, that could be a disaster for both her and her pups.

Tom glanced at Elizabeth. He shouldn't have, but he couldn't help wondering what it would be like to raise some pups of his own. Surely *his* kids wouldn't be as messy as Darien's.

Elizabeth had grown quiet and sat stirring her spaghetti with a fork. He reached over and patted her leg and smiled at her. She smiled back, but she looked exhausted even though she had napped all afternoon. He suspected she hadn't slept all that soundly.

Pack politics were discussed, despite Carol and Ryan being from another pack and Elizabeth being there too.

Jake and Alicia begged off after dinner to return home, claiming they were two tired, old wolves, which Tom knew meant that they were off to bed but not to sleep. Jake took Elizabeth's camera with him to try to repair.

Carol said to Elizabeth, "I'd stay overnight with you, but we have a problem coming up in the pack that Ryan and I need to deal with. Darien can call Nurse Matthew or Nurse Charlotte Grey to stay the night if he thinks you need someone to watch over you."

"No, I'm fine," Elizabeth said. "I just ache a little. With a good night's sleep, I should be great by morning."

Tom said, "I'll be next door if you need anything."

Elizabeth smiled at him. "I never knew ski patrollers made house calls."

Everyone laughed.

"If nobody minds, I'm off to bed. Thanks so much for dinner. It was delicious," Elizabeth said. "But I feel wiped out."

Everybody said good night except Tom, who walked up with her. "Can I help you with anything?"

"Like?"

"An ice pack on your back again?"

She smiled, walked into the guest room, and lay down on her stomach on the bed. "Okay."

Surprised she was agreeable, Tom hurried to get her a fresh ice pack. On the return trip, he raced up the stairs sounding like a pack of wolves and entered the room. "If you think of anything tonight that might clue us in about this, just let me know. You can wake me anytime." He placed the pack on her back.

"Hmm," she said sleepily.

He sat down next to the bed, waiting for time to pass before he removed the ice pack. Her breathing soft, her eyes shut tight, Elizabeth fell sound asleep.

Tom was glad she didn't have any trouble falling asleep because she needed complete rest to feel better.

Darien poked his head in the door. "She out?" he whispered.

"Yeah," Tom said, realizing twenty minutes had passed while he'd been daydreaming. He removed the ice pack from Elizabeth's back and headed out of the room to join his brother. As he closed the door, he asked, "What's up?"

"Peter called to say his brother's come into town with a mate in tow."

"Yeah, he told me earlier. I meant to mention it to you, but it slipped my mind. Is his brother in trouble already?"

"No...not yet. But Peter said he doesn't know what to think of them. He put them in his spare bedroom and told them to go ahead and fix themselves dinner while he conducted an investigation. When he came home, they were battling it out in the guest room."

"Case of mate abuse?" Tom asked, shocked. "Did he arrest his brother?"

Darien shrugged. "He said they were getting it on hot and heavy, a big-time sparring match. Peter asked if they could stay here."

Tom couldn't believe it. Peter was so good-natured, so how could he have a brother like that? "You told him no, right?"

CHAPTER 12

ELIZABETH WOKE IN THE MIDDLE OF THE NIGHT FEELING MUCH better. She wanted to check the footprints in the snow outside her room at the B and B before winds covered them up or the sun melted them away the next day. She was an excellent tracker, her father had said, because of her coyote heritage. She'd found a couple of lost dogs and several lost or runaway human kids because of her keen sense of smell and tracking ability.

She would have inspected the men's trail earlier if not for all the fuss Tom made about her accident. She'd leave right from the house, but she was so far out in the country that she'd prefer driving back into town and then exploring a bit while wearing her wolf coat.

She hated to wake Tom. But she was certain that if she asked to borrow his truck, he'd either say no to her going, worrying about her condition, or insist he go with her. She didn't need his help at tracking, which she almost always did alone. She really didn't want to trouble him at this hour of night, but she didn't have much choice.

She hadn't taken two steps out of the guest room when Tom walked out of his bedroom wearing only a pair of black-plaid flannel boxers. "Did you need something?"

She considered his nearly naked body and tried very hard not to stare and sigh. Well, kind of tried not to. He was in excellent shape, rugged and hot. She rarely thought of a wolf in those terms. She didn't think anything of a man being ripped if he was cruel to her. But Tom was so different. Actually, everyone in his pack was. Kind, welcoming, sincere. If only all families were like that.

"Sorry. Did I wake you?" she asked.

"Very light sleeper. So, did you need something?"

"Yeah. Your truck? Can I borrow the keys?"

He leaned against the wall and folded his arms. "It's three in the morning. You've been injured. You don't have your driver's license." He glanced at her wrist. "Where's your wrist wrap?"

She wiggled her hand back and forth. "All better. I want to take a run and do some tracking."

"At the B and B."

"Yeah. To see if I can learn anything."

"In your wolf coat."

"My back feels a hundred percent better."

One eyebrow raised, he gave her a skeptical look.

"Eighty-five percent."

He smiled.

"Seventy."

He didn't budge from the wall.

"*Nearly* seventy percent."

He exhaled heavily and moved toward her. She stood her ground, and this time *she* folded her arms. She knew that look on his face. He didn't believe she could track better than his wolves. Nobody ever believed it until she proved it to them.

"We've got pack members on it."

"I can do better."

He smiled.

She reached out her hand for his keys.

"Darien would have a fit."

"Don't tell him."

"I'm part of a pack."

"I'm not."

"I still have to tell him."

She sighed. "So tell him."

"He'll say no."

She turned and stalked toward the bedroom at the end of the hall. She didn't know which room was Darien and Lelandi's, but this one had more of their scent leading up to it. Others had been here also, probably doing what she was about to do. Bother them for pack business.

Tom said, "I'll call him. It's less likely to disturb Lelandi than knocking on the door."

He slipped into his bedroom and walked back out with his phone in hand. She'd already headed in his direction, and he put his arm around her. "Darien—"

"No," Darien said over the phone. "I heard everything. Wait until tomorrow."

Tom looked to see if Elizabeth had heard what Darien said.

Elizabeth made a face. "Help me strip out of my clothes."

Tom smiled just a little.

"I'm going running, no matter what Darien says. Since I'm only seventy percent healed, I might need a little help pulling off my clothes."

Tom still had the phone up to his ear, still smiling, but Darien didn't say anything.

"Okay," she said, "I can do it myself. I'm probably more like ninety-five percent fine."

She pulled away from him, and he hurried to join her.

"She can't run," Darien said.

"'Night, Darien. Sorry we disturbed your sleep." Tom shut off the phone and took Elizabeth's hand. "Come on. Let me get dressed." He glanced down at her stocking feet. "You're going like that?"

"I thought you might help me get my boots on."

"Are you sure you're able to run in your wolf coat?"

"Sure. If I start feeling bad, we'll come back here."

"You promise?"

"Yeah." *But only if she didn't get a lead.*

Tom and Elizabeth drove into Silver Town and parked in front of the B and B. Bertha met them at the front door, wearing a pink floral flannel nightgown, a big, fluffy pink robe and slippers, and a nightcap on her silver curls. "Darien called. Said you were on your way over here. Said it was a case of life and death."

"Yeah, mine, I'm sure," Tom said.

Bertha smiled.

Elizabeth and Tom went inside, intending to change in her room so they could shift in privacy.

Bertha shut and locked the front door. "Darien wasn't real happy you headed on over here. You can use another room. I've had to leave all the glass everywhere because he wants to see things the way they were first thing in the morning. Just leave the window open and come back in that way. The other guests are not like us," Bertha whispered.

"Thanks, Bertha," Tom said.

"Should you run as a wolf so soon after the accident?" Bertha asked Elizabeth.

"She's a better tracker than our people," Tom said.

Bertha smiled. "Good. We need the best."

Elizabeth was certain Tom didn't believe her, but she'd prove she was right.

"I'll be off to bed. Just close the window when you return and lock the front door when you leave. 'Night, folks." Bertha disappeared into her own suite of rooms.

Tom closed the door to the guest room and crossed the floor to open the window. "Are you sure you feel well enough to do this?"

"Yes, yes, I'm fine."

He considered her determined expression and then sighed. "All right. Let me help you off with your boots and socks, at least. I know what it feels like to go through what you did."

Yeah, and she'd bet nobody helped him undress afterward! Tom pulled off her boots and socks.

But he didn't stop there. He was unhurried while trying not to cause her any discomfort, but it was like stripping in slow motion, and she felt her skin tingle in embarrassment as he peeled each article of clothing off her body—jeans, formfitting sweater, bra.

Blushing furiously, Elizabeth realized she should have asked Bertha to help her.

Tom caught sight of Elizabeth in the mirror as he dropped the bra on the bed with her other clothes. Then he removed her panties. Before he could have more of his fill of her, she shifted.

He smiled. "You're beautiful."

She couldn't believe he meant it. She was still a wolf-coyote mix. She had more of her father's looks—a red wolf but smaller, in between a female red wolf and a coyote.

She turned to see Tom yanking off his clothes in a hurry and waited for him. When he saw she wouldn't tear off on her own, he relaxed a little.

Her jaw dropped as she stared at his toned body, tanned, ripped, and already aroused because he'd removed her clothes as if it were a prelude to something else.

Then he shifted. She expected him to jump out the window to lead the way. Instead, he joined her and nuzzled her cheek, her ear, sending a tingling interest rippling through her body. She really could get used to this kind of treatment.

Then he nudged her a little, as if asking her if she was ready. She headed for the window, but he jumped out first. He didn't look for scents on the snow. He watched her instead to see if she would collapse in agony. Even if she were still a little sore, she wouldn't let him see it and stop her from what she wanted to do. She put her nose to the ground while listening for signs of trouble. Tom could be her bodyguard. That way, she could concentrate on her job. *Tracking.*

She took off toward the ski resort in the direction the men had gone, then backtracked like they had done. They had headed around the building to the front where their vehicle had been parked, and she followed their trail there. The illumination of soft lantern lights along the street was blurred in a misty fog, the redbrick and wooden buildings topped with snow. She continued down the street, hoping that if any humans were around, they were all tucked quietly in their beds in the middle of the night or, if they happened to see her, thought she was a big dog. That was one advantage of being a smaller-sized wolf.

She headed toward the tavern, turned around, and loped back toward the B and B.

Tom continued to follow her, but he was looking for any movement in the area and not hunting for a trail.

She glanced across the street at the businesses there. An antique shop. A lingerie store with sexy nightwear and daywear. She glanced at Tom. He looked to see what she'd been observing. Fishnet stockings and crotchless underwear. Her warm breath mixing with the cold air, she felt heat course through her wolf-coyote body.

She switched her attention farther down the street to the abandoned hotel across from the tavern. She had a flashback to when she and Tom had gone into the tavern. She'd thought it odd that the dusty hotel window had one small clean spot. She studied it, looking for any movement inside the building. And saw something. She ran for the abandoned hotel.

With his longer legs, Tom bolted ahead of Elizabeth in protective big, gray wolf mode. When he reached the hotel, he placed his paws on the windowsill. He peered through glass so dirty that it was nearly impossible to see in. Someone had definitely wiped away a little of the grime to watch the street. Vagrants? Or was someone using this as a base of operations for something illegal?

Reluctantly, Tom turned and headed back to the B and B.

Elizabeth, however, took off down the alley. Tom woofed insistently at her. She was sure he didn't want her chasing down strangers, but she wanted answers. She got a glimpse of a white minivan tearing off behind the building. Lights off. No plates visible.

Rejoining her, Tom nudged her to return to the B and B. She wanted to track the men, and she wanted to check out the old hotel. If any of them were inside, she and Tom needed to stop them. But Tom wasn't budging.

He waited for her to comply. She growled at him, then raced to the back of the B and B. When she reached the guest-room window, she leaped inside.

Tom jumped inside after her and shifted. He yanked his boxers on, then grabbed his phone out of his pants pocket and called someone. After stalking over to the window, he shut and locked it.

Since he was on the phone, she could stay in her wolf form and wait for him to finish his conversation, then shift and he could help her to dress, or...

She shifted, climbed under the covers, and eyed Tom's gorgeous body. She could stay here the rest of the night just taking in the vision.

"Darien, get Trevor, Peter, and whoever else you can over to the Silver Town Inn. Elizabeth"—he glanced at her and smiled a little—"found our men's hideaway."

CHAPTER 13

TOM KNEW HIS IDEA WAS FAR OUT, BUT AS SOON AS ELIZABETH located where the men had camped out, he wanted to propose that she stay with his family. Whenever someone could really be useful to the pack, they wanted the person to join them. At least that was what he told himself.

It was essential that the pack members liked the wolf—everyone who had met her indicated they had—but skills that were important made all the difference to a pack like theirs that operated a whole town.

That wasn't the *only* reason he wanted Elizabeth in the pack, but he thought it might help sell the idea to everyone else before he could work up the nerve to expose how *he* felt about her. And how much he wanted to get to know her better. Elizabeth was so secretive about her affiliations with her own pack that he suspected she wouldn't want to be with their pack—or any other.

She'd curled up in the B and B guest bed, covers over her naked body.

Tom wanted to join her in that bed. Wanted to see her naked again, craved touching her, smelling her, tasting her. He just wanted to be with her. And kiss her like she'd kissed him on the slope.

With half-lidded eyes, she watched him. He needed to help her dress and return her to Darien's house. Yet he was torn, because he also wanted to check out the hotel and chase after the men who had been there. He wanted to catch them and make them pay for hurting Elizabeth.

"Go with the men when they get to the hotel," she said, her voice tired, her eyelids drifting closed. "You don't need to watch over me."

She was beautiful, her red hair spilling across the pale-blue pillow, the blue comforter resting at her naked shoulders that he wanted to kiss—that and her neck and her cheeks and her full pink lips. *She* would be his choice for dream mating if he'd ever had any dreams like that!

"I'll just sleep," she said.

"No. We need to return to Darien's place. It's better protected."

"Did you see them? When you looked through the hotel window?" Elizabeth asked.

"No. They shut the door to that room, so all I saw was the door close."

"We could have gone after them," she groused.

He smiled. "If you had been a hundred percent fine, yes."

She grunted.

"I'm serious." He sat on the bed next to her, running his hand over her thigh covered by the comforter, his gaze locked on hers. "At least two men are involved in this. Besides, I'm certain they were in the van when it took off, so it's not like we're going to catch up with any of them at the old hotel."

He was certain the minivan had been the same one that he'd seen passing in front of the hospital while he waited for Doc Weber to give him the findings concerning Elizabeth's injuries. Had they known she was at the hospital, so they had time to grab her things then? Most likely. A lookout could also have watched Tom take Elizabeth to the tavern for lunch and alerted the men when Tom and Elizabeth finished eating there.

"All right. Let me sleep then," she said.

"Not here." He rose from the bed and grabbed his jeans, then pulled them on.

By the time he yanked on the rest of his clothes, she was nearly asleep. He scooped her clothes up. He'd never expected to be undressing and dressing a woman he'd just met but who had his senses reeling. And not have his way with her the way he desired.

He tugged the covers aside, and she grumbled something. He smiled and slid on one of her socks, then the other. Slipping her panties on when she didn't move a muscle to help was harder than he expected. He grunted as he got the tantalizing ice-blue panties on. She smiled.

"You could help," he said, not really meaning it.

"You could leave me alone," she said, not opening her eyes. "Just let me sleep."

He pulled on the jeans very slowly. She winced.

"Sorry."

When he finished and helped her to sit up to put on her lacy blue bra, she held her breath.

"Maybe we should just put your sweater on and not bother with the bra," he said.

"Okay, you can carry it in your pocket." She smiled at him, the look one of pure delight. "You know, psychologically, kissing makes the hurt go away. Mind over matter. Not that I'm hurting that much."

He helped her on with her sweater, unable to keep from taking a longer look at her breasts as he tugged the sweater carefully over her arms and head and then down to her waist.

As concerned as he was about how she felt, he hoped he didn't look too eager. She looked at his lips and licked her own as if in invitation.

Vixen.

"I promise I won't bite too hard," she said.

He laughed and took her face in his hands, his thumbs caressing her temples, and then leaned down. "Here I was worried about *you* being hurt further. Certainly not *me*."

He kissed her. Softly, gently. Her lips opened to further exploration, but he didn't push it. Until she licked his mouth and smiled a little at him with the invite. He locked his lips over her lower one. Again, she smiled a little. Kissing her was like sampling a sweet, forbidden dessert, tantalizing and enticing the sampler to want more.

Her hands were on his neck, her thumbs caressing his jaw in a way that was provocative and incredibly sexy. He was already in full-blown arousal and had a devil of time keeping his feelings in check. He alternated between soft and unassuming kisses and inserting his tongue with teasing flicks and deepening the kiss. Trying hard not to lean her back onto the bed and press his interest further than was prudent, he smelled her excitement, her desire, and listened to her rapid heartbeat pounding as hard as his. He thought she wanted to go further as much as he did.

She was breathing fast and leaned away from his kiss to take a breath. He feared he'd overdone it and hurt her. Instead, she had her second wind, and this time, she gathered his sweater in her fists and pulled him close to get another kiss.

Instantly he obliged, their mouths fusing, their tongues caressing and appraising. He didn't want this to end. But he knew he'd better before they both regretted it. He broke off in the gentlest possible way and kissed her forehead, his mouth lingering there far too long. He didn't want to end this, and he needed her to know it.

"I have to help you dress and return you to Darien's house," he said.

"If you insist," she said, and the way she looked at him indicated that she wanted more too.

That was the reason he posed the next question, although he was sure what her response would be. But he had to. "I've never asked a woman this before, but…would you like to join the pack?" He knew he shouldn't ask. Not without getting Darien and Lelandi's approval.

"Thanks, but no thanks."

He wouldn't take her negative response at face value. "You're not a loner," he said, certain of it. She might have had to live alone, but she got along well with everyone she'd met here. She didn't act like a lone wolf. Not the way someone like Nurse Matthew did.

She didn't respond, just looked at his chest. He sighed and helped her on with her boots. "I have something back at the house that you can wear that's easier to get in and out of until we can pick up something else for you."

"Thank you, Tom." She seemed to want to say something else, given the way she looked at him and bit her lip. But she pulled her parka sleeve on one arm and didn't say anything.

He helped pull her parka on the rest of the way and then escorted her out of the B and B. They were ready to head for his truck when Darien stalked across the street, catching Tom's eye. Tom wasn't surprised to see Darien arrive when it looked like they might have found the men who had injured Elizabeth.

"Our men got her bags, ID, laptop, everything. At least we think it's everything. You'll have to look it over and see for sure, Elizabeth," Darien said, sounding pleased but still highly annoyed that anyone could have targeted her like they had in his pack's territory. And had been hiding right under their noses.

"Thank God. But…you didn't catch them," she said, appearing somewhat relieved because the villains had left her personal items behind.

Darien shook his head. He looked at Tom and said, "You say they drove a white minivan."

"Yeah. I saw it when we were at the hospital too," Tom said.

"Damn," Darien said, rubbing his chin as he looked toward the old hotel. "Those three outsiders at the tavern earlier today?"

"Were driving a white minivan," Tom guessed.

"Yeah, they were," Darien said.

Elizabeth let out her breath in an exasperated huff. "We just managed to chase them off."

Darien was quick to say, "We got your stuff back. That's what's important."

"They must have been afraid when they ran out of there."

"We didn't smell any fear," Darien said.

"Then what?" she asked.

"Not sure. Take her back home, will you, Tom?" Darien gave her a pack leader look that said she was his to command for now. "Sleep the rest of the night. No more running in your wolf coat or otherwise." He said to Tom, "If you have to, stay with her."

"He won't have to. I'm not waking up until I absolutely have to tomorrow."

———

Elizabeth could have been annoyed with Darien for saying what he did about Tom taking charge of her. Yet she swore more was being communicated than what was being spoken aloud—the way Darien cast a look at Tom and the way Tom gave him an almost imperceptible nod in response.

She even wondered if Darien had put Tom up to asking her to join the pack. In her father's pack, the leader would have decided such a thing. Certainly not a subleader.

"Thank you for the offer, by the way, Tom. Nobody's ever invited me to join a pack," she said on the ride back to Darien's house. She appreciated being asked and wanted Tom to know that her refusal had nothing to do with the pack or him but more to do with her past experiences and the problems with her uncle and half brother.

"You're not a loner," he said again.

"It doesn't matter."

He glanced at her. "It does. For a pack, it matters."

She wouldn't fight him on this issue. The point was moot.

When they arrived back at Darien's house, Tom escorted her to her room. "You might need a bodyguard tonight."

She smiled up at him, touching his sweater-covered chest. "Do you always like to live dangerously?"

He laughed. "Sorry, Elizabeth. I can't see that you would be too rough on me."

"You never know." She didn't want to be alone. She wanted whatever they could have just this once. No strings. No mating. Just a meeting of the minds. And their bodies, as far as they could take it and still not be mated wolves.

"'Night, Elizabeth." He waited for her response. A kiss. A hug maybe.

Trying to discourage anything more between them and annoyed with herself for getting so worked up over any man, she kissed him on the cheek. "'Night, Tom."

She walked into the bedroom and realized she couldn't take off her clothes without his help. She turned and frowned. He watched her, waiting for her to retire for the night. She wondered if he believed she might try to leave and do something further about the guys who had injured her. But she had no intention of going anywhere else tonight.

"Okay, I really, *really* hate to ask this because it's such an imposition, but…could you help me out of my clothes again?"

—————————————

Undressing Elizabeth one more time was way more than an imposition. It killed Tom to see her naked skin and not be able to taste it, to feel it, to smell her sweet scent and want more.

He waited a moment, trying to find the right words, and finally said, "You're killing me, you know?" He shook his head, smiling, and turned toward his bedroom. "I'll get one of my shirts for you. It'll probably be a while before they bring you your bags."

When he returned with the softest blue-plaid flannel shirt he owned, he found her sitting on the bed, her parka on a chair. He closed the bedroom door. She stretched her arms up to him so that he could remove her sweater.

"If I keep removing your clothes, something more is bound to happen," he said, hopeful yet practical.

"So…let it."

He raised a brow, not sure what she was agreeing to. He pulled the sweater over her head and stared down at her mouthwatering breasts, then shifted his gaze to her face. "If you kiss me again…" He let his words trail off, waiting to hear what she had in mind.

"You're supposed to kiss *me*—to make the hurt go away." She raised her foot. He pulled off one boot and then the other.

He thought she meant more than the physical pain. He wondered what she'd experienced that had made her a loner. He was so used to helping others that he wanted to help her too. But his feelings went deeper than that.

The cold wind blew against the closed window, but the room was toasty warm. He wasn't in any hurry to undress her or to help her into his flannel shirt or to leave her. She stood and he removed her jeans. He hesitated to take off her panties, thinking to help her put his shirt on, when she climbed onto the bed and pulled the covers over herself.

He picked up his flannel shirt off the bed. "Didn't you want me to help you into this?"

"Kiss me," she said.

"A good-night kiss," he said. Yet he didn't think she meant that. Her smile was wicked.

"If I kiss you the way I want to, it's bound to go a lot further than that this time." He had to be honest with her. He wanted a lot more. Not a mating, but something that said he wanted to go further later if they were both agreeable.

"I count on it," she said, reaching up to tug at his belt loop.

He was out of his clothes in a flash, making her smile. He pulled the covers aside, slid over to her side of the bed, and began kissing her again—cheeks, mouth, throat, shoulders—his hands sliding all over her soft skin. He kept telling himself he *wasn't* ready to mate her, but his body said otherwise.

————————

Elizabeth knew she was nuts to encourage this. The last man she'd trusted with her heart had stomped all over it and left her, so she hadn't felt this way toward anyone since. She knew Tom lusted after her because she was someone new and different, and this wasn't for the long term. Which suited her perfectly.

She thought she could do this—a bit of sexual release and then go about her business, return home, do her job.

She wanted this intimacy between wolves and her coyote half. Wanted to feel loved, if only for a fleeting moment. Wanted to savor the way his pheromones kicked up as he kissed her, touched her, lusted for her, making her own respond in kind. A wolf who would want a woman for a lifetime. Not a human who could ditch her for someone else at the drop of a hat. Not that any of this meant it was for a lifetime.

She kissed him back on the mouth, her hands curling in his hair as he molded a hand to her breast. She realized he observed her, studying her expression, analyzing it, wondering what was going on in her brain. She didn't want to consider that any further and pulled him down for another kiss.

His hand tightened on her breast as he moved his leg in between hers. He had removed all his clothes, even his boxers, and that had worried her a little. She hoped he didn't think she wanted a mating.

Still, she had left her panties on, which was a signal she didn't want to take this all the way. At least in *her* mind.

When he moved his leg in between hers, prying her open, she felt the exhilaration of sexual tension but also a little apprehension.

Caught up in the heat of passion, she rubbed her leg wickedly on top of his, his mouth not so gentle on hers now. She loved the roughness alternating with tenderness.

His hands moved between holding her face while caressing her cheekbones and sliding down her shoulders and arms in a way that said he loved touching her. Likewise, she felt her way up his toned muscles and enjoyed how they moved beneath her fingertips.

Then he kissed her again. Her mouth, the corners of it, her chin, her throat. Her willingness showed her acceptance of his touch. A wolf would never expose his or her throat to another without completely trusting that individual.

He slid his large hand down her belly. The tips of his fingers paused at the waistband of her bikini panties. She was already wet with need. He could smell her, just as she could smell how aroused he was. His stiff erection brushed her naked belly as they moved against each other, stirring up their hormones, pushing to go further.

She wanted so to slide his hand beneath her panties, to push his fingers deep inside her to make her come, as hot and needy as she was.

He waited a heartbeat. She didn't stop him. Didn't place her hand on his and move it out of bounds. She barely breathed, her hands stilled on his arms, his gaze locked on hers. As if he'd come to a decision, right or wrong, he slipped his fingers beneath her panties. He began to kiss her mouth, licking it, gently nipping her lower lip but not stealing her attention from the way his fingers moved to intercept the knotted bud waiting for his touch.

———————————

If Elizabeth wanted to live dangerously, Tom was all for it. He had no intention of mating with her, but he wanted to prove to her just how hot she made him. Especially since she was still wearing panties. Not that that would prevent him from giving her pleasure.

She seemed so needy. He slipped his hand beneath her panties, didn't sense she wanted him to stop, and plowed right ahead—finding the tantalizing bud that made her arch and moan and whimper as he stroked her. He'd never been with any woman who responded so easily to his touch, wanting more, letting him know just how good he was making her feel.

She raised her leg higher on his, spreading herself more for his easy access, and he wanted to yank off her scrap of silk panties and bare her to him. If he was mating with her, he would. He did consider removing her panties anyway, just to show her that he wouldn't take advantage of her even with them off, as much as he wanted to bury himself in her.

He was a little afraid he might do just that, with both of them losing their heads in the heat of the moment.

Instead, he stroked her, nuzzling her face affectionately at the same time and enjoying the aroused feminine scent of her mixed with his own musky scent, the heat of their bodies making him even hotter. He rubbed his penis against her soft belly and began kissing her again, so aroused that he wanted to end this now inside her, filling her, taking her.

His thumb stroked her bud, and he felt her come, the tiny ripples of orgasm, the soft mewl of pleasure escaping her lips. He loved bringing her pleasure.

He withdrew his hand from her panties and kissed her again, softly on the mouth this time, a farewell parting for the night. He wanted to go. He wanted to stay. If she wished him to remain here for the night, he couldn't. Not without craving more.

"I'll see you in the morning," he said, stroking her hair.

She looked down at his chest, and he lifted her chin to see tears in her eyes.

"Elizabeth?" he said, his voice low, concerned, shocked.

She gave him a smile, faked to reassure him. "I'll...see you in the morning."

"What's wrong?"

She just shook her head. "Nothing."

He knew something had upset her, but when it came to figuring out women, more often than not, he and his brothers didn't have a clue. "Are you hurting?"

She shook her head.

He thought she might be and didn't want to admit it. That she didn't want him to believe he was at fault.

He left the bed and threw on his boxers, then went into the bathroom to get her a glass of water.

He gave her the water and waited until she took a sip and seemed to feel a little better. "See you in the morning." He didn't think he could go to sleep again, as worried as he was about Elizabeth and the men and why she seemed upset.

The front door slammed shut. "Sounds like Darien." Tom had planned to grab his clothes and retire to bed, but he dressed instead. "Sleep, Elizabeth. We'll talk in the morning." He leaned down and kissed her on the forehead.

He smiled, but the smile she returned wasn't genuine, and her eyes swam with tears. Not knowing what else to say if she wouldn't help him out, he said, "See you in the morning."

He left and closed the door, wanting to kick himself for taking things too far with her. He hurried downstairs and met Darien in the living room. He had brought in Elizabeth's bags and raised a brow at his younger brother in question.

"She's gone to bed. I'll take her bags up to her. They've been dusted, right?" Tom asked him.

"Yeah. I can't figure it out. Why steal her stuff and then leave it there?"

"Maybe they weren't trying to get away with her stuff. Maybe they hoped that by bringing her stuff to the abandoned hotel, they could lure her there."

"And then what?" Darien asked. "It certainly wasn't just to talk. Breaking the window was an act of violence against Elizabeth. They could have jimmied the window open or attempted to pick the lock on the front door. They smashed her window as if they were angry."

"Because she took pictures of them?" Tom rubbed his whiskery chin. "They stole everything she had to learn who she was, but they don't want anyone to learn who *they* are. Her ID and airline tickets were inside the case of her laptop, so without having time to search through her stuff at the B and B, they just took everything. Why else would they need to ID her if she isn't some sort of mark?"

"Makes sense. But why leave her stuff and run when she showed up?" Darien asked. "Maybe they believed she'd come alone. That no one from our pack would watch over her. They probably didn't want to get in a fight and just had to cut and run."

"That's what I figure. I'll take her suitcases up to her and then go to bed," Tom said.

"I'm calling it a night too. Again."

When Tom reached the guest room, he saw the light still on underneath the door. He rapped on it. "Elizabeth, are you okay?"

"Yeah," she said. "You can come in."

He opened the door and walked inside, setting her bags on the floor. "Remember that Darien wants you to check them over tomorrow to see if anything is missing. Are you really all right?"

"Yeah, I'm okay. Have a good night's sleep."

He paused, feeling she wasn't sincere. He figured he could learn more about whatever was bothering her tomorrow when they were both well rested.

At least, that was what he planned.

CHAPTER 14

LATER THAT NIGHT, ELIZABETH WOKE FEELING MUCH MORE herself physically, but emotionally she felt bad. She hadn't realized how quickly she had become attached to Tom, and now she had to leave.

Despite the late hour, she called North to arrange another meeting, hoping he'd answer the phone. She had to get this resolved, get the evidence against her uncle, turn it over to Hrothgar, and return home soon.

Someone picked up, but when he didn't say hello or anything, she thought North might be half-asleep. She said, "North?"

No response, just someone's breathing. Her heart pounded, and she quickly hung up. Had someone learned North planned to meet with her to expose her uncle's secrets? Someone who didn't want those secrets revealed?

She paced across the guest bedroom's carpeted floor. She had to leave. She couldn't get Darien and Lelandi's pack involved in this. All she wanted to do was resolve this on her own. This was not the Silver pack's trouble. They already had enough problems with the other wolf strangers prowling around farms in the area.

She dialed another number. "I need the first flight out to Amarillo in the morning."

———————

The next morning, Darien greeted Elizabeth bright and early, but he knew something was amiss. He'd finished feeding the triplets, and a nanny watched them in the den while Lelandi ate eggs and toast before her first client session. She usually had one before this, but the woman had canceled because of the weather. Lelandi might be eating, but Darien knew she was trying to figure out what was wrong with Elizabeth, just as much as he was.

Being an alpha, Elizabeth told him how things would be right away. "I'm so sorry, but I need to leave. Could anyone drive me to the airport, or could I get a cab out here?"

She had three more days to be here, Darien remembered. Something was compelling her to leave this soon.

"Peter can take you. He's on his way here now anyway." Darien wasn't about to wake Tom and ask him. He suspected something was wrong between the two of them or Elizabeth would have asked Tom herself. "How are you feeling?"

"Great. All better. Thanks."

That was the way she'd spoken since she joined them. Brief. To the point. She wasn't sharing how she was feeling. The fact that she was downstairs so early after having been up half the night made Darien believe she was desperate to leave before Tom woke. He wondered if she'd slept at all.

"You're not afraid the men will come after you, are you?"

"No," she said so emphatically that he wasn't sure he believed her.

Lelandi was so good at psychoanalyzing patients and pack members, including himself and his brothers, that Darien wished she would speak up and get to the bottom of the trouble. She wouldn't. She just poured herself another cup of coffee while Elizabeth downed a glass of orange juice in a hurry, even though Peter was still on his way to the house.

"You spoke to Jake this morning."

"Yes." She looked out the window.

"He was pleased you did an interview of him," Darien said, trying to draw her out.

"Yeah."

"Did he manage to fix your camera?"

She shook her head.

"I'm sorry."

"Yeah."

He glanced at Lelandi. She raised her brows at him as if to say that the situation was in his court.

When Peter pulled into the driveway, Elizabeth hopped up from her chair—another indication she was physically fine—and hurried to slip into her parka. "Thanks for everything. You've all been…wonderful."

Darien heard the hitch in her voice and saw the way she turned away and wouldn't look at them.

She grabbed her suitcase handles and laptop, then hurried for the door, but Darien quickly snatched the bags from her hands and hauled them for her.

"I left a note for Tom on his computer," she said, trying to sound businesslike and not entirely succeeding.

Tom would be upset that she had left without saying goodbye face-to-face or allowing him to take her to the airport. Unless they had fought. But what he had smelled on his brother last night wasn't anger or upset. Worry and sex. That was what he had smelled.

"You always have a home here with us anytime you want to return," Darien said.

She offered him a faint smile. "Thanks."

When she looked away, he got the feeling she wasn't planning to return. He was disappointed, because he knew how much Tom liked her, and he'd seen the way she'd reacted to his brother in a positive, caring way. For that matter, everyone who had chanced to meet her had liked her. That video capturing Tom and Elizabeth kissing on the slope had totally surprised both Lelandi and him, and he knew more was going on between the two of them than they admitted.

He'd wanted to call Carol and ask if her talk with Elizabeth had revealed anything of her past, but Lelandi said what the two women discussed had been private. If Elizabeth wanted to share, it was her business to do so. It didn't matter that Darien had mentioned that this *could* have an impact on the pack. Lelandi had only shaken her head—an emphatic, nonverbal "No, butt out." He loved his mate, but sometimes, like now, she totally exasperated him.

He opened the door to find Peter standing on the porch, ready to knock. He smiled brightly at Elizabeth.

She hurried past him and headed for his vehicle.

"She's in a hurry to get to the airport," Darien said in explanation. "Could you take her?"

"Oh, sure." Peter took her bags, hurried out to the truck, and stuck them in the back seat of the cab. "See you in a little while."

Her eyes shiny with tears, Elizabeth waved at Darien and Lelandi. Then Peter got into the driver's seat, and they were off.

Darien knew that no matter what had happened between Elizabeth and Tom, this was not a good way to say—or not say—goodbye. Darien, for one, didn't want the job of having to deal with the mood he knew Tom would be in when he woke.

———————

That morning, Tom felt something wasn't right as soon as he got up. The sun was too high in the sky. He never slept this late, and he wondered why no one had bothered to wake him. He hurried to dress, then headed for Elizabeth's room. Her door was shut. He knocked. No answer. He opened the door a crack.

She was gone. The bed stripped. Her suitcases nowhere in sight.

With a sickening knot in his stomach, he ran down the stairs, expecting to see her eating breakfast with Darien.

The toddlers played in the den, squealing in delight, then

arguing—the way he and his brothers had done when they were that age—while a couple of wolf nannies watched over them. He thought Lelandi would be plying her psychology on a human client in the office they had built next to the house. The home was off in the woods, but this was the only way she wanted to work when the babies were still little. Bonding and pack dynamics were all too important, from the youngest *lupus garou* to the oldest.

To his surprise, Lelandi was sipping coffee with Darien. Jake and his mate were there too, which was odder still. They normally ate breakfast at their own home.

Elizabeth wasn't there. Everyone looked at him as though they didn't know what to say. Didn't know how to act.

"Where is she?" he asked, sounding much more growly than he intended.

"Peter took her to the airport," Darien said.

Tom turned and began to stalk out of the dining room.

"Tom!" Darien called out. "She's gone. She left two hours ago."

Tom scowled at Darien. "Why didn't anyone wake me? Tell me she was leaving?"

Why didn't she tell him herself?

"She didn't want it that way," Darien said.

Tom was the most even-tempered of his brothers, but right now he was so angry that he could have put his fist through the wall.

"What happened between the two of you?" Darien asked in a voice that was meant to calm him, but Tom didn't want his brothers' or their mates' sympathy *or* interference.

"Nothing," Tom said.

"Was she scared of the men? Afraid to stay?"

"Hell, no. She would have gone into the hotel after them if I hadn't stopped her."

Darien took Lelandi's hand in his. "Anything else that you can think of that happened, Tom? She asked if someone could take her to the airport, then had a glass of orange juice but no real break-fast. She was in a rush to leave. She barely said a word or two to us in response to anything I asked."

"She was supposed to be here three more days."

"You said yourself she had a job to do," Darien reminded him.

Lelandi said, "She was running away from something. She might not be afraid of the men, but maybe something else is going on that we don't know about."

Tom ran his hands through his hair. "I don't know about that, but... I asked her to join our pack. She didn't act interested in the idea."

Everyone stared at him as if he'd suddenly grown vampire fangs.

He folded his arms across his chest. "She's a damn good tracker. We could use someone with her expertise in the pack. And we don't have a newspaper. Maybe she could have started one."

"Is *that* what you told her?" Lelandi asked, her voice a little edgy.

"Not about the paper." Then Tom frowned at Lelandi. "Are you implying that if I had told her *I* wanted her to stay, she would have done so?" Lelandi's raised eyebrows indicated she thought just that. Before she could respond, Tom shook his head. "She was completely against the idea. She's not a loner, but she's afraid of belonging to a pack for some reason."

"Or making a commitment to a wolf possibly," Lelandi said.

Tom didn't want to mention he'd gotten a little frisky with her last night and that that had brought tears to her eyes. "Was she okay this morning? Hurting still?"

"She was fine," Darien said. "She moved fast and started haul-ing her bags out of here when she saw Peter arrive, so she couldn't have been feeling any pain."

Not physically. Then it dawned on Tom. She'd been emotion-ally upset—hurting. *Shit.*

Irritated with himself, Tom said to Darien, "Unless you have something else for me to do, I'm tracking those rogue wolves today."

No one said a word. Tom stalked out of the dining room, grabbed his parka and other cold-weather gear from the coat closet, then left the house.

Before he reached the garage, Jake joined him outside. "She left you something. She'd taken a picture of you helping an injured little girl on the slope, and she used it as your desktop picture. She also left you a note."

"Why the hell didn't Darien say so?" Tom strode back to the house. "Did you read what she said?"

"No. Not that I didn't want to, mind you, and it killed me not to. If it helps tell us why she rushed out of here, we'd all like to know," Jake said. "Lelandi said that the picture she left on your desktop has significance. Of all the photos she took, and she took lots, she put up that particular one. Lelandi believes your helping the little girl really touched Elizabeth. If you want to see more of her, you might have to take the initiative to make it happen."

"I already plan to," Tom said. He was so irritated at his brother for thinking he needed to suggest such a thing that he couldn't help snapping at Jake.

Jake smiled. "That's what we all wanted to hear. Darien got all her information—her cell number and home address—before he turned over her bags. Look, Darien and I have both been in the same position as you. We're with you all the way, however you want to deal with this. I'll see you later."

The little red wolf-coyote thought nobody cared anything about her when a whole gray wolf pack was ready to take her in.

Jake didn't join Tom in the den, giving him some privacy, for which he was grateful. Tom opened his laptop and turned it on. The monitor showed the picture of him crouching before the crying girl who had wrenched her knee on the slopes.

Looking at it now, it made him sick to think Elizabeth had

taken a Norman Rockwell-type picture of him and the little girl, and then some bastard had shoved Elizabeth down the slope right afterward.

On the desktop, she had created a folder of the pictures she had taken of her visit here, as if it were a gift to him. Which frustrated him even more. She couldn't come into his life like this and pop right out again without him having any say in it.

He opened the folder. A separate file was labeled "Elizabeth's Note to Tom." With apprehension, he paused, then clicked on the file and opened it.

> *Dear Tom,*
>
> *You are the nicest man I've ever met, for a wolf. You should meet a nice she-wolf and settle down. I think you'd make a great mate and father.*
>
> *I'm sorry for not saying goodbye properly. I just thought it would be easier this way.*
>
> *You said I wasn't a loner, and you're right. I love what you and your family have. But it's just not for me. It never has been.*
>
> *Thank everyone for me, will you? I won't be back, but I just wanted you to know how much I appreciated your kindness.*
>
> *Elizabeth*

Lelandi's words came crashing back to Tom: *She's running away from something.*

His thoughts in turmoil, he closed the letter. He wouldn't let her run away.

He stared at the scene she'd captured of him on the slopes. The central figures in the picture were Kemp, the little girl, and him. Off to the side, the distraught mother had her hand over her mouth. The father and son had still been on the slopes. A couple of skiers watched the scene—spectators interested in who had gotten hurt. One man, a few feet away, wore a black ski bib, hat, and balaclava and a blue-gray parka and reflective sunglasses—but he wasn't observing the scene with the little girl. Instead, he stared straight at the camera operator—*Elizabeth*.

"Darien!" Tom called out.

Everyone came, his brothers and their mates, all looking anxious. He pointed at the man in the photo. "Wasn't he the one seated on the chairlift behind Elizabeth? The one she thinks pushed her down the expert slope?"

———————

Elizabeth felt awful for leaving Tom behind without saying goodbye. She hadn't wanted to stay after her strange call to North. She had no intention of dragging Tom and his family and pack into her troubles. She'd tried twice more to get hold of North before she took off on the plane, but she only got his voicemail. She wouldn't leave any messages.

She'd finally found a safe haven away from her family. If they knew she lived in Texas, no one seemed to care. Staying in Silver Town would be a dangerous thing to do if her uncle knew she was there and decided he wanted her dead, again.

She didn't need to screw up her life by getting involved with a gray wolf, even as sweet as he was, who didn't know her past history. Making her uncle pay for his crimes seemed to be only a dream. She prayed North hadn't been hurt in the process.

Once she arrived home, she'd dropped her camera off to be repaired. Even though Jake was a pro with cameras, maybe the camera shop could do what he hadn't been able to. Then Elizabeth immersed herself in her job. She wrote the article for her paper about the Silver Town Ski Resort, making sure to mention their great ski patrollers and staff, and turned the story in.

After that, she started an article about red wolves. Her research showed that two theories existed: one that red wolves were a special species separate from gray wolves, and the other that red wolves were descended from gray wolves mixing with coyotes. She slanted the article toward the latter.

Carol had said that gray wolves weren't mixing with coyotes in the States, but Elizabeth found that Virginia coyotes *had* mated with Great Lakes gray wolves, and she found further articles stating that coyotes from other locations had a percentage of gray wolf DNA.

It made sense to her. Coyotes hunt in packs just as wolves do. They're also both predators, eating rodents that cause plagues. Both species are bound to their families and take care of their young as a group. The Native Americans thought coyotes were clever and savvy because of their ability to adapt everywhere. Elizabeth couldn't understand why some people were so strongly against them. Why was it so bad to recognize that some red wolves are just coyotes with a heavy dose of gray wolf DNA?

Intending to call her editor about the new article, Elizabeth realized she hadn't turned her phone back on since she flew home. She slipped it out of her bag and turned it on.

Twenty-two messages.

Surprised, she stared at the number before she clicked on it to see who had called her, hoping North might have tried to get in touch with her and was all right. She never got that many calls to her cell phone, and no one except her editor knew she was back in town.

She felt a pang of guilt, hoping Tom hadn't called some of those times. She hesitated for a minute, then clicked on the messages.

Tom had phoned her seventeen times, but he hadn't left her any messages. She closed her eyes. She had hoped he would figure out that nothing could be gained by the two of them speaking further. He needed someone who was local and all wolf, rather than someone like her.

Two of the calls were from Lelandi and the rest from Darien. Their messages were brief and just asked her to call them back. Maybe they'd caught the guy who pushed her down the slope. No calls from North. She should phone Darien or Lelandi, since they were the pack leaders. She shouldn't get in touch with Tom, knowing full well he'd be upset with her. She didn't want to explain what a mess her life had already been and why she was best being on her own.

So what did she do? She called Tom.

The phone rang several times. He didn't pick up. She reached his voicemail but didn't leave a message. He'd see that she'd called anyway. If he wanted to call her back, he could. This time she'd have her phone turned on. She tried getting hold of North again. Voicemail again.

She punched in the number for her editor, Ed Bloomington, and when he picked up, she could hear the smile in his voice, welcoming her home. But it wasn't home. Not for her. A shifter without family. She realized just how much she had been fooling herself ever to think so.

She put on her business persona, swallowed the emotions welling up inside, and said, "I just sent you the story about the ski resort, and I've got a great idea for another one that I got from…a friend in Colorado. It's a story about gray wolves not having mates, finding coyotes to love, and their pairings resulting in red wolves. Some call the offspring a coywolf. But evidence exists that's how some red wolves came to be. What do you think?"

"Sounds great. Send it to me."

She barely breathed as she emailed Ed the story and he read through it. "All right. Top-notch story. Love the angle, Elizabeth. I'll print it first," Ed said after a few agonizing minutes on

Elizabeth's end. "I'll print the other story at the end of the week. Damned glad to have you home. Got to run to a family birthday get-together. I'm surprised you came home so early though."

"I missed home," she said, even though Ed's mention of attending a family birthday party made her feel isolated and alone. She shrugged the notion off, not wanting to deal with it. Not wanting to think of Tom and his close-knit family. Not wishing to think of how she would have loved to have a family like that growing up. "I'll see you when I finish my leave." Even though she'd come home early, she was still using her vacation time, and she would attempt to enjoy it.

"All right. Talk to you later."

Later that week when her article about the wolves came out, she received an unbelievable number of hateful responses. She hadn't expected that. She'd only reported what scientists believed.

She was damned tired of burying her feelings. If gray wolves didn't have a mate and they found one in a coyote, what was the big deal? They were pack animals at heart. They deserved to find mates who would love them back.

But to get death threats?

Five emails, six phone calls. *Really?* The people who responded to her article in the paper were wolf lovers, maybe even red-wolf shifters. They didn't ID themselves. Of course, she got some irate calls from farmers and ranchers who said any of them—wolves, coyotes, and any mix of the two—should be shot on sight.

How would they feel if shifters felt that way about humans?

The phone rang again, with caller ID showing Caller Unknown. "Hello?"

"How dare you say the red wolves are part coyote," a man's voice said, though it was muffled and she couldn't identify him.

Her half brother Sefton? Uncle Quinton?

"How does it feel to know you're just like me?" she asked, chills running up her spine at the thought that they had her cell number, if one of them was calling her. Then again, if one of them had answered North's phone, that was how he got it.

She didn't know if the caller was really one of them. If he wasn't, the man had to have thought she was nuts.

The phone clicked dead and she felt shaky, as if she had just come face-to-face with her uncle. Goose bumps erupted on her skin.

The phone rang again. Another unknown caller. "Damned stupid article, if you ask me. Are you one of those animal activists? One of those vegetable eaters? Red wolves are beautiful and rare predators, while coyotes are sneaky scavengers. Damn coyotes are not part gray wolf."

Elizabeth ground her teeth, irritated that people were so hateful about the wolves and coyotes.

The caller hung up the phone. She guessed he didn't have anything more to say.

Elizabeth thought again about Tom. Every call gave her heart a little start. Every call might be from him.

She hadn't heard back since she'd phoned him a few days ago. He must have given up on her, which was for the best. So why did she miss him and his pack and Silver Town so much? Despite the misadventure at the ski resort, she loved how the pack members on the slopes had treated her, loved Tom's bossiness about taking care of her.

She would have given just about anything to eat more of Bertha's cinnamon rolls while talking to her about gardening. Elizabeth would have shared more with Carol. She wanted to know what had happened to Lelandi while she was with the red pack. She would have loved to go to the grand opening of Silva's Victorian Tea Shop and even see Silva and Sam get together as mates. She wanted to learn more about Peter's brother and if he was causing trouble for the sheriff during his visit.

Most of all, she wanted to see Tom again, feel his touch, experience his kisses, and so much more.

She'd never felt that way about any other wolves she'd met, never had any others act as if they'd already made her part of the family and she'd accepted the role. She had to quit thinking like that.

Uncle Quinton was still in the area. If she returned to Silver Town, he'd try to eliminate her. If she did and his pack leader was agreeable to hearing Elizabeth out, Quinton would be a dead wolf. He couldn't trust her to leave well enough alone.

When the sun began to set, she ran through Palo Duro Canyon State Park in her furry form. She scattered the two longhorn cattle living there, chased a cottontail rabbit, startled a white-tailed deer, and snagged her fur on the thorny mesquite. She ran and ran, trying to quit thinking about the article and Tom and what had happened to North.

She had nearly reached home when she spied a coyote.

That made her stop dead in her tracks.

Was it a shifter? Or a plain old coyote? Could he be family on her mother's side? Couldn't be. They lived in the Oklahoma Panhandle.

The coyote was a bigger male. He watched her, scenting the air to learn anything he could about her and what she felt. In this case, apprehension. Her heart rate had already kicked up a notch.

She didn't see any others, so he might be a loner.

What if he was a shifter? Maybe he was worried about what she was. He might be wary of her because she smelled like a wolf too. That usually kept any coyote shifters away from her.

A shot rang out, the bang sending a shriek of panic through her. She dove for the ground and watched to see where the rifle had fired from. The coyote ran off.

She waited for a long time, not moving, hoping that whoever had fired the round had given up trying to shoot the coyotes. If he came for her, thinking she had been shot, she wasn't sure what she would do. Shift before he could see her, so he'd find an uninjured, naked woman? Then what? She just hoped he'd go off looking to shoot something else, like a rattlesnake—though at this time of year, they'd be curled up in a den.

She thought of shifting and running as a human to her home, but the ground could be hazardous to her bare feet with its cactus, thorny senna, and rocky terrain, and it was only thirty-six degrees out today. Purple and pink stripes streaked across the sky as the sun began to set, but snow clouds quickly amassed.

She took a chance and raced through the juniper and scrub oak. Half an hour later, she plowed through her wolf door out back and entered the safety of the house. She panted, staring at the terra-cotta tile floor, barely feeling relief when someone knocked on the front door. Her heart skipped a beat. Now what?

She raced into the bedroom, shifted, and threw on some clothes. Peering out through the peephole of her front door, she saw no one. Wrong house?

A black sedan sat farther down the dead-end street. All the houses backed up on ten-acre lots, with a half acre between homes, so they had a lot of privacy. She couldn't see if anyone sat in the vehicle, and she didn't recognize the car.

To be on the safe side, she went into the kitchen and locked her wolf door so no one could get in when she least expected it. The coyote she'd seen would know where she lived once he tracked her scent. She glanced out the window with the lights off in the room and the black car was gone.

CHAPTER 15

EXPECTING A SNOWSTORM TO HIT BY NIGHTFALL, ELIZABETH needed some groceries to tide her over. The clouds had rolled in, white, voluminous, and filled with snow. She'd seen the weather reports, felt the change in the air pressure, and could smell the coming snow in the wind currents. If what she predicted would happen, they'd be in a whiteout by nightfall.

On the way to the grocery store, she spied a big sale sign in the window at a small butcher shop that she'd never visited before: *Rib-eye steaks 20 percent off!*

When she walked into the butcher shop, the strange scent of cat threw her. The odor bothered her because her first thought was that the butcher had supplemented his meat products with cat. Then she realized the smell was that of a couple of live cats. Feral. She would have sworn they were big cats, as in the predator-in-the-mountains type. The butcher couldn't have had house cats or any other variety in the store though, not when he sold food.

After buying the meat, she was still puzzling over the cat-scent mystery and didn't fully notice the people entering the shop behind her. She'd heard their footsteps, but their arrival hadn't registered as anything sinister. Until they quickly moved in close to her. Three men. Getting in her space. The distinctive smells of testosterone, cologne, and aggression surrounded her all at once.

Before she could object to their close proximity, one of the men quickly wrapped his arm around her shoulder and poked a gun against her ribs. "Don't make a sound," he whispered in her ear, as if pretending to be her lover, to her chagrin.

The butcher smiled. She had to have looked highly annoyed. Even wolfishly dangerous, if anyone had known what she was.

"You got the sale steaks, I see, honey," the man holding the gun against her side said, more to the butcher than to her. "I was afraid you hadn't gotten my message."

She opened her mouth to reply, but he quickly tightened his grip around her shoulder, warning her not to say a word. He nodded to the butcher and added, "Thanks."

Now what was she to do?

The article she'd written about wolves came to mind in a flash, but she couldn't imagine anyone kidnapping or killing her over it. Then she wondered if Uncle Quinton had found her that fast. Why go after her at a butcher shop? Why not when she was in her home? Alone?

The three men escorted her outside to a black vehicle with dark-tinted windows—the same car she'd seen near her home. The man acting as her lover attempted to force her into the back seat.

"You've mistaken me for someone else," she said to the man wielding the gun. She grabbed the car frame, not about to let him shove her inside. That could be the end of her.

And that was when she got her first look at the men.

None had shielded their faces from her view, so she could identify every one of them. Somehow they all looked familiar… Where had she seen them before?

Oh…my…God!

"You're the men who made a scene back at the Silver Town Tavern!" Elizabeth exclaimed, staring at the blond, bearded man in the group. She recognized his cold eyes glowering at her. He was the man from the chairlift.

"You bastard." She lunged forward to knee him in the crotch, but the dark-haired gunman jerked her back. She'd almost forgotten he still held her arm tight, but she recognized him as the spokesman of the group at the tavern. Since he was wielding the gun, she had a feeling he had also pushed her down the slope.

Instinctively, she tried to identify their scents. Nothing—as far as a wolf scent. They had to have applied hunter's spray and then cologne over that to make sure she couldn't detect them as wolves. Then everything clicked into place. She thought she hadn't been able to identify the blond man's scent on the chairlift because the wind blew it away from her. But she and Tom hadn't picked up any scents after her room had been broken into either. The men had to have been using hunter's spray then too. There was no other explanation.

She was certain they were wolves. They wouldn't have any other need to use hunter's spray in a nonhunting environment. Her heartbeat thundered in her ears.

If these were the guys who'd stolen her stuff back at Silver Town, they had to know exactly who she was. She *was* the one they wanted for whatever sinister purpose. She was certain it all had to do with her uncle.

The gunman tried to force her into the vehicle again. He jerked her from the car frame and shoved her inside the car. She fell forward, landing on her stomach on the back seat. Before she could turn and defend herself, he jabbed her in the buttock with a long needle, pissing her off. She lashed out with a kick of her boot to his right shin. He yelped in pain, shoved her legs aside, climbed in, and slammed the door shut.

"Drive," he growled to the blond man.

Her vision blurred. The driver and the other man, a redhead, looked back at him with smug smiles. "He warned us she'd be a wolf," the driver said, amusement coating his words.

Her heartbeat was slowing from the drug, but it did a little kick at his mention of "wolf."

"Uncle Quinton," she slurred.

"You sure you have enough hours under your belt to serve as copilot?" the redhead said to the driver.

Copilot?

"Hell, yeah," the driver said. "How do you think we managed to fly into Mexico so frequently? This will be a piece of cake."

Mexico?

"Hell," the redhead said, "you should have asked her where the deed was before you drugged her."

Elizabeth felt a stab of panic through the haze of the drug. Did they know she had been planning to trade the deed to her parents' property to North for the evidence he had against her uncle?

She had meant to return the deed to the safe in her home, but she hadn't gotten around to taking it out of the breast pocket of her ski jacket...that she was wearing. She'd forgotten all about it.

The gunman pulled Elizabeth around onto her back and searched her unceremoniously. She tried to muster a look of extreme disgust and indignation as he unzipped her jacket and patted her down a little too friskily. "We'll search her place if..." The gunman slapped the deed in his hand. "Not necessary. Got it right here."

The small plane soared high above snow-covered mountains, the flakes swirling around the windows and wings in such profusion that the sky and ground were no longer visible in the whiteout. God only knew where Elizabeth was as she shook off the effect of the drug her captor had given her. How could the pilot see where he was going? Or the copilot figure out where to take them?

"Damn it, Canton," the pilot growled. "You said there was a gap between the storm cells. You said we'd clear them before they hit us."

"If the damn cells hadn't moved as fast as they did, we would have," the dark-haired man said.

Where were they? Flying over Palo Duro Canyon? She didn't know how long she'd been out of it, but she couldn't see anything in the blanket of white.

She shifted in her seat and realized she sat in the tail of the plane, seat belted and handcuffed.

She had gotten into plenty of scrapes over the years as a wolf-coyote mix without a pack, and she'd always managed to get herself out of them. But this time…

Maybe she should have made more of a fuss in the butcher shop. Maybe she wouldn't be here now, but she had been afraid the men would kill the butcher—and her—and she hadn't wanted that.

Canton was half dozing in a seat across from her. When he realized she was watching him, he narrowed his gaze at her. What? Did he think she'd let the inner wolf loose again? That was when she noticed something…an unfamiliar scent. The scent of male red wolves. Their hunter's spray must have worn off by now.

She settled back against the seat of the small aircraft, glowering at the gunman wearing a blue-gray parka and a crooked smile—the one named Canton. She tried to appear more at ease than she felt.

His greasy dark hair swept his shoulders as he shook his head at her, that stupid smile firmly plastered on his face. His sharp eyes remained fixed on her while he slid his gun into his holster like he'd probably done a thousand times before—smoothly, like a gunman in an old Western. Same jeans, only the cowboy boots were grimy sneakers, and the dirty parka replaced the vest and old-time western shirt.

She glanced out the window. She didn't like to fly, and given the choice, she'd never set foot in a plane, ever. Certainly not in the middle of a snowstorm. She briefly wondered what they had done with her deed.

Canton chuckled, drawing her attention back to him and the fix she was in.

"Who ordered you to pick me up?" she asked, not that she expected him to tell her the truth.

Canton shrugged, then hollered to the red-haired pilot, "Hey, Huckster, when will we get there?"

Never. If Elizabeth had *her* way.

"Another half hour, but in this blizzard, it may take longer." The pilot sounded like he was trying to hide the anxiety in his voice.

That had her even more worried. If the pilot didn't think they would make it, what chance did they have?

She twisted her wrists again, wishing she had a hairpin or, better yet, her lockpicks to unlock the fool thing. She always carried lockpicks because her father said they had saved his butt a time or two, but the men had already patted her down and found the picks. That was part of the reason she had begun to wake up. Their hands on her, probing and searching, had brought her to a groggy state of consciousness.

Canton again turned to smile at her. "You're real pretty. Too bad. They didn't like that you got mixed up with the wrong people."

In the turbulent downdrafts, the airplane dropped again, her heart with it. She grabbed the seat back in front of her. Her stomach grew queasy. Neither wolves nor coyotes were meant to fly. At least not this one.

"Who?" she asked.

He shrugged. "We don't ask those kinds of questions. Besides, you think they'd give us their real names?"

Either he was lying or these three weren't with her father's pack. Rogue wolves for hire?

"Why did you knock me down the ski slope?"

"Nothing personal. Just getting paid for a job. The guy who wants you—and the deed—now that's personal."

Her uncle. And he must know North had evidence to prove he killed her parents.

The plane dove again, and she held her stomach.

"Getting seasick?" Canton chuckled. "Guess I should say airsick. We're just taking you to a nice little hideaway in the mountains so you don't think of slipping away from us until we can turn you over to the men who are paying for you."

Men. Plural. Her half brother had to be in on it.

If only she could shape-shift… She squirmed against the handcuffs again. If she could slip her hands through them… She wriggled and twisted. The skin around her wrists burned with the effort as the metal scraped the skin. No success. She growled under her breath. Then she nixed the idea of turning anyway. They could shift too, into larger male wolves. And even if she miraculously got the upper hand in a fight, what could she do? Kill them? She didn't want to contemplate that, but even if she did, what then? She couldn't fly a plane.

An engine sputtered. Her heart thudding, she listened to the sounds of a plane in trouble and smelled the stench of fear that cloaked the man closest to her. The plane abruptly angled hard right. One wing tipped down.

She fell from her seat into the aisle, smacking her left elbow hard against the unforgiving floor. Canton landed between the seats next to her while the others cursed up front.

She considered disarming Canton while he was off balance. If she could reach his gun—

Then she heard metal ripping, and she lost all sense of direction as she suddenly became weightless in a field of white.

Screams—*hers*—issued before she could stop the sound of panic and then silence. Everything—the wind, the cold, the snow blinding her—faded into oblivion.

CHAPTER 16

Out of range to call anyone on his cell phone, Tom quit attempting to get hold of Elizabeth and concentrated on tracking down the wolves stalking the livestock. He'd finally discovered what he thought was a lead: unfamiliar wolf prints in the snow leading into the woods near one of the farms. If he could just locate the wolves before the next snowstorm began...just a little bit farther. He didn't want to lose the trail this time.

The biting cold whipped at his face as he trudged through the Rockies, rifle slung over his shoulder. He suspected the rest of his gray-wolf pack mates would return to their homes in Silver Town, seeking hot showers, hot food, and if they were mated or had a human female to snuggle up to, hot sex. Which made him think of Elizabeth. He wished she was here.

Snowflakes dusted the evergreens with a sprinkling of white powder as fat flakes slanted sideways and were captured on the wind. The snow crystals covered his white parka and melted away.

Some of his pack mates helping with the search had run as wolves. With the approaching storm, he wondered if he shouldn't have also. Still, he was glad to have his rifle with him, and if he had to, he'd slip off to the family cabin about a mile away.

The wind howled through the trees, a ghostly, haunting tune, as he tried to listen for any other sounds—a howl from the wolves plaguing the farmers' sheep and calves or even his own people howling to say they had given up the search before it was too late.

The sun that had sparkled off the creeks and shone through the branches of the trees this morning had given way to mountainous blue-gray clouds that shadowed everything, muting the vivid colors and warning that the weather would worsen.

Almost as soon as Tom set his sights on the storm clouds above him, snow began to drift down upon his upturned face. The sudden snowfall got heavier with alarming speed, and Tom regretfully decided to give up the chase for the moment.

Despite the full-blown blizzard whipping about him, Tom loved the chilled air, the snow, the wind, and the sound of it as it shook the mighty firs. Yet he wished he were curled up somewhere warm with Elizabeth, her blue-green eyes challenging him—very much alpha, while she'd pretended to be a beta. He couldn't quit thinking about the way she had kissed him and then wanted him to go further, as if she'd hungered for more. He damn well wanted more with her. But she had been upset afterward. What had gone wrong? He should have sat down on the bed, gathered her in his arms, and flat out asked what the matter was instead of allowing her to get away with saying that it was nothing.

She hadn't returned one of his calls. He couldn't figure her out. Maybe that was why he was so hung up on her.

After a little while, the cabin he and his brothers kept in the mountains came into view. Though they were a close-knit family, sometimes having a little more privacy in a remote cabin appealed. Especially in a town like theirs, where no secrets stayed secrets for long.

Tom paused just outside the door, contemplating the meager woodpile, when the distant sound of an aircraft engine in trouble caught his ear. A sputtering, and then the engine completely cut out. Silence for a heartbeat. Then metal and tree branches ripped in discord and a muffled bang followed. He stared in the direction of the mountains hidden in the blinding snow.

No explosion, no flames shooting into the air or bleak, gray smoke curling up through the forest that he could see. Just silence.

He swore under his breath and charged into the cabin, slamming the door shut against the blizzard. He couldn't search for survivors in the middle of a blizzard as a human. But he hated to think what would happen if he found someone still alive and they panicked when they saw him as a wolf. Still, he had no other choice if he was to locate anyone still alive.

After ditching his clothes in a rush, he stretched his arms out, his body warming with the advent of the change, accepting the transformation, and welcoming it. His muscles and bones reshaped. Fur covered his skin in a warm pelt. The double coat would protect him from the frigid elements. He raced across the floor and dove through the wolf door.

Outside, the white bleakness obscured everything in a ghostly way. Whoever had chosen to be foolhardy enough to fly in this weather was out of their mind. Rich folks flying about in expensive private jets to see the spectacular Rockies, perhaps? Probably decided on a whim to witness the snow-covered peaks. Or maybe they didn't understand the air density at this altitude, mountain winds, navigating the ridges, the problems with radio communications, or even hypoxia, which could lead to altitude sickness up there. Or how suddenly a storm could move in.

The absence of the plane's engine hum ground on his nerves. A number of people had survived airplane crashes in the mountains. But without a way to keep warm, the cold would kill them if the crash hadn't.

If he found survivors who were near death, the only way he could save them was to bite them and share his *lupus garou* genetics. Darien would have a fit if Tom took it upon himself to make a life-or-death decision and turn a severely injured person or persons they knew nothing about.

Changing someone could prove disastrous. Some just couldn't accept being turned. What if Darien told Tom that the new wolf was *his* problem if the wolf became real trouble? Tom didn't want to save someone's life only to have to eliminate him later if he went rogue. Not only that, but the human's family had to be considered.

Tom focused on the sounds in the wind, trying to discern if he could hear anything in the direction that the plane had gone down. If the plane transmitted an SOS, search parties would begin combing the area, bringing more aircraft, people, media, and problems once the storm let up.

He dashed through the snowy woods in his wolf form. He thought he knew the general vicinity to investigate, but he sniffed the air, listening for any sounds that could direct him more precisely toward the crash site.

A sweep of metal tapped against a tree a long way off. He bounded toward the sound.

Gouges in tree trunks, broken branches, and needled twigs littering pristine snow warned of the plane's fatal path as he continued north.

No sign of bodies or—

A fresh depression in the snowbank caught his attention. He loped to the spot and peered into the indent in the snow. A gun.

The notion that the flight was way off course, carrying the crew and pleasure-seeking passengers to their deaths, became something else.

Who would have carried a gun aboard a flight? Even a private flight?

If they were government agents, the place would be crawling with rescue teams in short order.

Tom circled the area, listening. Sniffing the air, he didn't smell any blood or humans as the wind swept through the trees. The piles of snow were stacked so high on branches that they blew over and landed with a plop. A brown hare bolted out of a pocket of snow, startling him. Then Tom spied a section of plane: the tail ripped from the body, probably by force of impact with the trees. It was tilted on its side and stuck between two partially shattered trees, grounded in the forest floor forever.

No bodies anywhere though. No luggage, no personal effects,

nothing. He twitched his ears back and forth, listening for the soft moans of human passengers who might have survived the crash, but he heard nothing new.

He continued to search, finding a seat cushion. Several hundred feet from that, he discovered a man's mangled body, jeans ripped to shreds. He had a bearded face, shaggy blond hair, and the stare of death in his fathomless black eyes.

Tom discovered another body still belted to his seat, neck broken. Another man, maybe the navigator or copilot, was face-down in the snow. Tom nudged his nose under the man's body and flipped him faceup. This one was packing—a knife in his belt, a gun in its holster—and his appearance was as scruffy as the other two.

Drug runners maybe? Unless the guy had been undercover, although he didn't look like a government agent or cop type. But he looked...familiar. One of the men hassling Silva at the tavern?

Tom searched for a while longer but didn't find anyone else. He didn't know which situation he had feared more: finding no survivors or finding someone terribly injured.

The wind-driven snow covered everything in its path, giving the plane and its crew and passengers a cold, white burial. Deciding there was nothing else he could do, Tom bounded back the way he'd come, through the snowdrifts and past the tail of the plane embedded in the ground, intent on reaching his cabin...when he smelled blood. *Coyote blood.*

———————

Elizabeth was sure she'd died and gone to hell.

Except it was far too cold for that. Pain shrieked through her head, her shoulders, back, legs. She touched her forehead and found her fingers red with blood. She didn't think she'd broken anything, just had cuts and bruises. And just when she'd been feeling a hundred percent better too.

Beyond frustrated, she brushed her hair out of her eyes and surveyed the landscape. She couldn't see the plane from her vantage
point in a snowdrift at what looked like the bottom of a hill. The
last thing she remembered was the sound of metal ripping away
from the plane, but she didn't remember the crash. She decided
she must have been thrown from the tail before impact.

Her head pounded as if a jackhammer drilled into her skull,
and she was freezing fast. Heat could kill a body deader than a stiff
board, but cold... She knew she needed to move, but since she
was walking in blizzard conditions with no visibility and no way to
determine depth, she'd tumbled down a slope.

Cold, cold, cold!

As a wolf, she could protect herself from the bitter conditions.
But as a human in handcuffs and dressed, she couldn't shift.

Her jeans were in ribbons, snow clinging to every inch, her
sweater not much better. The wound on her forehead wasn't
bleeding as fast now. Her freezing skin helped to slow the bleeding, but she would be a Popsicle before long.

She forced herself up, stumbled, fell, and planted her bloody
forehead against the snow. "Ah," she groaned, the ice-cold snow
burning her skin. She pressed her cheek against a chilly mound of
accumulated flakes. Breathed the wintry air into her lungs, burning them in the process. She wasn't a quitter. She remembered
the steaks she'd bought on sale at the butcher shop. The bloody
steaks! And she wanted them!

She had to be hallucinating or out of her mind or something.
She wasn't even hungry. Willing herself to get to her feet, she
trudged through the ever-deepening snow, filling her boots with
the cold, wet stuff.

Freezing, she groaned. Then she heard metal slapping in the
wind. And propelled herself toward the sound.

Heart racing, Tom stopped, sniffed the air, searched his surroundings, and listened.

The wind wreaked havoc with his attempt to locate the scent of blood. He backtracked. Smelled it again. Faint. Circled. Nothing. He circled again, in a wider path this time.

There. Just a whiff of blood on the wind.

The scent of a female red wolf…blended with a female coyote. *Elizabeth's scent.* It *couldn't* be. His heart pounding, he lifted his nose again, sampling the turbulence. South. Toward the cabin. Smoke from his chimney mixed with the slight bloody scent. The scents swirled in the wind and shifted again. He stared in the direction of his cabin.

Nothing in the white blanket of snow revealed itself.

He raced in circles, widening his search to locate her, to rescue her.

He couldn't find tracks. If she had any sense, she would turn into her wolf self. She would most likely head toward the smell of the smoke from his cabin. If she smelled it.

He smelled blood again. He dug at the snow and found the blood already buried under a fresh layer of snowflakes. She'd been here. Recently. He began his search again. She'd headed away from the cabin, not toward it.

He howled. No response.

The wind whipped the smoke from the chimney around so much that she must be disoriented. Or the cold was making her lose her sense of direction. She must not have turned into a wolf. Why hadn't she? Too injured? That thought made him sick with worry.

He darted through a stand of firs, stopped suddenly, turned his head, and saw her. Staring back at him, blood dripping from a gash in her forehead, she watched him. Her clothes fluttered in snow-covered ribbons. Her cracked lips parted. She sank to her knees.

Elizabeth. His heart slammed into his ribs.

He focused briefly on the handcuffs on her wrists. What…was going on?

He let out a frosty breath, then headed straight for her. Only one thing to do.

Using his teeth, he grabbed one of the dangling pieces of her shredded jeans' fabric and tugged at her to follow him. If he could get her close enough to his cabin, he'd leave her, change, dress, and come back for her. If she could last that long.

He tugged all the harder to make her move as fast as she could, and he huffed out loud to encourage her to follow him before it was too late.

She stumbled in the deep snow, barely able to make any progress.

She tried to get up, tears freezing on her cheeks. Tom looked back at her, worried, not angered that she couldn't keep up. He couldn't shift and take her to the cabin in his human form without dressing in warm clothes.

He returned to her, nuzzled her face, and attempted to get her to her feet, but she couldn't move. She wasn't going to make it.

He hesitated for only a second, then dashed off.

"No," she moaned, the word barely slipping out on the stiff breeze.

Tom had never run as fast in his life as he did now, racing to get to the cabin, his mind sorting out just how quickly he could jerk on his clothes. Well, shift first. No, get into the cabin first. Hell. There was no planning this. He would do what he had to do as soon as he arrived.

Snow covered the cabin, the wolf door buried. Not having any choice, Tom shifted in the icy snow, threw open the human door, and slammed it shut. He tugged on his clothes, jammed his feet into his boots, pulled on his parka, a ski hat, and gloves, then grabbed a wool blanket and ran back out into the snow.

He swore he'd never reach Elizabeth in time. Not as slow

as his progress was while trying to run through the deep snow. No wonder she couldn't make any headway, being petite, barely dressed, and injured on top of that.

When he was close enough, he thought he saw her struggling to walk in his direction, but he couldn't believe his eyes. He expected her to be lying in the snow, half-buried before he reached her. She hadn't given up. She'd actually made it several more feet. Good. He tried to move more quickly but couldn't. It just wasn't physically possible to travel any faster through the deep snowdrifts. Her eyes widened a little when she lifted her head from watching her footfalls, following his trail, to see him. He couldn't even smile. The situation was just too grave.

When injured victims saw help arrive and quit the struggle to survive, thinking they were now safe, they died. She needed the adrenaline rushing through her blood, keeping her alive. She needed to keep trying, as if he wasn't coming to her aid.

To his relief, she trudged forward, but then she fell.

He thought he heard a choked sob. The disquieting sound made him feel as though an ice shard had stabbed him through the heart.

"I'm coming," he said. "Don't quit, Elizabeth!"

She struggled to get up, but she couldn't make it.

He was beside her before she could lift her head to try again. "Don't give up," he growled at her, angry at the weather, at the plane, at her if she succumbed to the elements before he could get her to safety.

He dragged his coat around her, intending for her to wear it, and remembered too late about the handcuffs. He cursed and grabbed the blanket, wrapped it around her, then the coat, and zipped it, folding her into it like a protective cocoon. He pulled the hood over her head and tightened the drawstrings until the fake gray fur fit snugly around her small face, nearly covering it.

She stared up at him with her blue-green eyes filled with tears and a look of gratitude. Her dry cracked lips parted, and he was certain she tried to say "Thank you."

"*Don't…give…up*," he said urgently, harshly. He lifted her into his arms and made the long trek back to the cabin. Her body was ice cold, but the parka and blanket and his body heat would help to warm her.

Carrying her made the journey nearly impossible as he tried to make headway through the knee-deep powdery snow. He knew the direction to go, even though he couldn't see the cabin.

"What happened?" he asked, not wanting her to go to sleep and never wake. He needed her to talk to him. To get this close to the cabin and lose her now… *He couldn't think of that.*

"Plane crashed," she murmured, her words slurred.

Not good. "Elizabeth, listen to me. *Stay…awake*. I'll have you to the cabin in just a few minutes. I'll have a warm fire blazing in the fireplace in no time. I'll get you some hot tea and chili—if you can manage."

"You…" she said weakly, straining to look at him, to watch his expression.

"Yes?" he responded, encouraging her to speak, to stay awake until he could get her to the cabin and ensure she would be okay.

"…will…warm…me," she said hesitantly, rasping out the words between clenched teeth, in pain, shivering.

"Yes, yes, I'll warm you."

"You'll…be…"

He looked back down at her, his feet trudging through the deepening snow. He had to hear what she had to say, even if she didn't make any sense. He really didn't expect her to make any sense. Not as hypothermic as she had to be. But he was glad to hear her speak about anything.

"…naked," she finally got out.

He raised both brows, unable to prevent the curve of his lips, the first time he'd managed to smile at her. "You…mean *us*? *Together*?

Naked?" He suspected the warmth of the fire, hot tea sliding down her throat, and being bundled in blankets and anything else he could wrap her in would do the job, if he could just get her out of this blasted cold weather. Lying with her naked? Yeah, he'd damn well like that, but he didn't know how badly she might be injured.

She smiled. And that one little smile sent his heart skittering.

CHAPTER 17

ELIZABETH WANTED SO BADLY TO SLEEP, BUT SHE KNEW SHE had to remain alert. The only thing that had made her stir a little from her grogginess was the thought that the big, sexy wolf would lie with her naked to warm her. After trying to keep some distance from him, she knew that was probably a bad idea in the long run.

Yet part of her hoped he'd say that was just what he intended to do. Because it was the only way she'd live. And maybe even take it further…

He'd seemed highly amused at her suggestion, and she was sure that if she hadn't lost so much blood and wasn't so chilled, her face would have been three shades redder. Her cheeks felt icy, so she hoped she hadn't blushed and given herself away.

He still smirked, the cad. She felt the difference in his footfalls, first through soft snow, then on hard wood, the porch to his cabin. She couldn't look that way though, not with the hood of his coat blocking her view of nearly everything except his strong jawline. Dark stubble covered the rigid bone, making him look strong-featured and sexy and able to warm her up just fine. Like he'd done before when she wasn't nearly this cold.

She shook her head at herself. He had to be angry with her for leaving him. And she had to look terrible. She had a gash in her forehead, and the skin around it had probably turned an assortment of rainbow colors. The rest of her had to be ice white otherwise, except for the blood dried on it. As much as her skin burned, she had to have a lot of abrasions. She was a mess.

"Elizabeth," Tom said, laying her on the floor as close to the hearth as he could safely get her. He was concerned when she closed her eyes. "Elizabeth!"

Her eyes fluttered open. He took a breath of relief. "Are you all right?"

"Yeah."

Another wave of relief washed over him. He'd had every intention of seeing her again—but not like this. He'd planned to locate the wolves stalking their livestock first, and then he was going to fly out to be with her in Canyon, Texas. To stay with her. To learn about her. To convince her to come home with him.

He wouldn't have let go of whatever had happened between them.

Before he unbundled her, he kindled a roaring fire in the hearth. Then he wondered what to do with her. Put her in a hot bath? Her head sported a gash and she had small cuts from the impact. Was she injured elsewhere?

As soon as he unzipped the coat and opened it and the blanket, he saw the damned handcuffs confining her wrists again. She was a prisoner. What was she involved in? Instantly, he'd thought the worst. This was why she hadn't wanted to keep in touch: she was involved in some kind of crime. Was that why she had plans to meet someone in Silver Town?

For business, she had said. Maybe that was why she wouldn't tell him what the business had to do with. Maybe that was why she had left so suddenly. Maybe she'd met whoever the man was at the airport and hadn't wanted Tom to learn of it. Then she'd been caught.

He frowned. The men in the plane crash had been the same wolves as at the tavern. What did that mean?

He covered her up again and stalked to the bedroom where he'd left his lockpicks, a typical *lupus garou* tool of the trade, on the dresser. Grabbing the lockpicks, he returned to the living room where the fire did a good job of keeping the place warm. The bedroom was ice-cold. The bathroom would be too.

Crouching beside her, he again moved the coat and blanket aside and began to unlock the manacles. After trying three different lockpicks and jiggling the last one, he succeeded: the lock clicked open. He tossed the handcuffs on the floor. He would have ripped through them with his wolf's canines, had *he* been trussed up.

Her wrists were red from the metal scraping at her skin. Her legs seemed fine, if her ability to trudge through the snow was any indication. "Are you hurting anywhere—ribs, any sprains?"

She shook her head.

"Good." He pulled off her wet boots and socks and wrapped a blanket around her feet. Once covered in snow, her clothes now dripped water.

He quickly removed her shredded pants. Then he touched the remnants of her pink cashmere sweater, which was stained with blood.

He wished he could absorb her cuts and bruises and make her feel all better.

"I'll take this off. Let me know if anything hurts."

He pulled the sweater over her head and tossed it aside, damned thankful she was okay.

"I'm fine, just…c-cold," she said through shivers, her teeth chattering.

The fact she was so cold worried him the most. He covered her up as gently and quickly as he could. "I'll get some warm clothes to put on you and something to bandage these cuts."

He grabbed some of his warm wool socks, a button-down shirt, and sweatpants out of a bureau drawer in the bedroom. Then he seized a first-aid kit from the bathroom and quickly returned to her side.

He slipped a double pair of the socks onto her ice-cold feet, then rewrapped the blanket around them. "I'll clean your cuts and then bandage them. They look pretty shallow, no debris, and should heal within a day or so."

He gently wiped down her wounds and applied antibacterial ointment as she shut her eyes and sucked in her breath. Then he bandaged all her scrapes.

"I'll take off your wet bra. If I can't get it off easily, I'll cut it off."

"It's the only one I have with me," she gritted out.

"I'll take care to remove it, but I do have your bra from before." Tom still had the bra she'd worn the day she arrived in Silver Town.

"I'd meant to wear it the next day."

He chuckled. "Sorry about that. It's home safe…waiting for you. You should have come for it." He glanced up at her to see her response. She wore a smidgen of a smile.

He shook his head. "You wouldn't have gotten far. I would have made sure of it." He would have found out just why she'd been upset and why she'd planned to run away. And he wouldn't have let her.

She might be cold, but the heat of the fire and the anxiety he felt from trying to take care of her and not hurt her further was making him burn up. He slipped off the bra and considered the thin material of the button-down shirt he'd taken out of his bureau.

"Cinderella," she said.

"Hmm?" He pulled his own sweater off and then unbuttoned his flannel shirt.

Her eyes widened, but she didn't say anything.

"I'll help you to sit and dress you in my flannel shirt. It's warmer than the one I brought for you from the bedroom."

She nodded.

"Cinderella?" he asked.

"Cinderella left her…glass slipper behind."

"With the handsome prince. Only Cinderella is a beautiful shifter, and she left behind a sexy, lacy blue bra," he said.

She smiled a little.

"And of course, she left behind the prince," he said, arching a brow.

"A wolf."

"A *prince* of a wolf," he qualified.

He couldn't be more relieved to see her smiling up at him. Once he'd pulled the shirt on her and buttoned it, he said, "Okay, now the panties come off, and I'll put some sweats on you."

She raised her brows. "Seems…we've been doing this a lot when we're together."

"Yeah, and for all the wrong reasons."

Her teeth chattered, but the shivers had lessened some and the color had returned to her pale lips. "Are you sure we shouldn't just strip down and lie together so I can warm you up?" He dropped her wet panties on the hearth, then pulled on the sweats.

"I bet you say that to all the girls…you rescue."

He chuckled. "You think that's what we do on ski patrol?"

She smiled again.

"How are you really holding up?" He applied some ointment on the scraped skin around her wrists.

She sighed, the shivers lessening. "Better. Thank you."

He wrapped the blanket around her. Then he zipped his coat up to her throat. "Good," he said, but he didn't like how cold she still was.

He began to clean up the gash on her forehead using a damp cloth. "It isn't too bad. Head wounds bleed a lot, so they can look really awful."

She grimaced as he wiped the blood away too close to the injury.

"Sorry." He cleaned her blood-matted hair as much as he could, then bandaged the cut on her forehead. "Nothing needs stitches. Your toes look good. Color's coming back. The same with your fingers."

She licked her lips. "Teeth," she said wearily.

He didn't want to discover that she had any missing or broken teeth. "Open your mouth."

She did, and he looked inside and smiled. "Great set of teeth. Nothing broken. Nothing missing."

"Good," she said. "Where are we?"

"My brothers and I own this cabin up in the mountains. I was up here tracking when the blizzard hit and I heard your plane crash. Do you…want to tell me about the handcuffs?"

===

Elizabeth stared at Tom for a minute, wondering why he would ask her about them. Then she realized he probably thought she was some kind of criminal.

Tom studied her, but she couldn't read his expression. He had the most beautiful brown eyes with amber flecks of light that sparkled from the flames flickering in the fireplace. He was a handsome devil of a wolf, his face a little flushed from the heat, his hair a little longish, and a couple of days' growth of beard making him look even more sexy. And she realized just how much she'd missed him.

A prince of wolves? He was that.

Her gaze trailed down his naked chest. She'd thought he was planning to strip and get naked with her until he put his warm shirt around her. It smelled so deliciously of him—the great outdoors, musky male, and wolf. She was glad he hadn't bothered to put on another shirt to hide his chest.

He gently tucked a strand of hair behind her ear and said, "Elizabeth."

Her gaze shifted back to his. She'd forgotten the question.

"The handcuffs?" he asked gently.

Oh. "Prisoner," she rasped out. As soon as his eyes widened fractionally, she realized her mistake. Annoyed with herself, she frowned and cleared her dry throat. "Hostage."

His expression changed subtly, transforming from annoyed wariness to surprise.

"Hmm. We'll talk about this later. You need to get some hot drink and food down."

He sounded as though he didn't believe her. She needed him to. As tired as she was, she didn't care even to give it a try right now. Later, there would be time enough.

"I'll get you some hot tea and some venison chili if that sounds good." He still crouched beside her, not moving, until she nodded slightly. "Will you be all right?"

"Yes, thank you," she said, her voice just a whisper. She wanted to fall asleep, to make all the hurts go away, to wake up at home in her own bed—with Tom in it—and her steaks in the fridge waiting for her to make a meal of them.

He caressed her uninjured cheek with the tips of his fingers in such a sympathetic way that it touched her deeply.

"You'll be all right." He spoke matter-of-factly, as though he knew what he was talking about.

He rose, looked at her for a while longer, then turned and walked across the living-room floor and into the kitchen. She felt alone and needy in a way she'd never felt before. She wanted to be with him, to share the space with him, to feel his body heat close to hers.

Without the energy to get up and join Tom in the kitchen, she observed him instead—the way his muscles stretched in his back and arms as he pulled open cabinets and found a pan, then moved to the stove.

From the kitchen, he said, "Did you know I tried calling you?"

"Not at first."

Holding the pan, he stopped and stared at her.

"I don't use my phone much. I had turned it off on the flight home and forgot to turn it back on," she said with effort.

"So you didn't know that I'd called?" Tom asked, sounding

doubtful and somewhat upset that he thought she had been avoiding him.

She looked away uncomfortably and instead took stock of what she could see from the floor of the living room—a large forest-green sectional couch blocked the view of the rest of the room. With all the pillows stacked on the velvety couch, it looked comfortable and inviting. Being as close to the fire as he could keep her so she could warm up more quickly was probably for the best. But that couch had its appeal.

The fireplace was made of red stone, the floor beneath her polished redwood, the ceiling crisscrossed by large timber beams. Photos of wildflower landscapes—probably Jake's—hung on all the walls, making the cabin look homey and well loved, an atmosphere she had missed almost as soon as she had left Silver Town.

She felt bad all over again that she had missed Tom's calls. She had thought he might have given up on her because of the way she left. Yet she still knew she had been justified. Things had just gotten too complicated. When she couldn't get hold of North, she could only think that her uncle was going to come after her again. She hadn't wanted the Silver pack to get involved in fighting her battles.

But if her uncle had anything to do with her abduction, then the Silver wolf pack was destined to get involved. Nothing that she could do about it now.

"I went to call my editor and realized the phone was off. I saw you had attempted to get hold of me. I tried to reach you then," she said finally, having settled on just telling him the straight truth.

Tom watched her closely, judging her.

"You didn't answer," she said.

He took in a breath. "I was probably in the woods. That's why I tried to get in touch with you before I left. Darien was out with the search parties too, if you attempted to call him. Lelandi was busy with patients."

"I only tried calling you." She couldn't read his expression. Was he glad she had wanted to talk to him?

"You shouldn't have left without saying goodbye." His gaze was fixed on hers, alpha-like, challenging her to agree.

She wouldn't look away this time. But she didn't say anything.

"You don't think you deserve to be loved? Is that it?" When she didn't respond, Tom said, "Well, you do, Elizabeth." He paused and took a deep breath.

He was still upset about her leaving him that way. She sighed.

She took a whiff of the smells in the cabin—the venison chili made her stomach grumble, and she realized it had been a long time since she'd eaten. The smell of several gray wolves and—she lifted her nose and smelled again—one red wolf, Lelandi, also filled the air.

The wind whistled around the cabin, reminding her just how chillingly cold it was outside, although she was beginning to feel a bit of warmth penetrating the marrow of her bones. The fire crackled in the large stone hearth, while she heard a teakettle whistling and then the water poured into a mug. She vaguely wondered if the cabin was part of a resort or isolated. How far was it from civilization?

"Are we close to Silver Town?"

"Yes and no. In this blizzard? With you feeling the way you do? No. If we had snowmobiles or you could run as a wolf, not too far out."

Even though they couldn't reach town easily right now, she was comforted by the fact it was nearby. That was a first for her. The town wasn't what made the nearness so consoling. The wolf pack that ran it bolstered her.

If she didn't hurt all over so much, she'd get up and watch him prepare the meal. Even offer to help him. That brought on another wishful thought of bumping against him as they worked in the kitchen making a meal together, sharing the moment.

She noticed Tom's scent in the room most of all—musky male, gray wolf, delectable. Why was he here all alone?

Then she thought about the first time she was in Silver Town and her luggage was stolen. So was her ID. She swore under her breath.

"What's wrong?" Tom asked.

"I don't have any ID again, and I don't even have any money to buy a plane ticket!" This was getting to be a recurring nightmare.

"Don't worry about it. We'll take care of it when the time comes."

She got the distinct impression that he had no intention of letting her out of his sight again, not like the last time.

Another thought occurred to her, one more worrisome. "Were any of the men who had taken me hostage still alive?"

"No."

On the one hand, she didn't want them coming to the door, armed to the teeth and ready to take her hostage again, because she knew Tom would protect her with his life. Still, freezing to death was a fate she wouldn't wish upon anyone, even criminals.

She shouldn't have fretted about them, not when she could have come to real harm—and would have, if not for Tom. Would whoever had paid her kidnappers send others to search for her once they learned the plane wasn't coming? Maybe they'd think everyone had died in the plane crash. *Including* her.

If Tom did get her on a flight back home, what if whoever had her taken hostage did it all over again?

———————

"Elizabeth, don't go to sleep on me. All right?" Tom walked around the room, bolting the door and the wolf door. He returned to the kitchen and finished heating up the chili, unable to quit worrying that she might have more extensive injuries that could cause her real trouble.

"I'll try not to," she said.

He wanted to get her to town, to the hospital, but traveling was too risky in this blizzard. After she had been so cold, he couldn't expose her to that again right away.

He stirred the chili. "So what was the deal with these guys?"

"At first, I thought they had grabbed the wrong woman." Her voice sounded more even now, her teeth not chattering as much. Good.

"Do you know who they were?"

"They were the men who made a scene in the Silver Town Tavern, the ones Darien told to leave."

"I thought I recognized them, even though they were pretty battered."

"One of them had ridden next to me on the ski lift. Another pushed me down the slope. The third broke into my room at the B and B. They said two men paid for the job, but they didn't know who."

"So why did you leave Silver Town instead of staying and letting us deal with this?"

"It was getting too dangerous," Elizabeth said.

Was she serious? She hadn't seemed scared. Upset, yes. But not fearful. Even Darien said she hadn't seemed afraid. In denial that she was running away from forming a relationship with a gray wolf? Maybe.

She had shut her eyes, and he couldn't tell if she was being earnest or not. "Don't go to sleep," he warned her.

Her eyes still closed, she wrinkled her nose at him in an annoyed way.

He smiled. "The picture you put on my desktop, the one of me crouching in front of the injured little girl, did you know the man who sat on the lift chair behind you had been watching you take the picture?"

She opened her eyes and frowned at him. "No, I didn't. Are you sure?" She sounded winded, sleepy.

"Yeah, we compared it to the photo in which he had his back to you right before you were pushed down the slope." Tom paused and looked in her eyes. "You suspect who's behind this, don't you?"

"I don't want you or your family involved."

"Damn it, Elizabeth, we *are* involved. Anyone who attacks a wolf in our territory—"

"I wasn't in your territory when they grabbed me."

He shook his head. "You were when they pushed you down the slope, and you were a hostage when they dropped out of the sky here."

She hesitated. "I think my half brother or uncle might be behind it."

Her words sent alarm bells ringing through him. She'd never mentioned she had family.

Processing this new information, he set the tray with a bowl of chili and a mug of tea on the coffee table. He pulled a couple of cushions off the couch and propped her carefully into a sitting position on the floor, still wanting to keep her close to the fire.

"Can you manage it all right? Or do you need my help?"

Her hands shook, so he steadied them with his own.

"I'll be all right."

He took one of her hands and inspected her fingers. "Make a fist for me."

She did, but her grip was weak.

"Grasp the spoon."

"I can do this." But her hand trembled as she took the spoon from him.

"Here, let me. By tomorrow morning, you'll be fine. Tonight, I'll take care of you." He held out a spoon of the chili to her.

She frowned at him.

"Humor me," he said, smiling. He could tell she really didn't like being waited on. But he was used to helping others—the pack, guests at the ski resort, or wherever wolves or humans needed him.

She took a bite of the chili. Once she'd swallowed, she said again, "I can eat on my own."

"I'm used to it. I help feed my brother's triplets. They don't hold still though, and we make more of a mess than anything. Darien usually has to wash the kids right afterward."

He noticed then that Elizabeth's expression was one of surprise. When she'd mentioned her half brother and uncle, he'd assumed Elizabeth was part of a pack, even though he thought she seemed too independent to have grown up in one.

Didn't her pack members all take care of the little ones? Built-in babysitters who loved their jobs? But maybe all packs weren't as close-knit as his. He wondered why Elizabeth thought her brother and uncle were behind all her trouble. What kind of pack would kidnap a member of their own family?

He was considering how to broach the subject when Elizabeth said, "I'm sorry for not saying goodbye. I just thought it would be easier."

He didn't want her to know how shook up he'd been, and yet he said just what he'd been feeling. "I was ready to punch the wall."

She chuckled. He smiled.

"Sorry," she said. "I just have a hard time seeing you taking your anger out on a wall."

He wanted to set the bowl down on the coffee table and kiss her, hold her close, comfort her.

Something banged outside. He looked in that direction. He thought he'd tied everything down.

"Let me check on that real quick." He grabbed his jacket and headed outside. The latch on the outdoor shutters had pulled loose in the high winds. He fumbled to close the shutters, noting that the latch was bent. He secured it as best he could. Nothing else he could do about it in this bitter blizzard.

He locked the door and returned to help Elizabeth. He frowned down at her bowl and saw that she'd eaten all her chili and finished her tea. He smiled.

"I told you I could do it." She paused. "You seem worried."

"The pack is still tracking the rogue wolves that have been stalking the livestock. We think they're *lupus garous*."

"So you think they're with your wolf pack?"

"They might be. But we suspect they aren't." He ran his hand over her cheek. "We've been keeping track of everyone's comings and goings in the pack since the second incident of wolf sightings, and everyone seems to be accounted for. They have to be rogue wolves."

She shook her head. "Has anyone left the pack recently that would want to cause you trouble?" She looked up when he didn't say anything. "Someone else?"

"Cousins. We had trouble before within our own pack. Our uncle was the sheriff and next in line to lead the pack, but he had murdered some of our pack members and we had to take him down. His four sons left the pack after Uncle Sheridan was killed, and we haven't heard from them since. We haven't been able to track down their last whereabouts."

"Your cousins. I'm sorry. And you're worried whoever it is might be out there. Somewhere in the storm."

"Yeah. I found wolf prints—fresh tracks before the blizzard hit. I had hoped I'd find evidence of where they were hiding after they made their strikes before the storm wiped out their tracks."

"You shouldn't have been out here by yourself," she scolded.

He smiled.

She narrowed her eyes at him. "I'm *serious*. You can't think you could take on four male wolves."

"I hoped to talk them out of whatever they've been planning. There must be some reason why they've been prowling the edges of our territory, and I don't think it's good."

Her lips parted in surprise, then she frowned. "You were trying to protect them—if it was them—weren't you?"

He didn't say anything for a moment, his gaze steady on hers.

Then he finally said, "It might be another pack causing trouble. Someone seeking revenge, perhaps. We've had trouble with another pack before. Some red wolf males thought they had some claim to a couple of our red wolf females who originally had come from their pack. Lelandi and Carol."

"Carol?"

"Yeah... You're not associated with any red wolf renegades, are you? They were part of the red pack now led by Lelandi's uncle Hrothgar."

"I'm not associated with...Lelandi's pack," she finally said.

Not with Lelandi's. She couldn't be. At least he didn't think so, because Lelandi didn't know Elizabeth. "There's one guy in particular we're not sure about. We never could tell where his allegiances lay. His name is North."

Elizabeth stiffened a little. "You told me the ones causing trouble were grays, not reds," she said.

Studying her, Tom nodded. She had evaded his question. What *wasn't* she telling him? She looked weary and he needed to get her into bed. Rest let the body heal faster. Yet he couldn't give up the notion that she knew something about the red pack, and that made him think of the wolf she'd mentioned the first time she was here. She'd said she needed to meet him on a matter of business, and he had been within driving distance.

"Elizabeth, who were you to meet but he couldn't see you because of the road conditions?"

Elizabeth heaved a deep breath, as if she were too tired to continue hiding her secrets from him. "North Redding."

CHAPTER 18

TOM COULDN'T BELIEVE THAT ELIZABETH HAD TRIED TO meet up with North, the rogue wolf who had caused their pack all kinds of trouble in the past.

North was the one who had tried to steal Carol back from Ryan, thinking a red wolf from his pack had more of a claim to her than Ryan, a gray from another pack. That concerned Tom. Would North attempt to claim Elizabeth? Tom didn't trust him.

"North was supposed to meet with me and hand over proof that my uncle had murdered my parents," Elizabeth continued.

Tom closed his gaping mouth. "Your uncle murdered your parents?" God, how could she have been dealing with this all alone? *The bastard better be dead*, Tom thought angrily but remembered that he couldn't be. Not from what Elizabeth said earlier—that she thought her uncle might have had something to do with her kidnapping.

"I always suspected he had," Elizabeth said. "He never hid the animosity he had for his brother, my dad, for taking a coyote as a mate. Both were widowed—my dad and my mother. And they found each other. Why was that so wrong?"

He took hold of her hand and caressed it. "Nothing was wrong with it, Elizabeth. Nothing if they loved each other and were free to do so."

"They were. I haven't been able to get in touch with North since first arriving in Silver Town though. Someone else answered his phone the night I was at Darien and Lelandi's. I was afraid whoever it was might come after me and"—she shifted her gaze to him—"cause trouble for your pack."

"I can't believe you were worried about *us*," Tom said, unable to curb his incredulity. She ran away to protect his pack? And for what? To put herself in a world of danger!

"I think…I think my uncle might have learned what North had planned. I'm afraid North might be in trouble, if he's not already dead."

"All right, let's go back over what we know. The chances of you dying on the slopes would be minimal. So why, if the men had been hired by your uncle or half brother, would they push you down the slope?"

"To make me easier to manipulate. They'd keep me out of the B and B by sending me to the hospital so they could steal my stuff from the B and B and lure me to the hotel, then take off with me. But you stayed with me, so that plan didn't work."

"So when they came to the tavern afterward, it was like they were taunting you. Telling you that they'd come for you anyway?"

"It was a way for the men to get in Darien's face—show they weren't afraid of him and would get to me some other way. But I'm sure they were pissed. They didn't think a gray wolf pack would help a red wolf-coyote."

"They had that scenario wrong. Everyone in the pack would take them on. Silva was at our table forever, and one of them looked straight at us. At you. *Damn it.* I remember being so pissed off I wanted to slug him, if only to get his attention off you."

She smiled a little at Tom, then grew serious. "One of the men who grabbed me said that I had been with the wrong company."

"Wrong company being the Silver pack leader and my brother and me." Tom squeezed her hand. "I won't let anyone hurt you. The pack won't. Lelandi's uncle Hrothgar won't stand for having a killer in his pack either."

Tears swam in Elizabeth's eyes. She reached out to Tom for a hug.

He knew she ached, but he pulled her into his arms and held her close. "You're not alone," he whispered against her forehead. "Never again." He separated a little from her. "We'll work this all out. I have another couple of questions though. Why did they steal your luggage and ID?"

"They wanted the deed to my parents' property, the horse farm where I grew up. Pretty valuable piece of real estate, I guess. I was going to sign the deed over to North in exchange for the evidence that would prove my uncle murdered my parents. I had taken it with me on the slopes because I was supposed to meet North at the lodge later."

"Damn him. He should have given the evidence to you freely."

"I don't care. If it means my uncle pays for his crimes, that's all that matters."

"Not to me." Tom took a deep settling breath. "So they grabbed everything you had at the B and B but didn't get the deed. I wonder if they knew North wanted it. They could have been monitoring his movements and cell phone conversations. Or he was in on it from the beginning."

"Sheriff Peter took me to the airport and stayed with me until my flight left."

"Which meant they couldn't get to you then either. But why kidnap you and bring you back here?"

Elizabeth considered that. "I don't think North was in on it. Otherwise, they would have just let me go through with my deal with him, so they could get me to willingly sign the deed over, but then withhold the evidence from me. The fact that I couldn't get in touch with North makes me think he went into hiding because he found out that they knew he had evidence against them."

Tom narrowed his eyes. "So they must also know he was going to exchange the evidence for the deed, and then they meant to use you to draw North out?"

"Yeah, they could kill two birds with one stone that way: destroy North's evidence and get me to sign over the deed. Except…Canton, the dark-haired one with the gun, took the deed from me. It's probably buried in the snow out there somewhere."

"We can order another copy later when you need it."

Something banged outside the window again. Elizabeth jumped a little, and Tom glanced in that direction.

"It's just the broken shutter latch. Are you ready for bed?"

Elizabeth cleared her throat. "Can I have some more of your chili first?"

"You really want more?"

She managed a small smile.

He smiled at her, not sure why the notion pleased him so. Everyone loved his venison chili, but he was really glad it seemed to make her feel better, considering what she'd been through.

"Sure." He kissed her cheek. "I'll get you some more."

"I can manage. Get some for yourself. Just a little more for me."

He returned with two bowls and two mugs of hot tea and joined her on the floor.

"After we eat, I'll make sure the place is secure again, and then we'll move into the bedroom. No heat in there. The couch in here turns into a bed, but it's lumpy and squeaky if anyone moves on it. The mattress in the bedroom is very comfortable. It has tons of wool blankets and a down comforter."

She cast him one of those you're-giving-me-a-guy-line looks.

He raised his brows. "Just so you know, no matter where we retire for the night, we're sleeping together."

Her lips parted. He expected her to protest, but he wouldn't buy any objection she might have. If someone broke into the cabin, he would be right beside her to protect her. Other than that, he intended to share his body heat with her.

The idea was hers in the first place.

"We're not getting naked?" she asked.

He swore that she almost seemed hopeful that they would.

He smiled. "If you think it's necessary."

"No," she said very quickly.

He fought the urge to laugh. "Just making sure."

"Thank you," she said, "for saving...me."

"You scared a ton of years off my life when I saw you out there, fighting to survive. All along, I figured I'd be up here by myself. I'm damned grateful to see you again, though I wish the circumstances had been a lot different. What about any other family you might have?" he asked, still wondering if she were part of another pack. "We'll need to let them know where you are and that you're all right."

She carefully shook her head.

"No other family?"

"No. But I had every intention of having steak tonight—at my home. *Colorado*," she said under her breath as if she couldn't believe her predicament.

"When I get you to Darien's house, steak will be the first thing on the menu. Guaranteed."

She smiled a little at that.

He hated that she'd gone through any of this and that he couldn't take her home with him this very instant. But he would get her there. He had no intention of her leaving him behind again.

She lifted her hands to his arms and took hold, her fingers now warm. "Take me to bed."

He couldn't help the wolfish grin that spread across his face, even though he knew it didn't mean anything other than that she needed to sleep.

Tom carried Elizabeth into the ice-cold bedroom and set her on her feet beside the bed. He pulled the flannel covers aside, then aided her in climbing onto the mattress. Once she was lying down, he covered her with all the blankets—a hodgepodge of colors, wool and warm. "You should be warm again in no time. I'll bank the fire and be right back."

———————

Elizabeth closed her eyes, but she didn't think that she could sleep with worrying about who might be outside.

"Just me," Tom said a few minutes later, quickly lifting the covers on the other side of the queen-sized bed.

"You don't have a mate yet, right?" she asked, her eyes still closed.

"Nope. So you don't have to worry about some she-wolf coming after you for sleeping with her mate."

Elizabeth couldn't help the way her mouth curved up a bit.

"That means I'm totally free and available," he added. He leaned over her and gave her a sweet kiss on the mouth. "If you get cold, just move closer to me. I won't touch you for fear I'd hurt you. Do whatever is most comfortable for you."

That was the last she remembered him saying as the hot tea, venison chili, warm covers, and heat radiated by Tom's body worked miracles.

———

Elizabeth half expected to wake and find that Tom had left the bed early to start a fire and make hot coffee. She hadn't expected to be lying against his naked chest, listening to his strong heartbeat, her legs straddling his—thankfully, he was wearing boxers—his arms wrapped loosely about her as if they were mates.

She didn't dare move. She hoped he'd wake, release her, and leave the bed while she pretended to sleep, not wanting him to think she was that needy to have sprawled all over him. But he held her close and didn't appear to be waking anytime soon.

She listened to his heart beating, smelled his masculine gray-wolf scent, and loved how he felt warm and protective of her. She hadn't felt that way since before her human mate had had the urge to stray.

She tried to assess the way she felt physically and opened her eyes. And took a soft breath of relief. Her muscles ached slightly, but she felt so much better. Her skin was still scraped a bit, lightly bruised, and her forehead still throbbed some.

Closing her eyes, she couldn't believe anyone who was a wolf would help her this much. Not given her history with wolves.

Tom didn't move. She thought to disengage from him, pretend she was just rolling over on her back and was still asleep.

Something banged outside the cabin. She jumped a little. Tom's arms tightened around her. Protective or maybe he feared she would leave him. Maybe he dreamed of having a little wolf loving. And she actually wished they could.

The room was cold and she didn't want to leave the warmth of Tom's embrace, the comfortable mattress, or the heaped-on blankets and comforter.

Maybe he had stolen the covers in the middle of the night, and she'd planted her whole body against him to ensure she got her fair share of the blankets.

Whatever banged outside—Tom had said it was a broken window latch on the shutter—did it again on the other side of the cabin. She wondered if it had done that all night long and she had slept through it or if the wind had picked up again and was blowing something around.

Tom groaned and rubbed her arm in a loving way, then kissed her on the forehead. He was awake. Had he been all along and waited for her to stir, not wanting to disturb her? Or maybe the noises outside had startled him from his sleep.

She looked up at him. He studied her, his dark-amber eyes roaming over her face from her forehead to her eyes to her chin, assessing her.

She parted her lips to tell him that she hadn't meant to be crawling all over him in the middle of the night and to apologize. Just as quickly, he kissed her on the mouth, silencing her, making her forget what she had in mind to say.

She gave in to the kiss, the sweet, loving, gentle way that he had with her as if he was afraid she'd break apart. "I'm okay," she said, and his mouth curved up against hers.

"Yeah," he said and deepened the kiss. "Better than okay."

Their tongues teased and tangled as he stroked her hair, his fingers combing the strands in a caring manner. She could feel his erection hard beneath her belly and knew this had to stop, but she didn't want it to. Yesterday, she could have been dead, just like the men who had taken her hostage.

She wanted this. She wanted him. A family. A pack.

Who wouldn't want this?

She'd managed to survive so many near-death experiences at the hands of wolves that she felt she had a guardian angel watching over her.

Whatever banged outside did it again. Tom didn't appear to be in any hurry to check it out, despite it being light enough to see now. He quit kissing her, his hands still stroking her hair, his eyes open as he considered her. "Beautiful."

She gave a soft, ladylike snort and tried to move off him, but his arms quickly wrapped around her back, and he held her tight. "Your forehead looks better. The area around the bandage is a little yellow and green, but the color doesn't look too bad on you."

"Yellow doesn't look good on me."

He laughed. "You look fine to me." He sighed, not loosening his grip on her like she thought he would. "This feels just right. I don't want to leave the bed. It's too cold out there."

She smiled at him. She loved this side of him. So he wasn't all alpha after all, or he would have taken charge, had the fire going, fixed coffee, and checked to see what made the banging noise. "You don't expect me to bring you breakfast in bed, do you?" she said.

He smiled at her.

She felt her whole body flush with heat. Why was it that men always thought of sex?

He still didn't make a move to leave the bed.

"You're not a late riser, are you?" she asked.

That got a chuckle from him.

She shook her head, placed her face against his chest, and let her breath out in a heavy sigh. "Your family will be worried about you. Then they'll come up here and find us in bed together and…"

"They'll know we're smart and kept each other warm during a blizzard."

"I'll have problems going home," she said, thinking again about her ID.

"Good," he murmured against her hair.

"I'm serious."

"So am I. You won't be able to tear off so easily." He moved his hands over her hair again. "I don't want you going anywhere until we resolve this."

"And I have no say?" She wasn't upset about it. If he was right, she wanted to learn the truth too.

"Sure you do. You can tell me if you like tea or coffee for breakfast. We've also got cereal and powdered milk."

"Tea, eggs, and *steak*."

He laughed. "Demanding wolf, aren't we?"

She snuggled against him and smiled.

"So tell me about this brother of yours." Tom stroked her hair as if trying to coax the information out of her.

She was silent, her smile gone.

"Elizabeth, tell me."

"Half brother," she said, her voice hard. "Sefton Wildwood, a pure-blooded red wolf. After his mother died, his father mated my mother. Everyone in the pack was upset with my father. Sefton and Uncle Quinton were even more furious when my parents had me. They wouldn't accept my mother or me, so we lived away from the pack.

"Years later, Sefton fell in love with a she-wolf from another pack, but when she learned he had a half sister who was half-coyote, she shunned him, called off the mating, and said he was tainted by association. Sefton tried to kill me then. My father came to my rescue and beat him off me. My uncle tried to murder me too and almost succeeded. Then my parents were mysteriously murdered, my mother first, then two days later, my father."

Tom barely breathed.

"Uncle Quinton was tired of the shame my father had brought to the red pack." She rolled off Tom and onto her back and stared up at the ceiling.

Tom moved onto his side and slipped his hand under the flannel shirt she wore and stroked her belly, reassuring her, telling her he would have been there for her. That he was not the same as the men in her family.

"What happened when Quinton almost…killed you?" he asked, his voice tight, when she didn't say anything further.

She looked at Tom. "He tried to drown me, but some random gray wolf teens came to the watering hole, scaring my uncle off, and I got away."

Tom ran his hand over her hair, his expression concerned.

"I moved far, far away. I thought I was doing damned good too."

"Until?"

Elizabeth sighed. "I avoided male wolves all my life. Twice, men got interested in me, but when their friends learned I was part coyote, they gave them a hard time and both times the men shunned me—as if I'd hidden some terrible secret all along. I thought that a human boyfriend wouldn't be as violent or mean-hearted as my own people, and I got the stupid idea to turn a human into a wolf to save his life and mate with him."

"You're mated," Tom said, frowning.

"Not anymore. He loved being a shifter, and he loved me. Until Gunner lusted after another she-wolf and the woman let him know he was an abomination—part wolf, part coyote. Then he came after me. I got lucky that time too. The she-wolf's brother went after Gunner for trying to take up with his sister—partly because Gunner already had a mate for life but also because he was part coyote. Gunner wasn't any match for the much bigger, much more aggressive full-blooded alpha wolf."

Tom ground his teeth.

She raised her brows at him. "Which means I'm free to find someone new, as if that is very likely to happen." No one could accuse her of not trying to find a suitable mate—at least in the past. But for years, she'd left well enough alone.

Tom's mouth curved up slowly.

"*No*," she said, elongating the word to emphasize that nothing would happen between them.

"You know how you told Silva to spread her wings."

Elizabeth opened her mouth to refute that idea, but Tom touched his lips to hers and kissed her.

"We're not all big, bad wolves," he said against her mouth and kissed her some more as if he wanted to prove to her just how much this one wanted her.

She pulled away from him to catch her breath, her hands on his bare shoulders. "You say that, and then the next thing I know, I'm fighting the wolf off and running for the hills and…"

"Finding a new home. With me. With my pack. We're a diverse lot, Elizabeth. Darien mated with a red wolf. Jake mated with a human who had been turned. There's no way I'd get mixed up with a plain, old gray wolf. It just wouldn't be right."

She laughed a little at that. "You might get tired of me and…"

"It wouldn't happen. Wolves mate for life. I'm not a human turned like the first man you took a chance on."

"You don't even know me."

"I know enough about you to know I want you. I haven't been able to get you out of my thoughts since the moment I picked you up at the B and B. You'll be safe with us."

She arched one brow at him.

"*If* we keep you at Darien's house until we catch these bastards who have hurt you. I'm not changing my mind about this. If you need longer for me to change yours, so be it."

She smiled then, just a little. She really couldn't believe it.

"Okay, look," he said very seriously, taking some of her hair and stroking it between his fingers. "After we finish with this business with the wolves I'm tracking, I had intended to find you, court you, and do whatever it took to convince you that you had lost your heart to one of the Silver brothers—me, in particular. I wouldn't give up on us. Why do you think I called you a dozen times?"

"Seventeen."

He smiled. "See?"

She'd lost her mind. Not that she hadn't done so before.

"So the only question now is whether this will be a long, drawn-out courtship or…" He waggled his brows.

"Just kiss me," she said, reaching up and grabbing his shoulders and pulling him down. "We can work out the details later."

———————

Before Elizabeth could change her mind, Tom unbuttoned the blue-plaid flannel shirt she wore. He was amazed at how many times he'd undressed and dressed her already, and every time seemed just as erotic as the first. And every time, he'd wanted to take this further. He parted the shirt and considered her breasts rising and falling, the nipples already tight with need, her long red hair curling about them.

His gaze shifted to her bandages. He peeled off each of the bandages all over her skin, ensuring she really was okay and glad to see that a light pink where her skin was nearly healed was all that was left of the abrasions she'd suffered.

"All better," she assured him, her hands combing through his hair, her fingers stroking his scalp in such a seductive way that he groaned.

Her skin was lightly flushed, her heart rate and breathing quickened, the smell of her woman's arousal kicking in. For a wolf, her scent was an aphrodisiac, calling to him, filling him with urgency, telling him she was ready and wanted him.

His cock already strained against his flannel boxers because of the way her soft body had pressed against him. The scent of her and her quiet breath drifting over his bare chest had filled him with desire before she'd awakened. When she'd stirred awake and moved that sweet body against his arousal, he'd stifled the urge to groan.

She needed family, him. But he needed her just as much. He'd realized how much so when she'd left Darien's home without saying goodbye. The heartwarming photo she'd left of him caring for the little girl made him feel that Elizabeth would have loved to experience the compassion and caring and being part of the scene. Not an outsider looking in.

Now he had every intention of making her his. No one would ever hurt her again.

He skimmed his hands over her breasts, feeling the soft mounds, the taut buds at the tips. He leaned down, and with a flick of his tongue, he licked a rosy nipple. She groaned.

He encircled the other breast with his hand, caressing, lifting, and then he took the nipple in his mouth and sucked. She writhed underneath him. He loved the way she responded to him, wanting his caresses as much as he wanted to touch her. Being with her like this felt so right.

The room was icy cold, the comforter and blankets cast aside, but he was burning up. Her hands stroked down his back, and he ground against her mound still covered in the soft sweatpants. *His.* It brought to mind the subtle thought that by dressing her in his clothes, he'd already claimed her.

She slipped her fingers underneath his boxers and scored his buttocks lightly with her nails. God, he was ready to come.

"Hurry," she whispered.

He was afraid she was in pain, but she smiled, her eyes dark with desire. He moved over and pulled the sweats off her gently, just in case she was still sore. She reached to tug off his boxers, watching when his cock sprang free.

He couldn't imagine wanting anything more than to love that sweet body of hers. To cherish her for who she was. To be with her forever.

He sank a finger between her feminine lips and felt her heat, wetness, and readiness. And then began to stroke her bud, his mouth on hers, his tongue penetrating, licking, teasing, playing with hers.

Her hands were all over him, touching, caressing, kicking up the heat, and he wanted more. He stroked between her legs faster.

"Harder," she begged.

He obliged, spreading her legs farther apart with his knee. He felt her tense and nearly stopped what he was doing, concerned she was hurting.

"Don't...stop," she implored, her voice tight with need.

Relieved that she craved completion, he stroked harder, faster, and felt her arch slightly beneath him.

"Ohh," she said, elongating the word on one satisfied sigh.

Smiling to see her needs met, he didn't wait, couldn't wait. He pressed the tip of his cock at her entrance and then plunged inside. Deeper, until he was buried to the hilt. Then he pulled out and charged in again, mating with her, loving her, wanting her. He took her with him, making her his.

———————

Elizabeth trembled with renewed need as she caressed Tom's skin, loving the feel of his hard muscles moving as he drove into her, so frantic to find release. Heat pooled between her legs, encircling him, welcoming him. She felt lifted again to that higher plane of existence, the exhilaration sweeping her over the edge until she couldn't hold on to the sheer joy of it and let go.

She thought she said his name as he came, filling her with a wash of warmth and wetness. Wonderful. Wicked. And she wanted to do it again.

Until the deep-seated worry that had haunted her own childhood came to bear—what about the trouble her own offspring would have when they were born part wolf, part coyote?

CHAPTER 19

LATER THAT AFTERNOON, THE BANGING OUTSIDE THE CABIN began again, and Tom groaned. "It's the damn outside shutters. The latch securing them is bent from the storm. I'll see if I can fix it and get some more wood for the fire." He climbed out of bed and hurried to dress. "You stay here."

Elizabeth felt chilled and anxious as soon as he left the bed. "Maybe you should shift."

"I'll take my rifle. In wolf form, I can't gather wood or do anything with the latch."

As nonsensical as the notion was, she couldn't help but worry that the men who had taken her hostage were outside waiting to pounce. Tom had accounted for all of them, but without seeing the dead men herself, she felt they were alive and still looked like they had before the crash.

She quickly got out of bed, searched through one of the drawers, and happily found some women's clothing mixed in with the men's—a sweatshirt and pants with Lelandi's scent. Because they would be a better fit for her, Elizabeth pulled them on, feeling as good as new.

She hadn't heard Tom leave the bedroom and turned to see him watching her, looking concerned.

"What?" she asked.

"Are you okay? You're really not hurting any longer?"

She smiled. "After what happened early this morning and again a couple hours after that, you have to ask?"

He chuckled. "Sorry about that. After you scaring me half to death that I might lose you, our coming together in a mating was long overdue." He sighed. "Sometimes you try to hide how you're feeling, trying to be all alpha. I just wanted to make sure you really are all right."

"Don't apologize. I wanted everything you gave me and more. I feel great this afternoon."

"Good." He crossed the floor and gathered her in his arms, ignoring the banging outside the cabin. He kissed her mouth, promising lots more where that came from. "Won't be too long."

She wrapped her arms around him and kissed him just as soundly back. "I'll count the seconds," she said cheerfully, but she worried about him being out there alone.

He smiled and kissed her nose, then strode out of the bedroom and grabbed his parka, hat, and gloves from the living room.

Still feeling insecure about him leaving, she pulled on some fluffy pink socks and followed after him.

He peered out the security peephole on the door, then walked over to the window where they'd heard the banging. He opened the inside shutters. The outside shutters were open and swinging in the wind. "Yeah, just like before. The latch has come undone. I'll see if I can fix it." He dug around in a kitchen drawer and pulled out a small hammer.

The floorboards creaked in a couple of places as Elizabeth crossed into the living room. She pulled the borrowed sweatshirt tighter. "Can I help you with anything?"

"No, I've got it. You don't need to be out in the cold." He unlocked the door and pulled it open, letting in a blast of Arctic air. She shivered. Tom shoved aside some of the snow piled up on the porch and closed the door.

She watched as he banged at the latch, then secured the outside shutters. She crossed the living room, closed the shutters on the inside, and started a new fire at the hearth.

By the time the flames took hold, she glanced at the door, wondering how long it would take him to gather some wood. The wind howled and the cabin creaked a little, but otherwise the place remained eerily quiet.

A scary-movie theme played in her mind, warning that she should not go outside. That she should wait for Tom to return. She thought of the woman in a movie who sees movement in her house and shouldn't go inside but creeps into the house to check it out. Or walks down the stairs into the scary, dark basement when she hears an unfamiliar sound down there. Or thinks someone might be hiding in the closet and yanks open the door. Or jerks the shower curtains aside to see if someone is there. Or…goes outside into the dark night because…she hears a noise.

The problem with being an alpha wolf, even if she was part-coyote—and truthfully that made her even more curious and bold—was that she felt driven to investigate.

Her boots were ruined. Except for a pair of Lelandi's warm socks, Elizabeth didn't have anything else to wear on her feet. Was there a spare coat, gloves? Hat? Nope. Even better than human clothes? Her wolf coat.

Elizabeth unlocked the wolf door and hurried to strip and shift. She didn't hesitate to push through the wolf door into the blustery cold. Her double coat of fur proved the best protection she had against the elements. The soft downy fur closest to her skin kept her warm and dry, while the outer coat caught the snowflakes. Her wolf pads protected her feet as she jumped through the drifts of powdered snow. She was in her element.

Tom was nowhere in sight. She circled the cabin, found his trail, and followed it.

A flash of something moved among the trees, catching her eye.

She hesitated. What if it was one of the rogue wolves who had been prowling the territory and now he was going after Tom?

Heart racing, she leaped through the snow and found that something had traveled in the snowdrifts like she had. The snow was too soft and deep, so she couldn't make out any tracks. But she could tell that whatever had made the imprints in the snow had headed away from the cabin.

Something moved to the right of her. Her ears twitched back and forth, trying to determine what she'd heard. The wind blew through the trees, ruffling the branches, whistling and howling like a banshee, the snow falling in soft plunks all around her.

The crunching of boots in snow? The breaking of twigs? Tom?

She loped through the snow toward the sound and stopped dead in her tracks. Tom had his rifle slung over his shoulder as he broke twigs off a dead tree, gathering them for more kindling.

Her heart jumped as she saw a big gray wolf watching Tom. If it attacked him, Tom couldn't get to his rifle quickly enough and wouldn't stand a chance.

She ran to intercept the wolf, growling fiercely, warning Tom to ready his rifle. The wolf turned, surprise lighting his amber eyes. He ran off.

She raced after him, instinctively pursuing him. This was now her territory, she realized. She was part of a pack, protecting their land. And damned proud of it!

"Elizabeth!" Tom shouted, his tone a definite "Come back here!" as he chased after her and the wolf.

With his longer legs, the male wolf soon outdistanced her. She did worry about him leading her into a trap, except that he had been watching Tom, not her. Still, he could be steering her straight to the other wolves, and they could rip her apart.

She lost sight of him, so she followed the path he'd made. Tom ran as fast as he could manage in the deep snow as a human, but he was still a long way back.

Then the wolf let out a pained yelp. He'd been hurt. But by what? Would she fall into the same predicament?

She loped off in the direction from which she'd heard his cry. The closer she got to where she thought he was, the slower she went. Humans could feign a cry of distress, but werewolves in wolf form couldn't fake such a pained sound.

Tom drew closer. He hadn't spoken her name again, just followed her trail.

The wolf panted hard out of her line of sight, just around another tree. Her heart in her throat, she edged around the snow-covered Colorado blue spruce, half expecting to see three gray wolves ready to make short work of her.

Instead, a *lupus garou*'s worst nightmare came into view. A steel leg-hold trap had snapped over the wolf's right leg. He struggled to get loose, his leg bleeding, his bone at an odd angle. Tom would have to spring him. The trap had broken the wolf's leg.

The wolf snarled at her. She barked for Tom to come this way, as if he wasn't already headed in her direction. She also alerted him that she'd found her prey.

It didn't take too much longer for Tom to reach them. He cursed under his breath as he considered the wolf. She hated to see the pain reflected in the wolf's eyes.

"What the hell are you doing out here, CJ?" Tom asked, sounding suspicious.

Was he one of Tom's pack members?

"I'm going to free you, but if you even think of biting me…" Tom let his words trail off threateningly. He stalked forward, set his rifle next to a tree, and leaned down to untie his bootlaces.

What was he doing?

The wolf, CJ, was growling low, but not at Tom, she didn't think. At the trap, his circumstances, maybe even at Elizabeth because he'd been running from her when he ran into the half-buried menace.

Tom dug the snow away from the trap, then slipped a bootlace out of the boot and tied one end of the lace to the top of the spring where it ran along the jaws. Then he ran the string through the bottom spring loop and up through the top again.

He stood on the chain that held the trap in the ground. He pulled up on the string, compressing it, and tied it off. Then he put the safety catch on. In a hurry, he did the same procedure with the other spring. Once he had finished, the wolf leaped back, freeing his leg. He snarled at the trap.

She was glad Tom had known what to do because she would have just tried pulling the trap apart. Probably unsuccessfully, and maybe to the wolf's further detriment.

"Okay, I've got to splint your leg now," Tom said.

While he searched for a tree branch he could use, she watched CJ, but she was sure he wouldn't run off.

Tom returned with a branch and dropped it on the snow. He untied his bootlaces and triggered the trap to snap shut so that it wouldn't catch any other animals. Then he made a makeshift splint the best he could for CJ. Elizabeth was glad Tom was trained on ski patrol to handle emergencies like this.

"Can you make it to the cabin on your own?" Tom grabbed his rifle.

The wolf stared at Tom, glanced at Elizabeth, then limped on three legs toward the cabin.

Tom tilted his chin down at Elizabeth and shook his head. "You were supposed to stay in the cabin."

She half expected him to tell her to run back to the cabin, but he didn't. She wouldn't have either. Whether he liked it or not, she would watch his back in case others were with the injured wolf.

CJ used the same trail that he and Elizabeth had made, but because of his injury and the deep snow, he kept falling, yelping, and suffering considerable pain, and he had a devil of a time traveling.

Tom finally gave in. "I'll carry you. But if your brothers attack…I'll dump you and shoot the lot of them."

Brothers. Tom sounded serious, but Elizabeth thought he also was upset that some of his pack mates could be the ones causing trouble for the rest of the pack.

He gathered the wolf in his arms. CJ growled softly, but he didn't snap or bite. Elizabeth breathed a sigh of relief.

"If you weren't my cousin…" Tom said under his breath.

Elizabeth stared at the wolf. Cousin?

When they reached the cabin, she dove through the wolf door, sniffed the air, ensuring no one had entered the house while they were gone, and waited for Tom to enter the cabin.

Tom shoved the door open, then kicked it closed and said to her, "Stay here. Don't shift back."

CHAPTER 20

ELIZABETH HAD NO INTENTION OF SHIFTING RIGHT AWAY when they entered the cabin. Her first thought was still that CJ's brothers could appear at any time. *She* would protect Tom in case anyone showed up.

Carefully, Tom crouched and set the wolf on the floor next to the fire. "Stay," he said to CJ, though she was certain he didn't need to tell his cousin that.

Panting, the wolf laid his head down. Blood matted his fur, and his leg was bent unnaturally. He had to be in a lot of pain, but he bore it stoically.

Tom locked both the wolf door and the human one. He went to the bedroom and then the bathroom. "Place is all clear," he hollered. "If the guys are wearing hunter's spray to hide their scents, I had to be certain we had no uninvited visitors hiding in here."

She'd forgotten all about that. No wonder he'd told her not to shift.

"I'll get you a robe so you can shift, CJ, and redo the splint," Tom said from the bedroom.

Before Tom returned, CJ shifted. He shivered on the floor next to the warm fire. He resembled Tom but was wirier in build, with curly sable hair.

And he looked eerily familiar.

Elizabeth loped over to the sofa, grabbed a blanket with her teeth, and hauled it over to him. He mumbled thanks and tried to pull it over his shoulders, but he accidentally moved his leg and groaned in pain.

She felt for him and wished she could do something more to ease his suffering.

Walking into the living room, Tom gave CJ an annoyed look. Tom might not like that Elizabeth was scrutinizing his naked cousin, but she was serving in guard-duty capacity for the moment.

Tom helped CJ into the robe, then turned to Elizabeth. "You can shift if you want to. He's not going anywhere. I'll be right back with something better to splint the leg." He grabbed the clothes that she'd left near the front door and deposited them in the bedroom for her.

She appreciated that Tom had offered, not commanded her. Especially since she'd do what she thought necessary. Not trusting CJ, she remained where she was while she tried to remember where she'd seen him before.

After a few minutes, Tom returned with a splint and something to wrap CJ's leg in, saline solution, and towels. He slipped a piece of plastic under CJ's leg, then poured the solution over the wound. "Trap was new, not rusty," Tom said, "but you'll still need a tetanus shot when we get you into town."

Gritting his teeth, CJ looked pale, but he didn't say anything.

When Tom straightened the leg a little, CJ swore.

Tom dried the wound, bandaged it, and wrapped the leg in gauze before he splinted it. He cleaned up the saline solution, then elevated CJ's leg with pillows and gave him a pillow for his head. "Why don't you lie down?"

CJ nodded.

Tom helped ease him onto his back, then covered him with the blanket. "Will you be all right?"

"Thirsty, nauseated," CJ finally said, wincing.

He was shaking too. Tom covered him with two more blankets and got him a glass of water, setting it next to him.

"We'll talk in a little bit. Just rest." Tom rose, then said, "Come on," to Elizabeth as he headed for the bedroom.

She growled at CJ, telling him she wouldn't hesitate to bite him if he moved an inch.

CJ grumbled, "Tell your wolf-coyote I'm not going any-damn-where."

"Come on, Elizabeth," Tom coaxed by the bedroom door.

She growled again at CJ, not about to let him get in the last word, then loped into the bedroom. She saw that Tom had placed the rifle on the dresser. He didn't shut the door to the bedroom, and she suspected he still didn't trust the man and was listening to ensure he didn't move from his spot by the fire. Tom had set her clothes on the bed. Then he headed into the bathroom and washed up.

She shifted and slipped on the sweatshirt while he put the extra medical supplies away.

"I'm sorry. I didn't mean to take so long, Elizabeth. Nice fire, by the way. You're pretty handy to have around, you know?" He looked around and shook his head. "I knew I shouldn't have turned my back on you and missed seeing you shift."

She smiled, loving him. "Yeah, well, you might get other ideas." The sweatshirt was long but barely covered her buttocks.

"I always get those other ideas when I see you—naked woman, wolf, coyote, or otherwise." He came to her before she could pull on the sweatpants and wrapped his arms around her.

"Oh, you're so cold," she said, trembling in his arms, the chill of the air outside clinging to every inch of him. Her skin was still warm from having been in her wolf coat. She took in deep breaths, smelling the crisp, clean air on him.

She noted she did not smell CJ on him. Hunter's spray, camouflaging his scent.

"That's why I came over here to hug you—to get warmed up."

She curled into him, wanting to rub his arms to warm his icy body, but he chilled her and she folded in to him instead. "He's your cousin?"

"Yeah," Tom growled. "I figured we'd stay here until some-one worried about me being caught in the snowstorm and came looking for me. But now we've got to get CJ to the doc. His bones will knit together too quickly but not correctly, and Doc would have to break them again to set them right."

"Your cousin. I can't smell him. He's one of the ones that's been prowling the territory then?"

"Looks like it."

"Great. Do you have something we can haul him in?"

"Yeah. Got a toboggan for emergencies."

"So when do we leave?"

"Tomorrow, first light. If no one comes for me before then, we'll head out on our own." He rubbed her arms, looking into her eyes. "I'm sorry about everything that's happened. That you're in the middle of all this."

She sighed, cuddling with Tom. "We don't know anything for sure." She reached up to help him out of his parka.

"You know, if you change roles and start stripping me out of *my* clothes..." Tom said.

"Just your parka."

"Aha, then next you'll want to remove my sweater and jeans, and who knows where it will end."

She smiled as she peeled off his jacket and tossed it on a chair.

"So now that we have that out of the way and you know what you could be in for..." Elizabeth's voice trailed off. She pulled off Tom's ski hat and dropped it on the wooden floor, then cupped his face and looked up for a kiss.

His lips were just as cold as his coat had been, his nose too. She quickly warmed his face, her hands cupping his chilled cheeks, her kisses turning his mouth hot and insistent. He slipped his hands into her hair and held her close.

They took a breath and he leaned his forehead against hers. "You shouldn't have left the cabin, Elizabeth. I can't lose you."

"I'm okay. Really, Tom. Are you sure we can't leave now to get your cousin into town?"

He pulled away to look down into her eyes. "It's too late in the day to attempt to leave the cabin with CJ in his condition. We'll have to start out in the morning. How do you feel?"

"A hundred percent."

He chuckled under his breath. "Seems I've heard that somewhere before."

"I am. Really. I don't need any more help dressing and undressing."

"As far as the undressing part goes? You might not need my help, but I'm happy to oblige anytime. In fact, I insist."

She chuckled. "What will we do about him tonight?"

"I'll tie him up. Even if he's not going anywhere on his own, he could manage to unlock the door to the cabin and let in some of his buddies. No sense in taking any chances."

She pulled free to finish dressing. "I'll fix us something hot to drink and warm up some more of that venison chili. Sorry that you missed getting the kindling."

"That's okay. We might have caught one of the bad guys. I'll talk to him before he falls asleep. Join me when you're ready. After we eat, we'll pick up where we left off."

"You don't think we could get down the mountain sooner?" She still worried that CJ's brothers would show up and huff and puff and threaten to blow the cabin down. Most of all, she wanted to get CJ to the hospital.

"I hiked up here looking for wolf tracks, so I don't have a snow-mobile or I would have taken you down as soon as the weather cleared up a bit."

"We could both turn into wolves. You could tow the toboggan. We both could. It would be easier for us to run in this snow and—"

"Farmers are antsy about wolves. Darien doesn't want us running in our wolf coats anywhere near town in the farmers' vicinity. I know some have risked running as wolves out here. Nearer to the town, no. The farmers and ranchers have been told not to shoot any wolves they might see, but that doesn't guarantee they'll abide by the rules. Besides, I'll be armed with my rifle just in case. You can run alongside in your wolf coat, and we'll pretend you're my new dog."

"The things I do for you."

"Yeah, but that's not really what I want you to do for me."

He kissed her again and then left the bedroom.

———————

Tom closed the door to give Elizabeth privacy while she finished dressing. He was concerned about CJ, yet he wanted to wring his cousin's neck if the cousins were up to no good and CJ had had any part in it.

Tom stood over his cousin, watching him as he appeared to be sleeping.

Elizabeth quickly left the bedroom. "Asleep?" she whispered.

"Seems to be."

She entered the kitchen and looked into a cupboard. Tom joined her, moved around her, and opened another cabinet. He brought out a couple of mugs. "Coffee? Tea?"

"Tea, plain." She poured hot water into the mugs.

"About your half brother and uncle… We take care of our own, Elizabeth," he said seriously. If they had been in his pack, her uncle and half brother would have been dead the first time they laid hands on her.

"I could have used a champion."

He leaned up against the counter, his mug in hand. "Where do they live?"

"You can't go after them now. I need the evidence to turn over to Hrothgar. He can take care of it."

"*Where do they live?*"

She chewed on her lip.

"We'll find them," Tom said.

"I don't want the Silver pack fighting with the red."

"Okay, fine. We'll get Sheriff Peter and Deputy Trevor on it when we get back."

She let out her breath. "Twenty miles west of Bruin's old home."

Tom's face hardened. "Damn it, Elizabeth. You should have told me all this already."

"I knew it. Already you're having second thoughts about us." She slammed her mug on the countertop, stalked out of the kitchen, and headed for the fireplace.

Taken aback by her response, Tom didn't react at first. How could she think he'd ever have second thoughts about them? For a moment, he watched her as she stood near his sleeping cousin in front of the fire, rubbing her arms as if she'd suddenly become chilled to the bones. Tom set his mug down with a clink on the counter, then crossed the living room to join her.

She stiffened. He wrapped his arms around her, his chest to her back. Not to be put off, he buried his face in her hair, nuzzling her ear and cheek and neck. She deserved tenderness and loving. "I'm not having second thoughts. I'm just surprised. You told me you weren't related to the reds," he said gently.

"I'm *not*. My uncle and my father joined Bruin's pack as adults. None of us are blood-related. I wasn't *ever* part of the red wolf pack—or any other, for that matter."

"What about North or any of those red wolves? Do you think it's possible they're the ones that have been prowling our territory?" He'd much prefer believing it was them and not his cousins.

"I don't know anything about that, but maybe it could have been the men on the plane, circling the area for a way to get to me."

"Possible." Yet Tom had seen a gray wolf near the last set of prints circling a farm. And now he had found CJ out here. Tom had to have been tracking him and his brothers before the storm hit. Why else would they be out here, trespassing in Silver pack territory and wearing hunter's spray? That had to mean they were up to no good. "I guess we'll just have to ask CJ after he's recovered some."

Tom took her back into the kitchen to warm up the chili, then spooned enough for the two of them into bowls. She took the mugs to the kitchen table. They ate in silence, the only sounds the wind and the fire crackling at the hearth. After they finished eating, she went to clean the dishes.

"I'll make sure my cousin is secure." He kissed her on the temple and headed for the living room.

Recalling Elizabeth's handcuffs, he retrieved them from the floor near the fireplace where he'd left them yesterday.

CJ opened his eyes. "You don't have to. I'm not going anywhere. I can barely move, and I hurt like hell," he growled.

Tom smiled. So CJ wasn't really sleeping after all. "Better safe than sorry." Tom snapped one of them on CJ's wrists, then attached the other to the sofa leg. CJ couldn't lift that heavy sofa bed with his leg paining him so much. "Are you okay? Need anything else?"

"Hell, Tom, I'm not going anywhere."

"Yeah, I know. Sleep. We'll talk later." He wanted to give his cousin time to rest up after his ordeal before he questioned him.

Tom returned to the kitchen and helped Elizabeth dry the bowls, silverware, and mugs, and then they retired to the bedroom and shut the door. "Since we have some time to kill, I'll make love to you. Snowstorms are meant to produce pups."

"They'll be mixed," she said, sounding as if they might be regarded the same way she had been.

He hated the way that some of her family had treated her, but he would prove that he and his family were different.

He scooped her up in his arms and set her gently on the bed. "You, me, and one whole pack of wolves will adore them."

CHAPTER 21

TOM HAD PLANNED TO MAKE LOVE TO ELIZABETH IN THE living room on the sofa by the warm fire. He'd never expected his cousin to be confined right where she had rested—and suffering from an injury too.

He wanted to see every inch of her when he made love to her this time instead of being buried in the blankets. But the bedroom was too cold.

Then again… His gaze skimmed over her in the pale-blue sweats as she smiled up at him, took his sweater in her hands, fisted them around the soft wool fabric, and drew him close.

"Hmm, Elizabeth." Already his blood heated and the room seemed a lot warmer. Even so, he didn't want her chilled like she'd been yesterday. He slipped his hands up her sweatshirt and caressed her breasts, his mouth moving over hers—soft, pliable, appealing—as she kissed him back.

He moved her slowly backward toward the bed, the covers still thrown aside from earlier in the afternoon. When her legs bumped into the mattress, she smiled. He rubbed her nipples with his thumbs, his mouth still fused to hers. She let go of his sweater and tugged to pull it up.

He quickly shucked his sweater, jeans, socks, and then boxers. Watching her as she slid into bed wearing the sweats, he yanked all the blankets over her. At least the sheets were flannel for this time of year and softer and warmer than cotton. Her eyes feasted on his body, and her interest made his body come to life.

"Hot," she said, focusing on his erect cock, her mouth and eyes smiling.

"And getting hotter." He pulled the covers aside so he could join her. He yanked them over him and reached down to pull off her sweatpants, their mouths again kissing. He struggled to keep his mouth on hers, not wanting to break contact as he tried to yank her pants down. She finished the move by kicking them away, burying them in the sheets.

She ran her tongue across his lips as he slid his hand underneath the sweatshirt and cupped a breast again. He loved how her breasts were soft and cushiony and sized just right for his mouth and hands.

Her leg slid over the side of his, her heel brushing the back of his calf. A frisson of heat shot through him as he slipped his hand down her soft skin until he reached the curly hair between her legs. And stopped.

Her mouth suckled on his lower lip, and he groaned with ardent need. He claimed her, his fingers stroking her wet, ready flesh, his mouth nipping her lips with a gentle teasing. She attempted to take off the sweatshirt. He would have helped, but he was busily stroking her and making her writhe with pleasure. The sweatshirt rested above her breasts when she came, his mouth covering hers to muffle the cry of ecstasy.

She smelled divine, sex personified.

He climbed over her, between her legs, not entering her yet but pulling off the sweatshirt. He feasted his eyes on her breasts and then set his mouth on one—sucking hard and caressing the other at the same time with his hand.

Her fingernails raked through his hair and scalp, tightening on strands of his hair as her nipples became taut, sensitive peaks. He rubbed her mound with his erection, and she bent her knees and spread her legs, inviting him to enter.

Not yet.

The urgency throbbed within him to take her, to finish this, to fulfill the wolf's need, the primal urge to claim, but he wanted it to last.

She didn't make that easy as he kissed her again, and she

inserted her tongue and stroked the insides of his mouth. His other head took charge, his cock pushing between her wet, slick folds, burrowing deeper until he couldn't go any farther.

She reached up and flicked her fingernails over his taut nipples, and he let out an inhuman growl. She smiled. He kissed her again, licking and tangling his tongue with hers until he was close to the edge, trying to hang on, suspended, and then he came, striking it rich as the firestorm hit.

He hadn't needed to dream about this to know she was the one for him. He couldn't imagine suffering the dreams and waking to find she wasn't with him.

He collapsed on top of her and she laughed. "I love you, you tired old wolf."

He smiled at her but didn't make any attempt to move off her after what she'd called him.

"You're heavy."

"You're sexy. And I claim you for my own, forever and ever," he said very seriously.

"Good, because I'm not letting you go." She wrapped her arms around his neck. "You're still heavy."

He laughed and moved off her, then pulled her against him. "You're beautiful," he said, stroking her hair.

"You are too. I didn't know gray wolves could be that big."

He chuckled. "I love you."

"I love you too, Tom. I didn't think I ever could love a wolf or another man, whatever kind he was." She cuddled against him, the two of them buried under the covers, snuggling.

He caressed her shoulder, loving just being able to touch her in this way. To lie together. To be together.

He had planned to sleep, but he couldn't just yet, wanting to know more about her brother if she wasn't too tired. He needed to know what he and his pack were up against when it came to her family. "Do you mind telling me more about your half brother?"

She sighed. "Sefton doesn't see me as his sister. He claims my father couldn't have mated with my mother because my father was already mated to *his* mother."

"She was already dead though. Right?"

"Yes. That didn't matter to Sefton. I don't think he would have cared if my father mated again, if his new mate had been a wolf and not a coyote."

"So your uncle took him in?"

"Yeah. My father turned him over to my uncle to raise after Sefton tried to burn down the house."

Tom blew out a harsh breath. "Do you think your uncle was angry he was saddled with raising your half brother?"

"Not that I ever saw. He raised Sefton like he was his own son. At least that's the way it appeared to me whenever I saw them together. I think it was more that my uncle hated that both he and Sefton had trouble finding mates of their own because of their association with my mom and dad."

"It couldn't have been because of the way *they* were? That maybe it had nothing to do with your parents or you?"

Elizabeth didn't say anything for a while as he stroked her silky hair.

"What about Bruin? He's dead now, so no longer a problem where you're concerned, but would he have sanctioned your parents' murder?"

"He might have. I never saw him. I don't know how he treated my uncle and half brother."

It didn't really make much of a difference, Tom thought. All that mattered was learning who was responsible for her parents' death and everything concerning her parents' murderers and their involvement with Elizabeth.

He wanted to know everything about her. He smiled at the thought that she was his mate now. "Tell me about your father."

She laughed a little. "He was a character. Good-natured.

Loving. He was a perfectionist, and when he showed me how to do some job, he'd go into long-winded detail, indicating exactly how I was to do it. When he was done, I'd ask if he could show me again. And he would. So instead of having three cast-iron pans to wash, I'd only get stuck with one."

Tom chuckled.

She smiled. "It got to be a joke with us because he was like that with everything. Every time, he'd do the job again, digging a second hole in the garden to plant a tree, or whatever. Usually by the third time I asked him to demonstrate again, he'd smile and make me do it."

"I would have liked him," Tom said.

"Yeah, you would have. And my mother. She baked cinnamon rolls like Bertha does." She sighed heavily.

Tom didn't know what to say. He was afraid the memories were too sad for Elizabeth, but before he could attempt to change the subject, she said, "She didn't take any guff from my father, wolf that he was."

"That must be where you get it from."

"Yeah," she said dreamily. "Just *you* remember that."

They snuggled for a long time, and when she fell asleep, he followed. A few hours later, he heard something in the living room—a scraping sound, he thought—that jarred him awake.

Tom quickly extricated himself from Elizabeth, not meaning to wake her, but she quickly sat up as he left the bed. He grabbed the rifle, hurried to the bedroom door, and yanked it open.

CJ stared at the door, still manacled to the sofa but sitting up now. "I'm not going anywhere, Tom," he said. "But I'm hungry. Any more of that great chili you make? I've smelled it all evening."

"I'll get you some in a minute." He closed the door, set the rifle on the dresser, then dressed. He watched Elizabeth dig around in the bedsheets for the sweatpants she had been wearing. "Showtime."

"Do you think he'll tell us anything that we don't already know?"

"I sure hope so."

When they were both dressed, they left the bedroom together, and Tom joined CJ by the fireplace, adding more wood to the fire.

"Can I get him anything?" Elizabeth asked Tom.

"A glass of water and a bowl of that chili, if you don't mind."

"All right." She hurried to get them.

"Start talking, CJ," Tom said, crossing his arms as he looked down at his cousin. "What do you know about the wolves harassing the livestock?"

"I didn't have any part of it."

Tom grunted.

Elizabeth rejoined them and stood quietly nearby with the bowl of chili and glass of water. CJ stared at Elizabeth as if seeing her for the first time. Was he surprised Tom had mated with her even though she was part coyote? CJ's father had had issues with Lelandi being a red wolf and not gray, so maybe so.

"Yeah. We're mated," Tom said defensively.

CJ glanced at Tom, then back at Elizabeth.

"You know me from somewhere, don't you?" Elizabeth asked quietly.

That took the wind out of Tom's sails. Maybe that was why CJ had been staring at her.

"Yeah. Yeah, I do. A long time ago."

"When?"

CJ cleared his throat. "I mean, at first I wasn't sure. I didn't know you're the one Tom got interested in." He shook his head. "But when I heard you talking about Bruin's pack and... Well, my brothers and I were the ones who found you at that watering hole when that man nearly drowned you.

"We didn't know what to do. We weren't in our territory, but we'd decided to take a swim there because it was a hot day, and then we saw you struggling with some older guy. We made a lot of racket as we headed for the water, hoping the creep would let you go. After the guy took off, we followed him to make sure he didn't come back."

Tom studied his cousin and couldn't believe that at one time, CJ and his brothers had saved Elizabeth's life.

"Thanks," she said softly, "for coming to my aid."

Tom scowled. "You and your brothers should have killed the bastard."

"We weren't in our territory. If Bruin had learned we were there, he would have killed us. You know what he was like."

Tom shook his head. "You should have killed him." Hell, if they had, Elizabeth would never have had all the troubles she'd had lately. Then again, she probably wouldn't have done the story on their ski resort if her main goal hadn't been to meet up with North. Tom wouldn't have met her. "Who's behind stalking the livestock then? The farmers are all up in arms. Somebody could get killed."

"Damn it, Tom. You know my brothers will want to kill me."

"Better them than me."

CJ looked mutinous but didn't say anything. Tom changed tactics.

"We were friends once," Tom said, trying to coax CJ to explain everything to him.

"I know. Why do you think I didn't go along with any of this?"

"Any of what?" Tom wanted specifics. Had CJ really not had anything to do with the problems the pack had?

"The livestock scares." CJ looked down at the floor.

"We suspected it was the four of you," Tom said, though only three wolves had been spotted. But the brothers did everything together, or had in the past.

"Not me," CJ said defiantly.

"Why not you?"

"Eric, Brett, and Sarandon all have a grudge against Darien because he murdered our father. If our father had taken over when yours died instead of Darien… I was angry, but you were still my cousins. We were still a pack."

"No longer. You abandoned the pack," Tom said.

"I know, Tom. It was a mistake to leave the pack. All right?" CJ sounded exasperated. "I didn't like Darien's first mate. She was a cancer in the pack. I liked Lelandi. What my father did was wrong, but he was still my father, and my brothers felt like we couldn't stay. I didn't want my only family to leave without me. But I grew up with most of the people in the pack. They're my family too, and now I wish I'd never left with my brothers."

"Why didn't you just come back to the pack?" Tom asked, still hoping that his cousins would. Darien would make them pay in some way for putting pack members in danger by scaring the farmers, but no one in their pack had been hurt because of it so far.

"I wanted to, but Eric wouldn't hear of it."

"So why were your brothers stalking the livestock?"

"We've been looking for a way to come back into the pack and still save face. We knew what our father had done reflected poorly on us, as had leaving the pack. We thought if we could help the pack in some way, it could work in our favor. I don't know why my brothers thought stalking the farms was a good idea, but I don't control what they do."

Tom breathed a sigh of relief. "Hell, CJ, we thought you were getting ready to cause trouble. Revenge against the pack or something. Why else would you wear hunter's spray?"

"Because we didn't want you guys to know it was us before we could come up with a good reason not to just kick us out of the territory."

"For a while, we thought you might have been the ones behind all of Elizabeth's trouble because we couldn't pick up those men's scent either."

CJ glanced at Elizabeth. She handed him the water and chili. He took it but didn't thank her.

"We weren't but Eric talked to a wolf who was also wearing hunter's spray up on the ski slope."

"You were up on the ski slope?" Tom asked.

"Yeah. Hell, just because we left the pack, it didn't mean we didn't want to hit the powder during the first big snowfall of the season. We saw you with Elizabeth and were curious about who she was. Especially when we saw her kiss you. I'll admit it killed me to see the two of you kissing like nobody else in the world existed, and I couldn't even rib you about it."

Tom glanced at Elizabeth. Her cheeks turned rosy.

"Anyway this really nosy guy approached us. Asked why the woman was getting so much attention. Naturally, we tried to smell him and couldn't. He had to have been wearing hunter's spray like we were. And he was covered up like we were. Not that it wasn't cold, but it just seemed odd that he was hiding his identity from other wolves like we were doing. And we saw him getting into a white minivan in a big hurry. Also odd.

"Right after that, we heard that someone had shoved the lady down the slope. We all hung around and questioned staff to see if she would be all right. We knew that you were interested in her and were ready to hunt down the dude who had pushed her, hoping that maybe bringing him to justice would give us points toward getting back in with the pack. But we weren't able to track him, and then Elizabeth left town, so we were back to square one."

"So what were you doing out here then?" Tom asked.

"Been living in the area. We knew Elizabeth had left on a plane in a real hurry, and I wondered why, seeing how close you two had become in such a short time. When I heard the sound of a plane in trouble, I knew I shouldn't mess with it because I was in my wolf coat, but…you know how we are. Too curious for our own good.

"When I searched for survivors, I smelled Elizabeth. I knew

you were also looking for her. Between the two of us, I figured we'd find her. Then you did. I wanted in the worst way to learn if she would be all right. I came to see you when you were trying to gather wood. You know the rest."

"Did you mess with the latch on the cabin's outdoor shutters?"

"I thought I could peek in and see that she was all right. Even though you'd managed to get her to the cabin, I still didn't know if she had made it. The damn latch was frozen shut and I had to jimmy it loose from the ice. I thought if I left the shutters open, you would come out to secure them, and I'd catch a glimpse of her. I...didn't mean to bend the latch."

"Damn, CJ. You could have just knocked on the door. Where are your brothers now?"

"I don't know where they are. If we head for Silver Town, we may never run into them."

"If we did try to make it into town and they found us before we reached it, what would they do?"

"Help us, I'm certain."

Unless CJ was lying. Or didn't know what his brothers were really up to.

"Thanks, Tom, for helping me out." CJ glanced at Elizabeth. "I'm sorry. I never thought you'd be hurt. We should have killed that guy at the watering hole when we had the chance."

CHAPTER 22

MUCH LATER THAT NIGHT, ELIZABETH HELPED TOM MAKE UP the foldout sofa bed for CJ to sleep on after they'd fed him and were ready to retire. "Maybe he should sleep in the bedroom," Elizabeth said. "If this bed is too lumpy, maybe he'd be more comfortable on the other."

"He'll live," Tom said, trying to sound gruff and mean, like his cousin was still on his bad side, but she knew it wasn't so.

Tom had tried to find a reason to acquit his cousin of any wrongdoing, and she guessed CJ had been a good friend growing up. Finding friends like that was difficult, and she didn't want Tom to lose him.

She plumped a pillow and set it on the sofa bed. "His leg will most likely keep him awake most of the night. If he could sleep—"

"In here." Tom put another log on the fire.

CJ smiled. "You can't put on the tough-guy show for her, Tom, and *not* tell her your reasons."

Elizabeth raised her brows at Tom. "What is he talking about?"

Tom took her shoulders and rubbed them, then leaned down and kissed her forehead. "He'll stay in here on the lumpy mattress and the squeaky frame because the fire will keep him warm. We can't bury him in blankets in the other room when he doesn't have a more protective cast on his leg. Any pressure on that makeshift splint would really hurt. He wouldn't be able to sleep in the bedroom because it would be too cold without covering up."

"Why didn't you tell me that in the first place?" She threw another pillow on the couch and straightened the blankets again.

"Because I was trying to act like a tough guy for you, Elizabeth. I knew it wouldn't work on CJ. He knows me too well."

She shook her head. "Maybe the two of you should sleep in here together."

CJ chuckled. "You've got a winner, Tom. I envy you."

Tom helped CJ onto the sofa bed, and Elizabeth covered him up, except for his leg. "Let me get some socks for your feet," she said.

She hurried out of the room and was grabbing a couple of socks when she heard CJ say, "You're damn lucky to have her."

"Thanks for saving her when she was a girl."

"Yeah, well, I wish I'd killed the man who was trying to hurt her."

Elizabeth wished he had too. She went back into the living room with the socks. One was black and the other navy blue. "Hope you don't mind that they don't match. I guess the washing machine ate the matching ones. These were all I could find."

Tom snatched them out of her hand, startling her. "I'll dress him. You can get ready for bed, and I'll join you in a minute."

Elizabeth frowned at Tom, annoyed that he'd worry about her being with his cousin. She said to CJ, "Sleep well."

She turned and headed for the bedroom and just barely caught herself before she slammed the door. When she leaned against the door to listen to what was being said, she overheard CJ and Tom reminiscing about funny mishaps, fishing trips, hunting as wolves, and mischief when they were young. Their conversation brought tears to her eyes. She would have given anything to have had family like Tom had. She got the feeling CJ was still hiding something, though, and only hoped his brothers would see the light before they permanently ruined any chance to be part of the pack again.

Unless they already had.

Tom sat on the edge of the sofa bed and pulled the remaining sock over CJ's right foot. He was trying really hard not to hurt his cousin's leg, but CJ let out a strangled sound that revealed he was in pain no matter how careful Tom was. He resituated the blankets again to ensure everything was covered except his cousin's splinted leg.

"Remember the time we fished and you caught Eric?" CJ asked.

Tom smiled. "Yeah. He was madder than a stirred-up yellow jacket. My dad pulled the fishing hook out of his back, telling him he was one mighty fine catch and making your brother even angrier."

"Until the she-wolf felt sorry for him, and then he made out like it wasn't any big deal. Whatever happened to her?"

"Parents moved away two months later."

CJ nodded. "Remember when you and I took on your brothers and mine? I don't even remember what it was about, do you?"

Tom snorted. "Hell, yeah. They were picking on us because we were the 'babies' of the family. We gave 'em hell. Proved we weren't at the bottom of the heap."

"What were we? Five?"

Tom chuckled. "Yeah. We were scrappers even back then." He sighed. "I want you back in the pack, CJ. But you know it's not up to me."

"It's up to Darien. I know. Thanks for saving me out there. You didn't have to."

"Yeah, I did."

"Tom," CJ said, his eyes drooping a little, "watch out for her. I'm not sure that North is the one you have to worry about."

"What do you mean?"

"I think…he might be the fall guy."

Elizabeth wished Tom would leave his cousin and hurry to bed. She needed his hot body to warm her up. The sheets were flannel, thank heavens, but she still needed to snuggle with him.

The door opened, and she watched as he closed it behind him and stalked toward the bed.

"Is he okay?" she asked.

"Yeah, Elizabeth, he'll be okay. Soon as we get his leg seen to in town." Tom slipped out of his clothes, pulled the covers aside, and joined her.

She sighed. "Silva's still planning her grand opening?"

"In a few days. She'll be thrilled if you can go to it," Tom said.

"I wouldn't miss it for the world, now that I'm here again. How's Sam taking it?"

"Not well. He pretends it doesn't bother him. Three she-wolves applied for Silva's job, but he—"

"Turned them down because they're not Silva," Elizabeth finished for him.

"Yeah. Truthfully, I think he'd do it all himself rather than have anyone take her place."

She yawned. "Why don't they just mate?"

"They both have issues."

"Don't we all," Elizabeth mused as she stroked Tom's arm.

"Not me."

She looked at him askance.

"Not since you came back to me."

"Under duress, I might add. You have no deep, dark secrets?"

"I ran away from the pack once."

"You? Who is loyal to the core to your family?"

"I was four. I was going to start my own pack. I was mad at Darien and Jake for ganging up on me since I was the young-est—by only a few minutes. But it was enough."

She laughed. "So you and who else intended to form a pack?"

"CJ and me. He had the same trouble with his brothers. If you'd been there, I would have been set for life."

She smiled. "At four years old."

"Yeah. I finally realized running away wasn't the solution. Standing up to them was all they wanted of me." He caressed her cheek. "Some in our family, Darien and Jake included, were dream mated. I always thought I would be, while neither Darien nor Jake believed in such a phenomenon."

"Dream mated? That's what Silva mentioned in the tavern. I'd forgotten about it, but I've never heard of it before."

"They dreamed of having mated with their women before they even met them. And Lelandi and Alicia dreamed of Darien and Jake in the same way."

"That didn't happen with you, did it?"

Tom kissed her cheek. "I found you—a dream in the flesh. I didn't need to fantasize about you."

"Hmm, maybe if I'd been gone longer…"

"You wouldn't have been. I already told you. I was coming for you as soon as I took care of business here." He pulled her into his hard embrace and held her tight. "CJ thinks North might be the fall guy."

"Great. Which means…?"

"Maybe your uncle or half brother planned to get rid of you and pin the blame on him. Maybe he was set up to get in touch with you in the first place."

"Like they made the evidence available to him to lure me here." Great. She loved being her uncle's pawn. *Not.*

━━━━━━━━━━━━━━━━

Early the next morning before Tom or Elizabeth had awakened enough to realize the sun would soon rise, someone banged on the front door, giving Tom a near heart attack. He yanked on a sweatshirt and a pair of jeans, grabbed the rifle, and hurried for the bedroom door, hoping to hell it was someone from their pack and not the rest of his cousins, if they meant to cause trouble.

Elizabeth whispered, "Not CJ's brothers."

"I don't know. Stay here."

He entered the living room and crossed the floor to the front door.

CJ had raised his head off the sofa bed, looking anxious.

"Just stay there and don't move," Tom warned him. Not that CJ would, being handcuffed to the sofa leg and at a distinct disadvantage with his broken leg.

Tom looked out the peephole first and smiled to see Kemp and Radcliff standing on the porch, stomping on the snow and rubbing their gloved hands.

"Just a minute!" To Elizabeth, Tom hollered over his shoulder, "Ski patrol's here!"

CHAPTER 23

TOM JERKED OPEN THE DOOR AND LET KEMP AND RADCLIFF in. Both men grinned at him, snow clinging to the fur around their hoods. He smelled the fresh, crisp air and pine on them.

"I didn't hear you coming. No snowmobiles," Tom said.

"We used snowshoes. Quieter. We could hear any trouble in the area."

"Am I damned glad to see you," Tom said.

Kemp slapped Tom on the shoulder with warm regard. "Darien asked for volunteers to see if you were here. Glad you were instead of stuck someplace else in this weather."

Radcliff entered the cabin and shut the door and locked it. "No coffee on yet? Blizzard hit town hard. Everything is snowed under. Electric lines and trees are down. So we've had a time of it there too, and—"

They all caught a glimpse of Elizabeth pulling on a sweatshirt as she rushed to shut the bedroom door, her cheeks crimson.

Kemp and Radcliff stared at the bedroom door, their jaws hanging open.

Tom said, "How about one of you getting the fire going again? The other can get some coffee water ready. I'll be right back."

"Need any help?" Kemp asked. "You make better coffee than I do."

"That's not what you said when you complained last time about my coffee-making ability," Tom said, smiling. He knew the brothers would rather check on the she-wolf.

"I've changed my mind," Kemp said.

"Yeah, I bet." Heading for the bedroom, Tom motioned to his cousin and said, "Just don't bump the sofa bed and jar CJ."

Both brothers glanced at the living room. "What the..." Kemp said. He yanked off his jacket and gloves, tossing them on a chair, then pulled off his ski hat. "Here we worried all the way up here that Tom would be safe. All this time, he had a real setup going. Though I'm not sure about CJ."

Radcliff shook his head as he ditched his parka, hat, and gloves on the dining-room table and started the coffee. "This will be one for the history books on Silver Town."

Tom knocked on the bedroom door. "Elizabeth, can I come in?"

Elizabeth opened the bedroom door a crack.

"Can you hand me the lockpicks for the cuffs?" Tom asked. Now that he had backup and CJ was still incapacitated, he figured he didn't need to keep his cousin confined. Last night, he'd hated to do it, but Elizabeth's safety came first in case whoever wanted her came here to get her. Though he mostly trusted CJ, Tom hadn't wanted him to open the door to visitors in the middle of the night while he and Elizabeth slept.

"Sure." She hurried to get the picks and handed them to him. "We can go now, can't we?"

"Yeah, we sure can. Just holler if you need anything."

"Thanks." She shut the door.

Kemp stood over CJ. "Looks like you had some trouble." He got a fire started. "So what's the dice with Elizabeth? And...*him*?" he asked as Tom removed the handcuffs.

"CJ caught his leg in a trap. We need to get him down to the hospital."

"Has he been involved in the livestock situation?"

"No, I haven't been," CJ said, sitting up in bed, rubbing his wrist, and sounding tired and irritable.

Tom and Kemp joined Radcliff in the kitchen.

"I didn't think she would be returning *that* soon. How in the hell did she end up here? Or...was that really the plan all along? To rendezvous with her?" Kemp asked.

Radcliff frowned. "Yeah, what *is* she doing here?"

"In a blizzard?" Kemp asked.

"With you?" Radcliff leaned against the kitchen counter, crossed his arms over his chest, and raised his brows.

"Long story, but essentially she fell out of the sky."

Radcliff poured cups of coffee for all three of them. "You want any, CJ?"

"Yeah." CJ still looked pale except for the dark circles around his eyes.

Tom figured he hadn't slept well last night from the pain and probably from the confinement.

Both brothers stared at Tom, waiting for him to say something further about Elizabeth.

"Plane crash. Elizabeth was kidnapped."

"Kidnapped," Radcliff said, not asking a question but mulling it over.

"She's okay though?" Kemp said, glancing back at the bedroom door.

"Yeah, she's like an angel without wings and as close as I'll get to heaven."

Kemp turned to his brother. "I told you, didn't I?"

"Yeah, yeah, that her leaving like she did wouldn't mean she was gone forever. And there wouldn't be any chance for us when she came back."

"Hey," Kemp said, "next time a woman like that is at Bertha's B and B and needs a ride to the slopes, have her call *me*."

"But give Bertha *my* number," Radcliff said.

Getting serious, Kemp cleared his throat. "Are there any more survivors?"

"No."

"If somebody's looking for Elizabeth, we need to get her to town just as much as we do CJ," Radcliff said.

"My thoughts also. The weather seems much better today.

Now that you're here, we'll have safety in numbers. After we have some breakfast, we'll head out. Is anyone else up here looking for me?" Tom asked.

"Are you kidding?" Kemp said. "Half the town is searching for you. Even farmer Bill Todd, though Darien asked him to stay at home. The man insisted he had to look for you, saying it was all his damned fault you were such a blamed fool."

Tom chuckled. He liked the farmer, but he knew why Darien didn't want the human out searching. "Someone from the pack is with him, right?"

"Sam is. And to ensure nothing goes wrong, Deputy Trevor is sticking close to him in case Bill sees a wolf and gets trigger happy."

"We just got a jump start on the rest of the searchers." Radcliff sounded proud of himself and his brother. "As soon as we learned you were missing and the storm had cleared, we put on our ski-patrol hats and were on our way."

"Thanks, guys. You don't know how welcome your arrival is." Tom glanced at CJ, pinning him as the man who could still cause the most trouble if his brothers intercepted them on the way home.

———————

Elizabeth couldn't find enough warm clothes—no boots, no parka or gloves, not even another ski hat—so she opted to be a wolf for the run into town. Tom wasn't happy about it, even though he had suggested she might have to do that, but it was the only thing she could do. The men had a devil of a time dressing CJ. His leg throbbed really badly, though he tried not to show it. When they pulled sweats over his injured leg, he passed out. They quickly wrapped him in blankets and strapped him onto the toboggan before he came to.

Eager to run, Elizabeth paced back and forth in the living area, out of the men's way. She couldn't contain her excitement.

"You stay close to us, Elizabeth." Tom crouched beside her and ran his hand over her head. "Don't stray."

"No rabbit chasing," Radcliff said with a wink as he zipped up his parka.

"No deer chasing." Kemp smiled at her while he slipped on his gloves.

"No chasing wolves down," Tom said, ultraseriously.

She licked his mouth and the brothers chuckled.

Once they had bundled up, they carried the toboggan outside.

Tom shut the door to the cabin, then joined the men and Elizabeth in the snow. Wearing snowshoes, the men trudged through the drifts while Elizabeth ran ahead. She had to. Walking at a snail's pace next to the men wasn't an option, as far as she was concerned. Besides, she'd keep an eye out for CJ's brothers, and if she smelled a whiff of anyone she didn't know, she'd warn Tom and the others.

Tom slung the rifle over his back, while Kemp pulled the toboggan for the first part of the journey.

Tom and Radcliff hollered out every once in a while to let the searchers know they were all right, if any of the searchers could hear their voices. They'd have a fight if CJ's brothers came after them and meant to cause trouble.

Elizabeth was certain the brothers wouldn't come for them though. Too many people were out combing the area for Tom. And if the brothers did come upon Kemp pulling the toboggan and Radcliff and Tom, what could they do? If they wanted to take CJ with them, they'd still have to transport him to the doctor. So she felt the brothers would leave them alone.

She dashed ahead, jumping into the snow with exuberance and having the time of her life. She'd love to do this again when Tom was a wolf and could play with her.

"Elizabeth!" Tom yelled at her.

She turned her head, snow clinging to her fur, a few flakes

sitting on her nose, and woofed back. Then she bit at the snow, having wanted to play in it since that first time she visited Silver Town. Now she was finally able to do it.

She rolled around in the snow, then shook it off. When she looked back again at Tom, he was shaking his head as he and the others trudged after her. The brothers smiled.

Kemp said, "You sure are one lucky SOB."

"I sure am," Tom said.

Elizabeth smiled in her wolf way, right before she tore off again. She would laugh if she could.

"Elizabeth!"

She was quite a distance ahead of the men and hidden by spruce trees when she saw Sam, a rifle resting on his shoulder, staring straight at her. She did her best impression of a dog as she observed the two men with him. Deputy Trevor and the one who had to be the human farmer. *Great.*

The gray wolves wouldn't recognize her in wolf form, and she could smell *their* scents, but she stood downwind of them.

She woofed and wagged her tail vigorously. Then she leaned down with her front legs, her butt up in the air, still wagging it in play, but didn't move any closer.

"It's a wolf," the farmer said, pulling his rifle off his shoulder.

CHAPTER 24

Sam grabbed for the farmer's weapon, hurriedly saying, "It's one of our dogs. Don't shoot!"

Trevor likewise hurried to disarm the man. Why in the world would they have allowed the farmer to be armed?

Elizabeth's heart pounded like crazy as she went into pretend dog mode. Having a devil of a time *not* lifting her chin like a coyote or wolf that was about to howl or even a coyote when it barked, Elizabeth woofed in response—a nice dog-sounding bark.

"Elizabeth!" Tom said, winded as he tried to run on top of the snow in the snowshoes.

She turned her head in his direction, though she could only hear his approach and not see him. She did a happy bark, then raced back for him like any loving dog would who wanted to please its master. Okay, so she could do this and make it convincing because she didn't want to get shot. She'd been through enough already.

Tom came around the trees and saw Sam, Trevor, and Bill just as Elizabeth jumped on him and bit at his clothes like an unruly, overgrown puppy thrilled to see her master.

"Good dog," Tom said, his voice relieved but hard.

He tried to pet her, but she nipped at his gloves and woofed. She was good at this playacting, she thought.

Looking anxious, Radcliff quickly joined them, huffing and puffing, his warm breath mixing with the icy air and turning into wisps of vapor. "Oh good, you caught up with her," he said, glancing in the farmer's direction and then stating the obvious. "Hey, we found Tom."

"And his dog," Trevor said, a brow raised. He didn't smile, but she could hear the hint of amusement in his voice.

Sam stared at Elizabeth. She woofed back at him in greeting and, for good measure, wagged her tail.

"We found more than that," Kemp said, joining them, still towing CJ on the toboggan.

"What happened to him?" Sam asked.

"He stepped in a leg trap," Tom said. "We need to get him to the hospital and call off the other search parties. Bill can come with us. Trevor, you and Sam can locate the rest of the teams and let them know we're all right."

Trevor nodded.

What was Tom thinking? Elizabeth didn't want to have to play like a dog the rest of the way to Silver Town. Then again, that was just what she'd looked like as she'd frolicked in the snow. She suspected Trevor and Sam didn't want Bill to come across any other wolves, if some of Darien's people tried to locate Tom in their wolf forms. This was a way to get Bill back to town, still supervised, before he caused any trouble.

She ran off and Tom shouted, "Elizabeth! Stick close!"

"Cute dog," Bill said. "I didn't know you owned one."

"Yeah, but she definitely needs to go to *obedience* school," Tom said.

Radcliff and Kemp laughed.

He'd pay for the obedience-school comment later. But for now? She dove into another snowbank. She came out covered in the cold, wet white stuff, shook it loose from her fur, and dashed off again. She was having the time of her life as a wolf, coyote, dog, whatever.

Bill chuckled. "She sure is cute."

"Yeah, she stole my heart as soon as I saw her," Tom said.

"If he hadn't caught sight of her first," Kemp said, handing the trace to the toboggan to his brother so he could haul CJ for a while, "*I* would have claimed her."

She woofed. No one was claiming her! She had done the claiming—and Tom was the one for her.

Before long, several searchers came to join them—Sheriff Peter, the two Viking-looking twin brothers from the ski resort, Cantrell and Robert, and a slew of others she didn't recognize.

Everyone was curious about her and probably also about the fact that the farmer was with them and hadn't shot her.

"Tom's new dog," Kemp said to the sheriff. And so it was. Elizabeth became Tom's new pet dog for the duration of the trip into town. She would be there already if she hadn't had to move at the humans' slow pace.

"Get the word out to the alert roster. We've found Tom, his dog, Elizabeth, and CJ, who has a broken leg and is being brought in on a toboggan," Sheriff Peter relayed over his phone as they got near enough to town and had reception. "Yeah, hold on." He handed his cell to Tom.

"Yeah? Hey, Lelandi. CJ has a broken leg from an animal trap. He's in a lot of pain. Conscious, but barely. Have Doc ready. I'll tell you the rest when we get there. Bill Todd's with us."

Elizabeth knew that said it all. They had a human with them, and Tom couldn't tell Lelandi everything that had happened, including how Elizabeth came to be with him.

"They're calling off the search teams. We'll be to the road in about half an hour. If you can have a car pick us up and an ambulance for CJ, that would be great. Peter will accompany him." Tom glanced at Elizabeth as she waited for them to catch up to her. "Yeah, Elizabeth is fine. I'm sure she'll be happy to see you too." He gave coordinates of where they'd meet up at the road. "Okay, talk to you in a little bit."

He ended the call and handed the phone to Peter. "Lelandi says she can't wait to give you a hug, Elizabeth."

She woofed.

Smiling, Bill shook his head. "She's one smart dog. I don't care what you said about the obedience training. Sometimes you just need to give them a little extra leash. You can tell she's intelligent."

She woofed at Bill and wagged her tail.

He grinned. "See?" He turned to Tom. "If you ever need a home for her, I'll take her in."

The guys laughed.

"You'd have a fight on your hands over that one," Cantrell said.

"I don't doubt it," Bill said. "A really good dog is hard to come by."

She enjoyed the teasing. Everyone made her feel as though she was part of the pack.

When they reached the road, several vehicles waited. One of the men waved to Bill and said, "I'll take you to your truck."

Elizabeth swore everyone held their breaths until Bill left. Then the questions began in earnest.

Tom said, "We'll talk later. I want to get Elizabeth to Darien's house so she can shift and dress, and we'll figure out where to go from there."

They loaded CJ into the waiting ambulance. Peter was on his cell. "Yeah, I'll tell Tom." He ended the call and said to Tom, "Darien and Jake are on their way to the hospital to meet with Doc and CJ. All the search teams have been accounted for and are on the way back here. I'll see you all later."

"See you in a bit," Tom said, opening the back door of a black SUV.

Knowing Darien would question CJ, Elizabeth didn't want to be in his place for anything. She jumped into the SUV and hopped over the middle seat to sit in the rear one. She was glad someone had draped blankets over the seats. She wasn't muddy, but she was a little wet. She smiled to see the driver was Bertha, owner of the B and B.

"My," Bertha said, "you're back. Not that I doubted it for a moment." She gave Elizabeth a heartwarming smile.

Tom got into the vehicle and saw her panting in the very back seat. "Good dog, my ass, Elizabeth. You nearly gave me a heart attack when I realized you'd run into Sam and Trevor with Bill. We're just lucky the farmer didn't shoot you when he saw you before someone could stop him."

She woofed and wagged her tail. He was right: she wasn't anyone's obedient little dog. But she knew she had scared him—and herself—when she came upon the farmer armed with a rifle, so she wasn't annoyed with Tom for scolding her.

Tom wrapped his arms around her in a bear hug of an embrace. She licked his face. He chuckled, and she snuggled the upper part of her body against his lap.

Sam, Kemp, and Radcliff climbed into the SUV.

Sam glanced over the back seat and said to Tom, "You're keeping her for real, aren't you, Tom? I wouldn't let her slip away again."

Elizabeth wagged her tail, wanting to tell Sam it was the other way around. She was keeping Tom for herself; no other she-wolf need apply. She wanted to tell him that he should see what he had in Silva and do something about it!

Tom stroked Elizabeth's head and back in a loving way as he explained to Sam and the other men what had happened. He left the part out about them being mated wolves. She wondered if they had all guessed as much.

She sighed and promptly fell asleep on the ride to Darien's house, despite worrying about what was coming next.

———————

As soon as they drove around the circular drive to the front door, Lelandi hurried out of the house to greet them. Elizabeth raised her head and woofed. Watching her playacting, Tom knew he loved her.

Sam got out of the vehicle so that Tom and Elizabeth could leave the back seat. "I'm staying," Sam said, "for Elizabeth's protection."

"Me too," Radcliff said.

Kemp followed him out of the car. "Thanks for the ride," he said to Bertha.

"Sure thing. If any of you need a lift later, just holler. My guests are all at the ski resort, so no need for me to be home at the moment." She drove around the circular drive and the long way through the trees to the main road and then headed to Silver Town.

Lelandi gave Tom a hug. "I'll take Elizabeth up to the guest room and get her some clothes. Get anything you'd like to eat or drink. I'll be down in a little while."

Elizabeth had already raced up the stairs.

"Come on, guys. Let's make some sandwiches for everyone," Tom said.

"I'll make them." Sam was so used to doing so at the tavern that no matter who offered, he always took over the task. "What will we do about your cousins?"

"I wish it was anyone in the world but them," Tom said. "But it's Darien's call." Tom said so, though he knew his brother would ask Jake and him what they wanted to do since they were all blood relatives.

When Elizabeth came down dressed in clean clothes from Lelandi, Sam and everyone were making sandwiches, but Tom seemed distracted, a contemplative look on his face. Elizabeth pulled him aside.

"I don't think CJ told us everything."

"I was thinking the same thing," Tom confessed. "I wanted to stay here with you to make sure you're safe if your uncle has a death wish and tries to steal you away from here"—Elizabeth shot him a look—"but now I'm thinking we should go to the hospital and see if CJ changes his story. I have something I want to ask him."

"He needs morphine," Doc Weber said to Darien as he looked at the X-ray of CJ's broken leg. "I'll rebreak the bone where it has knit together wrong and realign it properly."

"I need to question him about his involvement in the problems we're having," Darien said.

"You're welcome to question him," Doc said, "but I still need to give him morphine."

Tom and Elizabeth slipped into CJ's hospital room as Nurse Matthew inserted an IV into CJ's hand. Jake and Peter stood nearby, arms folded across their chests.

Jake finally said to CJ, "Okay, so you say you didn't have anything to do with anything, yet you knew about everything."

"I overheard my brothers talking."

"And you were where at the time?" Darien asked.

"Mr. Winston's place on the outskirts of town."

"And just what did you overhear?"

"Their plan to scout out the perimeter of the territory, around the farms, to see what they could see."

"Why would they want to do that?"

"I don't know," CJ said. "But why would they lie? They didn't know I was there."

Darien said, "Or they knew and they fed you a line of bull in case we picked you up and you spilled your guts about what was going on. Or you're lying to save your ass."

"No, I swear that's all that I know," CJ insisted.

"That's all?" Darien asked.

CJ hesitated. "Yes."

Tom spoke up. "CJ, at the cabin, you said you knew I was looking for Elizabeth. But when I heard the plane crash, *I* didn't even know Elizabeth had been on it until I found her, so how did *you* know that?"

CJ didn't say.

"I could break your uninjured leg," Jake said. "You know, to take your mind off the pain when Doc rebreaks the injured one."

CJ eyed the syringe filled with morphine.

Doc withheld it, waiting for Darien to give him the go-ahead.

"Damn it. I didn't have anything to do with it, but after we found out Elizabeth had gone to the airport in a hurry, we went back to Mr. Winston's and the guy that Eric had talked to on the slopes was there. He asked to talk to Eric alone. Of all of us, Eric was always the angriest at Darien for everything that had happened. As I said, he wouldn't even consider just coming to Darien and asking to rejoin the pack.

"So I was worried and went to listen at the door. I heard the guy say he knew Eric had a grudge against the Silver pack. The guy said his employer wanted to bring back the woman Tom was with—Elizabeth—on a private plane and asked Eric if he wanted in on the job." Everyone's eyes were glued to CJ.

"What did he say?" Tom asked threateningly.

"I don't know. I heard Brett and Sarandon coming down the hall, and I had to get out of there. The creep left right after that." CJ said, looking pained. "Eric might still be angry about our father, but no matter what, I *don't* believe he would have agreed to help kidnap Elizabeth. He couldn't have. We were trying to help Elizabeth! We were still trying to find the guy that hurt her on the slopes only hours before this guy showed at Mr. Winston's."

"I recognized all three men who kidnapped me," Elizabeth said. "No one else took part in my kidnapping in Canyon."

CJ looked at Elizabeth gratefully.

"You should have told us about the kidnappers' plan," Tom said through gritted teeth.

"I wanted to," CJ said, "but I didn't want to rat out Eric. I didn't know what to do."

"Where are your brothers now?" Darien asked. "Still at Mr. Winston's place?"

"I don't think so," CJ said. "After Elizabeth left, we argued about what to do. I wanted to find another way to get back in the pack.

Eric said maybe we should just give up altogether. I left the cabin in my wolf coat to run through the woods, and that's when I heard the plane in trouble. Since the snowstorm hit and I didn't go back to Mr. Winston's, they're probably out looking for me. They could be anywhere."

CJ winced at the pain in his leg.

"Give him the morphine," Darien said to Doc, wishing that CJ had stayed with the pack but still not positive his cousin hadn't been involved in any of the pack's recent troubles.

Tom certainly looked like he could just about strangle CJ. He whispered something in Elizabeth's ear and moved to leave. Elizabeth followed, casting CJ a sympathetic look, and they walked out of the hospital room.

Darien shook his head. "And knock him out before you break the leg," Darien added.

"You got it," Doc said.

Darien turned to Peter on the way out. "Let me know when he wakes up. All right? Come on, Jake."

As they headed out of the hospital, Jake said to Darien, "I think he was telling the truth."

"I don't know. If our cousins were looking for a way to get back in the pack, why scout out the human farms? I feel like there's something we're still missing. Let's go home and learn what more we can from Tom and find out how Elizabeth ended up with him in the woods during the blizzard."

"You know he's got to have mated her by now."

Darien smiled. "If Silva thought she was done knitting baby booties, she's got another thing coming."

CHAPTER 25

WHEN ELIZABETH WAS WEARING A PAIR OF COMFY SLIPPER boots, she and Lelandi joined Tom and the others in the living room. Tom wished he hadn't been so antsy about Elizabeth taking so long. But he suspected they'd had a lot of girl talk and Lelandi had gotten the whole story from Elizabeth.

Noticing how tense he was, Sam, Radcliff, and Kemp had cast amused looks at each other, but they hadn't dared say a word.

Tom quickly handed Elizabeth a plate with a ham sandwich, chips, and a pickle. "Compliments of Sam."

They took their seats, Elizabeth sitting as close to Tom as she could without being on his lap. He loved how she wanted to be as near to him as he wanted to be to her. He wrapped his arm around her shoulders as she ate her sandwich.

"So the next step is to find CJ's brothers," Lelandi said.

"I...think we need to find North." Elizabeth bit off the end of a pickle spear.

"North?" Sam said. "How do you know about him?"

Elizabeth looked at Sam. "My father was in the red pack when Bruin was pack leader."

Lelandi frowned at her. "When? I...never met you."

"I guess I was a well-kept secret. Did you know Sefton? And Quinton?"

"Why, yes. They were in the pack. Quinton's brother was said to have died. That's why Quinton was raising Sefton, his nephew."

Elizabeth stiffened a little. "I guess that explains why the pack never had anything to do with us. We didn't exist. Quinton was my uncle and Sefton my half brother, though he wouldn't wish to admit it to anyone."

"I can't believe they conned all of us. But…you knew North?" Lelandi asked.

"Yeah. I was running in my wolf coat one day, and North followed me home. He was curious about who I belonged to. When he learned I was related to Sefton and Quinton, he was shocked. Quinton found out North was coming to see me and threatened him with bodily harm. That was the last I saw of North. Recently, he discovered evidence that could prove my uncle's part in my parents' murders and learned where I'd ended up. I wanted the evidence to turn over to Hrothgar so my uncle could get his just rewards."

Lelandi shook her head. "If only I'd known." She got her phone out and called someone. "Hello, Uncle? It's me. Lelandi. Yeah, we found Tom. And someone else. Someone related to a couple of people in your pack. Elizabeth Wildwood. She's the half sister to Sefton and she's Quinton's niece. The possibility exists that her uncle murdered her parents. But we don't have the proof. Another of your pack members, North, was supposed to give it to her."

"I haven't been able to get in touch with him," Elizabeth said. "I don't know if he's come to harm or not."

Lelandi passed the information to her uncle. "She's staying with us now. I believe…permanently." She raised her brows at Elizabeth, waiting for confirmation.

Before she could respond, Tom said, "Damn right." He wanted the whole world to know Elizabeth had a home with him, with his pack, that she wasn't going anywhere. She would never again be in a situation where she *didn't exist*.

Elizabeth smiled. "We're…mated, if no one guessed."

Everyone cheered them, then Kemp said, "I don't know what I'm cheering for. Tom got the girl."

Everyone laughed.

Sam's smile faded and he said, "Excuse me for a moment, and don't say anything important until I get back." He walked into the den and pulled out his phone. "Silva? Did you...need any help with the opening of your...tearoom?"

Elizabeth smiled up at Tom. He leaned down and kissed her mouth, glad he hadn't waffled around about wanting Elizabeth for his own.

Lelandi said to her uncle, "Yes, Elizabeth is now part of our pack. Permanently. If you can check into the whereabouts of three of your pack members—North, Sefton, and Quinton—we'll be grateful. Thanks so much. Love you, Uncle." She ended the call.

———————

Elizabeth reached up and clasped her hands around Tom's neck. She kissed him with passion and longing, claiming him for her own in front of some of his pack. It felt good to show off that she was loved and that she loved someone back just as much. That she was mated, but this time to a real wolf who wouldn't stray. That she was accepted for who she was and that her relationship with Tom was just as well received.

No one could take that feeling of elation away from her. She knew mentioning North bothered Tom, but he had nothing to worry about. No one could steal her away now.

Sam returned to the living room, frowning, but he didn't say anything.

"Why go after North first?" Tom asked Elizabeth.

"We need to learn the truth," Elizabeth said, but what concerned her most at this point was whether North was even still alive. "Given North's disappearance, I don't *think* he was involved, but we don't know for sure what part he plays in all this. CJ didn't seem to know if Eric was working with the men who kidnapped me or not. Where were they headed? Must have been somewhere that they could land. One of the kidnappers said they were a half hour from their destination. Unless they were way off course." Elizabeth paused.

"Uncle Hrothgar will put the word out to his pack about the three red wolves. We'll also call the alert roster about them. Anyone who sees any of them will detain them, if they can, or report their whereabouts. We also need to track down CJ's brothers," Lelandi said.

"I can help track them. I want to do this," Elizabeth said.

Tom furrowed his brow, looking concerned.

The front door opened, and Sam and Tom jumped to their feet in protective wolf mode.

"Just us," Darien called out as he shut the door.

"Did you get anything more out of CJ?" Tom asked as his brother entered the living room.

Darien snorted. "That he's sorry he left the pack. I've called in the plane crash. They have investigators coming who will take care of it. I told him you didn't find any survivors, Tom."

"What if they find my ID? Or my deed?" Elizabeth asked.

"Stolen," Darien said. "We'll come up with a story when the time comes."

"Good," Tom said, taking hold of Elizabeth's hand. "We don't want to have to explain to the media how she came to be with the men or how she survived the crash." He took a deep breath. "Elizabeth wants to help track the wolves."

"You mean our cousins, right?" Darien asked.

She stood. "I've done this kind of thing before. I've worked with special teams who search for missing hikers. I'm good at what I do. Of course, most of the teams I worked with didn't know I had a unique ability to smell trails. Some would tease me about being a bloodhound in another life. As if I would have ever been a dog."

That earned a couple of chuckles from the men who had been

with her as she played the perfectly lovable but—according to Tom—disobedient dog.

"Okay, she's with us," Jake said, as if he was in charge instead of Darien.

Darien, however, looked to Tom to see if he was agreeable, which surprised Elizabeth. Why wouldn't the pack leader just make the decision?

"I think she should rest up a bit more from her ordeal," Tom said.

Elizabeth was about to say she'd go it alone if she could help— just to prove her worth because she was desperate to let the others know she really could be an asset to a pack and not just a liability. But before she could respond, Lelandi cleared her throat.

Everyone looked at her. Lelandi said, "She should go. She'll be a welcome resource."

Darien smiled at her. Elizabeth loved the way he treated his alpha-leader mate. Elizabeth couldn't be annoyed with Tom though. She suspected he was just worried about either her previous injuries or the possibility of one of the red wolves injuring or trying to kill her. She *was* a good fighter. She might not be as hefty as a gray wolf, but she had a set of wicked canines and was extremely wily, like a coyote.

"All right," Tom said. "Our team should probably start at Mr. Winston's, see if he knows anything, and then branch out from there."

Darien nodded. "Tomorrow morning. We'll have four tracking teams. I want everyone to report at regular intervals. Oh, and while you were gone, Tom, we met Peter's brother. The guy's likeable. I'll give him that. He said he and his mate are not staying, that they've settled down on the Oregon coast with a gray pack out there. He just wanted to see his brother and have him meet his mate. But he did say he'd like to give us a hand with tracking down these men. His mate, Anna, also wants to help. They should be here any moment."

A knock on the door sounded and Jake said, "Right on time."

He headed for the door and returned with a man and a woman. Elizabeth gaped at Bjornolf Jorgenson. *He* was Sheriff Peter Jorgenson's brother?

"Bjornolf Jorgenson?" He was just as hot as she'd remembered, only his burnt-sienna brown hair was cut short this time, military style. His mouth curved up as he saw her, but a white parka hid his tanned muscles.

"Elizabeth Wildwood, I'll be damned. You get around, woman." He appeared to want to give her a hug, but he glanced at the feral expression on Tom's face and just smiled a little.

"The two of you know each other?" Tom asked, mentioning the obvious and not sounding really comfortable with the notion.

"Yeah," Elizabeth said, slipping her arm around Tom's waist. He reciprocated by wrapping his arm around her shoulders. She hoped he would get over his newly mated possessiveness soon, but she didn't mind for now. Then again, Bjornolf was an unknown to Tom. Not part of his pack. If it had been someone from his pack, he probably would not act as possessively.

"We worked together on locating a kid one time. The boy was autistic and had gotten separated from his parents on a campout. I was doing a story on Palo Duro Canyon, and Bjornolf was there for some reason. He never told me why. He scented what I was right away, of course. He was practically the only male wolf I ever met who didn't act like he wanted to kill me. Prior to coming here."

Bjornolf shook his head and slipped his arm around *his* mate's shoulders.

"That's because he reserves those feelings for *me*." Anna had silky auburn hair tied back in a tail. Her eyes were a lovely shade of green, her smile infectious. She wrapped her arm around Bjornolf's waist.

He laughed, leaned down, and kissed her. "Anna, this is my

tracking partner, Elizabeth Wildwood. Between the two of us, we found the kid. Only he wouldn't come to me."

"You were a much bigger, badass wolf," Elizabeth said.

"You were just a pretty red dog," Bjornolf said, smiling.

"You'd better smile about the dog reference," Elizabeth said. "I didn't know you were Peter's brother."

"I didn't know you knew Peter."

"I didn't. I only just met him a few days ago."

Bjornolf bowed his head a little to Tom. "Will you be on our team?"

Before Tom could say anything, Elizabeth said, "Yes. For old time's sake."

"Jake, Tom, Elizabeth, join me. I need to talk with you," Darien said. "Sam, you want to fix Bjornolf and Anna some lunch? Make them welcome?"

"I'm on it. If…you're discussing the teams." Sam ran his hand through his hair. "Silva wants to go with us. With me. On…the same team. The…two of us."

Darien smiled. "You got it."

He waited for his brothers and Elizabeth to enter his office, then shut his door. "Lelandi wanted to sit this one out because she won't be on the hunt tomorrow and is off to see to the kids. So tell us what's going on, Elizabeth. We've heard bits and pieces, but we need to know everything." He took a seat in a chair in front of the coffee table where two love seats were situated.

———————

Tom sat next to Elizabeth on one of the love seats as Jake sat on the other. Tom pressed his leg against her, unable to keep from showing his possessiveness, despite both brothers being mated wolves. It was just instinctual. He would have held her hand, but she was using her hands to explain her situation, family, what had happened to her up until now. So he just sat close, watching his brothers' expressions, reading them as they listened to all that she had told him already.

Until she came to one minor point. *North Redding*.

Tom turned to look at her. She blushed.

"All right, so for once in my life, a red wolf was interested in me. But he couldn't stand up to my uncle. He didn't protect me from my brother or my uncle."

Tom took Elizabeth's hand and squeezed gently.

Elizabeth continued, "But he said he would give me evidence of my uncle and half brother's involvement in my parents' murders in exchange for me giving him my parents' horse farm. I was willing to do it, since I didn't ever want to go back there. All I want is to see my uncle brought to justice. Anyway, I called North the morning I left here and there was no answer. I'm worried that Quinton might have learned North's plan and gone after him. Or worst-case scenario, they deliberately let him find the evidence and are using him to lure me to them."

Darien nodded grimly. "And we still have CJ's brothers to find. Since you and Tom agreed to go with Bjornolf and Anna, that'll make one team. Peter will head up another. He's taking Radcliff and Kemp and somebody else, whoever he decides on. Trevor will be in charge of a third. He's taking Cantrell and Robert and someone else he chooses. Jake and I will have Sam and Silva on our team."

"Will you be able to manage the two of them on the same team?" Tom asked. "They've been out of sorts with each other, even if there appears to be a truce between them for the moment."

"Yeah," Darien said, "just to ensure they don't kill each other." He took a deep breath. "So the two of you are really mated."

Thrilled that they were, Tom leaned over and kissed Elizabeth's cheek. "Yeah. I had to beg her to mate with me."

Elizabeth cocked a brow at Tom. "Don't believe that. He told me we were mating sooner or later, so just plan for it."

Darien and Jake smiled. "Welcome to the pack, Elizabeth," they both said at the same time.

"Thank you. I have a home in Canyon, Texas, and a job there though." Not that she wanted to go back to it and abandon what she could have here, but she did have to settle things there.

"We'd love for you to start up our first newspaper here," Darien said, jumping right in as if he was afraid he would lose both his brother and Elizabeth to Texas. "Lelandi said she'd love to do a weekly advice column on psychological issues. Silva wants to advertise her new Victorian tearoom. The new owners of the old Silver Town Inn want to too. And Bertha said she'd pay to have her B and B included. Mason said he'd give tips on savings and financial investment tips. I could go on and on. Suffice it to say, everyone's excited about it if you'd like to start up a paper."

Elizabeth couldn't believe it. Before she was even part of the pack, they'd been making plans to include her. "Thank you. I'd love to."

"I was going to look for a house, come spring, but we'll start right away," Tom said, kissing her cheek. "I'll return with you to Canyon to help you get your place ready to sell as soon as we can." Tom asked Darien, "What are we eating tonight?"

Darien looked at Tom like he couldn't fathom why Tom would bring that up right now. Elizabeth also wondered why the interest in dinner. They'd just eaten lunch.

"I believe chicken is on the menu."

"Chicken," Tom said. "Do we have any steaks?"

Elizabeth smiled. "Chicken sounds great."

"I promised you—" Tom said.

Elizabeth shook her head. She didn't want them to hear the whole story of how she'd been taken hostage. "Chicken is fine."

Darien and Jake still waited for an explanation.

Tom cleared his throat. "Elizabeth had bought some steaks at a butcher shop and—"

"It's all right, really," Elizabeth said, taking his hand and squeezing it. If she was going to be alone with Tom, sure, then she'd want steaks. But whatever his family had planned was fine with her.

"She lost them when they took her hostage," Tom said, sounding angry now that they had kidnapped her. "I promised her when we reached your place, I'd fix her a steak."

Darien and Jake smiled.

"Yeah, steaks. Yeah, that's what really appeals to me," Darien said. "You, Jake?"

"I'm always interested in a tender, juicy steak."

Elizabeth felt her face flush with heat. "I was just a little angry that I'd paid for the steaks, good price too, and…" She shrugged. "Lost them."

"Whatever you'd like is fine with all of us. That's about all I have to say about the tracking tomorrow. We'll get together for dinner in a few hours, call it a night early, and leave before dawn," Darien said.

CHAPTER 26

As soon as Darien ended the talk, Tom sequestered Elizabeth in his bedroom, and she knew they hadn't come up here merely to take a wolfish nap.

She noted he didn't have antique furniture like in her guest room. Everything was modern. A dark chocolate-brown padded headboard stretched halfway up the wall. A white duvet covered a king-sized bed, and a brown satin padded bench sat at the foot of the bed. The covers were in disarray, half tossed over the bench and half on the floor.

"Restless night?" she asked.

"Woke really late and worried about you, then found you were MIA the next morning."

"Ah." She didn't want to get into that again. She'd disappeared on him, and she guessed he'd left to look for the rogue wolves after that and didn't have time to clean up.

Two large, matching armless chairs were situated one on either side of an entertainment center—wide-screen TV, computer, and stereo. A thick, plush brown carpet made her want to kick off her shoes and roll around on the floor because it looked so cushiony soft.

She toed off the slipper boots.

"Are you sure you trust Bjornolf?" Tom asked, closing the door behind them as she looked at the rest of his bedroom and saw one of the pictures she'd taken at the ski slopes framed and sitting on his dresser. He cleared his throat. "Jake must have had the picture turned into a print. To remind me to chase you down."

She chuckled. "I doubt you needed the reminder."

"I didn't."

"As for Bjornolf, yeah, I'd trust him with my life. He's a retired SEAL, you know. Anna works on 'projects' with him. I suspect both of them know lethal moves without even turning into a wolf."

Tom laughed, turned on some soft instrumental music, then raised the volume.

"What's so funny?"

Tom joined Elizabeth and wrapped his arms around her back. He slowly danced to the music with her. "Peter thought his brother had been involved in illegal operations all this time. He said he caught the two of them sparring in the guest bedroom of his home. We all thought it was a case of mate abuse."

She laughed. "I guess they were keeping in shape."

"*Speaking* of keeping in shape..."

Elizabeth had never danced with a wolf before, and she loved Tom's moves as he held her close, rubbing his body against hers and claiming her, just as she was claiming him back. "Great dancer."

"Hmm," Tom responded, his hands slipping all over her back, sliding the soft wool sweater against her skin. His warm hands slid up her sweater, his fingers pausing at her bra. He smiled. "Did you find it in my room?"

"I had to look a bit. It was tucked away in your underwear drawer between two pairs of black briefs."

"See how I even share my drawers with you?"

She smiled and rubbed her body against his, loving the feel of his cock coming to life, firm, ready. "I love how much you share every bit of you with me."

That earned her a smile. He leaned down and nuzzled his face against her cheek, lower until he could kiss her neck, her throat, her breasts. At the same time, his fingers unfastened her bra at the back. When he straightened, she pressed harder against his erection, wanting to feel his firmness, touch him, caress him, take him inside her.

He groaned as she moved her pelvis, grinding against him.

He slid his hands around to her waist, traveling up her skin and making her tremble with expectation. She loved how he responded, his heated gaze, his hot touch. His fingertips traced the wire cups of her bra, but then he pushed it out of his way and cupped her breasts with his hands, the sweater still covering her.

His mouth was on hers, not soft and gentle and refined but taking what he wanted—knowing she craved the same. The lust driving them both. The need to conquer and possess, to fulfill the hunger that chased them.

Her sex was already aching for completion, and she was wet for him. His eyes were filled with desire, his lips insistent, his tongue stroking the inside of her mouth. She savored the feel, sucked on his tongue, and made the big gray wolf groan with entreaty. And she loved it.

His hands slid around her back again, lower and lower until they were on her buttocks. He pulled her hard against him, making her feel his feral need for her.

She didn't hear the music any longer. Their feet were still walking to the beat on the soft plush carpet, but she concentrated on how he made her body turn into a burning furnace. He unzipped her pants, plunged his hand into her panties, and felt the wetness between her legs, then smiled.

An all-knowing, smug smile. He might make her wet, but she made him rock hard. She slid her hand over his jeans and the rigid bulge eager for release and stroked, telling him she wanted him. His kisses grew more urgent, his hands tightening his hold on her ass. He was about ready to strip, forget the foreplay, and get on with business.

She thought she heard him mutter how hot she was, and then he pulled off her sweater and her bra. He tossed them to the floor, then yanked off his own sweater and shirt. She loved the way he made her feel desirable, wanted, needed. Growling low with a little bit of a purr, she ran her fingers over his chest. She felt his sleek, warm, hard muscles under the palms of her hands and saw how his nipples pebbled.

She hadn't been able to see him like this, hadn't been up this close to touch him—every bit of him—without being buried beneath blankets and covers to keep the chill out. The room was comfortably warm, though she was burning up as she skimmed her hand over his skin, feeling his muscles, smelling his hot, musky all-man scent. He encouraged her to take her pleasure first, experiencing how her hands slid over him while she cherished him.

That didn't last long as his mouth drew down to hers, slanting over her lips, his hands now cupping her naked breasts. His tongue licked the seam of her mouth as she attempted to unzip his pants. He slid his tongue into her mouth again. She concentrated on pulling his jeans away from his lean hips, trying to enjoy the way he invaded her with his tongue and sent her senses reeling.

She struggled, tugging at his jeans, wanting to stroke that enticing part of him that his pants and boxers still held hostage.

She managed to jerk his jeans down to his knees and reached for his boxers. His alpha wolf came into play. He kicked off his jeans and quickly dispensed with hers. Her panties and his boxers hit the floor next.

Naked, skin to skin, he continued to slow dance with her, his hot, hard body rubbing against hers. She was in heaven as she raised her arms and looped them around his neck, letting her breasts skim his chest, her hips swaying, her mound rubbing against his full-blown erection.

His darkened brown eyes were clouded with lust as he stroked her back with his large hands, sliding them down until he cupped her buttocks again. She felt his whole body tense right before he lifted her, and she wrapped her legs around him. He slowly carried her to the bed, kissing her, loving her.

He was a wolf dream come true.

He set her on the bed, but she didn't release him, her legs wrapped around his hips, and he smiled. More than one way to do this, she thought his expression said.

He slipped his hand down to her wet sex and stroked her nub until she released him. She moved onto the mattress, wanting him on the bed with her. Like a predator wolf approaching his mate, ready for a joining, he prowled across the mattress to reach her. His fingers renewed their strokes, his free hand pushing her legs apart.

He was so beautifully naked, the light hair trailing down his torso to his pubic hair, his cock jutting out so proud and large and eager to please and take pleasure.

She dug her heels into the mattress, enraptured with the way he was making her feel—the joy, the headiness, her body thrumming with pleasure.

She let out a small cry as the fireworks showered her with hot, warm gratification. He wasn't done as he lifted her legs over his shoulders and separated her with his fingers, stroking as she writhed to his touch, waves of renewed carnal need washing over her.

He replaced his fingers with his cock, burying it deep, seating himself. He pulled out and thrust again. He pounded against her ass, his muscles straining as he worked up the heat, their breathing heavy, the smell of wolfish sex permeating the air.

"Beautiful," he managed to say, his voice ragged as he climaxed, the tremors of her own orgasm clutching at him.

He sank down on top of her, his face buried between her breasts, his breath warm against her skin, his tongue licking the valley. "Salty and sweet." After a moment, he added, "And spicy."

Sometime later, Elizabeth woke in Tom's arms in his bed, the covers over them, and she realized they'd fallen asleep for a couple of hours. "Do you think your cousins might be changing their minds about joining the pack?"

"Maybe. They would be mad at all of us—Jake and me, Darien, and Lelandi. Probably Peter too, since he took their father's place as sheriff. I don't know if they're out looking for CJ or if that's just CJ's wishful thinking. I'm worried that they might have turned tail and given up on trying to come back to the pack."

"You think they'd leave CJ?"

"I wouldn't want to think so, but I wouldn't think Eric would entertain notions of helping kidnappers just to get back at us either."

"Too bad I wasn't able to track them while we were in the forest."

He pulled her tighter into his arms. "Best little tracker in Colorado."

"And Oklahoma and Texas. Not that I'm bragging," she said with a smile.

He kissed her forehead and smiled a little, but a crease marred his brow.

"What's wrong?"

"I wonder what evidence North could have of your uncle's involvement in your parents' murders."

"He wouldn't tell me. I think he wanted to see me."

Tom scowled at that. "I suspect to convince you to stay with him. What triggered the killings? Do you have any idea?"

She took a deep breath and let it out. "My parents were getting ready to celebrate my sixteenth birthday." She gave a soft snort. "Sweet sixteen and I didn't have any friends around my age to celebrate it. You know what my father gave me? I mean, it was sweet, but not exactly what I had expected."

Tom caressed her arm and shook his head.

"A boot knife. To protect myself with. Like I said, it was sweet of him to worry about me, probably because of the trouble I'd had with wolves who didn't like what I was. But still, I was thinking more of a mare. A boot knife? I was away from home both days when they were murdered. If I had been there either day…" She shuddered.

Tom rubbed her arm. "Your father wasn't home when your mother was murdered?"

"No. He had broken some horses for someone, and he went to deliver them. I was at the mercantile that day, picking up some goods my mother wanted. I–I returned home after my father did and found him in a state. He was just numb. I've never seen him so…shocked. He wouldn't let me see her body. He buried her alone. I had…a sense that he knew who had done it. I asked, but he just shook his head.

"Two days later, he sent me into town for some supplies. I–I didn't want to go. He insisted I take the boot knife with me. He was acting really strange. I wanted him to go with me. But he said he needed me to do it. I begged him to go with me. I was scared. I didn't take the knife with me. I hadn't wanted it. When I was halfway to town, I almost turned around. I had like a sixth sense something bad would happen."

"He was meeting someone. Meeting the person he suspected killed your mother. Family," Tom guessed.

"I think so. He didn't want to tell me. I believe he confronted whoever it was, and that person got the best of him. He was stabbed to death. It was awful. Maybe that's what had happened to my mother and that's why my dad didn't want me to see her. I was terrified. I was certain whoever had done it would want me dead next. North arrived and—"

"North?"

"Yeah, he was excited and said he had something for my birthday, but he needed to speak to my dad first. Then he must have seen my tears and how distraught I was. Once he learned my dad had been murdered, North never said anything more about my birthday and the two of us quickly buried my dad. He helped me pack, and I planned to take the remaining five horses and sell them. I still own the property, but I used the money from the sale of the horses to buy a small house out of the pack territory and lived there for a while. Then I moved to Oklahoma, close to my mother's family, and from there to Texas."

"Okay, back up a moment," Tom said. "You didn't smell who killed your mother? Back then, no one would have had hunter's spray to use."

"My dad wouldn't tell me where he'd found her. I was caught in a torrential downpour before I made it home with the goods for my mother. My dad had been outside, probably trying to calm one of our more skittish mares. I–I did smell a hint of what I thought might have been my uncle's and Sefton's scents. But I couldn't be sure. Not with the way the rains had washed everything away. Since I suspected they had a hand in it, I thought I might have imagined it."

"So nothing triggered your mother's killing that you knew of? If your father confronted the killer, that would explain his death."

"The only thing I remember that seemed significant was that I'd had my birthday."

"And the boot knife you got."

She thought about that for a moment. "I wasn't really grateful… I mean, I tried to show how much I loved it. But it was a stretch. I wanted a mare. Once I found my dad…" She shook her head. "I didn't appreciate why he wanted me to have it until I had to leave and I wanted to have it for protection. Only I couldn't find it. Dad had another. I took his and the rifle he owned, and North gave me his boot knife. I didn't think I needed another, but he insisted."

"The one your father gave you—was it new? Or something passed down through the family?"

"Passed down from my father's grandfather. It had a lovely bone handle, but still…"

"You wanted a horse."

She nodded, feeling guilty about it still. "I was in such a rush to leave and so distraught that I didn't think anything of it. I just wanted to get weapons, some clothes, food, the horses, and leave."

"Do you think the killer had it? Used it?"

Elizabeth closed her eyes. She didn't want to think that her father giving her his treasured family heirloom had resulted in her mother's and father's murders.

"Would either your half brother or uncle have known that your father gave it to you?"

"They might have talked about it. I could see my uncle being upset that my father, who was the firstborn of the two, had gotten it from their father and then passed it down to me instead of Sefton. Uncle Quinton…might have even asked my father when he would give it to Sefton."

Tom kissed her cheek. "I can't imagine how hard that would have been for you." Tom took a deep breath. "I need to discuss something else with you though. Jake said you interviewed him for a story. He didn't tell me right away, afraid I'd be upset you'd talked with him at length and hadn't said a word to me before you left."

She snuggled against him. "I did conduct an interview with him early that morning, all about his photography. He left to be with his wife. Darien and Lelandi came downstairs for breakfast. Jake's article won't be published until next week."

"We didn't know that."

Elizabeth barely breathed. Had Tom and Jake been looking for her article and come across the one she had written about coyotes and wolves? She hadn't wanted *them* to read the article. Sure it was available online, but she hadn't thought they would have looked for Jake's interview already and found her other article.

Tom stroked her hair. "Gray wolves came first."

She thought she heard a hint of amusement in his tone of voice and looked up at him. He gave her a smug smile, as though he was delighted to learn that he and his gray wolves had been right.

Her stomach tightening, she worried how Lelandi would view it. "You won't tell Lelandi, will you?"

"She found the article first."

Her heart sinking, Elizabeth groaned. "I never meant for her to learn of it. I'm so sorry that she saw what I'd written."

"Don't be, Elizabeth. If she has some coyote roots, she says that makes the two of you even more like sisters. She's very happy for that."

Elizabeth took a deep, grateful breath. The reason she had made the trip to Silver Town in the first place was to make things right concerning her rotten uncle, and she had ended up finding a home, a pack, and a mate who gave her a whole new outlook on her kind.

Not that they didn't still have real problems.

CHAPTER 27

EARLY THE NEXT MORNING, THE BITTER COLD AND north-chilled breeze stirred up the snow, creating a white mist-like world as Minx, Cody, and Anthony trudged along in their snowshoes to reach Mr. Winston's house out in the country. Like the others in the pack, they were homeschooled. Some of the pack members had better teaching skills than others, and Mr. Winston was the best calculus teacher anyone could want.

"You know our parents won't be happy with us if they learn we're headed out this far when they think we're skiing at the resort," Minx said to Cody and Anthony as the two boys hauled a sled carrying groceries—bread, milk, OJ, tuna fish, and a few other items they thought Mr. Winston might need.

"So we don't tell them. If Old Man Winston lets it slip, we'll at least have done the deed, and what would they say about it then?" Cody asked, his jester ski hat jingling with every step he took. "It'll be too late."

"It won't be too late to ground us," Minx warned.

"You didn't have to come with us," Anthony said.

"Of course I did."

They both looked back at her. She couldn't keep up with their longer stride, no matter how hard she tried, even though *they* were pulling the sled. But Anthony and Cody were always thinking up new schemes, and Minx wouldn't be left out of an adventure for anything. She liked old Mr. Winston too and was just as worried that he couldn't get into town to replenish his food when the snowstorm had hit. Not that several members of the wolf pack hadn't offered to help him out. He had his pride. Since they were just kids, they figured he wouldn't mind them bringing him food and giving him some company. As long as they didn't have to do any math problems while they visited.

Cody and Anthony smiled at her.

"Your parents are betas," Anthony said to Minx, continuing to move through the deep snowdrifts. "You never get into trouble. When we all fell off that cliff that time, I figured you'd get grounded forever since you're a girl."

"Nah, not Minx," Cody said. "Not even for one hour."

"Like the two of *you* should talk. Your parents didn't punish either of you."

"That's only because we promised we'd never do it again. Otherwise? Dad said he would have had us mucking out Doc Mitchell's horse stalls for two months."

"Well, you *didn't* have to clean out the vet's stalls." Minx stopped in her tracks. "How much farther is it? I don't remember Mr. Winston's home being this far out."

"In the spring, it isn't. Or at least it doesn't feel like it. Trudging through powder snow, it is," Cody said.

Minx waded through the snow after the brothers again, trying to think about anything other than how much this was wearing her out. "I like Elizabeth."

Neither Cody nor Anthony made a comment.

Minx let out her breath. She was still thinking about meeting Elizabeth at the ski resort when she remembered something. "My dad thinks Eric Silver was at the ski resort."

Cody glanced over his shoulder. "Why does he think that? They left the pack months ago."

Minx wasn't sure if her dad knew what he was talking about either. But what if he did?

"Okay, so how does he know?" Cody finally asked.

"Well, my dad's not sure, but he thought he saw Eric in the men's room at the ski resort after he dropped me off there to join the two of you. Eric, if it was him, was moving really fast and had his mask down for only a moment. Dad only got a glimpse of his profile. Dad was a little surprised to see him, thinking the brothers had moved far away. But he could have sworn it was him."

"Did your dad tell Darien?" Anthony asked.

"Of course, but because he couldn't be certain and because the Silvers have no idea where their cousins are staying, there wasn't much they could do about. Hey, is that smoke? Yes! We're getting closer."

She stopped again. "Cody," she whispered, since he was closer to her than Anthony.

Both brothers stopped to look at her.

She pointed to wolf tracks in the snow.

Per Darien's orders, all the searchers would remain in human form. Darien worried that the farmers or ranchers in the area would find out about the hunt for the wolves and try to tag along, although Elizabeth would have preferred tracking as a wolf. On Elizabeth and Tom's team, Bjornolf and Anna had split off in another direction to look for any wolf or human footprints.

"Were your cousins really well liked?" she asked Tom.

"Yeah, they were. Everyone felt really bad about their dad. And about them leaving."

"So it makes sense that Mr. Winston would give them a place to stay while they figured out how they wanted to attempt to return."

"I guess so," Tom said. "But Mr. Winston probably would have told them that we weren't mad at them and would have welcomed them back, so the fact that Eric was so against just coming clean from the start makes me worry they're up to something. And now that they've put the pack in danger, they've actually hurt their chances."

Elizabeth wished they could spread out a bit, but he wouldn't leave her for a second, and she knew he still worried someone might attack her.

"Lelandi is the psychologist in the family. What has she said about any of this?" Elizabeth examined a cluster of spruce branches, noticing some of the snow had been brushed off as if someone had walked into them recently. It could have been a searcher, but then again, Bjornolf and Anna were farther away, and the other search teams even more spread out. This was really recent, new snow-flakes not having had time to cover the blue-green needles again.

Her heart sped up a little.

"Lelandi says it's possible they're acting out. Or maybe seeking revenge for their dad. Or they might not even be involved in any of this, like CJ said."

"Or they just want attention."

"It's one damn stupid way of getting it," he said, glancing in her direction.

Elizabeth understood his anger, the betrayal, only too deeply. She turned away from him and studied a footprint in the snow, sit-uated among the branches of the spruce. "Haven't you ever done anything to get someone's attention and afterward you regretted it? Some will do anything to get some notice, negative or other-wise. Since they're angry that your brother put their father down, maybe they've been fuming about this and lashed out."

"It's dangerous for the pack. We can't have our farmers reach-ing for their guns every time they see a wolf in a wolf-run town. We might have welcomed them back before, but now I don't know if we want to have pack members whose decisions place all of us in danger," Tom said, joining her as she measured her boot size with the one left in the snow.

"Man's, recent," she said. "He stood here, hiding among the branches of this spruce tree."

Tom pulled his rifle off his shoulder and searched around the trees.

Someone was hiding nearby, listening, watching. If it was one of Tom's cousins, she desperately wanted to talk him into giving himself up.

"They had a pack. They can't let go of it. They want to be part of it again, but they don't know how to come back and still save face," she said.

Tom moved off into the trees, but Elizabeth didn't follow him. He quickly came back for her. "Aren't you coming?"

"They deserve a second chance, Tom. Maybe some intervention sessions with Lelandi. I never had a pack to grow up with. I only had my mother and father to learn from. I can only guess what it would be like for them to play and fight and be part of a pack growing up—and then lose their father, you and your brothers, and the rest of the pack all at once. Let them return to the pack. Show them what you've all shown me—tolerance, acceptance, and unconditional love."

Tom looked around at the ground, searching for more footprints. "It's up to Darien to make a decision like that." His expression tight, Tom stalked across the snow, shouldering his rifle. He took Elizabeth into his arms and hugged her tight. He whispered into her ear, "They're here, aren't they? Listening."

She nodded, tears misting her eyes. She never cried if she could help it, and she'd been more misty-eyed around Tom and his pack than she wanted to admit. "You wanted to protect them, Tom. They knew if anyone would listen to them, it would be you. What they did *was* stupid. It all needs to end now."

Tom gazed into her eyes. He shook his head. "You're beautiful, you know? Inside and out. Despite all you've been through."

"CJ turned himself in."

"That was *only* because he stepped into the trap and couldn't run any farther."

"I think my charging after him, growling and snapping, spooked him. I think he came to see you when you were gathering kindling like he said, trying to find a way to get your attention and show you he didn't mean you any harm. Only…I sort of ruined it by suddenly coming on the scene."

Tom heaved a deep breath but didn't say anything. He wasn't convinced yet.

"Let them come in on their own and square things with Darien and Lelandi. Get back to being a pack. I like CJ. I want to have the biggest family I can have."

Tom smiled at her, holding her still, looking down at her with wonder and admiration. "It won't be easy. For any of us."

"Time will heal."

"But not in your uncle's case," Tom said vehemently. "That bastard will pay for attempting to kill you."

"I also want to know if he murdered my parents. I want the proof, and Hrothgar can deal with him. As harshly as he sees fit." Quinton didn't deserve anything better.

Movement by one of the trees made Tom raise his rifle as Elizabeth turned to see who it was.

"Brett," Tom said, sounding surprised, despite having assumed that one of his cousins was nearby.

Brett was wearing a white parka and ski pants that made him blend in with the snow, with only a hint of dark bangs showing beneath the hood of his coat and dark-brown eyes. He studied Tom, waiting to see his response. He had Tom's stern jaw, and she wondered if when he smiled, his expression would be similar to Tom's.

Bjornolf and Anna came behind Brett, weapons pointed at the ground.

"We were watching him," Bjornolf said, "while he listened to the two of you talk. I didn't know what was going on until I realized you knew he was there."

"Thanks, Bjornolf, Anna," Tom said, then turned his attention on his cousin. "Where are your brothers?"

"They're not here. We spread out so that we won't get caught in a cluster. We knew you were searching for us, so we split up. We've been trying to find the damned wolves scaring the livestock. It wasn't us. But we knew you'd suspect us first. We've tried damned hard to find the bastards and turn them over to Darien."

"Why did you keep CJ out of this?" Tom asked, sounding suspicious.

"Hell, Tom. You know him. The minute he left the pack, he regretted it. He had his own ideas about how to get back in with the pack. Took us a lot longer to come to terms with everything. We know Darien had no other choice, but still..." Brett took a settling breath. "You're still family, our pack. We knew the farmers would hunt any wolf, and one of our people could be killed. We had to hunt the rogue wolves ourselves. Prove that we weren't anything like our dad."

Elizabeth felt all misty-eyed again.

"All right, say I take your word for it. But CJ said he overheard Eric talking to the guy who kidnapped Elizabeth. Did you know about that?"

Brett creased his forehead. "No, Eric never told us what they talked about. But I suspected that guy was up to no good."

"Do you have any clues?"

Brett snorted. "They're red wolves. They use hunter's spray. We saw the three of them clustered in the distance, spooking some calves. They're big wolves, but they're definitely reds. We took chase, but they disappeared into the mountains. Easy to do when we couldn't scent them."

"You wore hunter's scent camouflage too," Tom accused.

"Hell, yeah. If we hadn't, you would have only smelled *our* scents at the farms. That would have assured you we were the culprits."

"What now?" Tom asked.

"I'll go into town. Settle the score with Darien. Where's CJ?"

"Injured, leg trap. Doc's taking care of him."

Elizabeth saw the concern wash over Brett's face.

Tom turned to Bjornolf and Anna. "Take him into town, will you?"

"What? I'm being treated like a prisoner?"

"Let's just say that until Darien has a talk with you, this is the way it's going down."

Brett shook his head. "So who are *you*?" Brett asked Bjornolf. "I've never seen the two of you in the pack before. Leave for a short time and everything changes."

"Sheriff Peter Jorgenson's brother, Bjornolf."

"He's a retired Navy SEAL," Anna said.

"Damn, I didn't know Peter had a brother who was a SEAL. I thought you were trouble."

"I am…for the bad guys."

Brett chuckled, but Elizabeth thought the amusement was a little strained. "Didn't know they sent you guys on missions like this."

"I owed Peter big-time for not keeping in touch. See you later," Bjornolf said to Elizabeth and Tom, and the three of them headed back through the woods in the direction of the town.

"He sounded sincere," Elizabeth said to Tom, searching for new tracks, smelling the breeze, looking for any signs Brett's brothers had been with him at some point.

"Could be. But why were the red wolves causing trouble for us?" Tom asked.

"The guys who kidnapped me were red wolves. I was able to smell them once their hunter's spray wore off after we'd been flying for a few hours. They have to be the same ones."

"If they're the ones who kidnapped you, why would they want to harass our farmers?"

"What if they instigated the situation with the farmers to distract the pack from North and me? It's clever, really. They created a situation that not only kept the pack occupied but made the farmers antsy *specifically* about wolves, thus making Darien want to limit the pack's shifting," Elizabeth said.

"So they thought that by distracting us with the farmer problem, they could slip under our radar and get away with stealing your deed and North's evidence," Tom said, nodding. "But they weren't planning on you and me getting involved."

Tom cast her an elusive smile.

She kissed his cold cheek. "You're right. And all this time, you were tracking down your cousins and not the wolves actually spooking the livestock."

"I suppose so. But we still don't know for sure if Eric is up to something."

"True," Elizabeth agreed.

Not finding any sign of the others, she and Tom had been walking for about an hour when she paused, spying a footprint half-hidden by snow. "There." She pointed to another place beneath a tree about three hundred yards from the other. "Smaller boot. Wait a minute. Look at the track marks. Somebody's been hauling something fairly heavy." She studied the snowshoe prints. "Three people. A girl and two men."

"A girl? Silva's out here. Anna too, but she was with us." Tom studied the girl's footprints. "Small. Lightweight. She sat down over here and took off the snowshoes, then continued to walk without them."

Elizabeth sniffed the air. "Minx?"

Tom sampled the air. "Cody and Anthony are with her. I bet none of them had permission to come out here. Not with the problems we've had with the rogue wolves. The boys haven't given the pack any grief in the past six months, and next year, they're supposed to work as ski instructors. We hoped that would give them enough to do to keep them focused and out of trouble."

"They're good kids," Elizabeth said. "It looks like Cody and

Anthony pulled a sled…" Elizabeth paused and turned, looking off to the side where the girl's footprints stopped. "Wolf tracks, Tom." She felt a chill race up her spine. Whoever hauled the sled had left it some feet from the first sign of the wolf prints.

"Darien said no one was supposed to be in wolf form," Tom said.

"Groceries and one set of snow…wait, three sets of snow-shoes," she whispered, getting a really bad feeling about this.

———————

Tom wanted Elizabeth to stay with the groceries, but he couldn't leave her alone. And he didn't want her to continue following the tracks in case they came across real trouble. When Bjornolf and Anna had been with them, that was one thing. Tom had felt a sense of security when he'd thought the rest of his cousins would also turn themselves in.

Tom and Elizabeth followed the trail, both of them trying to be as quiet as possible. The kids wouldn't have left the groceries behind unless they had run into trouble or had gone after the wolf tracks quietly, trying not to catch anyone's attention.

They should have returned to Silver Town at once with word of what they'd found. Not that Tom or his brothers wouldn't have done the same thing when they were the kids' ages.

Elizabeth whispered to Tom, "Any reason they would be haul-ing groceries this way?"

"Nothing here but Mr. Winston's house. He lives way out. He's a wolf, but when he got cut off from the pack during the snow-storm, he said he didn't need any help. Looks like the kids thought to take something to him anyway."

"But the wolf tracks?" she asked, glancing at Tom.

He shook his head. "The house is just beyond those trees. The kids wouldn't have left the groceries back there without some good reason. Like they were in trouble. Or Mr. Winston was."

"We should get backup, or I should shift," Elizabeth said.

Tom listened for any sounds of people or wolves moving about in the trees. Nothing. "Let's get closer to the house. Mr. Winston should be the only one there, except for the kids."

"Unless your other two cousins are here. Brett said they had split up, but I'd assumed he meant they were all out looking for CJ."

"Yeah," Tom said.

Moving in closer, Tom and Elizabeth used the shelter of the snow-laden spruce to study the one-story log cabin. The living room curtains were open, smoke drifting out of the stone chimney, lights on in the living room and kitchen. Eric paced across the living-room floor.

"Eric," Tom said.

Of all the cousins, Eric was the tallest, six one, and the most muscled. He wore a gray sweatshirt and jeans and appeared highly agitated.

A girl wearing a bright-blue sweater and with blond hair in braids crossed in front of the kitchen window. She peeked outside, turned, and walked out of view.

"Minx," Tom said under his breath. Something had to be wrong. The kids wouldn't leave the groceries out here without having a good reason. They wouldn't have forgotten them. "Damn. Cody and Anthony must also be in there."

"Eric and his brother wouldn't hurt the kids, would they?" Elizabeth asked, her voice soft and concerned.

"No. But why would the kids leave the groceries in the snow—" Another man crossed the living-room floor. Not Eric's brother Sarandon. And it wasn't Mr. Winston. Tom didn't know the gray-haired man.

"My Uncle Quinton," Elizabeth whispered, her rosy cheeks losing all their color as a shudder ran through her.

Was Eric working with Quinton?

CHAPTER 28

ELIZABETH'S BROW WAS FURROWED DEEPLY, AND TOM SAW THE fear in her expression as they crouched in the trees surrounding Mr. Winston's house. He reached out and touched her cheek with his gloved hand. "I don't know what's going on. Maybe Eric was caught unaware and taken hostage." Though he didn't look like it. "I...don't...can't believe my cousin is in cahoots with your uncle. I want you to return to town for help."

"You can't confront them alone." Elizabeth was ready to give him hell if Tom even thought to do so.

"I won't. As long as everyone seems relatively at ease, I'll leave them alone and just keep an eye on them. If anyone exits the house, I'll make plans. But I want you safely in town."

She glanced at the small shed where Mr. Winston kept his tools and gardening supplies. "I could shift and wait with you here."

"No, Elizabeth. I want you as far away from your uncle as possible." Just thinking of her being anywhere near the bastard gave him heart palpitations. "We need reinforcements."

The front door squeaked open. Tom's heart pounded faster. They turned to see who had opened the door. North and Minx. North sported a black eye and it was half-shut.

A chill slid up Tom's spine as he watched Minx with North. How many were in the house? He had to get Minx away from North.

North shut the door behind him and followed Minx through the fresh tracks, directly toward Tom and Elizabeth.

"What will we do now?" Elizabeth whispered.

New plan. His blood pumping furiously, Tom grabbed

Elizabeth's hand and squeezed, hoping this worked. "Elizabeth, I'll take out North. You grab Minx and take her home. And get help."

From Elizabeth's reluctance, Tom could tell she didn't want to leave him. She finally nodded and squeezed his hand back.

Minx looked furious. She swung her arms back and forth, matching the pace of her hat's swinging pom-poms as she stalked through the snow. "Darien will make you all pay for this."

"I haven't done anything wrong," North growled.

"You're going along with the others, and that means you're in the wrong as much as they are. You can help us stop this before it's too late."

"Just tell me where that sled is and—" North didn't say another word except, "Oof," as Tom lunged for him and slammed the butt of his rifle against North's temple, knocking him out.

Elizabeth had moved just as swiftly to clamp her hand over Minx's mouth and muffle the scream that escaped.

"Oh, oh, oh," Minx whispered after Elizabeth let go, tears collecting in her eyes. "I am so glad to see you."

"Shh," Elizabeth whispered, giving the girl a quick hug. "How many others are in the house?"

"Eric, Cody, and Anthony, and Mr. Winston. And some guy named Quinton." Minx looked at North as Tom dragged him to the sled. "And him."

Tom untied the ropes keeping the food on the sled, then whispered, "Help me dump the groceries."

Elizabeth and Minx assisted him in turning the sled over, depositing the groceries into the snow. Using the ropes, Tom tied North to the sled. "Change of plans. You and Minx take North back to town with you."

"Okay," Elizabeth said.

"I don't want to leave Anthony and Cody," Minx said, tears streaking her red cheeks.

Elizabeth gave her a hug. "I don't want to leave them either, but we won't do them any good if we stay here. Let's go before my uncle Quinton wonders what's taking you and North so long. We'll send help."

Glad Elizabeth wouldn't argue with him any further about staying here with him, Tom embraced her and kissed her lips. Afterward, he gave Minx a reassuring hug. "Take care of each other. I'll be waiting."

"No heroics," Elizabeth said, frowning at him.

"Only if I don't need to be a hero."

———————

Elizabeth reluctantly nodded, hating to leave him behind, but she didn't want Minx to be in any danger either. She and Minx took hold of the tow rope and moved as quickly as they could through the snowdrifts.

"Why do they want you?" Minx asked.

Elizabeth said, "Shh, Minx. We need to be really quiet all the way back to town."

If Tom's other cousin, Sarandon, wasn't with Eric, he could very well be out in the woods somewhere. Maybe he and Eric hadn't planned to have a truce with Darien and the pack. Or they had changed their minds.

The going was slow as they lugged the sled. Elizabeth wished they could move faster, but leaving North behind with Tom would have been a mistake. If North came to and yelled for help while Tom watched the house, Tom would have to face down at least three of them—Eric, North, and Quinton. Maybe Eric's other brother and her half brother too.

Minx's comment continued to plague Elizabeth as they trudged through the snow, and she finally whispered to the girl, "What do you mean that *they* wanted me?"

"North arrived at Mr. Winston's house right after we did,"

Minx said, her voice ragged as she tugged the sled with Elizabeth and they tried to move as fast they could. "Eric was already there. Mr. Winston let North in, and then Quinton and some other guy barged into Mr. Winston's house waving guns. I guess they had followed North. Quinton said that North would pay for having brought you here and the plane going down. Then Eric got really mad and punched North in the eye."

"Eric did?"

"Yeah. He said that was for thinking he'd want to get back at the Silver Pack. He said he'd kill North for nearly getting you killed. North said he didn't know what Eric was talking about and that he'd been in hiding from Quinton. He said Quinton was the one who had you kidnapped," Minx explained breathlessly.

"How did North end up at Mr. Winston's?" Elizabeth asked.

"It sounded like North found out Eric and his brothers were looking for you because they had been asking about you at the ski resort. North had followed them to Mr. Winston's place to ask them if they knew where you were."

"That must be why Eric thought North was the one who had hired kidnappers," Elizabeth said.

Minx nodded. "Then the other guy who came with Quinton—no one ever said his name—asked why we were there. Said he figured a bunch of teens wouldn't come out all this way for nothing." Minx paused to get her breath.

"We had to tell him about the groceries. We hoped if anyone saw them there, they'd know someone was in trouble," she said.

"We assumed as much."

"But...what happened? Were you really in an accident?"

"Yes." But Elizabeth didn't want to discuss that now. "What happened after you told him about the groceries?"

"Quinton told North and me to go get them. And not to do anything stupid."

"Like run away?"

"Yeah."

They walked for another good twenty minutes. Elizabeth's mind continued to run through all that had been said and not said. "The other man. What did he look like?"

"Ohh," North groaned.

Elizabeth glanced back at him. His eyes were still closed, but he began to stir. She whispered to Minx, "Keep moving."

"What...what happened?" North mumbled.

This wouldn't do. If he started yelling, they'd be done for.

Elizabeth stopped pulling the sled and hurried around to the left side of it. She unwrapped her long woolen scarf from around her neck and was about to tie it around his mouth when he opened his eyes and narrowed them.

"Elizabeth. I'm...I'm on your side."

"Maybe you are, but I can't trust you right now." She tied the scarf around his mouth, then returned to Minx, whose eyes were huge. Elizabeth tugged on the rope. "Come on. Let's go, Minx."

They hadn't trudged very far when Elizabeth thought she saw movement beyond one of the spruces. Adrenaline shot through her veins. A wolf, she thought.

In a rush, she began removing her gloves, hat, and parka and piling them on the sled.

"What are you doing?" Minx whispered.

"Shifting." *If* Elizabeth could only strip out of her clothes fast enough. Her wolf teeth, stealth, and speed were the only protection she could offer to keep Minx safe. "Keep moving toward town. If you can't pull him," she whispered to Minx, her teeth chattering from the cold as she removed her sweater, "leave him and get to the nearest safe place from here." She fully intended to watch Minx's back while she attempted to track down whoever was out here with them.

"Darien's house," Minx said.

"Yes," Elizabeth said, peeling off the last sock. *Cold...cold.* "Go."

Elizabeth shifted into her wolf form, thankful for her winter-coat protection. The warmth surrounded her so quickly that she nearly forgot she'd been freezing seconds earlier.

She bounded into the trees, searching for whoever had come upon them. She hoped it was someone with one of the search teams, though that would mean he was in wolf coat when he wasn't supposed to be. She thought from the quick flash of fur that it was a red wolf, not a gray.

She saw Minx run as fast as she could toward town. She'd abandoned North.

Glad for it because Minx could make more headway that way, Elizabeth made a wide circle around Minx, trying to catch sight of whoever was out here with them. She saw a flash of a black-tipped tail. Red wolf. North was tied to the sled. Quinton was at Mr. Winston's home, unless he had left the house and gotten ahead of them. Only one other person who was a red wolf could be in on this. Sefton. Her dear, sweet half brother.

Minx screamed. Elizabeth's heart dropped into the pit of her stomach. Her fur stood out in aggression as she bolted for Minx.

As soon as Elizabeth saw the wolf, she recognized him. It was Sefton. And he was trying to corral Minx in the direction of Winston's house.

Elizabeth didn't care if he was bigger than she was or a full wolf when she was only half. She lunged at Sefton, biting him in the neck before he knew what hit him. She feared that would be the only good bite she'd get in, but she hoped it would give Minx time to get away.

Sefton tore loose and snarled and growled. But he didn't attack. Minx ran off. Thank God.

Sefton's failure to attack her made Elizabeth pause. He'd wanted to kill her before when she was little. Why not now when she had attacked him?

Fine. She'd run into town and get help for North and Tom and make sure Minx got in safely.

As soon as she bolted off, Sefton lunged at her. She saw the furred body flying at her out of her peripheral vision. She had only a second for her heart to give a start, and she made a startled yelp. Right before he slammed into her.

———————

Darien had discovered tracks that indicated someone had been hauling supplies somewhere, and he and Jake started following the trail.

Sam and Silva were a few feet away searching for more tracks.

Sam finally said to Silva, "I know why you're doing it."

Silva looked over at him. "Yeah?"

"You've been wanting to remove that old glass mirror from behind the bar forever, and I didn't want to. It gives the place character."

She snorted. "*You* give the place character."

He smiled, then grew serious again. "You've wanted to update the windows. Even the ceiling fans." He paused and glanced at her. She waited for what he had to say next. "Well, it's time to make a few changes."

"You can do whatever you want with your tavern, Sam. But I'm opening my tearoom on Saturday, eleven o'clock sharp."

Darien took a deep breath and shook his head at Jake.

Jake gave him a small, knowing smile back.

Sam didn't say anything for a while as they trudged through the snow. "For a long time now, I've thought of the tavern as being *ours*. You've worked *with* me for years."

"I've worked *for* you for years. There's a big difference."

Darien didn't think they'd ever resolve their differences. He didn't remember it being this difficult between him and Lelandi, and for that he was eternally grateful.

"I can't find anyone to replace you," Sam growled.

She didn't respond, but she smiled.

"Don't look so smug," he said.

"You're looking for someone who's just like me. Am I right? Find someone who's not. You know. Hire someone who's blond and tall, with green eyes."

He stopped in his tracks and seized her arm.

She raised her brows at him. Darien and Jake came to a halt, warily watching the two of them. Darien knew Sam and Silva had to resolve their issues on their own, but he wanted to step in as pack leader and as a friend and tell them to get it over with and mate already.

"I don't want anyone new, Silva. I want you."

"I'm not working at the tavern anymore." She jerked her arm free and stalked off.

Sam stared after her, then as if he realized Darien and Jake were watching them, he glanced in their direction. With a furrowed brow and a frantic wave of his arm, Darien encouraged Sam to go after her.

Sam scowled and hurried after her. "Silva, wait up."

She didn't, of course, and instead walked faster. "We're supposed to look for tracks. Not air our personal business out here."

"I don't want anyone else. I want *you.*"

"I'm not working at the tavern any longer. When will you get that through your thick—"

Sam pulled Silva into his arms and kissed her. Darien and Jake stared, jaws hanging open. It wasn't that they hadn't seen them kiss before, hot and passionately and way too often for them not to have mated by now, but Darien just hadn't expected it here and now.

Darien nudged Jake to follow him, and they continued to look for the sled tracks.

"What was that for?" Silva asked, sounding out of breath and awed.

"I want you back."

"Sam, I won't give up my tearoom."

"I didn't say you had to give it up. This is the happiest I've seen you in ages. I want to share in your new venture."

She looked skeptically at him. "Somehow I can't see you wearing frilly Victorian wear while you serve ladies special tea in tiny antique teacups."

Darien stifled a chuckle, poking Jake in the ribs when he didn't manage to control his own chuckle.

"Besides, you have your tavern to run," Silva said to Sam.

"I want to help you in any way that I can. But I don't mean just that. I want you with me at night. Every night. The tavern will have new hours—closing down early so we can spend more time together."

If Silva and Sam settled things between themselves, it would be a cause for celebration.

"Why didn't you say so before?" she asked.

Sam scrubbed his gloved hand over his nearly black beard. "You were always with me. Always nearby. I got to hear your smart-ass comments all day long from the time we opened until the time we closed. I could deal with not having you in bed with me at night, believing that we'd get there eventually. I want to be with you when our places aren't open. Sundays our establishments will both be closed. You're only operating from eleven to three for lunch the rest of the week. Maybe you could come over—"

She folded her arms and frowned up at him.

"This is *not* just about you working *with* me, damn it. It just won't be the same without you. Half my clients—sheriff, deputy, our pack leaders, everyone—will go to eat lunch at your place just to see *you*. You know they will, Silva. You're the biggest draw there is."

Darien couldn't believe it. *Foot-in-the-mouth Sam.* He could have slugged him. Jake cast a glance at Darien and shook his head. Darien let out his breath on a heavy sigh.

To Darien's astonishment, Silva smiled. "You…think you could live without me until four?"

Sam grabbed Silva, swung her around as he gave her a bear hug, and whooped and hollered.

Darien said under his breath, "Hallelujah."

Grinning, Jake said, "I was beginning to think it would never happen."

"You and me both."

Darien heard what he thought was someone running a long way off, sobbing. A girl.

They all took off in that direction at a run—as much as they could through the deep snow.

Tom hated waiting to see what would happen next. Eric stared out the living-room window, most likely watching for Minx and North's return. Eric turned his attention to the front door. It opened.

Tom tensed. Cody stood in the entryway, surveying the trees in front of him and listening for any sounds. Tom remained hidden, not wanting to catch Eric's eye as he watched out the living-room window again.

"Hurry it up," an older man growled. Had to be Quinton. Tom didn't recognize his voice. "Get them back here."

Cody closed the door and trudged through the snow toward the trees, following the path that Minx and North had taken. The bells on the tassels of his rainbow-colored jester hat rang with every step he took. The hat would have to go. He moved slower than Tom knew he could manage. A worried frown creased Cody's forehead.

As soon as Cody reached a point where the trees hid him from anyone watching from the house, Tom intercepted him, covering his mouth before the teen could cry out.

Tom quickly released him and Cody whispered, "Oh my God, Tom, I'm so glad to see you." The teen looked around at the trees. "Are you it? No one else? Where are Minx and North?"

"Minx and Elizabeth hauled an unconscious North back to town on your sled. See if you can catch up to them and help them out. Their trail should be easy enough to follow."

"What about you?"

"Maybe I can send Anthony on his way in a bit."

"That Quinton guy said he'd kill Anthony and Eric if I didn't bring North and Minx back with me."

"You say Eric isn't in on this with him?"

"No. He was using the place as a safe house. After Minx, my brother, and I arrived, North came. He had come to see Eric because he and his brothers had been searching for Elizabeth. North thought the brothers knew where she was. Believing North was involved in her kidnapping, Eric socked him in the eye. Quinton and some other guy arrived and took us all hostage. He has got a gun."

"Okay, good to know. I have a rifle and a Glock."

"The other one isn't in the house," Cody warned.

Tom's blood chilled. "What other one? Where is he?"

"Some guy named Sefton. After North and Minx left the house, Quinton muttered to himself that Sefton was taking too long to get back. I don't know where he is. He went out in his wolf coat after they took us hostage."

Tom prayed one of the search teams had picked Sefton up. He was torn between going after Elizabeth and Minx and ensuring they stayed safe or remaining here to try and take Quinton out.

"All right. Hurry and find the women. Send reinforcements this way if you see any of the search teams."

"Search teams?"

"Yeah, three others are out here."

"Okay, I'll take good care of them. Just…don't let any harm come to my brother. Okay?"

"Yeah, you know I'll do anything I can to protect him, Cody. Go."

Cody glanced back in the direction of the house, then nodded to Tom and started to take off, jingling.

"Wait, leave your hat here. You can use mine."

Cody looked torn. He loved that jester hat. On the other hand, wearing a pack subleader's hat was an honor. All the other guys would be envious. They exchanged hats, and Tom set the jester hat on one of the tree branches as Cody hurried off.

Tom hoped Cody was correct and that Eric hadn't pretended to be something he wasn't. Gambling that Eric had planned to explain what was going on to Darien, Tom moved out of the trees for a moment. He caught Eric's eye as he watched out the living-room window in the direction Cody had gone.

Eric's eyes widened and his jaw dropped.

Now or never. Either he would alert Quinton, or he would keep Tom's presence here secret.

Eric smiled, wearing one of his evil smirks.

What did that mean? He would get Tom back? Or he was glad to see him?

CHAPTER 29

TOM REACHED MR. WINSTON'S SHED AT A DEAD RUN, PRAYING that Eric wouldn't reveal his presence. Tom ran behind the shed and around to the back door of the house. If everyone remained in the living room, no one would see him. His biggest problem would be picking the lock to the back door.

If everyone talked, it might cover up the clicking sound he'd make with his lockpicks. If not, Quinton could very well hear him with his enhanced wolf hearing. The wind whipped about and the old cabin creaked, which helped somewhat to disguise his work.

"You can't kill us, Quinton," Eric said suddenly. "The red pack and the Silver pack will want your heads."

Good. Eric was covering for Tom.

"I have no intention of killing anyone here," Quinton said.

"So why do you want the woman so badly?"

"I have a business arrangement with my niece. I'm having a time getting together with Elizabeth."

"You can't hurt her. I suspect she's Tom's mate by now," Eric said.

Quinton growled, "No wolf in his right mind would take her for a mate."

Tom wanted to wring the bastard's neck. He was glad Elizabeth wasn't here to witness this.

"What kind of business arrangement?" Eric asked, louder this time as Tom continued to attempt to pick the back-door lock, his gloves lying on the porch, his hands sweating despite the frigid weather. "Is that why you had her brought back to Colorado?"

"I told you, North brought her here," Quinton snapped a little too quickly. "He wants her for his own. Always has. He was always mooning over her."

The lock clicked open. *Keep talking, Eric.*

"Why take us hostage?" Anthony asked quickly, his voice raised as if everyone in the house had hearing problems.

"You can be my witnesses. You're not hostages."

"So what's the business deal? If you want us to be witnesses, you might as well tell us what the situation is," Eric said.

"Can I fix anyone anything? Coffee? Sodas?" Mr. Winston suddenly asked.

"No, just sit where you are," Quinton said.

"I gotta pee," Anthony said to Mr. Winston. "Can I use your bathroom?"

The back door led into a laundry room, and Tom tried to close the door as quietly as he could. He was afraid to leave it open as the cold wind blew in, and he knew they'd soon sense the change in the temperature and smell the fresh snowy breeze. Thank God the door hadn't creaked when he opened it. He set down his rifle and pulled out his Glock, but he stopped moving across the laundry room and waited for a response to Anthony's request.

"Be quick," Quinton snapped.

"This way, Mr. Winston?" Anthony asked.

"Yeah, second door on the right."

"Thanks. I'll be real quick. Sorry." Anthony hurried off down the hall and gave Tom the coverage he needed as he left the laundry room.

Tom gave a nod to Anthony, who said softly to him, "He's got a gun."

Tom showed him his pistol. Anthony's eyes widened. He turned and pushed the bathroom door open and whispered to Tom, "Good luck."

"Stay in there."

Anthony looked rebellious, like he wouldn't let Tom do all the fighting if he needed help. Tom didn't want Anthony getting shot. "Stay," Tom whispered again.

"Elizabeth still owns her parents' property. She's going to sell it to me," Quinton said from the living room as Tom continued down the hall one step at a time, trying to ensure he didn't make a board squeak beneath the carpet.

"So why do all this?" Eric turned his head a little in the direction of the hallway leading to the laundry room, bathrooms, and bedrooms, but he didn't look, knowing that would cause Quinton to glance in that direction and see Tom.

Tom quickly assessed the situation. Quinton stood near the couch armed with a 9mm revolver. Mr. Winston sat on the opposite end.

"Are you sure nobody wants anything to eat? I'm hungry," Mr. Winston said.

"No!" Quinton snapped. "Eric, look out the window. See if Anthony's brother or the others are coming."

Anthony flushed the toilet and ran the water full blast in the sink, making more noise for Tom. He'd have to thank the kid later. And Eric.

As soon as Eric moved toward the front window, Tom had a clean shot. He aimed at Quinton's gun hand and fired.

The sound reverberated through the house. The bullet hit Quinton in the hand. He screamed in pain and dropped his weapon.

Eric swung around and dove for him, taking the older man down. Quinton whacked his head hard on the sharp edge of a table with a *thunk* and crumpled to the wooden floor.

Anthony rushed out of the bathroom. "I missed all of it! You should have waited for me!"

"That was the whole point—to ensure you missed all of it," Tom said. "Thanks for the help though. You did a damn good job, Anthony, Eric." Tom stalked over to check on Quinton.

Eric examined him for a pulse.

"I'll get some rope out of the shed," Mr. Winston said, heading for the front door.

Anthony glanced out the window. "Holy crap. Wait, Mr. Winston! North's pulling the sled and headed toward the house."

Tom's heart pumped double time. How did North get loose?

"Elizabeth, Minx?" Tom said, hurrying for the window.

"A red wolf is on the sled. Small. Female," Anthony said. "And another red wolf is running alongside the sled. I think it might be that guy Sefton. No sign of Cody or Minx."

Tom started stripping as soon as he heard Anthony say a red wolf was on the sled. Once he was nude, he shifted. Anthony ran to open the front door for him.

Tom charged out of the house and across the snow to tackle Sefton, figuring that was who the wolf had to be, hoping North would stay out of it. At least North was unarmed unless he shifted. Elizabeth was tied to the sled, blood on her mouth. She gave a little whimper in greeting when she saw Tom. He wanted to free her, but first he had to deal with Sefton.

The fight with Sefton wouldn't be fair, but from what Tom could see, her half brother had already injured Elizabeth, and he *had* tried to kill her before. Sefton's right flank was bleeding, which meant she must have gotten in a good bite first. Tom was damned proud of her. He noted that North was trying to untie Elizabeth.

What was he doing? Whose side was he on?

Tom clashed with Sefton, snarling and snapping his powerful jaws, but he only managed to grab a mouthful of fur before Sefton scampered away. Growling, Tom smelled fear on the red wolf. He should be fearful. Tom wouldn't let him live.

He charged again at Sefton, trying to get the wolf's neck, but Sefton bolted out of his path. Tom wanted to get the red wolf pinned down so he could fight with him wolf to wolf. He finally maneuvered Sefton against the trunk of a spruce, heavy snow on the branches shaking so hard from the wolves' movements that it created a makeshift snowstorm. Tom bit into Sefton's flank, drawing blood. Sefton yipped and jumped through the branches, snow collecting on his fur as he escaped another chomp of Tom's wicked canines that missed him by inches.

"Tom, watch out! Sefton killed Elizabeth's parents!" North shouted.

Sefton had killed them. Not Quinton. Though Quinton's attempted killing of Elizabeth made him just as guilty. With the way Sefton avoided clashing with Tom, he wondered how the red wolf ever had the guts to kill his own father.

Tom and Sefton both panted as they circled. Tom angled for another charge. He leaped for Sefton, but Sefton dove through more branches. *Stay and fight, you coward!*

Sefton licked his wounds a short distance away. Tom glanced at North, who was still trying to untie the knots in the ropes keeping Elizabeth in place. She lay still, eyeing Tom, but suddenly she glanced in Sefton's direction.

Sefton had crept closer to Tom while he'd pretended to be distracted. Tom was tired of chasing down the red wolf. When he swung around to confront the wolf, Sefton lunged at him. Tom jumped back out of the path of Sefton's sharp canines as they snapped shut near his ear, just missing the leather.

North untied the last knot securing Elizabeth. She sat up for a second, then jumped off the sled.

Don't come near us, Tom wanted to tell her. *Stay put.*

She circled around the fighting male wolves.

Eric ran out of the house, Glock in hand. Mr. Winston and Anthony followed. *Someone should have stayed with Quinton!*

Sefton leaped at Tom again. He was agile and strong, but Tom was more muscular, a bigger gray. He tore into Sefton again, ripping at his uninjured flank. The wolf moved so quickly that Tom lost his hold on him.

Tom went for Sefton's throat at the same time the red went after Tom's, but teeth met teeth, and Tom tasted blood. Sefton's. Maybe a little of his own.

Tom eyed Sefton, the two of them drawing the frigid air into their lungs, panting, readying for the next bout.

Sefton went for Tom's leg but he jumped out of Sefton's path, the red's teeth clamping together on thin air with a menacing threat. A red blur of fur dove past Tom.

No! Stay away, Elizabeth!

Elizabeth sank her teeth into Sefton's tail. He yelped. And swiftly turned to retaliate.

Fatal mistake. Never turn your back on a bigger wolf.

Tom leaped onto the wolf's back, bit him in the neck, and held on until Sefton sank into the snow, his blood coloring it cherry.

Worried that Sefton would still try to shake him loose and hurt Elizabeth, Tom didn't let go until the wolf took his last breath.

That was when he saw Eric holding the gun on North.

Anthony shouted at North, "Where's Cody? And Minx?"

"Minx got away. I saw Cody spying on us from the trees when I had to tie Elizabeth on the sled. I motioned with my head to him, letting him know which way Minx took off, and he went after her," North said, smiling.

"I'm going after them," Anthony said.

"No," Mr. Winston said. "You'll stay here until Tom says what you'll do."

Tom trotted over to join Elizabeth, nuzzling her face and neck and licking her nose. He didn't smell any blood on her except Sefton's, and he breathed a sigh of relief, damned glad for that. He didn't believe the wolves had planned to let Elizabeth *or* North live.

"I swear I didn't have anything to do with any of this," North said. "You screwed things up for them by going to Silver Town, Elizabeth. They thought they'd catch you at my place because I'd planned to meet you there. I got this weird feeling my phone was being tapped, which is why I hung up on you real quick that time. They must have learned I had the evidence against Sefton, and I went into hiding. I was in such a hurry to clear out of there that I left my phone behind."

That was why she never could get hold of North. Tom wished to God she'd just told him what had been going on with her, why she'd been there in the first place, and what the business meeting had been all about.

North said to Elizabeth, "Then I worried Quinton and Sefton were going to go after you, so I made it to the ski resort and asked around. Some ski-patrol guys told me Eric and his brothers had asked about you too, and I came here to find them. Quinton and Sefton must have been following me the whole time.

"He paid to have you brought here and tried to make everyone think it was me. Quinton didn't want anyone to know he was behind this. Then after he killed you, they'd think I did it. He didn't plan to let either of us live. Especially since I found the evidence of Sefton's guilt."

"What evidence?" Eric asked North.

"Sefton's murder weapon. Elizabeth's father planned to give her a boot knife his father had given him. He treasured it. I saw her grandfather use it once. It had a beautiful hand-carved bone handle. But I knew Elizabeth wanted a horse. It was all she ever talked about when we met up. I wanted to buy one of the mares Elizabeth's father was breaking in because I knew her father wouldn't give her one. Horseflesh was his business. Catching them, breaking them, and selling them. He didn't give 'em away free. So I planned to buy her one. I had the money in hand and was going to meet with her father on her birthday to pick out the one her father thought she cherished the most."

Tom glanced at Elizabeth. He couldn't read her expression. He'd buy her a whole herd of horses if she wanted them.

"When I arrived that afternoon, Elizabeth was in a state of shock. Her father had been stabbed to death. I helped her bury him, then pack and saddle up one of the horses. She couldn't find the boot knife her father had given her. We were so frantic to get her out of there that we just figured it had been misplaced. I gave her one of my own that she could use for protection. I–I couldn't tell her that I was buying one of the horses for her. Not after her father had been murdered. After she was gone, I looked for the knife, intending to send it to her wherever she settled, but I never found it.

"A few weeks ago, I was out fishing with Sefton, and he used that same knife to clean and fillet the fish. Why would *he* have it? Then I made the connection. Sefton was furious his father had given it to his daughter instead of his firstborn son. Sefton often had groused before about the knife, but after the murders, he never mentioned it again." North swallowed hard.

"I looked Sefton squarely in the eye at the fishing hole and asked where he got such a beautiful knife. I tried really hard not to show how much I was sweating or that my hands shook. Sefton said as proud as could be, 'My father gave it to my uncle to give to me,' then smiled. The look was pure menace. I knew he was lying to me and that either her uncle or Sefton had killed her father. No way would he have willingly given the knife to his brother or Sefton. Not after he had given it to Elizabeth.

"I stole it from Sefton's house. I was over there all the time, so he never suspected I'd slipped in when he was gone. After that, I had to track Elizabeth down and tell her the news. I knew she'd want to know. Her uncle had covered for Sefton, given him an alibi, so he was just as guilty. And Bruin, the pack leader at the time, backed them up.

"When I heard Elizabeth was alive and well, I hoped she might return. Once her uncle and Sefton were dealt with, I thought maybe she might agree to start a new pack with me on her land.

I guess Sefton and Quinton watched me the whole time to learn what evidence I had on them, and they intended to force her to sign the deed on her property over to them."

"Where's the knife?" Eric asked.

North pulled it out of his boot. "Where a boot knife belongs. Now we just have to get Quinton's confession and—"

"About…Quinton," Mr. Winston said, sounding like they might all be in trouble. "We have a problem."

CHAPTER 30

In his wolf coat, Tom raced into Mr. Winston's house, Elizabeth on his tail, and everyone else running to catch up. Quinton lay on the floor by the table—no heart rate, no breath. The man was stone-cold dead.

Mr. Winston and Eric stood nearby. "Sorry, Tom," Mr. Winston said.

No need to be sorry, Tom thought. Quinton had been living on borrowed time for far too long.

Anthony grabbed Elizabeth's clothes from the sled and Tom's in the living room and left them in a bedroom where Tom and Elizabeth hurried to shift and dress.

From the living room, Anthony shouted, "Darien and Jake are here!"

Anthony raced outside to meet them and give them all the news. Eric and Mr. Winston had brought Sefton's body into the living room and covered it and Quinton's with sheets.

Elizabeth joined them and cast a look at Eric, who openly stared at her.

"Don't I know you from somewhere?" Eric said to her.

"A long time ago," she said.

"The water hole. My God." Eric looked back at Quinton's dead body. "He was the one who tried to drown you."

"Thanks for stopping him," Elizabeth said.

"Yeah, sure. I wished we'd killed the bastard then."

"Watering hole?" Darien said.

"Fill you in on it later, Darien." Tom quickly enfolded Elizabeth in his arms, noting that she wouldn't look at her dead relations. He wanted to get her out of there as soon as he could.

"How convenient it was for you to find the knife," Elizabeth said to North. "I'm curious why Sefton would have made the mistake of showing it to you. He knew you had been seeing me and might have known Dad gave it to me for my sixteenth birthday."

North's face lost all its color. "Hell, you mean they used me to get to you?"

"Yeah, to ask for the deed and to meet with me to give me the evidence in person. And they would have grabbed both of us, the evidence, and the deed."

North let out his breath hard. "Yeah, I can see it all clearly now. I'm so sorry, Elizabeth. I would never have called you if I had known."

Tom gave him a killing look. As Darien and Jake joined them in the house, Tom said, "About time you guys got here. We've got to find Minx and Cody."

"We came across Minx already," Darien said. "Sam and Silva took her to my house and will alert her parents to pick her up. We ran into Cody a short while after that and sent him in the same direction. We didn't know what the situation was here. What happened?"

Eric said, "I guess when I took the man down, he hit his head too hard and… Anyway, he's dead."

Darien nodded. "One fewer issue to deal with."

"Elizabeth's half brother's dead also," Tom said.

"What about Sarandon?" Darien asked.

Tom shook his head. "No sign of him."

"All right. We'll take care of things here. Meet me at the house," Darien said.

"You sure you don't want me to help with this?" Eric offered. When Darien hesitated to say anything, Eric added, "I'd really like to help out."

"Okay, we'll turn Quinton's and Sefton's bodies over to Hrothgar since they were with his pack. What about North?"

"I don't want the deed to your property," North told Elizabeth. "I just…wanted to see you again. And though I wanted to give you the evidence about your uncle's and half brother's part in your parents' deaths, I'd hoped you might consider seeing me." He glanced at Tom, then said to Elizabeth, "But I didn't want your property unless you lived there with me."

"Thanks for trying to help me learn the truth about my uncle and Sefton," Elizabeth said. "I appreciate it."

North appeared as though he wanted to hug her or kiss her or both, but Tom gave him a look meant to discourage the notion. The man had *not* protected Elizabeth when she could have used his help.

North bowed his head a little, acknowledging he wouldn't be able to get any closer to her, then turned on his heel and left.

Darien listened to Mr. Winston's reasons for having given Eric and his brothers refuge when they needed it. Mr. Winston had still believed in the men and had tried to talk them into telling Darien what they were up to. But Eric had always been as stubborn as Darien.

Anthony said, "Hey, we almost forgot. Where are the groceries we had on the sled?"

Tom told them where they had dumped them in the snow, and Eric and Anthony went to get them for Mr. Winston.

After they left the groceries with Mr. Winston, when Anthony, Elizabeth, and Tom headed for town, leaving the others to take care of things, Anthony led the way, pulling the sled. Tom grabbed Cody's hat from the tree branch. Elizabeth smiled as Tom jingled with every footstep he took, wishing he had his own hat back. "We could trade hats, you know," he finally said to her.

She raised her brows. "You'd wear a soft fuzzy pink hat over a jester's?" She shook her head. "I like it on you. Lets me know where you are at all times."

When they finally reached home, they gave the news to Lelandi and everyone else there—Sam, Silva, the kids, and some of the other teams that had arrived.

After the news broke that Sefton and Quinton would no longer be any trouble, Silva beamed. "Remember the tearoom's opening on Saturday."

Sam stood there, his arms wrapped around her like a big bear holding a gray wolf. "Tavern will open a little late that day. We'll serve drinks after her tearoom closes at three, and we'll continue the party at the tavern. All drinks will be on me." He smiled. He was one happy wolf.

"On us," Silva said. She pulled away from Sam and gave Elizabeth a big hug. "As soon as you learn what you're having, let me know and I'll work on those baby booties."

Tom loved the way Elizabeth blushed.

"What about you?" Elizabeth asked, finally finding her tongue.

"No, not me. Sam and I have our businesses to run."

Sam waggled his brows at Tom, indicating he had other plans.

Lelandi called Carol to fill her in, and she put her on speaker so Silva could hear. "I'm coming to the tearoom opening and want to get together for a girls' night out with you all."

Tom shook his head.

"That's okay," Sam said. "We'll have beer and pizza and game night after the ladies leave to have their girlie party."

CJ was sitting on one of the couches, his walking cast propped up on a pillow on the coffee table nearby—compliments of Lelandi. Brett sat beside him. Tom watched as they gave each other surreptitious smiles. They were happy to be home with the pack and the family.

Tom was glad his cousins had returned to the pack. Darien called to say they were on their way back to the house and had located Sarandon, who was all too happy to be coming home. He had been out searching the plane wreckage before a search team arrived in the area, and he'd found Elizabeth's deed and ID inside one of the kidnappers' pockets.

Tom sighed. His cousins were proving they were valued members of the pack once again.

But before Darien and Sarandon arrived, the kids' parents came to take them home.

Anthony and Cody's father said, "I ought to ground you for two months and make you muck out Doc Mitchell's stables for all that time. But because you were trying to help out Mr. Winston..." His voice faded as they left the house.

Minx's father was so choked up that he couldn't say anything. He just hugged her and kissed her and finally left the house with her apologizing, saying she wouldn't ever go with the boys unless she had her father's permission.

Only time would tell if she'd stick to that.

As soon as Darien returned home, Tom took him aside. "We're leaving first thing in the morning to take care of Elizabeth's home and so she can say her goodbyes at work. I guess we'll also need to take care of her property near Hrothgar's pack. We'll be back to find a place here. We'll return before Silva's grand tearoom opening, no matter what."

Darien said, "Come with me, you and Elizabeth." He escorted them into his office and shut the door. "Elizabeth doesn't know this, but I need you home as soon as you can return."

Guessing what this was all about—a new problem for the pack—Tom said, "Because...?"

"The new owners of the hotel will be here this weekend to start renovations on the place. I need to make sure we don't have any trouble with the pack when the owners show up."

Tom folded his arms. "Our cousins can help out there."

"*That's* what I'm worried about," Darien said ultraseriously.

"Maybe it's Peter's turn to watch out for the new she-wolves in the pack." This time, Tom wouldn't ensure that an unaccompanied she-wolf—in this case, three of them—didn't stir up trouble with the pack. He already had his own.

When they arrived at Elizabeth's place in Canyon, Texas, the next morning, Tom loved the coziness of the two-bedroom, one-bath home surrounded by land and mesquites and junipers. He decided the warmth of the home was all because of her.

"Kind of small," she said, glancing around at her place, "compared to Darien's house." She smiled up at Tom. "Then again, you make the house seem small. I hadn't really thought of it that way before."

"I like it." Tom gathered her in his arms. "In a place this size, you couldn't get very far from me." He kissed her lips. "I'm hungry. We had no food on the plane, and I feel like having a steak."

She looked wary, as if she already knew where this was headed. "I don't have any steaks in the house. The last time—"

"The last time, you weren't with me. You know they say that you should revisit the place where you experienced something bad to get over your fear of going there again," Tom said.

"But if they have sale steaks at the grocery store…" she said.

"Nope, let's go to the butcher shop. I want you to have only good memories before we leave here. Besides, we need to pick up your car if it's still parked there."

"All right, but if the steaks are full price, you're paying."

He laughed, then hurried her out to the rental car and drove her to the butcher shop.

She sighed with relief as he parked at the shop. "My car's still here." She glanced at the butcher's window and with an I-told-you-so look, she said, "No sale signs."

Smiling, he patted her leg. "Steaks are on me."

When they walked into the store, the butcher's blue eyes rounded. "I wondered when you'd come back to get your car." He eyed Tom as if he was speculating about whether he was the *new* boyfriend. "What will it be?"

"Rib-eye steaks sound good to you?" Tom asked Elizabeth.

"Yeah." She turned to stare at a sleek-looking woman wearing an ivory sweater, tan jeans, and high-heeled boots, who was checking out grilling spices on a rack, a package of meat in hand.

The woman glanced at them. She sniffed the air, the action so reminiscent of a wolf shifter that she stole both Tom's and Elizabeth's attention.

The woman frowned at them and stuck her nose up in the air, hurrying past them and out the door. Tom swore she hissed, "Dogs," under her breath.

Tom and Elizabeth watched her leave.

She frowned up at him. "Did she smell like—?"

"A cougar?"

They both shook their heads and said, "Nah."

———————————

A short while later, Tom grilled the steaks on Elizabeth's back patio while she made arrangements to have her household goods shipped and lined up a Realtor to sell her house. She'd also picked up her camera from the repair shop, delighted that it worked again. She would need it to take pictures for her new newspaper, though maybe Jake would shoot some pictures for her too. Tom intended to get her another camera—as a spare.

At her insistence, so he wouldn't splatter steak juices on his sweater, he wore Elizabeth's bluebonnet floral apron. It got him to thinking about Darien wearing Lelandi's brown and pink ruffled apron when he fed his toddlers. Tom realized that Darien didn't need a manlier apron. He himself wasn't bothered about wearing Elizabeth's flowery one if it meant being with her and keeping her happy. He could even envision feeding oatmeal mush to *his* toddlers in another year or so, wearing this same apron.

That had him smiling.

When Elizabeth joined him with a platter covered with raw vegetables to grill, he turned and saw she was looking out at the vista. A male coyote off in the distance watched them.

"Looks like you have an admirer." Tom flipped the steaks, keeping his eye on the coyote.

Elizabeth set the platter of vegetables on the table next to the grill and wrapped her arms around Tom's waist. "I think he was interested in me before, but he was afraid of my wolf half."

Tom set the tongs on the sideboard, turned, and drew Elizabeth into his arms. "Well, now he can be afraid of your *other* half too, who's a *whole* wolf."

She smiled up at Tom. "I have to admit I thought I'd made the biggest mistake, shopping at that butcher shop."

"Sometimes our worst mistakes can turn out to be the very best thing for us. I know your being in my life has been the very best thing for me."

Elizabeth couldn't believe her half brother and uncle were dead, and she had nothing to worry about in returning to Colorado, all because Tom had been there for her. She loved him.

And she knew from Tom's expression that he was ready to skip the steaks and prove just how glad he was that she'd come back into his life. But she wasn't giving her steaks up for anyone or anything *this* time.

"Steaks first. Dessert after," she said.

"Did I ever tell you how hard you are on me?"

"Once or twice," she said with a smile. "And you love me for it."

"Damn…right." He quickly tossed the food on the plates, gathered her in his arms, and started kissing her—and she was reminded of that kiss on the slopes when they'd become a video sensation for the whole pack.

Except for the cool Texas breeze and one coyote witness off in the distance, this time, they were alone. And she decided that life was too short.

She wanted dessert first so she dragged him toward the house, plates in hand.

"What about our steaks?" he asked.

"Priorities change," she said, smiling up at him. "Some things just won't wait."

"Amen to that."

SEAL WOLF PURSUIT

A SEAL WOLF NOVELLA

CHAPTER 1

Becky Woolworth was busy scheduling a dinner engagement for her employer, liquor heiress Pamela Tynan, so she was surprised when Pamela barged into her office with a proposition that had nothing to do with her own life or commitments but instead Becky's! She couldn't believe it when Pamela said, "Becky, dear, how long have you worked for me?"

Pamela was wearing one of her royal-blue business pantsuits. She always looked so together, and the pantsuit's color complemented her warm blue eyes and short blond hair in a chin-grazing bob. Becky often went shopping with her, and her boss was always telling her to grab anything she liked at the most expensive dress shop. Becky never felt she needed to dress as smartly as her boss, but Pamela insisted with a wave of her hand, saying Becky needed to look her best in her employ. Which was a way of saying Pamela wanted her to have expensive clothes too, not that she was embarrassed with her hired help's couture. Pamela was just nice that way.

"Over three years, ma'am," Becky said, putting the restaurant owner on hold. The owner or manager of restaurants where Pamela was a guest often wanted to be the one called to ensure they reserved the best seating for the heiress.

"Yes, over three years, three months, and so many days. Yet in all that time, you haven't once dated anyone," Pamela said.

Which had all to do with Becky's wolfishness. She was a gray wolf shifter, and finding a wolf like herself to date was a problem, especially in Mountain View. But also, she really didn't have a lot of free time off from work to just enjoy herself. Every time Pamela told her to take some time off, she called Becky in a fluster, wondering about this problem or that. Becky was always there to help sort out her life. And she loved working for Pamela.

The perks were great. A lovely guesthouse on the estate, very private in the woods. All paid health and dental insurance, and a lovely forest to run in as a wolf. Becky even had her own garden she loved to cultivate. Great pay. A great boss. She couldn't have asked for more. Pamela might be an heiress with money to burn, but she was also very down-to-earth, and when it came to charities, she had a big heart.

"I haven't really found anyone I want to date," Becky said, hoping to get back to the owner of the restaurant to finish the reservation. She imagined he had plenty of work to do and couldn't sit on hold forever.

"Right. And it's all my fault," Pamela said.

Becky had to smile. It was no one's fault that there weren't any wolves around here to date, but she quickly lost the smile and cleared her throat. "I've got Rizzo's owner on the line—"

Pamela waved her hand in dismissal. It wasn't that she didn't appreciate that people had other things they needed to do with their time, but when she decided something, she wanted it done now. "I will take care of it."

"The reservation?" That would be a first.

"No, no, *you* deal with that. Dating. I'll make sure you have a date and time off for it." Then Pamela smiled as if she were making the best charitable plan of the year and headed out of Becky's office.

Becky's jaw dropped. Not only did she not want to go out with any old human, but she didn't want to disappoint Pamela when she had to tell her it wasn't working out between her and said human. No one knew she was a wolf shifter, and she had to keep it that way. And there was no turning a human, even if she really, really liked one, because then he would have trouble shifting during the full moon, and if he had a family, well, the repercussions would have a rippling effect. "Hello, Mr. Binghamton, I'm so sorry to keep you waiting. Yes, six tonight, and Pamela said she will decide on her meal when she gets there. Yes, one guest."

"The guest's name?" the owner asked, which was par for the course because they wished to greet their VIPs by name when they could.

"Uh, no name." Pamela rarely said who she was taking with her or who was taking her to a restaurant or some social engagement. It lent a bit of mystery to her and that made it fun. But the owner or manager always asked, and when Pamela told her to do so, Becky would let the person know too.

Sometimes, Pamela even took Becky as her guest, which made it extra special for her.

Max Browning couldn't believe it when his boss at the PI agency, Ryan McKinley, also his wolf pack leader and the mayor of Green Valley, Colorado, called him into his office, told him to shut the door, and said he had a job for him—a blind date with a woman. No particulars at all. Not what she did for a living, her name, who she worked for. Nada. The thing was that if he had a name, it *wouldn't* be a blind date. Max could learn almost anything about a person if he knew his or her real name. Aliases took a bit more work to run down the real person's identity, but he was good at doing that too.

"For real? Okay, so is this an agency job?" Max asked.

"Yes. The client asked for one of you to take a woman out on a blind date. *You*, in particular."

Max opened his mouth to object, but Ryan waved his hand in dismissal. "Don't ask Asher. She specifically checked you out apparently, liked what she saw, and wanted you to take out the woman."

Asher Wells was one of Max's coworkers and a friend. Max let out his breath in exasperation. He would do anything for his pack leaders—Ryan and his mate, Carol—but this wasn't something he'd ever thought he'd have to do, or he might just have to set some limits next time on the terms of his employment. "When and where?"

"Tonight, at six at a restaurant in Mountain View, so it'll take you about twenty-five minutes to get there. The client is paying for both of your meals. Take a raincoat. It's supposed to pour tonight. Take an umbrella for the lady, just in case she's unprepared. The woman's name is Becky, and the client said that was all you needed to know."

Max shook his head. "How many years have I known you now?"

"Plenty. There's a first time for everything. Have fun, enjoy yourself, make the most of it. Remember, it's a free dinner out."

"Where?"

"Rizzo's Italian Restaurant. They're high class, so don't dress down too much."

Max saluted him. "I've got a case I'm looking into. A missing German shepherd, but I'll be ready when I need to be with raincoat and umbrella—for the lady, just in case."

Max took off to do another neighborhood search for the dog, posting more flyers, checking with animal clinics to see if anyone had contacted them. At least the dog was chipped, so if someone took him in to have the vet check it, they would locate the owners. The dog had been wearing a collar with his name and address and vet clinic name on it, but the owner had found the collar hung up on a low-hanging branch and realized the dog wasn't wearing it when he got out. If the yardman hadn't opened the gate at the wrong time, just when Bear was out doing his business, none of this would have happened.

Max loved animals, and he was always taking the cases of missing pets. Not that Asher or Phoenix, their newest PI agent, didn't like animals, but Max jumped on the cases. Everyone he talked to was sympathetic to his cause when he went looking for the missing pets. Well, except for the occasional pet thief but that was a different story.

When Max arrived at the restaurant that night, he didn't know what to expect. A woman who was so shy she couldn't meet anyone on her own. Or one who worked with mostly women and there were no work-related romances to be had. He wondered who had set up the woman for a blind date through a PI agency. A friend? A relative? How bizarre was that?

All these thoughts were running through his mind when he saw a woman who looked a little uncomfortable standing all alone. She was pretty, with short dark hair and green eyes that widened a bit when she saw him studying her. She was wearing a silky green dress, presenting an image of softness and curves, and the neckline dipped a little, showing a tiny bit of cleavage, enough to be enticing but not too much to be suggestive. The white sandals that completed the outfit were high-heeled and sexy, emphasizing her shapely legs. Was she the woman?

He just hoped they enjoyed the dinner and the night wouldn't drag on. The good thing was that she was here even before he arrived, and he'd come early. He hated late dates, as if the woman had to make a big entrance if he hadn't picked her up and brought her there in the first place.

He cleared his suddenly gravelly throat and realized he was feeling a bit awkward, when he rarely felt that way. He was a Navy SEAL after all. He headed over to her side of the entryway to see if she was his date since she wasn't making a move in his direction. And as soon as he did, he smelled she was a gray wolf like him. He was shocked, thrilled, and he smiled broadly at her, hoping she *was* his date. He'd never met her before, probably due to her living in a different city that he didn't come to very often, and they probably didn't travel in the same circles.

She looked shocked to smell that he was a wolf. She didn't smile, just quickly clamped her lips closed, took another deep breath of him as if to reassure herself he truly was a wolf, and then gave him an almost imperceptible smile—of relief, he thought.

"Well, this is a pleasant surprise," he said, trying not to sound totally gobsmacked that he had a much more appealing dinner guest than he thought possible. And then he wondered if his pack leader Carol had set this up. She was much more likely to try her hand at matchmaking than her mate, Ryan.

"I, uh, agree," his date said and stuck her hand out to shake his with a formality he hadn't expected. "I'm Becky Woolworth."

"Max Browning." He shook her hand with a gentle firmness.

He wondered if she'd ever gone on blind dates before. He'd gone on one a time or two, nothing that had ever worked out, but those had been with wolves. He had never expected her to be a wolf. At least they had a chance to make something of it if they liked each other.

Max was beginning to wonder if this had been a job at all.

"So who set you up on a date?" he asked Becky as the hostess seated them at a booth.

"My boss."

He laughed. "My boss did the same to me. He's like us, but he didn't say you were too. I just assumed you weren't."

"Oh, me too about you. My boss isn't one of us, so I really figured you weren't—" She quit talking when the server brought them menus.

"Thanks," they both told the server, then opened their menus to check out the selections.

"So why did he think you needed to go on a blind date? And what does your boss do?" Max wanted to learn more about Becky in a social way, but he couldn't help also using his PI training to learn all there was about her and her boss.

"Um, Pamela Tynan is my boss's name and I'm her personal

assistant. I thought I was scheduling an appointment for *her* for dinner with a guest tonight, but it turned out I was the one she wanted the table saved for, and you are *my* guest."

Max smiled. "She has good taste in restaurants."

"She can afford them." Becky set her menu aside. "So what do you do?"

"I work for Ryan McKinley as a PI in his investigative agency, and he's the one who set me up. Now, if I'd known you were a... well, one like us, I would have believed my boss's wife, Carol, was behind it."

"She's kind of a matchmaker, I take it."

"Yeah. So why did your boss think you needed to have a date for tonight?"

"I've been working for her for over three years and not been on a date for all that time. I mean, it's not easy finding one of our kind just anywhere, and I do have a job that keeps me busy. I don't understand why she would have contacted your boss to arrange this through a PI agency though."

"I don't know. And the thing of it is, she chose me, no one else. We have four other guys who work at the agency. One is recently married, but truthfully, I had thought of passing this off to another single guy."

Becky smiled. "I'm glad you didn't. Not that I know anything about the other guy, but this is fun. Now that I know you're a wolf too," she said, when no one else was around to overhear them.

The server came back and Becky ordered veal scallopini. Max decided to order the same thing. And glasses of red wine.

"If you have the time, maybe we could go to Green Valley tonight and run, and then I'll return you here after that," he said.

"Or I could follow you there so you wouldn't have to drive me back here. Sure, I would love that. I'll have to make sure my boss doesn't need me. She's pretty good about letting me have my nights off, but there are times when she's got all kinds of things she wants me to do, so I never know. Then too, sometimes she'll give me the time off and then need me to take care of business that just came up or look for things she can't find."

"Okay, so we'll ask her first."

"Right."

"I hope your drive to her place isn't too out of the way if you have to be at her beck and call all the time," he said.

"No. She has a veritable mansion, and I live in one of the guest-houses on the property. It's really nice and I love it. She has a lot of acreage so I can run as a wolf when it gets dark."

"I don't blame you. Ryan and Carol have a lot of acreage, so we'll be safe there."

Their wine, glasses of water, bread, and salads were served.

"Have you ever been here before?" Becky asked Max when their server left.

"No. It's expensive. Not that I can't afford it, but I generally stick to—"

"Fast-food places?" she asked.

He chuckled. "Not on a date. But this wouldn't have been my first choice. It's great though." He clinked his wineglass with hers. "To your first blind date, right?"

"Yeah. Is this yours?"

"I've gone on a couple that friends set up. Always wolves though. Nothing panned out."

"So what do you do as a PI?"

"Serve as a bodyguard when I need to. Search backgrounds. Look for missing pets, children, wives, and husbands. Investigate to see if someone's cheating a company out of money or cheating on a spouse. Determine the truth in paternity suits. Just a whole lot of different stuff. And I can add blind dates to the list."

Becky smiled.

"And you? What does your boss have you doing?"

"Oh, everything from keeping up with her financial advisors

and lawyers to maintaining her social and business engagements. The list goes on, kind of like yours, but in a different way."

"Did she make the dinner reservation for us?"

Becky chuckled. "No. I always set them up. Talk about a surprise when she said she was sending me to the restaurant to meet my blind date. The owner was here to greet her and her important guest. Imagine *his* shock when he saw me and no boss. I was afraid he would think I had played a trick on him to get the best seating in the house for a date of my own."

"I hope he greeted you with as much respect."

"He did. Because he knows it would get back to my employer if he hadn't and she would not be happy about it."

"Well, at least that's good. I would have a word with him otherwise."

"And that would have been reported back to my boss. No thanks! I really like working with her and want to keep it that way. What about your boss?"

"Yeah, I like him and the other guys I work with." But Max couldn't quit thinking about why Becky's boss had singled him out to go out with her. Why not someone else? Someone who lived in Mountain View? Puzzles always made him want to unravel them. Why, if Ms. Tynan thought a PI would be a good guy or match for Becky, not one who was located closer to home? Maybe Ms. Tynan thought Becky needed to meet someone somewhere else since the pool of eligible bachelors was not as acceptable? Who knew? He had to just enjoy dinner with the she-wolf and then he would run with her.

Their meal was served to their table then.

He carved off a bite of veal and ate it. "This sure is good."

"It's my favorite when I've come here with my boss. So what are you working on right now? Anything exciting? If it's okay for you to talk about it."

"I'm trying to track down a missing German shepherd. He raced out of his backyard when the yardmen came in to mow."

"Any leads?"

"No. I'm afraid someone found him and just kept him. According to his family, he's super friendly and will go to anyone who has a kind word to say to him."

"Oh dear. I love animals, so I know how hard that would be for a family to lose one. Maybe I could help you look for him after we run. With our enhanced sense of smell, we would make a great team."

"Sure, if you don't mind looking for a missing dog on a date."

"No, I'd love to help you."

He appreciated the offer, and it would be nice to have the company. They finally finished their meals and Max said, "I'll need to thank your Ms. Tynan for both a delightful dinner and dinner companion."

"She'll be thrilled it worked out. Not that anything more will come of this…" Becky quickly said, as if she was afraid to sound like it was a given that he would want to see her again. Especially if it was on his own money.

"Yeah, well, I was thinking about that. No time like the present to make another date. How about… Well, I guess we need to see if your boss can release you for another date first."

Becky smiled. "I'll text her now to ask her. Don't pay a tip," she quickly said when he pulled his wallet out of his pocket. "She has already done so." Becky got a response right away. "My boss is okay with it, but she insists that the only time she can afford to lose me this coming week is tomorrow night. Is that too soon? I just need to make a reservation for her and a companion at this restaurant for tomorrow night and I'll be free. She also said to enjoy my time with you tonight. I hope she doesn't think I'm into one-night stands."

He chuckled. "I know that's not the case, not when we are what we are. Are you ready to go?"

"Oh, yes, I can't wait to run."

Just as she said she would, she followed him home in her car, and he wondered if she was surprised he owned a place with acreage that adjoined his boss's place. Then he showed her the guest room where she could strip and shift, and he went to his bedroom to do so. He met her in the living room where she was waiting for him, a pretty black wolf, her tongue hanging out, appearing to be eager to run with him. Just as much as he was eager to run with her as a wolf.

They took off through the wolf door and raced through the woods to the river beyond. The property had wildlife cameras all over it, and anyone monitoring them could see that wolves were running on the property. They would know him, but they wouldn't have a clue who the pretty black wolf was. He was so glad Ryan had told him he *couldn't* swap with Asher to take the assignment. Asher would be disappointed that he hadn't gotten the job, once he learned of it. Who would ever have thought it would have turned out this well?

They ran with each other, him leading the way, her exploring and smelling the scents of rabbits and deer, of other wolves, and he imagined she would be surprised to smell all the wolves in the area. Was there a wolf pack in Mountain View? He wondered too where her family was. He hadn't mentioned his either though. He had to remind himself they'd had just one date. He couldn't expect for them to know each other's life history after one dinner out.

CHAPTER 2

BECKY REALLY LIKED MAX, AND SHE HOPED SHE COULD continue to date him without it interfering with their work. Cute smile, great dimples, dark hair and dark-brown eyes that melted her heart defined him. His hair was a little longish and he wore a trimmed beard. He looked like he was about six two, like her dad and brother were, while her mother and sister and she all were five seven.

His suit was light gray; his shirt was even lighter and complemented his hair and eyes. The shirt was open at the collar and a couple of buttons below were unfastened, which made him appear both dressy, casual, wolfish, and sexy.

He was the perfect gentleman at dinner...and then offering for her to run with him on his pack's property? She knew he liked her well enough to extend the date night a bit. She would never have thought a blind date could be this nice and lead to a wolf run.

She smelled all kinds of wolves that had been in the area, and that made her wonder how big the pack was. She'd belonged to one when she was growing up, but they only had six other wolves in their pack. What would they think of her going on a blind date? They wouldn't have approved. But it turned out all right, hadn't it?

They were running toward a river. She could hear the sound of it flowing and smell the water when suddenly rain began pouring down. She loved the rain, so she didn't mind getting wet. Their outer coats would repel much of the moisture, their inner coats keeping them warm and dry, though it was a nice warm summer evening, so getting cold wasn't an issue.

She wondered if they would run into any other wolves out here.

But she also wondered why her employer had contacted Max's boss to hire just him. Pamela couldn't know he was a wolf, but she suspected, from the way Max spoke of them, that his boss hired only wolves. She was feeling great, excited about running with a wolf. Max's dark-gray saddle was surrounded by lighter gray fur, his belly fur and under his chin all blond and his muzzle a light gray, though he had a dark-gray mask on the top of his head and face. He seemed to enjoy running with her as much as she enjoyed running with him.

The rain didn't make any difference to her, and she was glad Max hadn't stopped to return her home as if she was so fragile she would melt. Maybe he was afraid she would end the date with him, but she was serious. She wanted to help him look for the missing dog first. She loved her job, but she didn't do anything like this, nothing where she could use her special wolf skills. Sometimes, she wished she worked for someone who was a wolf and would know how important that was to her.

They reached the river and drank from it, and then he nuzzled her in a way that said he was glad she was with him. She reciprocated, and then he indicated he was ready to return home if she was.

She agreed and they raced off to see who could reach the house first. She hadn't raced with a male wolf on a date ever. He gave her the lead, and she thought he was cute for doing so. Though she was fast, so he might not have needed to. They would have to test their speed some other time. For their first date, this was perfect.

As soon as they arrived at the house, they heard both their phones ringing. She'd known the bliss couldn't last long. She hurried into the guest room, shifted, and shut the door. She was so hoping Pamela didn't need her home right away. "Hello?"

"Hey, I didn't want to interrupt you about anything, but I was just checking on you to make sure you're all right."

Becky smiled. She'd be even better if her employer would give her the whole night off. "Yes, we're having fun. He's a PI and is looking into the disappearance of a family's German shepherd. I offered to help him look for the dog." After telling her boss that Max was a PI, she realized Pamela already knew that.

"Oh good. I just wanted to make sure I hadn't done anything wrong in setting you up on a blind date you hadn't enjoyed. Though I guess if you're having another date tomorrow night, things are working out."

"Yes, thanks, Pamela. We're having fun."

"Enjoy the rest of your time with your date. And good luck with finding the dog."

"Thanks." Then they ended the call and Becky sighed with relief.

As soon as she was dressed, she joined Max in the living room. She was eager to help him look for the dog.

"Here's Bear's scent." Max handed her the collar. "I kept it with me in case I find him, and I've got his leash in the car. We'll park at the homeowners' home and then take off on foot from there. I'll let them know we're coming so we can park in their circular drive."

"Okay, good idea." She so hoped they could find the dog. "When you find their dog, then what? You'll have another assignment to work on?"

They climbed into his car and took off down the road.

"I always have several cases I'm dealing with at the same time. Like the missing dog case, the blind date mission—"

She laughed. "Hopefully, you'll see that as a mission accomplished."

"Yeah, in the best of ways, and I'm going to tell my boss to refund Ms. Tynan's fee for hiring me for the job, if Ryan had accepted one."

She laughed. "Pamela would not take a refund, believe me. She hired you in good faith."

"Was that a call from your boss?"

"Yeah, she was just checking to see if we were still enjoying our time together. What about your call?"

"From Ryan, asking the same thing of me. He was astounded and glad to hear you are a wolf."

At least the rain had stopped when they finally reached the dog owners' two-story brick home and its big circular drive and parked. Becky was surprised they didn't have an ornate fence and electronic gate out front, but none of the other fancy homes in the area did either.

"Do you worry that a thief stole the dog to resell?" That was what she would be concerned about.

"I worry more about someone in the neighborhood calling the police because two people are roaming through the neighborhood looking for a dog."

"Oh, I hadn't thought of that."

"We have a couple of gray wolves on the police force, and everyone knows the mayor and that his investigators are good at their jobs—if the police get called to check us out. And I'm sure you have nothing to worry about since your employer is someone important."

"Right. I just don't want to drag her name into it if we are picked up for looking suspicious, if I can help it."

"I don't blame you."

After he texted the dog's owners, they got out of the car. With collar and leash in hand, Max and Becky began walking through the neighborhood, searching for Bear's scent.

"When did he go missing?" Becky asked.

"Just yesterday afternoon. I came right away, but I couldn't find any sign of him."

"Did they take him in any particular direction when they took him for walks?"

"No. They left food out for him, but raccoons ate it."

"Oh, that's not good."

They had walked about two miles around the houses, though all of them had fenced-in backyards. Unless the dog jumped one, he wouldn't be in someone else's yard. Unless someone took him into their yard or home.

Max finally said, "We could be at this all night—"

"Wait, I hear something. Scratching? Bear! Are you there?" She thought she heard some noise from the garage of the two-story stucco home they were approaching.

A dog yipped in the garage.

"Bear!" Max called out.

The dog barked. But it wasn't alerting its owners that someone was trespassing on their property. It was a happy bark that said he recognized his name but couldn't reach them to greet them properly.

"That's got to be him," Becky said. "I don't smell his scent here, but if they picked him up in a vehicle, they could have brought him here and left him in the garage."

"When I went by yesterday to ask all the neighbors if they'd seen any sign of the dog, these owners weren't home. I checked again earlier today, same thing. No one was home. No barking either though." Max went to the front door and knocked.

A dog in the house was barking, and so was the one in the garage. They sounded similar in breed and size.

No one answered, and Becky was afraid the owners didn't want to open their door to strangers. She didn't blame them.

Max called out, "I'm a private investigator searching for a missing German shepherd that goes by the name of Bear. I believe he's the dog in your garage."

A man came to the door then and frowned at him. "Have you got some ID?"

"Yes, sir." Max showed him his ID and a picture of Bear and his collar and leash with his name and address on them. "You can verify with the pet owners that they hired me to locate him." He gave the man the owner's number.

"You're with the mayor's PI agency?"

"Yes, sir."

"Come on in," he said. "I just brought my wife home from the hospital. The dogs were staying with friends. I didn't have time to locate the owners."

"No problem. They'll be thrilled to get him back."

The man led them into the garage and Bear greeted them all. Max put on his collar and leash.

"Where's your vehicle?" the man asked.

"We've been walking through the neighborhood, searching for Bear, hoping he was still in the area." Max explained how the dog had gotten out of the family's yard.

The man shook his head. "My yardmen were here when Bear came into the yard to greet them. They thought the dog belonged to me so they shut him up in the yard. Imagine my surprise to find an extra German shepherd at my house. Sally, my German shepherd, was in the house at the time and she adores Bear."

Max and Becky smiled.

"I'm glad you came to get him. At my age, I'm too old to have a bunch of grand puppies."

They laughed.

"Thanks for taking care of him," Max said.

"Sure thing."

Then Max and Becky headed back to the owners' home about a mile away.

"I ought to take you on more of my cases. You're my good luck charm," Max said to Becky.

"I'm glad we found him, and I can't wait to see the happy reunion." She couldn't think of a happier moment for all parties concerned.

But before that could happen, Max was texting the owners the good news.

"I bet they're excited."

"Yeah. They wanted to drive out and pick him up, but I told them we're giving him a good walk home," Max said.

"He smells like he could use a bath," Becky said, wrinkling her nose.

Bear wagged his tail at her, looking to be having the time of his life. New friends, a nice long walk. Yeah, nothing could be better until he returned home to his family.

When they finally reached the house, the man and his wife and three boys of about seven through ten years of age rushed out of the house to greet Bear. He was just as happy to see them as they were to see him, his tail wagging hard, his tongue licking their faces, then all giving him affectionate hugs.

"We can't thank you enough," the man said.

"We're just glad we finally found him," Max said.

Then they said their good nights and Max drove Becky back to his place. He got them some glasses of water, and after they had their fill, she had to head home.

"I've had a lovely time with you tonight, Max. It couldn't have been better."

"I agree." He kissed her lightly on the lips, and she kissed him back and smiled. "'Night, Becky."

"'Night." She got into her car and drove home feeling heavenly. She thoroughly enjoyed a fantastic dinner with Max and a lovely wolf run, and the perfect culmination of the events tonight? Finding and returning a beloved pet home to his family.

She finally arrived home and had barely gotten inside when Pamela called. Becky was so ready to just call it a night and bask in the delightful evening she'd spent with Max. She didn't want to think about work right now.

"Hello, Pamela."

"Did you find the dog?"

"Yes, we did. Seeing him with his family was truly heartwarming."

But Becky suspected that wasn't why her employer had called her.

"Does he seem like a...good PI?"

"Of course. I'm sure that the mayor would hire only the best for his agency's reputation." Not to mention, Max was a wolf.

"You're sure?"

"Well, yes." Becky wondered what this was all about. Pamela seemed so serious.

"Okay, I want you to hire him for a job for me."

That was why Pamela set Becky up on a blind date with a PI? So Becky could investigate the PI for her? That was hilarious. Wouldn't Max be amused that Becky had been investigating him even though she hadn't known it either!

"I need him to find the man who was to be my husband, but I don't want anyone to know about it. No one, all right? Can Max be fully trusted with this confidential information?"

"Husband?" When in the world did that happen?

"Yes, yes, it's something no one knows about. I'm an only child, and when I fell in love with Christopher Anderson, my parents were furious with the both of us. They said if I insisted on marrying him, I would lose all my inheritance in the event of their deaths. Well, I've finally received the rest of my inheritance, and I'm going to do what I have always wanted to do. Be with him. He's kind and generous, and I think he still loves me like I love him."

The first thing Becky wondered was if the man truly loved Pamela or if he was a gold digger, waiting in the wings for her to come into her inheritance.

"In heart we were all but married, but we couldn't risk actually getting married. If either of my parents learned the truth about it, they would have given all of my inheritance away to a cousin. Now, I know it sounds cavalier, if I truly loved him, I would have given up the inheritance to be with him—"

"But it was his idea for you not to throw it all away for him, right?" Becky hadn't meant to sound like she didn't trust the guy's motives, though she didn't in the least. When a woman fell in love with someone, she could easily be swayed into believing the guy loved her too. Becky had been down that road, so she knew something about it.

"Right. I know how it sounds. If he'd wanted to marry me without hesitation, casting aside the money, and all that mattered was me, it would seem more legitimate. I understand that. And I'm no dummy."

No, Pamela was shrewd in her business dealings.

"So you want Max to try to find him? He wasn't just waiting for you to get in touch with him and marry you?"

"Yes and no. He's been waiting for ten years. But in the last six weeks, I haven't been able to reach him. He says it all has to do with his work."

"Ah, so you want Max to not only locate your husband-to-be but also to ensure he's a safe bet to marry."

"Exactly. That's why I need to know if Max is going to be close-mouthed about this whole business. I don't want even the mayor to know about this job. I'll pay Max handsomely, rest assured, and he'll have to dedicate himself to just this high-priority case.

"Christopher waited so long for me that I can't, with a good conscience, end things between us without knowing what he's been up to and if he's seeing someone else and ready to move on or if he's truly ready to make a full commitment to me."

"Ten years is a long time, and you haven't been seeing each other in all that time?" Becky couldn't imagine the relationship they'd had. If she was hooked on a guy, no way would she be able to wait to be with him, money or no. And if he wanted her to wait and marry her when she had the money instead, that made him suspect to Becky's way of thinking.

"We had been seeing each other up until six weeks ago. We stopped when Christopher thought someone was spying on us, but then I just couldn't get in touch with him. My dad could very well have had a PI watching either one of us earlier on."

"What if Max has other important cases he's working?" Becky couldn't expect him to drop everything for one person. It wasn't fair to the people whose cases he was already working on, nor to him or anyone else with the firm that would have to take over the cases.

"We'll come to that when we come to it."

"When was the last time you actually saw Christopher?"

"Six weeks ago to the day. I told him that the settlement would be through soon, back then, but he didn't believe it. He thought I was just stringing him along. He said he had a job in Europe for the next few weeks and then he would be home. As soon as I learned I would get the rest of the inheritance, I figured it was time to tell him, but something just doesn't feel right. Actually, I probably could use a full-time investigator."

Becky sighed. Max was a wolf and she suspected he would prefer working for Ryan since he was a wolf too. She could imagine how nice it would be to talk about cases when they were all wolves and could relate to one another so well.

"Okay, so you want me to ask Max to look into this boyfriend of yours, who was to be your husband, and see if there's anything fishy going on and report back to you. Max might need to talk to you further to see if he can learn any other details that you might not have told me." Either because her boss didn't want to say or she just didn't think the information was relevant, but it would help Max with the case. Becky hoped he would take the case and she'd see more of him.

"Yes. Call him tonight, if you don't mind, and let me know what he says."

"Yes, ma'am." Becky ended the call and called Max. "Hey, my boss wants to hire you for a job." Then she explained everything she knew about it.

"Seriously? Okay, no running it by my boss? He's going to get suspicious if I transfer my cases to the other agents and won't tell him why."

She chuckled. "You know? You're a wolf. Of course you'll tell him, and of course the word won't get out to anyone beyond those that need to know. I'm not worried about that. You have to do what you have to do to keep yourself from getting backed into a corner."

"True. I didn't want to lie and tell you I wouldn't. Ryan needs to know what's going on with the agents in his office. We have a daily briefing, letting him know about the more important cases we're working on, though sometimes what seems to be less important might be extremely so."

"Where does this case rate?"

"I'd say, considering who is hiring me for the job and the concern to her reputation, it's extremely important."

"Did you need to speak to her about Christopher?"

"I do. I'll give her a call."

"All right. I'm going to get ready for bed. 'Night, Max, and thanks so much for doing this."

"Wait, was our dinner a case of you checking me out to see if I was reliable enough?"

She smiled. "Well, for *me*, it was just a blind date. Apparently, Pamela had an agenda of her own. That's kind of a switch for you, isn't it?"

He laughed. "I would never have guessed it in a million years. She's great at this business."

"I think what sold her on you, besides my putting in a good word, was that you found the dog for the owners."

"And you had a lot to do with that."

"We make a great team. I'll see you tomorrow."

CHAPTER 3

Max didn't know what to think of this new mission of working for Ms. Tynan. He was certain his boss would be fine with it, but he still needed to check with him because Max would have to transfer all his cases to the other guys. And Ryan needed to know where Max was if he wasn't working on regular cases. He called Ryan right away and explained what he needed to do.

"All right, Max, you sure got yourself into something that sounds intriguing. Mum's the word. Tell the other guys they need to take over your cases, and if anyone gives you grief, have them come to me. I would rather this stay between you, me, Becky, and Ms. Tynan."

"Yes, sir."

"How did the date go? I guess Ms. Tynan was checking you out."

Max smiled. "Becky and I had fun. And yeah, that was sure a surprise to both of us."

Ryan chuckled. "That's good. See you tomorrow morning then."

"Thanks, Ryan." Then Max called Asher. "Hey, I've got a job to do—boss approved—and it means not working on any other cases."

"Well, hell," Asher said. "I bet the pay is better than the cases you were working on. So what do I need to take on now?"

Max was glad his friends at the agency agreed to take his other cases on such short notice. He really wanted to do this right, and he couldn't have if he'd been worrying about taking care of cases he'd set aside, though he knew Ryan would have made sure someone did them. They all worked together, and if someone was having trouble with something, they all chipped in to assist. It helped that they were wolves and belonged to the same pack.

The good news was he was going to be seeing more of Becky, and that really played into his plans perfectly. He would enjoy every minute he could with the she-wolf!

Then Max called Becky back. "We're all good. I made arrangements with Asher and the others to take the rest of my cases, and I've talked to the boss and he's fine with it. Do I need to call your boss and tell her?"

"No. As her personal assistant, I handle all the stuff like that. If she feels differently about this, she can tell me if she wants to deal directly with you."

"That works for me."

"I'll tell her you're for sure working strictly on her case. She'll be pleased. Don't be surprised if you solve this for her in a way that makes her happy enough that she might just want to hire you full-time."

He chuckled. "She might not like to hear what I learn."

"I totally agree. I'll see you tomorrow then."

"You will. 'Night, Becky." This sure had been a strange turn of events that he'd never expected. He stripped off his clothes and took his shower, climbed into bed, pulled his covers up, then grabbed his laptop resting on his bedside table. He set it on his lap and checked his special databases for anything relating to Christopher. He had so many hits that he would have to speak with Ms. Tynan again to get some more details on him.

Max set his laptop aside and turned out his lamp, settled against his pillow, and closed his eyes. He suspected that if the other single guys ever met Becky, they would be hounding the boss for a blind-date assignment. But Max didn't believe they would ever get as lucky as he had on a blind date. And solving a case tonight with her? It couldn't have worked out any better, not only for the family, the dog, the ones who had found Bear, and him and Becky, but it probably helped him snag this new assignment that looked like it could get interesting really quick.

———

First thing in the morning, Max called Becky's boss. "Ms. Tynan, this is Max Browning. I don't have enough information for Christopher Anderson. Do you have any other details about him that will help me narrow the search? Birthplace? Birth date? Parents' names? High school attended? All these things will help with reducing the number of names I have to comb through."

"Yeah, sure. And please call me Pamela. Christopher and I went to school together. We graduated from Vander High School, class of 2008, and he was born June 21, 1990. I was in some of the same classes with him. He's a natural strawberry blond, has the nickname of Red, and his parents' names were Fred and June Anderson. Both of them still live in Mountain View, but they are adamant he shouldn't have anything to do with me since I wouldn't give up my fortune to marry him. It's a decade later and they could have had grandchildren by now. They felt that once I received my inheritance, I wouldn't marry him, so my relationship with them is as bad as it was with my parents with regard to Christopher. Also, he was born in Kansas City."

"I'll start the search on the databases again. I don't want to ruffle feathers, but I do want to speak with Christopher's parents to see if they have any clue where he might have gone."

"I don't believe they will be helpful at all with this. If anything, they will lie about his whereabouts so that I can't get ahold of him, if they know where he is."

"I'll let you know if this helps. Talk to you later." Max and Pamela ended the call, and he began to narrow the search down. Using Christopher's parents' names, his birth date, and his high school, Max was able to narrow it down pretty quickly. Even though he'd thought this was going to take a lot longer, now it looked like it wouldn't take any time at all. But one of the things he learned was that Christopher's biological parents had died in a car accident when he was two in Kansas City. The Andersons were his adoptive parents. Max wondered if Christopher knew that.

Becky called him back. "Hey, I'm free for lunch if you want to come here, and you can tell me how things are going. Pamela is busy for most of the day, so she wanted you to update me if you have any news."

"Yeah, sure, I'd love that."

When it was time for lunch, Max arrived at Becky's home on Pamela's estate, a lovely little brick one-story home surrounded by woods, but Becky had planters around the house that were filled with flowers. He wondered if she loved gardening and had planted them.

Becky had made a delightful lunch of Indian spiced chickpea wraps, something he'd never had before.

They sat down to eat, and he told her how good the wraps were.

"Thanks. I should have asked if it was something you might like first. So what did you learn?" she asked.

"I called Christopher's parents, and they wouldn't tell me a thing about his whereabouts. Either they figured Pamela wants to know, or they're worried he's in some trouble and they don't want to give him up."

"Who did you say you were working for?"

"I say I'm a private investigator, and I don't name my client."

"Okay, that's good. But they still suspected something was wrong?"

"Sure, when a private investigator gets involved, usually

something is up. Though if he has nothing to worry about, there shouldn't be any problem. I also learned the Andersons are his adoptive parents, and I don't know if Christopher realizes that or not. He was two when his parents died."

"Oh, that's sad. So what do you do next?"

"I'm trying to learn who his friends are and where he's worked in the past. I'm coming up with nothing. No current location for him."

"Hmm, I'll text Pamela and see." Becky quickly pulled her phone off the dining table and texted her boss, then waited. When she got a return text, she said, "Okay, she said no, that he was an investment counselor, did investments overseas, but he never told her which firm he worked for. I wonder if she didn't ask or look into it further when she was seeing him because she didn't want to believe he could be a con man or seeing another woman."

"She's more interested in learning the truth. Nobody likes to believe they're being conned, and when emotions and relationships get in the way, it can be really hard to keep reality and relationships separate," Max said.

"So gut feeling, what do you think?"

"I don't know enough about him to give a guess yet. Sure, I can speculate, but I would rather be more well informed first. Speculation won't help my investigation, unless it comes up with new leads I can look into."

"Pamela's really open about a lot of things, but when it comes to relationships, she is really tight-lipped about them. I had no idea she had been dating Christopher. Not that I blame her. She has been in the tabloids any number of times, and she really tries to avoid anything about her love life getting into them. Particularly while she was trying to get her inheritance. If her parents hadn't been so adamant about who she was seeing, she might not have been so secretive. In any event, I don't blame her. It's different for us. We are able to see each other when we can anytime, and we don't have to worry about paparazzi reporting our every move. Of course, they did report about Christopher early on, but then she was careful because her parents were so angry with her."

======================

Later that afternoon, Max was back at the office, looking up news stories about the Tynans, and one caught his attention. He thought he might see some references to the boy Pamela Tynan had dated, but this was a story of when she was a little girl and she had cried wolf! According to the news story, she had broken through ice on the pond on her parents' property and a wolf saved her. Only the wolf shifted into a woman and fished her out before she drowned. And then she carried Pamela off to a cabin somewhere where she warmed the girl up and then took her back to her property and vanished.

No one believed the young girl, but Max thought it was too much of a coincidence that Pamela had seen a wolf shifter who had saved her when she was young, hired a personal assistant later who was a wolf, and then picked Ryan's PI agency to hire a wolf to check into the missing boyfriend. Knowing the woman who rescued her was a wolf shifter was one thing, but how did Pamela know about Becky, if she did?

Then what about the business with him and the other wolves in the Green Valley pack? He remembered the incident they'd had on their Green Valley pack land recently. The case where hunters had shot one of their wolves on the pack leaders' land. And the hunters had sworn they'd shot at wolves. Of course the wolves said they were walking along the river on a date when the hunters started shooting at them. It was in the news all over the place. Several of the wolves had been involved in the whole affair, including Max and the rest of the PI team as they tried to gather evidence against the hunters. Some had testified against the hunters; some had been in the courtroom watching the proceedings.

Pamela could have seen the news at any time since it was so widespread, given the nature of the hunters' accusation—that they'd been shooting at wolves who had turned out to be humans. He could see where she might have put two and two together and figured it out that the couple the hunters had said were wolves had truly been shifters too, since she'd had the earlier wolf experience at the frozen pond.

Then there was Becky. Why did Pamela assume Becky was a wolf, if his assumptions were correct? He called Becky up to ask her. "Do you ever run as a wolf on your employer's property? Somewhere you would feel safe?"

"Yes. She has hundreds of acres that are never used for anything. She doesn't allow hunting or anyone to trespass on the property. It's really pristine, and it makes for a great place to run in. Why?"

"I found an article about her when she was a young girl. She was rescued by a wolf."

"What?"

"Yes. I have no idea who the woman who rescued her might have been, but she pulled her out of the frozen pond on her parents' property when Pamela fell through. The wolf shifted to save her. The girl told everyone, but of course no one believed her."

"Ohmigod, the woman carried the girl to a cabin and warmed her up and—"

"Yes, you found the same article I was reading," Max said.

"No, my mother told me the story. She saved a young human girl, despite her people chastising her for doing so. She couldn't let the girl drown, even though she risked detection. She carried her toward home, but then my dad, who wasn't mated to her yet, came to help Mom and the girl, so my mother could shift back into the wolf. At the house, they warmed Pamela up, dried her clothes and hair, carried her back to her property, and told her to stay off the pond in winter or spring thaw and run along home.

"My dad said that he mated my mother shortly after that

because she did what was right, and he would have done the same. Still, the other wolves in their pack didn't agree. My mother wouldn't have done anything differently, and my father was always proud of her. Then she had me, my sister, and brother, triplets, and it made her doubly glad she'd saved the girl. No one deserved to die like that."

"Pamela Tynan was the girl." It all fit.

"My boss," Becky said. "She knew who my mother was then? That was why she hired me?"

"I don't know. Not for sure. But, well, I don't believe in that many coincidences."

"Okay, I have to agree. Wow, now I don't know what to do. The others in the pack always said that humans who knew about us would have to be turned or eliminated. We couldn't risk that anyone would learn about us."

"I agree. But because of her wealth and how well known she is in the area, I don't think that's a viable option either way."

CHAPTER 4

BECKY WAS SO SHOCKED TO LEARN THAT A WOLF HAD RESCUED Pamela when she was a girl that she didn't know what to think. That her mother was the one who had saved Pamela was even more of a surprise. That Pamela might know that Becky was a wolf just blew her mind.

She immediately wondered if Pamela had seen her running as a wolf on her property. But then Becky thought that maybe Pamela had wildlife cameras about. Becky had never realized they could be set up in the woods. *Great. Just great.* She would never be able to run as a wolf out there again. She hoped that Max wasn't right in his assumptions, but she didn't think he was wrong. It was just too much of a coincidence that Pamela set her up with Max and that she'd hired Becky after her mother had saved Pamela's life when she was a girl. Becky wondered just what Pamela had thought of her when she hired her. She'd had to wonder if Becky was a wolf too, unless Pamela's family had convinced her that werewolves were just imaginary creatures.

Becky wanted to talk to her about it. She wanted to quit her job and leave town. She felt conflicted. She loved her job and had never wanted to leave it. Pamela had made her feel like a friend and confidante, yet she knew so much more about her than Becky knew about Pamela. She couldn't believe it. She sighed and knew she had to just focus on the current job, learn what she could about the boyfriend and the new guy, and go from there. Becky wanted to tell Pamela she knew and understood and hoped Pamela would keep their secret. But maybe she would anyway. Maybe she realized that Becky needed someone in her life—a wolf—just like

Pamela wanted someone in her own life. If that was the case, Becky appreciated her boss all the more.

"What do we do now?" Becky asked Max.

"We do just what we planned to do. We learn about Christopher, and beyond that, we talk to Ryan and Carol, my pack leaders, about what's going on. They need to learn the truth when it involves anyone knowing about wolf shifters in the pack, and in your case too."

"I just can't believe this."

"I can't believe your mother rescued her. But it sounds to me like Pamela wants to pay her back in some way by taking you in, giving you a job, and finding a mate for you."

Becky smiled. "She doesn't know anything about our kind. That we mate for life and relationships have to be for a lifetime."

"I agree, but I think that's what this is all about. The date bit and to see what you thought of me as far as looking into her relationship."

"Do you think that's all on the up and up? What if she doesn't really need anyone looked into? That you can't find anything about this Christopher boyfriend?"

"In the kind of work I do, anything is possible."

"Okay. You're coming for dinner?"

"Yeah, sure. I can't wait."

That night, Max drove to Becky's house for dinner, eager to enjoy her company again, and she made pork chops, fried dollar potatoes, and a cauliflower and broccoli blend.

After dinner, she took away the dishes and put them in the dishwasher. "What if Pamela has wildlife cameras set up on her property and she has recorded where I've been running as a wolf?"

Max frowned. "Wouldn't you have noticed that she was having them set up? You're in charge of all that, right?"

"Normally, yeah, but if she wanted to catch me at it, then maybe not. Maybe she had them set up before I interviewed for the job. Then again, it would have been smarter to have done so on the trail I normally take."

"Let's take a walk. You show me where you usually run. I don't see a dog door, so she didn't have one installed for you."

"No. But she's always said I could have a dog and have a dog door installed if I would like."

Max raised a brow as they headed outside. "You made a trail where you walked?"

"Yeah, I never thought anyone would be watching me going on my runs. I would always shift way out in the woods."

"Always at the same place?"

"Yeah, I'm totally a creature of habit. I always felt safe there, never ran into any problems, and moving to another location might not have been the same for me. So I didn't want to chance going somewhere else."

He thought it was a nice night for a walk in the woods with Becky, though he would have loved to run here with her as a wolf too. Every chance he had at changing into his wolf form when he could do so safely was something he loved to do. He was looking up at the trees for any sign of trail cameras along the path Becky always took, the grass worn down here, evidence that a hiker's trail had been made.

He smelled her lingering scent in the woods, and if he'd come upon her scent before, he would have wanted to find the wolf that it belonged to. A she-wolf, sweet and saucy. He smiled down at her, but she was looking a little worried, and he realized this wasn't just a pleasant walk in the woods with him but an investigation into whether she'd been observed as a wolf running through the area.

"Have you ever seen her on your runs through the woods as a wolf?" he asked. As wolves, they saw movement and were really observant of their surroundings. They had to be, since they were wary of danger to themselves, so he figured Becky wouldn't have just run through the property without thinking of that, no matter how vast the land was or how little it was tramped on by anyone else.

"No. And yes, I naturally watched for any sign of anyone. Even though it's posted all over that no hunting is allowed, it's always a concern that hunters will ignore the signs and try to hunt on the property. So I'm always cautious when I go out. I haven't seen anything that looks like a camera in a tree, have you?"

"No." But that didn't mean Pamela didn't have trail cameras watching for wildlife in other locations or just for security. Even if she just had them up to watch any wildlife—cougars, deer, anything that might move around on her property. "You could ask her."

"Then she might suspect that I realize she knows about me."

"You could smell her scent and see her reaction." As wolves, they were much more attuned to changes in people's behavior and their corresponding scent. "Um, not that I want to worry you, but I think I'll go over your home with a bug detector to make sure there are no listening devices in your place and no hidden cameras either."

"Oh, great. I never thought of that."

"I've been hired to check a home, office, vehicles over for that very thing."

Becky's eyes widened. "Did you find any?"

"In one client's office and home, yes. But it wasn't what I thought."

"Like espionage? Someone trying to learn about their products or something?"

"FBI surveillance. They called me in and told me what was up. The surveillance was legit and what the client was doing wasn't."

She arched a brow, waiting to hear what the client had been doing that wasn't right.

"Drugs. He was running a big pharmaceutical drug ring, and I nearly messed up the sting operation."

"So what happened?"

"I had removed the devices and destroyed them, then the FBI took me into their confidence and had a little talk with me. I could be charged with obstruction, or I could agree to plant new devices."

"Did you?"

"Sure. I work for the good guys. I told the client that I needed to do another sweep in a few days to make sure I hadn't missed anything, then slipped in several more bugs than the FBI had managed to plant the first time around. I was off the hook and they arrested the bad guy, who had incriminated himself fully." Max shrugged. "All in a day's work."

"Wow. I'm glad you didn't get charged for a crime."

"Well, Ryan wasn't happy about it. He doesn't like it if we end up with a client who's a bad egg. It's bad news if we look like we're helping a scoundrel get away with illegal stuff. So yeah, we started screening clients better. Though they can slip through the cracks sometimes. Like with Pamela. Digging deeper, I found the connection with our kind. On the surface, she seems to be just a nice woman who cared about you having a date out. Then it morphed into me looking into a guy she'd been dating. And now? Maybe something even bigger—as it relates to us. Has she ever said anything to you that would lead you to believe she knows about you? Or us?"

"No, this is all a shock to me. I mean, she's always so nice to me. She can be a bear when it comes to other people who work for her. I don't mean in a bad way, but when people do her wrong, she doesn't let it slide. I admire her for it. It's not that she expects perfection. People make mistakes and she's forgiving, but man, if you knowingly do something to undermine her or steal from her, she will really come down on you. For instance, we had a maid who was selling Pamela's stories to a tabloid. It was hitting too close to home for it not to be coming from someone who was on staff.

"Pamela trusted me, as if she thought I had a bigger moral compass, and I guess as a wolf, I do, because none of us want to end up in jail. So I set up a situation where I would give staff members different stories, nothing that would hurt Pamela but that sounded juicy and were so far-fetched that no one would believe them. But coming from me, the people who worked for her would. Only one person, the maid, knew the story I had shared with her, and it went straight to the tabloid. I gave her one more story, though by this point, I knew it had to be her, and then I followed her around, just out of sight like a wolf would, until she made the mistake of calling the tabloid on her phone. Our enhanced hearing being what it is, I was able to listen in beyond the wall. I looked up the man's name, Mr. Quinlin, and found him to be one of the reporters for the tabloid."

"The maid could have been talking to him about something else."

"No, she was sharing the story I had given her. Pamela was at a luncheon in town at the time, and I think the maid thought she was being covert about the whole thing. In truth, she had shared several stories before we caught her at it."

"Hell, you would make a great PI."

Becky laughed. "It only worked because I'm a wolf and I work for Pamela. Anyway, Pamela fired her. She wouldn't give her a referral, and if anyone asks her about her employment with Pamela, she'll tell them the truth. If a prospective hirer wants his or her life exposed to the tabloids, the maid is the one to hire."

Max smiled. "I doubt anyone of consequence will hire her. It's ironic that the maid wanted the extra money but was too short-sighted to realize she had a steady income all along."

"And lots of benefits. Pamela believes in educating her employees. Some are high school dropouts. She doesn't care. She wants them to have the best opportunities in life they can have, like she had, when they leave her employ. One girl, who had been a maid for her, had dreamed of being a nurse. She's an RN now. Pamela made that happen."

"She sounds like a really great employer to work for." Max continued to search the area, walking with Becky to all the usual places she ran as a wolf. They reached the pond where Pamela could have died. "I could have missed trail cameras set up in areas where you don't go that frequently," he admitted. He didn't want Becky to believe he had been totally successful just because he hadn't found any cameras. He was hoping that Pamela hadn't set up any. If she had and she was willing to keep the secret, someone like the corrupt maid wouldn't. What a story for the tabloids—and actually for any of the news sources—that would be. He wrapped his arm around Becky as the air chilled.

"Well, I guess I'll just have to come to your place to go running from now on," Becky said.

Max smiled down at her and then leaned in and kissed her. She wrapped her arms around his waist and kissed him back, and they opened their mouths to each other, tasting the bouquet of the wine they'd had with their dinner. This was an even nicer end to a date. He hadn't expected to kiss her again.

Then they heard movement in the woods and Max turned. He saw a tan-colored cougar watching them, and he yelled at it to go away. But it just stood there with its amber eyes aglow, looking like it was eyeing them as a meal. "Remain standing upright. I'm going to grab a stone and throw it at him, but we don't both want to lean down. With a cougar, we need to look big and menacing."

"Then I'll get the rock and you remain standing tall. You're taller than me after all."

He agreed. "Sure, go for it."

She moved a few paces away from him, but he followed her to stay close, and she grabbed a big stone. Max yelled at the cougar again, but the big cat was keeping his distance and not moving a muscle to leave. Becky returned with the rock and Max pitched it at the cougar. The big cat jumped back but didn't run away like they had hoped. He was stubborn, hungry, and he probably thought humans should be on the menu. Becky got another couple of rocks and gave one to Max. This time, he ran at the cougar, throwing the rock, and she did the same. Hers didn't go as far as his, but still, with two wolves running at him, albeit in their human form, they scared the cat off. At least for the moment.

"Let's head back to your place, but keep a lookout for the cat. Sometimes they'll begin stalking someone once they have their back turned to them," Max said.

"I've never seen one here before."

"He might have come to drink from the pond and we're in his way, or he could be adding us to his meal-to-go along with a drink from the pond." Max gathered some rocks, and so did Becky.

"I would have smelled him before when I went for a run."

"He might be new to the territory."

"I'm definitely running as a wolf at your place."

Max began thinking about the issue with Pamela again. He had to learn the truth from her about whether she believed wolves were real or not.

"I think what you do is fascinating," Becky said. "It's remarkable how you connect all the dots between these news stories concerning wolf issues."

He smiled at her. "It has its ups and downs. But I do like what I do."

Max heard something moving through the woods behind them. They both glanced back at the same time, and he knew Becky had heard the same thing. The cougar was back. "I guess he wasn't looking for water like I had hoped," Max said.

They began walking backward, to keep an eye on the cat. They couldn't run, climb trees, or turn their backs as that could make him chase them down and kill one of them. He was eyeing Becky, the smaller of the two targets. They yelled at him but kept their ammunition in case he got too close. He was following them, keeping the same distance. Max wanted to change into his wolf coat and tackle the cougar, but then Becky would need to also. And he was afraid there still might be trail cameras. Before he could even mention that to her, Becky was stripping off her hiking boots, socks, and jeans. He watched the cougar while she stripped the rest of her clothes off and shifted in a blur of forms. As a wolf, she growled low at the cougar while Max quickly stripped out of his cargo pants, boots, socks, and T-shirt and shifted. Now the cougar had two much more ominous characters to threaten.

Still, the cougar didn't run off. Not until both Max and Becky ran at him. Max wasn't sure she wanted to at first, but then she charged, and he was ahead of her in a second, not wanting her to have to face the threat of the cat's wicked claws and teeth. The cat jumped straight in the air and took off running. Max thought they would run after the cat for a short distance until they figured it had enough of two wolves chasing him. But Becky wasn't stopping so Max kept up with her, racing through the tall grass and feathered, needled pines. They kept running until the cougar was well away from the pond, and then she slowed her run, and so did Max. He figured she was done now.

He assumed the cougar would stay away and wouldn't try to follow them any farther. It was one thing to lob rocks at him. Another to give him a race with death. Not that they planned to kill him, but they had to impress upon him that this territory was theirs.

They licked each other's faces in camaraderie, telling each other they had done good. Then they watched for the cougar for a little bit longer, but it didn't seem to be returning. Max motioned with his head and a little woof to say they needed to get back, and Becky woofed at him. They both raced off, the wind in their fur, their tails straight out in an alpha posture as they headed back to their clothes. He realized even in the face of danger, they worked well as a team. Even as fast as they were running, it took them some time to return to where they'd stripped out of their clothes. Then they shifted and hurried to shake out their clothes and dress. Once they were done, they hugged and kissed each other.

"Outings with you are fun," he said.

"Ditto for me. I never thought I would run into another predator on the prowl out here. Thanks for helping me look for cameras and chasing off the cougar." Despite Becky saying so, she gathered her rocks back up. "Just in case."

"He would be dumb to return to stalk us." But Max picked up his rocks too, because it was better to be safe and prepared than sorry.

They finally reached her house and set the stones in a pile around a tree where Becky already appeared to be nurturing a sedum rock garden.

"I think we need to speak with Pamela about this wolf business," Max said.

"I was afraid you might say that, but are you sure? The notion of letting sleeping dogs lie comes to mind."

"I'm certain you're going to feel differently about her now. You can't help but think she might be watching your every move as a wolf. I propose we somehow bring up the situation with her nearly drowning at the pond. I'll run it past Ryan because wolf stuff like this needs to be discussed, but if you think we could do it, we will. If you think you would have a better chance at it alone or that I would, we can talk about that too. I just think from now on, you'll behave slightly different around her. We need to learn if she truly knows about us or not."

CHAPTER 5

BECKY KNEW MAX WAS RIGHT. WORRYING THAT CAMERAS could have caught their actions tonight, that listening bugs or cameras could be in her home—though Max said there weren't any—made her feel unnerved. And she didn't want to feel that way working for Pamela. But what if they did discuss what Pamela knew about wolves? She would still be an outsider, still have the ability to expose them if they let on that wolf shifters did exist and she wanted to share that news with the world. Becky just felt disquieted about the whole thing.

After Max left, she was going to call her mother and talk to her about the incident.

"I've got to be on my way," Max said. "I'm sure we'll have a pack meeting over this, because it does affect all wolves."

"I agree." This time when they kissed goodbye, it was a long, lingering tongue kiss. He warmed her to her toes and spread the warmth throughout her body to the tips of her fingers that were clinging to him.

He continued the kiss, and she was thinking that, if they could, she would like him to stay here with her tonight. Because of the way Pamela called on her so frequently, she was afraid staying at his place overnight would present a problem.

"You know, it's getting harder for me to give you up for the night," Max said, kissing her cheeks reverently.

"I was feeling the same way about you and wondering if it would be better for you to stay here because of my job or safer for me to stay at your place, because of us both being wolves. But not tonight. I think you need to discuss this business with your pack leaders."

Max sighed. "Yeah, as much as I would love to just stay with you tonight, I agree."

Then they said good night, and he left her home and drove off. She really enjoyed being with Max, and she couldn't believe how swept up she'd become in his job too. She sighed and took a shower, but when she was coming out of it, her phone was ringing. Naturally.

She answered it, and yes, it was from her boss. "Yes, Pamela?"

"Invite Max to have lunch with us tomorrow. I want to hear what he has learned about Christopher."

"Okay, sure, I'll call him and see if that works for him." He was on Pamela's case after all, and Becky didn't know where he would be while he was in the middle of it. Maybe that was another reason Pamela wanted him to work only on her case. Because she was still pulling the matchmaking strings.

"When I said 'us,' I of course meant you too," Pamela said. "I just wanted to clarify that."

"Thanks, Pamela." Becky did eat with Pamela sometimes—because her boss enjoyed her company, Becky figured—and then they would discuss some of the ongoing situations Becky needed to be made aware of or that Becky needed to talk to Pamela about.

"Did he learn anything?" Pamela asked as if her curiosity was getting the best of her and she couldn't wait to hear about the investigation from Max.

"He might have. He had some promising new leads, and he wanted to check into them further."

"And you?"

"Me?" Becky's cheeks heated. She was certain her employer was referring to Max and her dating, but she didn't want to assume as much.

Pamela chuckled. "Coming along fine, I hope."

"We've been enjoying each other's company, yes, Pamela."

"Good. If you ever need any time off to have dates with him, just let me know."

"I will, thanks." But Becky didn't think she would. She would just do her job, and she and Max could be together around their work schedules for meals and maybe some overnight get-togethers. She didn't think she would have to take any extra time off to do that. Her boss really needed her to keep her schedule straight for her. It made Becky feel useful in a good way.

"Well, good night, and I'm glad things are working out. We're having chicken salad for lunch."

"I'll tell him. What time?"

"Noon. Maybe that will give him more time to learn more about the situation with Christopher. And, Becky? If Max needs to go to some other location to run more leads down, I'll send him, all expenses paid."

"I'll tell him. Thanks."

Once they ended their call, she called Max. "Lunch with Pamela at noon; a chicken salad is on the menu. And I'm invited. Also, she'll pay for your expenses if you need to go anywhere else to track Christopher down."

"I'm still trying to learn where he ended up. I'm calling Ryan now about this wolf situation. I'll talk to you later."

"Okay, good luck and good night."

—————————————

On the way home from Mountain View, Max called Ryan and told him about the business with Pamela and the wolf who had rescued her.

"Becky's mom rescued her as a wolf?" Ryan let out his breath. "Okay, we need to talk to Carol about this and get her take on it. We'll have to decide with the rest of the pack how we're going to handle it. I'm sure Carol will want us to meet tonight about it. Then you'll have your decision when you have lunch with Becky and Pamela. If Pamela has any plans to mention the wolf business to you, we need you to be ready."

"Right, though I suspect the lunch date has to do with Christopher and not anything to do with wolves, but you never know. Already this has gone in so many different directions that it's hard to say."

"Correct. I'll give you call in a little bit." Ryan ended the call but called back only a few minutes later. "The meeting is scheduled in fifteen minutes. Everyone's headed to my place now."

"All right. I'm almost there." That was one thing Max loved about his pack leaders. They weren't wishy-washy about taking action. They got things done right away.

When he arrived at the pack leaders' house, several wolves were already there. Some lived close and others lived across the town, but it still would only take them about ten minutes to get there. No traffic issues in Green Valley, especially this late at night.

Max explained the situation to the pack members. Some of the older wolves shook their heads. He took that to mean they thought that Becky's mother shouldn't have rescued the human girl. But if it had been him, he would have done the same thing. Carol had been more recently bitten and turned, so she was more sympathetic to the human equation. They could very well have eliminated Carol after *she* had been bitten. She was also a nurse, so her goal was to save people and not let them die without doing everything she could in her bag of tricks to get them through. Ryan felt the same way.

Most everyone did, except for five of the elders, one female, four males.

"So we let Max tell her straight out that she was right all along? A wolf shifter saved her?" one of the elders asked.

"I think we'll let it ultimately be Max's call. He's seeing the woman tomorrow for lunch, and we assume they'll be discussing the case he's working on for her. But if the other situation comes up, we want everyone to be in agreement on how it's handled," Ryan said.

"Kill her or turn her?" the she-wolf elder asked.

"Or let her live among us as she has all along," Max said.

"Okay, so do we put it to a vote? Three different options. We let her live as she has before, we eliminate her, we turn her. I think everyone knows what the repercussions are for each of the options. She's not some drifter, so if she's turned and can't fight the shift, that's going to be an issue for someone as important as she is. The same if she somehow just vanishes. Or if we leave her be, she might tell on us," Ryan said.

"But she hasn't before," Carol said.

"She did in the beginning, but she was just a kid, scared, and nearly drowned," Max said, having to be perfectly honest about it. If she learned they were really wolves, if she only suspected so now, then what? Would she want to tell everyone who hadn't believed her before? They couldn't trust that she wouldn't. Then too, if she decided she wanted to marry Christopher, the husband would be her closest confident. Would she tell someone who had such a special place in her heart the truth? It was hard keeping secrets like that from someone you loved, even if it could protect them.

Carol passed around pieces of paper and pens for everyone to write down their choices. Then once everyone wrote a 1, 2, or 3 down to choose their selection—let her be, death, or turned—Carol collected them in a bowl. Then she said, "Okay, so this is only in the event that she truly knows what we are. If she doesn't or doesn't make any hint to Max and Becky that she does, we take no action."

Everyone agreed. That was one thing Max liked about their pack. They had a really tight-knit pack. Ryan and Carol made a good team. The pack members had been a little worried that Carol might be a problem with her shifting issues, but she was a nurse and well liked, so they couldn't have been more pleased with the way things had turned out between her and Ryan.

"So what about you and Becky?" Asher asked before Carol could read the votes off the papers in the bowl.

Max smiled and everyone laughed. Yeah, he wasn't giving her up to any bachelor wolf in the pack or anywhere else.

Then Carol began reading off the notes, and at the end, not one person voted to have her eliminated. Most wanted her turned. Five were willing to let her live as before.

If Pamela wanted to be turned, the good thing about that was Becky would be there to help her out. Max would too. Well, the whole pack would, if they turned her. But the boyfriend could be an issue unless someone who was in their pack appealed to her and became the boyfriend.

"Okay, so if we turn her, she would need to date one of us," Asher said, smiling. "Forget your quest to look into Christopher for her. She would have us there to watch over her every step of the way."

"Can we have another vote?" Stephan Wright, one of the single males, asked. He was only twenty and not old enough to be Pamela's mate, Max was thinking.

Carol smiled. "We'll have another vote as soon as we know what's going on with Pamela. For a decision that affects all of us, we want this to be unanimous."

Max agreed and so did everyone after a fact. Then the meeting ended, but Ryan and Carol wanted to talk to him further before he went home.

"Asher does have a point as far as turning her and then keeping her in the family, so to speak. If she knows about us or highly suspects, she has already set in motion a plan to work with us. Still, we have to cover all bases, and keeping her as one of our own would assure us she wouldn't talk. Unless she made a mistake in appearing in public when she couldn't stop the shift, she would be okay," Carol said.

"I agree," Ryan said. "For the sake of the pack, for the sake of our kind, I think that Asher is right, actually."

Max took a deep breath and let it out. "We have another issue.

If she truly loves Christopher and wants to be with him, what do we do about him? Turn him too?"

"Well, if we talk to her about us being wolves, maybe we can convince her she wants to be one of us, and she shouldn't be with Christopher," Ryan said.

Carol shook her head. "If Pamela is in love with Christopher and she knows about us as wolves for sure, we've got another stumbling block in our path and it's back to the drawing board for us."

CHAPTER 6

BECKY WAS ALREADY APPREHENSIVE ABOUT HAVING LUNCH with Pamela this afternoon, but when Max called her to say he had canceled with Pamela already, she just felt it was bad news.

"I'm still trying to get a lead on Christopher and hope to have some information for her soon. Tonight or tomorrow," Max said.

"Uh, sure."

"I'm so sorry, Becky. I know how difficult this is for you what with worrying if she knows about us."

"No problem. I'll ask if she wants to cancel lunch with me too. Hopefully she will." Becky had managed a number of tasks this morning for her employer, and so far, everything was fine. But sitting down with her at lunchtime? Becky was afraid it would be too tension-filled, since she now knew about Pamela's past experience with a wolf shifter. It was just something she couldn't forget.

Then she called her boss. "Pamela, since Max is in the middle of chasing down leads on Christopher and can't make it for lunch, do you want to cancel our lunch date?"

"Heavens no. It's about that time. Why don't you join me in the dining room?"

Becky could imagine ominous music playing in the background as they had their lunch.

When she finally sat down with Pamela and the server set their dishes of chicken salad, a teapot and teacups, and glasses of water on the table, Pamela said, "I'm glad Max is working so hard on this case and might have some good news one way or another soon. Has he told you about any of what he has learned?"

The server left them to have their lunch in privacy.

"No, but I'm hopeful it all turns out the way you want it to." Talk about being put on the spot! Becky wanted to spill the whole story—that Max and she were wolves. That the wolf who saved Pamela as a girl *was* her mother and that her father and sister and brother were all wolves. Instead, Becky concentrated on eating her lunch, feeling uncomfortable when normally she enjoyed meals with her employer. Becky wondered if she would have felt any better if Max had been there explaining some of what he'd learned during his investigation.

"My staff has been dismissed for the lunch hour so they can go off and enjoy a lunch in town for a couple of hours."

Becky took a bite of her chicken salad, trying for nonchalant, but she was afraid of what that meant. Pamela wanted to discuss something private with her, and that probably meant about them being wolves.

"I wanted to mention the reason I'm always reticent about you going to the pond in winter. I fell through the ice there when I was six."

"Oh, that's awful." Becky's blood felt chilled.

"Yes, and a woman saved me."

"A woman?" Becky hoped she was sounding as surprised as she was trying to let on that she was.

"Yes. I learned later that she was your mother."

"My…mother?"

Pamela smiled. "Yes. It's not the reason why I hired you. Well, I mean, certainly, you were my choice over seven other candidates because of it. I can't lie about that. It did help me to make my decision." She took a sip of her water. "Did your mother ever tell you about it?"

"It must have been before I was born."

"So she never mentioned it?" Pamela asked again.

"I…I vaguely recall some talk of it. As a kid, I wasn't paying much attention, I guess. And she didn't boast about it or anything.

I just remember her warning us when we were kids not to cross frozen lakes or ponds in the event they weren't all the way frozen. She didn't want us falling through the ice. We used to ice skate on a pond in a park, so she just made a point to remind us of it every winter. There was a case of two kids falling through the ice one year, about the time I was learning to ice-skate with my brother and sister and friends, so I had believed that's why she kept mentioning it to us."

"She had saved me before that. She took me to her home to warm me up and dry my clothes."

"Oh."

"Nobody believed me."

"That she saved you? Why wouldn't they?" Becky acted as sincerely as she could that she had no clue that a wolf had saved Pamela.

Pamela smiled. "I had a big imagination back then—according to family and friends."

"You are very creative. That's why your liquor line continues to be such a success."

"Right. I…" Pamela shook her head. "If it wasn't for my imagination going wild on me, I would swear that what I had seen was all true." She took another bite of her salad. "You went for a walk with Max in the woods yesterday."

"Yes. We had a great walk. Lots of fun." Becky was dying to ask if Pamela had any security cameras set up anywhere.

"Good. You'll have to swim in the pond together. When I was a kid, I swam there all the time."

Becky smiled. "Sure, if you don't mind, we could do that."

Pamela sighed. "I just wish you knew something about Christopher's whereabouts and what he's doing."

"Hopefully, Max will have something substantial for you tonight."

"Do you believe in the paranormal?" Pamela asked.

"Uh, psychics? Sure. Not that all people are sensitive to things that some experience, but I believe some can see or hear things the rest of us can't." This was so not good. Paranormal as in werewolves? She bet that was what Pamela was getting at.

"Right."

"What about you?" Becky asked. Pamela had never said anything to her about any of this before. She always seemed the most levelheaded kind of person.

"Well, I do believe that there are those who sense things that the rest of us don't. Not me. I don't have a paranormal cell in my body. But what if what I thought I had experienced was real? That a werewolf saved me from the pond when I nearly drowned."

"A werewolf?" Becky's mouth dropped open. It wasn't an act either. She hadn't thought her employer would *really* come out and say that to her.

"Yeah, it was in all the papers when I was a kid. I told everyone I saw that a wolf had run to the edge of the pond and turned into a woman to save me."

Becky ate another bite of her food, unsure what to say.

"I have to admit, I wanted to see if you would turn into a wolf and run in the woods."

"Me?" Becky's heart hitched. It was a good thing Pamela couldn't smell her nervousness or hear her thumping heartbeat. "That would be scary." Not only that Pamela would see Becky do that but that Becky would learn she had. But then she frowned. How had Pamela known who had actually saved her? The woman could have been anyone.

"I always wanted to thank her," Pamela said.

"Why do you think she was my mother?" Becky had to ask, because in the article, it hadn't said.

"My parents hired a private investigator to find her. He found her home, though she denied she had done anything so heroic. But I had remembered the direction she had taken me from the lake. I used to play in the woods all the time. The investigator showed me a picture of their house and of her, and they were the same as I had remembered them. My father offered her fifty thousand dollars for saving my life. Your mother refused to accept the money, saying she hadn't done anything, and if she had, she wouldn't have asked for money for it.

"But my father could be just as stubborn. A year after the incident, your mother had triplets, and he set up an account to fund you and your brother and sister's education. He knew I wouldn't have been alive if it wasn't for your mother's brave heroics, and he wanted to do something for her children."

"And then you hired me because of that?"

Pamela smiled. "You have a great education, you're fun to be around, and you're really great at your job. I knew you would be. But what I still want to know is, can you shift into a wolf like your mother can?" Before Becky could answer her, Pamela got a call. She took it and said to Becky, "We'll talk later." Then she hurried out of the dining room.

All Becky wanted to do was get on her phone and tell Max what had happened. She had half expected it, dreaded it, and when she heard Pamela talk all about it, that changed everything for her.

CHAPTER 7

ONCE BECKY HAD TOLD MAX WHAT HAD HAPPENED DURING the lunch with Pamela, he felt bad that he hadn't been there to help her handle the issue. It wasn't easy dealing with someone who knew what wolf shifters were and finally admitting to it and being put on the spot. "I'm on my way over."

"No, you need to keep working on finding Christopher. That's your job."

"I should have been there for you."

"And done what? You couldn't have done anything more about it."

"I should have been there for moral support, and yes, I could have at least talked to her about this wolf business."

"Will you have enough information to share with her about Christopher tonight?"

"He's running me ragged. I'm not sure that I will have."

"Okay, well, I want you to come tonight and have dinner with me anyway. And if it's not too soon, stay the night."

He smiled. "Yeah, I'll do that."

"But for heaven's sake, learn something more about Christopher."

"I learned he's working for an investment broker at a bank."

"Where?"

"In a town in Kansas, but he's gone to Europe, so I don't know what that's all about. But this business with Pamela changes everything if she's totally hooked on him and doesn't want to give him up for anything."

"We can't turn him too. If we decide—the pack decides— Pamela needs to be turned for her own peace of mind and ours."

"I'll have to call Ryan about this latest development."

"Okay. I'll wait to hear what he has to say."

"He and Carol are busy with their jobs for now, so it will be a while before I can talk privately with them. I can't wait to see you tonight though."

"I'm glad you came into my life. I just wanted to tell you that in case you didn't know."

He smiled. "I feel the same way about you. And I've been trying to keep you a secret as much as I can."

"From whom?"

"The other bachelor males."

She laughed. "I'll see you tonight then."

"I might still be trying to track down Christopher while I'm at your house, if you don't mind."

"No. I might have to field a call or two from Pamela, if it doesn't bother you."

"Not in the least."

"Okay, good. Chicken for dinner?"

"You read my mind."

Then they ended the call and he was glad he had let her know how he'd felt about her going it alone with discussing the wolf business with Pamela. He talked to Asher about the situation at the PI agency after that.

"That's all the more reason for one of us single wolves to meet up with Pamela and tell her how much we're glad she understands us and can be our friend," Asher said.

"You would try to become her boyfriend, but I think she's still hung up on this Christopher."

"Right, but you know what a relief it is when we meet up with another wolf and we can talk openly about what we are? After all these years with living with what had happened to her, don't you think she's going to feel the same way? That she can finally discuss what she has had to bottle up for decades?"

"True. We'll just have to see what our pack leaders say about it." Max certainly didn't want to start encouraging the rest of their wolves to meet up with her and make friends when Pamela wasn't a wolf. What if she decided she'd made a big mistake? That she should have kept her mouth shut all this time?

They couldn't risk exposing more of their wolves' identities to a human.

"Well, I want to be the first in line to offer my bite."

Max chuckled. "What if she isn't your type? You have no idea if the two of you would be compatible. Not that you would have to mate each other if you bit her, but still, what if she felt beholden to you, and you realized she wasn't the woman you were interested in mating? It could be a disaster."

"You're right. I wouldn't bite her. I just would get together with her for a date or two and see if there was any spark between us. Speaking of which, what about you and Becky?"

"We're enjoying some time together." Max didn't want to tell him he was staying over at her place tonight. That would sound like the beginning of something deeper, but he didn't want to take anything for granted. What if it didn't work out? Then Asher might be interested in dating her. Max just felt it was best to keep mum about it all.

"More than some time together, I suspect," Asher said, then got a call on a case he was working. "Yes, Mrs. Probst. I've got some photos to share with you if you think you're up for it."

Asher was working on a husband-cheating case where the wife had all the money, so she was ready to kick him to the curb if what she suspected was true. But she had to have proof so she wouldn't have to lose too much money on the deal. Luckily, she did have a prenuptial.

Max packed his overnight bag with a couple of days of clothes and his laptop to do his research. Then he headed over to Becky's place to have dinner with her. She'd already told Pamela he didn't have enough new information to discuss with her tonight, and Pamela had made other plans for dinner. Becky hadn't thought she would need to tell her boss when she was having dinner with a friend, but since he was working Pamela's case and would be on her property, he wanted Pamela to know that he was going to be there.

When he arrived at Becky's home, she gave him a warm hug and a big kiss, which he immediately deepened, wrapping his arms snugly around her. "I know we haven't been seeing each other for long, but this feels so right," he said.

"I agree, which is why I wanted you to stay the night. Not to mention that all this business with Pamela has me worried. I wanted to talk to you in person and not on the phone or be texting you all the time."

"I feel the same way." He carried his bag into the bedroom, and then he set his laptop in the living room. "I should have mentioned it, but the reason I might be doing a little bit of work on this case tonight is because of the time differences."

"Certainly. What did Ryan and Carol say about this whole matter?"

"They were both working at their jobs. I figured I would call them once we were together and we could all talk to one another on speakerphone, particularly since you were the one who actually spoke with Pamela about this."

"That's true. Are you ready for some chicken?"

"Yeah, and if you would like, and I'm not getting way ahead of myself, I could grill us some steaks tomorrow night. I noticed you have a grill on your back patio."

"Oh yes, I would love that. And a wolf run tonight? When I feel unsettled, I really like to run as a wolf. And now that there's a cougar on the property, I really want to do it with you and not by myself."

"Absolutely."

"Do you think we should go in a different direction? Just in case we missed seeing any cameras in that area?"

"Yeah. I mean, we've checked it over, but the chances she would have them all over the place, rather than where you always run, seems to be unrealistic. We'll have to scent-mark the new territory so the cougar knows he has got the two of us to deal with."

She smiled. "I never scent-mark my territory."

He tsked. "That's half of who we are."

They sat down to eat the chicken and the Mediterranean vegetables she'd cooked in a spicy sauce—zucchini, potatoes, red bell peppers, peas. It was great.

"I love your cooking."

"Thanks. I can't wait to eat your grilled steaks."

"Corn on the cob sound good? Baked potatoes? I can make them with the steaks." He forked up some more potatoes.

"Sure, that sounds great."

"And for after we eat our chicken, I made us mocha treats topped with whipped cream and raspberries."

"Now that really sounds great."

Once they were done, they had dessert, and then Max needed to call Ryan and Carol. He'd already sent Ryan a text telling him that he needed to discuss the situation with them about Pamela after dinner.

"Okay, so here's the deal," Max said and then he motioned for Becky to tell them everything that she could recall that Pamela had told her.

"It sounds as though she wants to be one of us," Carol said.

"I agree, but is that prudent?" Ryan asked.

Max and Becky took a seat on the couch together to snuggle while they talked over the speakerphone.

"I think it all depends on Christopher," Becky said. "If she is truly in love with him and he is with her, then I don't think turning her is a great idea. Not unless you're ready to turn Christopher too."

"And Christopher does have parents who are living. That would be an issue," Max said. It could have a snowball effect. They didn't want to have that many newly turned wolves to deal with. It was bad enough turning just one person.

"If she wants to be turned," Ryan said, "her whole staff would have to be terminated in a financially acceptable way. She can't be around a bunch of humans on a daily basis if she has trouble shifting during the phase of the full moon. The only way it would work is if she hired all wolves from our pack to fill her various jobs. Some of her positions would be easy enough to fill, I'm sure. But some jobs could take some training. Still, she would have to agree to all that. She might be partial to some of her staff and not want that."

"Then it goes back to eliminating her," Carol said.

Everyone said no to that. Max knew that Carol was the most adamant about not doing that since she had been turned and still had difficulty at the time of the full moon. And she couldn't shift and play as a wolf with her mate or the rest of the pack members during the new moon either. But it was different for her because she had a loving wolf mate and she was part of a whole pack who watched out for her. Even her job as nurse meant she worked in her own clinic with only her own people. They were still trying to get a wolf doctor to work for them as they expanded their wolf base, but for now, sick or injured wolves who needed to be seen by a doctor went to Silver Town.

"So what do you want me to do?" Becky asked. "I think she suspects how dangerous her knowledge of us is to both her and to the wolves in general. But we owe it to her to tell her what her options are."

"We still need to find Christopher. I'm hoping that if I can make contact with him, he'll tell me he's not interested in her any longer and has moved on. I haven't learned if he's in a relationship, but if he is, I hope that would help her to see that he has moved on. The thing of it is, if he really wanted her money, he could have approached her right after her parents died and she had inherited all the estate. Why wait?"

"To make it appear that he wasn't after her money?" Becky asked. "I mean, if he had jumped right in after their deaths, don't you think it would have looked like he had been waiting in the wings all that time for the day to come?"

"I agree," Carol said.

"All right, well, I want you to learn what you can about Christopher. Find him, talk to him, and then we'll go from there," Ryan said.

Ryan was one of the best investigators there was, and Max trusted his advice. The same thing went for being a great pack leader.

"You two enjoy your night," Ryan said, and Carol echoed the sentiment.

Then they ended the call and Becky sighed. "I will feel like I'm sitting on pins and needles until we resolve this."

"I'm doing everything I can to locate Christopher so I can start up a dialogue with him. I just hope he's honest with me when I'm able to talk to him."

Becky left the couch and began gathering up the dishes, and Max joined her to help clean up the kitchen.

"But about us," Becky said.

Max smiled. "That's more of a sure thing."

She smiled, raising a brow.

"I wouldn't leave you hanging about whether I would want to be with you or not. I definitely am all for being with you."

She chuckled and put the dirty dishes and the silverware in the dishwasher while he cleaned the baking dish.

Becky sure hoped Max was ready to take their relationship

further. Not all the way. They needed some time to get to know each other better. She was going to suggest a movie, but she wanted to make love to him—unconsummated, of course. Consummated meant mating for life, and they weren't ready for that.

She washed her hands and he followed suit. Then she cleared her throat, wanting to propose going to bed, and hoped he was thinking along the same lines.

She reached up and cupped his face, and he instantly placed his hands on her hips, pulled her close, and leaned down to kiss her. Yes! That was just what she had in mind.

They kissed, the heat building between them, but she wanted him to know she wanted more. Not just an after-dinner kiss. She ran her hands over his T-shirt. He was wearing shorts and a T-shirt, nice and casual, though she liked seeing him all dressed up too. He had nice legs, well-toned from running, and in shorts, he was hot.

She kicked off her sandals and he smiled. Yeah, he knew where this was going.

He nuzzled her cheek with his, his body pressed lightly against hers, but then he hugged her closer, letting her feel his burgeoning arousal. He was such a hot wolf. She shifted her hands down to his buttocks and pulled him even more firmly against her, wrapping one leg against the back of his, caressing him with her bare foot, offering herself to him in an erotic way.

He cupped her buttocks then and lifted her against him, and she wrapped her legs around him. Man, she wished they could just go all the way, the sweet, achy longing between her legs just coming to bear.

"To the bedroom?" he asked, kissing her cheek.

"Yeah," she said, her voice breathy, sounding sexier than she had thought it would.

He carried her into her bedroom, her legs still wrapped around his hips, and the whole time he was kissing her, hugging her tight, making her wet.

When he reached her bedroom, he set her down on the carpeted floor, then she removed his shirt, and he pulled her shirt up and over her head. He kissed the curve of her breasts and placed his hands on them, squeezing a little, then kissing her again, though he kept his hands on her breasts, massaging, making her feel sexy and irresistible.

He slid his hands down her bare tummy and found the fastener on her shorts, then undid the button and unzipped the shorts. She wriggled out of them before she began working on *his* shorts. She loved summer. Fewer clothes when she wasn't working, which meant less to have to peel off for making love to a wolf.

He kissed each of her breasts through the sheer bra cups. She wore them for support, not for padding, but she liked the sheerer ones on hot days. They made her feel cooler, and for being with a hot wolf, the bra was sexier than others she had.

He seemed to think so too and rubbed his thumbs over the fabric and her nipples and smiled as they peaked and poked at the fabric. She only wore bras like that when she wore T-shirts or other heavy materials that no one could see through, but when her shirt was off in the presence of a hot wolf that she was eager to seduce—perfect.

Then he dipped his head and licked a nipple through the fabric, and she sucked in her breath. She was already soaking wet for him, and if they could make love to each other all the way, she would just pull him into bed and get on with it.

He lightly scraped his teeth against one nipple, making her groan with need, his thumb still rubbing the other as if to keep it satisfied. She was feeling the erotic ache in her groin grow. Then he reached down and unfastened the clip in the front of the bra, unsnapping it and freeing her breasts like she wanted to do with his erection.

Her bra straps were hanging off her arms, while she pulled down his unfastened shorts and released them. They slid to the floor, and she dropped her bra and started to pull down his boxer briefs. Then he was doing the same with her boy-shorts panties, and they were totally naked, their pheromones engaged and their hearts beating frantically.

They ended up on the bed, all skin and muscles and legs and arms, never-ending kisses and tongues and hands. Stroking and kneading, passionate longing claiming them both.

For a moment, he paused on top of her, his hands on the sides of her head, gazing at her with lust and—dare she say it?—love. Then he took a deep breath and kissed her again.

She kissed him back, tonguing him for entrance, and he gave way, took her in, and held on with his lips in a sexy way, sucking, making her even wetter down below.

She ran her hands over his back, and then he changed position again. This time, he was behind her, his hand reaching between her legs and stroking her. His body was angled over hers so he could still kiss her. This was better than nice.

He kissed her neck and back and stroked her and every erotic nerve he could reach. No man had ever pleasured her like this before. She was thinking he was really a keeper!

He was rubbing his body against her back, his erection swollen with readiness. She placed her hand over his and made him rub her nubbin harder, faster, eager for completion. She felt the momentum building, the anticipation driving her crazy, their arousal making it all the steamier. The orgasm was just beyond reach, so close, so far. If only she could just grab hold and ride it to the moon. Then she shattered and cried out, feeling awash with pleasure.

Max pulled her over on her back and smiled down at her, his gaze filled with lust. He kissed her mouth and played with her breasts, skimming his hand over the nipples, teasing them with delicate sweeps of his hand. She didn't want to let go of the earth-shattering moment, wanting to remember it for always, just in case it never happened to her again.

But then she pushed him on his back and climbed on top of his legs. She took hold of his rigid arousal and then smiled as she began to stroke him, thinking just how beautiful he was lying against her pillow, her bed, and she would remember this always.

Max was so grateful it had come to this with Becky. He had hoped they could continue to make love to each other as they got to know one another. He swore she'd never climaxed with another guy before, and she seemed thrilled. Seeing her sitting on his legs, her own spread for his viewing pleasure, her breasts beckoning him to mold his hands around them again, he settled against the mattress, feeling the overwhelming need to climax as she continued to ply him with magic, one stroke at a time. She smelled divine, of musky woman and she-wolf, and he vowed to bring her to climax again— tonight, later.

But for now, he was caught up in the way she was stroking him, taking him to the top and bringing him to orgasm. She continued to milk him, and he wished they were further along in their relationship when they were mated, and they could go all the way. Yet this was great too, and he would be ready to do it again soon.

When they were finished, he climbed out of bed. "Man, Becky."

"Yeah, wow, Max."

He smiled. "I'm going to shower. Do you want to join me?"

"No, another time."

He smiled at her, leaned down and kissed her, and headed for the shower in the master bathroom. He thought she wanted to build up to all this. But someday, he hoped, he would shower with her and make love to her in there too.

He washed himself with her tangerine body wash, since his toiletry bag was still in the guest bedroom. Then he joined her in bed, and she was smiling at him, looking pleased, beautiful, sexy, and like she'd had a good romp. He wouldn't mind going another round with her later. When they both wanted to. And they did.

As to Pamela, she had dropped the issue of the wolves, to Becky's surprise, and when she had tried to talk to Pamela further about it, her boss had dismissed it as silliness on her part.

For two weeks, Becky and Max worked and played and made love, while Max searched for Christopher and she continued to do her job. Then Max learned Christopher was now living in Green Valley, to his astonishment.

"Christopher is in Green Valley, working as a librarian," he told Becky over the phone.

"What? He's no longer an investment counselor?" Becky sounded disheartened by it. "I'd kind of hoped he really had waited to be with her all this time and that he was doing well financially himself. Though we would still have the wolf issue."

"Right, but remember, that doesn't necessarily make him a bad guy."

"He might not want to share where he's working with her, believing she wouldn't want to be married to someone who wasn't in a higher income job."

"Correct. He might be embarrassed to tell her the truth. And if she knew that's what he did, he might be afraid she'd really think he was after her for her money, since he probably doesn't make that much on his own. But with this information, I can learn about his income, investments if he has any, and who he might be seeing."

The next morning, Max went to see Christopher at the library to learn what he could from him in person. When Max arrived there, he went inside and saw a tall, strawberry-blond-haired man sitting behind a desk, looking just like the picture on Christopher Anderson's driver's license. "Hi, I'm Max Browning, and you're Christopher Anderson?"

The man smiled at him. "I am. What can I do for you?"

That was when Max smelled that the man was a wolf. *Hell.* "I know an acquaintance of yours, and she was under the impression that you were in Europe as a financial advisor of some sort."

His expression turned dour. "Yeah, well, no longer."

"Pamela?"

"Yeah. There's nothing between us." He took a deep breath. "You're like me, and you know nothing could come between us, if you know what I mean."

"Okay, but you couldn't tell her you weren't interested in her any longer?"

"Listen, when we were young and dumb, I had the idea she could be mine. But it couldn't happen because we're not the same. Did you know about the accident she had when she was young? The near drowning incident?"

"Yeah, and she thought a shifter had saved her."

"Yeah, a shifter *had* saved her. So she loves wolves. She loved me, though she didn't know I was, um"—he spoke more softly—"one. Like I said, I was young and dumb. I wasn't in her social class, and that wasn't just because of how much money my parents made. It took a lot of time for me to get over her, but I finally realized that I couldn't do anything about it. We're just too…different. I couldn't…turn her. For years, I'd considered it."

"Okay, so you need to tell her it's not going to work out between you. You need to meet with her, tell her—"

"What? That I lied to her because of what I am? I can't. You know that. It's better if I just don't say anything." He frowned at Max. "Who are you anyway?"

"A private investigator she hired to find you."

"To tell me it's over?"

"Yeah, if you weren't who you said you were or you were seeing someone else, I figure."

That made Christopher smile. "Well, then you've done your job."

"No. She needs to hear it from you. We have another issue though." He explained a little about their pack and Becky.

Christopher's eyes widened. "Are you certain?" He sounded a little uplifted to hear the news.

"Yeah, I'm certain."

"What if I spoke with her?" Christopher asked.

It appeared Christopher still loved her. "She apparently doesn't know about you. And I'm not talking about your job situation," Max said.

"Right."

"You weren't waiting for her because of the money, correct?" Max didn't want to help an opportunistic wolf mate her just because of her wealth and prestige.

"What do you think?" Christopher asked, frowning at him in annoyance.

"I honestly don't know. But I do know she has waited for you all these years, and she still wanted to see you before she decided if it would work out between the two of you. She wouldn't have hired me if she hadn't wanted to find you. She could have just moved on, but she felt she had to make things right between the two of you first."

"And discover if I had waited around just to get her money? I didn't, you know. It was the…other issue. That's something you can't explain away."

"What about you? Have you been seeing anyone else? You're not part of our pack here."

"I just moved into town last weekend and started this job. I didn't realize there was a pack located here. But no. I haven't been dating anyone."

"Well, it's a great pack, so I'll make sure you can visit with the leaders and—"

"Learn what's expected of me?"

"They're very open-minded, but I'm sure they'll offer some advice about the lady in question too."

"All right. Thanks. Sorry I've been kind of brusque. This has been a sore spot for me for so long—"

"Because you love her?"

Christopher nodded. "I tried dating other women, but no one held a candle to Pamela."

Because she is an heiress?

"It's not about the money," Christopher said as if he knew just what Max was thinking. "I know that's something everyone will believe no matter what I say about it."

"That's true." Max wasn't going to sugarcoat it, but he suspected Asher was going to lose out before he even had a chance to speak to Pamela if she still loved Christopher too.

Max wanted to go with Christopher to speak with the pack leaders, to learn what they all had to say, but he suspected Christopher couldn't just take off from work. Maybe at lunchtime, if Christopher could go with him and if Max didn't have lunch scheduled with Pamela and Becky. Then he wondered if he could get the lunch switched to dinner and meet with the pack leaders and Christopher at lunchtime.

"I was meeting with Pamela for lunch to discuss what I've learned about you."

Christopher looked saddened by the prospect.

"I think you need to speak with the pack leaders first, so I'm going to propose to Pamela that we have dinner instead, if she's free. At lunchtime, you and I can meet with Ryan and Carol, talk about the best way to handle this, then have dinner with Pamela this evening. You will have to meet us there too. What do you think?"

Christopher's expression brightened, then he looked glum again. "What if she doesn't believe me when she learns I don't make that much money but I still don't care anything about the inheritance?"

"I think her reaction to you and the way you respond to her will tell all. Are you free for lunch and dinner?"

"Yeah, I am."

"I'll have to make sure the mayor doesn't have anything planned for lunch also."

"All right." Christopher looked hopeful, but then he frowned again. "What if Ryan doesn't think I should do it? Or he thinks I should call it off?"

"Let's just see how this all goes. Who knows? She may be over you. I don't want to sound harsh, but we just won't know until we're there."

"Okay, let's do it."

"Oh, one other thing, I talked to your parents on the phone. They were against you marrying Pamela."

"They were my adoptive parents and didn't have any clue that I was a wolf. They'd raised me since I was two in Kansas City and moved with me at that time to Mountain View. I had to sneak out to run as a wolf whenever I had the chance. Not that the phases of the moon force me to do anything, but it's just in our blood. I never met any wolves there while I was growing up. But my parents felt that Pamela was just leading me on and never planned to marry me because I didn't have the kind of money she had."

"Okay, gotcha."

After he left Christopher, Max called Pamela. "Is there any way we can get together for dinner? I'm still looking into the situation and should have more information by dinnertime."

"I have a dinner with a couple in town."

"Okay, can we switch it to tomorrow then? Lunch or dinner?"

"I'll cancel on the other couple. We'll have dinner tonight if you think you'll know something about Christopher. And tell Becky to join us."

"Okay, see you tonight."

Then Max called Becky with the surprising news. "It turns out Christopher is one of us."

Silence.

"Becky?" He thought he'd lost the call.

"A wolf?"

"Yeah."

"Ohmigod."

"Yeah, we want to speak with the leaders about it before he sees her. So we thought we could talk to them at lunchtime, and he'll actually meet with Pamela for dinner. I already arranged to have dinner with her tonight and you're to come with me."

———————

Becky couldn't believe that Christopher was a wolf! No wonder he couldn't commit to the marriage and he hadn't wanted to tell Pamela where he'd gone. She suspected he hadn't been able to give her up though, or he would have just told her he was over her.

Becky called Pamela then. "Hi, I guess we're not doing lunch, just dinner."

"You can have lunch with me, if you're unable to have it with Max because he's working the case."

Becky smiled. "I would love to." After they ended the call, she texted Max: I'm still having lunch with Pamela.

> **Max:** Okay. I spoke with Ryan. We're meeting with him at lunchtime.
> **Becky:** I sure hope this works out today.
> **Max:** Me too. I'll let you know how it goes after we talk to the pack leaders this afternoon. Look forward to tonight.
> **Becky:** All right. See you at six.

Becky sure hoped it all worked out. She wished she could be at the meeting with Max, Christopher, and the pack leaders to prepare herself for the dinner engagement. Still, maybe they would have this case resolved tonight. She hoped it was a good resolution for all concerned, and that could mean that Christopher was finally able to tell Pamela he couldn't see her any longer, or the whole truth was going to come out. It was a scary proposition no matter what.

She really hoped Pamela could find true love, but who knew when it would hit? All Becky knew was she had really gotten lucky on her one and only blind date.

Then she went to the mansion and to her office. She called up Pamela and said, "How did you want me to handle the situation with your other dinner guests?"

"Tell them we'll reschedule. You don't have to give them a reason. They're good people."

"Okay, I'll do that." Becky prayed everything would turn out for the best.

CHAPTER 8

MAX MET CHRISTOPHER AT THE PACK LEADERS' HOME FOR lunch, though Ryan had to shift a lunch engagement around that had to do with his mayoral duties. When it came to wolf business, that took priority. Carol was off, having made arrangements to make sure she didn't have any patient appointments. She saw only wolves, so her patients understood if she had to switch appointments around when they had a pack situation she needed to help deal with.

Both she and Ryan were sufficiently shocked to learn Christopher was one of them, but they quickly welcomed him with open arms to join the pack, first thing.

Carol had fixed them roast beef stew that had been simmering in a slow cooker since that morning.

"The way it works is you can join us, but you don't have to," Ryan said. "We don't force anyone to join the pack. Everyone does, because we have so much to offer, but we've had a lone wolf or two who would wait and see, check out the events we're having, and feel if it was right for them or not. We haven't had anyone move on, and we're trying to build up our wolf base here in Green Valley."

Christopher smiled. "You could be a salesman."

"Being a mayor can be like that sometimes. So you can think on it, and even if you do join us and feel it's not right for you, you don't have to stay with the pack."

"We have to tell you how surprised we are to learn you're a wolf though," Carol said. "I imagine Max has brought you up to speed on the business with Becky and how her mother saved Pamela as a child when she was a wolf?"

"Yes. I was friends with Pamela back then. Not as in boyfriend and girlfriend that early on, but we were just friends in school. When that happened, it was all over the school. You know how mean kids can be. They teased her about her story. I told her that it was probably a good idea not to mention the woman was a wolf."

"Because you are." Carol smiled.

"Yeah, and because she couldn't prove the woman was, which meant everyone just thought Pamela had made up the fantastical story. No one wants to be treated that way in school. Anyway, it brought me closer to her because she'd witnessed one of our kind shifting. But another part of me wanted to be with her, to support her when everyone else jeered her. It was so hard for me not to tell her what I was and confirm that what she saw was true. I also wanted to make sure she didn't continue to spread the story."

"So what did you say to her?" Ryan asked.

"Well, I told her anything really was possible. But that she had to remember she'd had hypothermia when the woman saved her, so her brain probably wasn't registering things quite right. Of course I said it in a way that a six-year-old would, as my parents explained it to me."

"What did she say to that?" Carol asked.

"She agreed. But even so, she said the woman was a wolf, shifted, and raced across the ice to save her. That she didn't have any clothes on. That when the woman grabbed her hand just before Pamela went under the ice, she managed to pull her out and made sure she was breathing. Then naked, the woman ran through the snow to reach a cabin beyond Pamela's family's land. Pamela said she should have been frostbitten. Then the woman howled as a human, as if telling her pack she needed help. Pamela never told the paper that a man came running to help them. He was wide-eyed as if he couldn't believe the woman would be carrying a half-frozen, sopping-wet kid, and the woman was naked.

"But he quickly took Pamela from the woman's arms, and then

he turned and ran as fast as he could to the cabin. Pamela wanted to see the woman, but she was behind the man. Pamela thought the woman had to have turned back into a wolf. When they arrived at the cabin, Pamela didn't see the wolf again. But sometime later, she heard the woman making hot soup in the kitchen, telling her everything would be all right. The cabin looked normal, no wolf decorations or photos or wolf beds lying around. She did notice that the door had a large doggy door, which Pamela suspected was for wolves, not dogs. She never saw any sign of dogs. So that was the story she had to tell, and I had to listen and assure her everything was all right."

Max was feeling like they just needed to turn Pamela. He couldn't imagine anything worse than knowing about the wolves and having to be quiet about them her whole life. Yet she seemed to have respected Becky's mother for what she had done. Would Pamela feel the same if they turned her? Would she want to be? Would she be happy being one of them?

He doubted she would know the answer to the question until she was one for a time and could process how it felt. She would have problems with wanting to shift during the week of the full moon. She couldn't shift during the new moon.

Then he wondered how Becky was getting along with Pamela while she was having lunch with her.

He was enjoying the meal Carol had prepared, but he wished he could have had lunch alone with Becky. In fact, he was feeling like that all the time. Like during their breaks from work, for any reason—meals, the end of the workday—he wanted to spend time with her. It was as if the lovebug had bitten him hard and he didn't want the feeling to go away.

In the middle of the lunch, Becky called him. "Hey, I hope I'm not interrupting your lunch or anything, but Pamela had an emergency board meeting to go to. I need to meet her there and I'm driving over as we speak."

"Thanks, Becky, I'll let everyone know. She told Christopher when they were kids that she also met your father when your mom was carrying her home. She didn't mention him in the report. He was in his human form. So just something else you should know."

"Okay. I'm thinking Christopher, if he still really loves her, should turn her. But only if she really wants to be one of us and loves him back. If not—which means we need to know how she feels about him before we tell her he's a wolf—then I think we need to rethink things."

"How do you feel about keeping your job there?"

"I'm staying here as long as I can."

"Tell Pamela I've found Christopher and talked to him. If she would like, he could join us tonight for dinner with her, or if she prefers, she could have dinner with him alone." And then Max would wish he could be a fly on the wall.

"Are you sure you don't want to talk to her over dinner first?"

"Yeah, I'm sure. I think the best thing to happen is that we get them together now. If he doesn't want to be with her, or she doesn't want to see him further, or if they're free to date now and they can see how things work out between them, it's for the better."

"What about us? If you've closed your assignment, you won't have any need to come out here." She sounded serious.

"Are you kidding? I just found you on a blind date, and I'm losing you now? Just because the mission might be accomplished, we won't know that for sure until we see if things work out between them. But for sure, I'm telling my coworkers I'm busy seeing a she-wolf every chance I get."

She sighed. "Good. Because I didn't want to have to quit this job so I could see more of you."

He chuckled. "We'll be together. And if things work out between Christopher and her, she's going to be busy too. Though that might be more work for you, come to think of it."

"As long as we can spend time together, I'm game. I'll talk to her after her emergency meeting."

"Okay, you have a deal. Just let me know if Christopher is coming or if we're going to have the night off instead. I'll bring something for us to eat if we're not eating dinner with Pamela tonight."

"All right. Sounds good. After the meeting is through, I'll call you." Then Becky ended the call.

CHAPTER 9

AFTER THE MEETING WAS FINISHED, BECKY HAD SEVERAL business calls to make, but she said to Pamela, "Max called me with good news. Christopher lives in Green Valley, and if you want, we can make arrangements for him to have dinner with you, with or without us present."

Pamela's eyes filled with tears. Becky probably shouldn't have done it because she had a professional employer-employee image to keep up, but she gave her a hug. "It's up to you. Max and I are happy to do whatever you want."

Pamela chewed on her bottom lip. "Come to dinner, all three of you. We planned it already, and Christopher will be just another dinner guest. Since Max is an investigator, I want to know his professional opinion about Christopher's responses to my questions tonight."

"Okay, sure, thanks. I'll let Max know and he can get in touch with Christopher, if you would like. Or you can if you would rather."

"No, I have too much to do. Max can let him know. It's his case, after all."

Becky smiled. "Sure. I'll see you at the house." She thought Pamela really wanted to call Christopher herself but was afraid to get too emotional over it. Becky hoped she would be fine at dinner. Pamela could put on the most serious of expressions no matter what was going on in her life, but Becky wasn't sure she could when it came to matters of the heart.

Becky called Max. "We're all on. Tell Christopher he's also invited. Six sharp."

"I think he's kind of nervous about seeing her."

"I think she's feeling the same way about him, or she would have called him herself. I've never seen her like this before. I'm sure she still feels something for him. Oh, and why don't you bring an overnight bag. You can spend the night and we'll watch movies, run as wolves, whatever our hearts desire." She always asked and he always said yes.

"You're on." Max sounded thrilled.

Then she ended the call and drove back to the house. She was excited about having Max stay over, but she was still concerned about what would be said between Pamela and Christopher. Part of her wanted to be there to support Pamela, but part of her wanted to leave the couple alone so they could really get to know each other again and she and Max could do the same. She was hoping they could run as wolves tonight—as long as they didn't run into that blasted cougar again.

Becky thought that Pamela was doing a flurry of business, more so than usual, as if she was afraid to think about dinner tonight. Becky wanted to go home and straighten up her place a bit more, though she had cleaned up pretty well. So many things were left up in the air.

―――――――――――

That evening, Becky got together with Pamela before Max and Christopher could arrive, running a bit late, and she seemed to be nervous. But Becky wondered if it was about the business with the wolves or it had all to do with Christopher.

She was helping Pamela to set up things for dinner. Sure, the chef made the beef Wellington, and the kitchen staff served the meal, but Pamela was in such a state, wanting everything to be perfect.

"Was Christopher really in Europe?" she finally said to Becky, after readjusting the fresh roses on the side table for the fifteenth time.

"Yes, ma'am. He just started working as a librarian in Green Valley."

Pamela immediately had her phone out and was looking up the library to see if he was pictured as part of the staff. She frowned at first, which Becky took as a bad sign, but then smiled. "He doesn't look much different from the last time I saw him. I wonder why he told me he was an investment counselor." She readjusted the silverware again, so they were completely uniform as they sat on the placemats.

"I think he was. But now, maybe he doesn't believe being a librarian would live up to your expectations. Not that it wouldn't, but you know how men can be. Especially since you're so successful."

"Libraries are important. Librarians are just as important. When I was a girl, I often went to the library. Sure, my parents could afford any book I wanted, but I just loved the children's programs and reading so many different stories, some of which I wouldn't have wanted my parents to know about."

Becky smiled. "Oh?"

"Yes, I read a lot of romance books when I was a teen. My mother…and my father would have frowned on it. It was just silly fluff to them, when I needed to learn all about the business. But we have to have time to enjoy other worlds and, well, I have to admit I ended up reading quite a few shifter stories. I couldn't help it. I just fell in love with them."

The butler announced that Max Browning and Christopher Anderson had arrived.

Pamela's eyes misted when she saw Christopher, and Becky saw the slight curve of his lips as if he was thrilled to see her but didn't want to overreact in front of Becky and Max. Again, she wondered if they should have had dinner alone tonight.

Normally, Pamela would meet guests in the great room, but this time she had them ushered straight to the dining room. She showed them the seats they were to take, and then once they were seated, the salads and wine and bread were served.

"Becky tells me you're a librarian, Christopher."

"Uh, yes, Pamela. I'm sorry I didn't tell you sooner. I only just got the job."

"And the part about being an investment banker?"

He snorted and buttered a slice of bread. "The broker I worked for was picked up by the feds for not paying his own taxes. I was disillusioned by some of the illegal things that were being done, and I just wanted to do something else. I didn't tell you I'd switched occupations because I didn't think you would approve."

"Are you happy?"

"It's a decent job. I was in Europe on business, but once I quit that job, that was the end of Europe for me."

Max was quiet, letting Christopher and Pamela do all the talking. He winked at Becky. She felt her face flush with heat. He was no doubt thinking about tonight.

"I've wanted to see you," Christopher said.

"You wouldn't tell me you were close by. I had to hire Max to locate you."

"I've been only working for three days at the library." Christopher let out his breath. "I just didn't know how to break it to you that I was close by and was afraid to meet with you."

"I…" Pamela smiled. "I'm so glad to see you. I was about to give up on you."

The beef Wellington was served and then Pamela gave the staff the rest of the night off.

"I have something to confess," Christopher said.

Pamela's face fell.

"You know when you told me about the woman rescuing you in the pond when you were six? You said she was a wolf?"

Pamela glanced at Becky. Becky remained quiet, not sure where this was going.

"Yes. I know it was silly of me," Pamela finally said.

"It wasn't. I've seen them too."

Pamela's eyes rounded.

"I guess you know that Becky is one."

Pamela looked at Becky as if she was seeing her in a new way. "Uh, I figured she was, but I was afraid I'd said too much already."

"Max is too, but you knew that also, didn't you?"

Her gaze shifted to Max. "Yes. I suspected that might be the case when I had read all about the happenings in Green Valley with the hunters claiming they had shot at wolves and they turned out to be people. How…did you piece it all together like I did? I mean, after I told you about Becky's mother being one. Wait, how did you know Becky is one?"

"I'm one also," Christopher said.

Pamela's face lost all its color.

CHAPTER 10

BECKY WASN'T SURE PAMELA WAS READY FOR THE NEWS THAT Christopher was a wolf too. That Pamela knew everyone else was seemed fine. She'd known about it for a while. She had come to grips with it. But with Christopher, he had been her boyfriend. And she seemed to still care deeply for him.

"That's why I stuck up for you in school. That's why I wanted to protect you from the others who were giving you such grief. I was one, am one, and I knew you were telling the truth. I knew that they existed—" Christopher said.

"Because you're one." Pamela said the words in almost a hush, like she wasn't sure she should speak the truth out loud now. Not when she was among all wolves and they all knew she knew about them. "So what happens now?"

"It's totally up to you, Pamela," Christopher said. "I've loved you from the day I first met you, even as a young boy, because you had loved the wolf who had saved you. Over the years, I wanted to turn you, but I couldn't. I innately knew it was wrong. It went against everything we believe in, I figured."

"You could turn me?"

"Yes, but while your parents were alive, no. I learned so much from a guy I met in college who was a wolf, and he was surprised I didn't know all this stuff, until I told him my biological wolf parents had died when I was two and I'd been raised by humans. That's when I learned that most wolf kids homeschooled and all the rest of the stuff I should have learned while growing up. If you are turned, you would have trouble shifting without a choice during the full moon. During the new moon, you couldn't shift at all. I'm what is known as a royal. I can shift anytime I want because I have few human roots mixed up with the *lupus garou* roots."

"*Lupus garou*?"

"That's what we call ourselves, or wolf shifters."

"Oh."

"I wasn't part of the Green Valley wolf pack, but now I am. I guess what I'm asking is can you continue to keep a secret?" Christopher asked.

"Or be bitten and become one of you?" she asked.

Becky was trying to see where her employer was coming from. Yes, she wanted to be turned? No, what a horrible idea? She didn't know which it was. She felt bad for Christopher who'd had to hide what he was all those years growing up too.

"If it's something you think you can live with. We live longer than normal human lives," Christopher said.

Pamela's lips parted. Who wouldn't want more longevity?

"But—" she said.

"We mate for life. For all time, unless we lose our mate and then we can mate again, but no divorce."

"I–I realized telling Becky about the wolves had been a mistake if I found you and wanted to be with you and didn't want to get you involved in what I suspected. But…well, you're one too. So what do we do now?" Pamela asked.

"I hate to say it, but normally if someone has seen us shift, we have to turn them or eliminate them. We can't hope that they would refrain from telling anyone else about it," Max said.

"Just think of your former maid who was selling stories to the tabloids. What if she had known all about it? It would be the perfect story to sell, only once the press learned it was real, they would have been all over it," Becky said.

"So what does that mean for me? I could have just continued on, knowing but not saying anything. You know how well that worked out when I was a young girl. No one believed me," Pamela said.

"Well, that means that you need to be turned," Christopher said matter-of-factly. As if she had no choice in the matter, and nobody was going to do anything differently.

She arched a brow, he smiled, and the smile was devilishly wolfish.

"I would turn you. I could bite you, or we could do a nonbiting method. I have to tell you that we heal twice as fast as humans," Christopher said.

"Okay, but what about my staff? They're not all wolves."

"That would be an issue," Max said. "If they're wolves, everyone could watch out for you. But if they're not, you're putting yourself and others at risk."

"You could give them huge severance packages, enough to make it worth their while, and generous recommendations for new jobs for their service to you. You wouldn't have to explain why you can't keep them on unless you want to make up a story," Christopher said.

"Do you have any knowledge about investments? Really?" Pamela asked.

"I do. I was just unhappy with the crooks I was working for."

"Then you're hired. Will you stay with me, Becky?" Pamela asked.

"Absolutely. I love working for you."

"Good. I would be devastated if you left my employ. Max, I would love to hire you on as my personal security advisor and private investigator. You can tell me who in your pack—that you belong to, right?—might be able to fill my other household staff positions—wolf only, of course. Would that be acceptable? You and Becky, if things are working out for you, could have the house she lives in now as a home of your own."

"I'll have to talk to my boss, and I'll have to make sure it's okay with Becky to move in with her, but yeah, I'm all for it." Max reached over and squeezed Becky's hand.

She was over the moon with the news, and yeah, she was ready for it!

"We need to put security cameras up all over the place so that we can be sure your staff, who live on the property, can also run as wolves when they are off duty," Max said.

Pamela nodded. "I was hoping I was right in setting up the blind date between you and Max."

"Why him? And not someone else in the agency?" Becky asked.

"Remember the day when I was talking to you about the kind of guys who appeal to us—physically? I know there's not much to that as far as making a connection, but that was my start. All the men in Ryan's agency had photos on the agency site. I just looked them up, found the three who weren't married, saw that Max had been a Navy SEAL, and because of my near drowning experience—that still haunts me—I just thought he would be perfect to keep you safe."

"What if I had left you instead of any of us telling you about this? What if Christopher hadn't been a wolf?" Becky asked.

"I might have lost you as my personal assistant, though I had hoped not. As far as Christopher was concerned, I knew in my heart I wanted him no matter who he was, what he was doing. It just didn't matter as long as he felt the same for me. Max was really only supposed to find him for me. Beyond that, I wanted to renew our dream. But I'm glad Christopher's a wolf too. It's like living with this secret forever and finally being relieved to know others not only believe it but are some of the same kind and accept me.

"I–I think you and I need to discuss more of this alone, Christopher. Becky and Max, you have a good night. Max, thanks for finding Christopher for me. Becky will have my finance officer pay for your services tomorrow. I hope the two of you have some plans for tonight. I think Christopher and I do," Pamela said.

"There's no charge for the services I provided," Max said. "Just a welcome to our pack."

Christopher smiled and it was truly a happy smile. Becky thought things would work out between them, if they were honest with each other and they showed each other how much they cared. But for now? She and Max were going to have their own party.

And then they said their good nights, and Becky and Max walked to her home.

"I never dreamed I would meet a wolf like you. One who was there to help me with my boss's problems, yet there for me too. Protective. It could have been a disaster when I went to run with you as a wolf if I had been alone and had to face the cougar," Becky said.

He smiled at her. "You are so fierce as a wolf, it scared me. But I would have worried about you if you'd been walking alone as a human. Then you could have been in trouble. Once a predator like that thinks you are supper, you have to be fiercer than it, bigger, scarier, show you will win in a battle between the two of you."

"That's true. It might have turned out differently if I had wanted to strip off my clothes and fight him as a wolf if you hadn't been there for me."

He agreed. "So, about us—"

"When are you moving in? Permanently?"

He smiled and kissed her. "As soon as you say the word."

"I'm ready. It's amazing how many things can fill your life and keep you busy, except for the one thing you *really* need in it. I was so busy doing things for Pamela, I hadn't realized I needed more. You are that for me."

"I feel the same way about you. When we had another PI join our agency, he was seeing a wolf that I thought I might have a chance with. But the two were a couple from the beginning. So when I met you, the feeling was mutual. That we had something going for us that I've never had with any other she-wolf. I feel I can let down my hair when I'm around you."

She chuckled. "If your hair was longer. I can talk to you about anything and I feel comfortable, not judged. I enjoy being with you like this, or just taking walks, eating, playing. It's added a whole new dimension to my world."

"Yeah, if anyone had told me going on a blind date would end like this, when here I thought you were human, I would never have believed it."

"When you were in the service, did you have a lot of dangerous missions to go on?" she asked Max as they entered her house and shut and locked the door.

"Yeah. I stayed in until I retired, then started working for Ryan. As many years as we live, we have to be so careful about exposing the fact we live so long and don't age as quickly as humans."

"Well, I'm glad you left the service, ended up working for Ryan, and Pamela decided you were the one she wanted to have date me. I want you. I love you, Max," Becky said, running her hands over his dress shirt, toeing off her heels.

"I love you, and if you're truly ready for a mating, no more waiting, I'm all for it." He yanked off his shoes.

"I am."

"Good." He cupped her face and began kissing her mouth with gentle presses, then conquering, as if he'd found the one he'd wanted and he was claiming her. But she kissed him passionately right back, letting him know she wanted the same of him—to have him for always. He was smart, wily, protective, and loyal, and she needed that in a man. It was the kind of relationship her parents had and she'd always wanted. Loving, caring, interested in what the other was doing. Yet for her, it was the hot passion between them that stirred her blood too, making her want more. Not just the unconsummated sex but fully committing to a mate—Max, her mate.

He began to unbutton her blouse, but he was still kissing her mouth, and she began unbuttoning his shirt, ready to strip him down and get to the nitty-gritty. She pulled his shirt out of his trousers, bared his shoulders, and kissed his solid pecs. He was so sculpted, like art in the flesh. She licked a nipple as he freed her blouse from her skirt and cupped her silky bra-covered breasts, massaging, kissing her lips again as if he didn't want to be separated from that part of her for anything.

Her panties were wet, her body ready for him, and she began to work on his belt. His hands slid down her skirt, searching for the fastener. "Side," she said, their lips parting for a moment, and he glanced down at her skirt.

The zipper was hidden, and she patted her hip, then resumed work on his belt. He found the button above the zipper on her skirt, unfastened it, and pulled down the zipper. Then he slid the formfitting skirt down her hips and let it fall to her feet. She stepped out of the puddle of blue linen fabric and kicked it out of their way.

She slid his zipper down and pulled his trousers off his hips, and he jerked the pants off the rest of the way and kicked them aside. He slid her blouse off her shoulders, still holding onto her blouse, and kissed each shoulder softly. His tongue swiped over her neck, then her jaw, and he kissed her mouth again, his hands sliding her blouse off her shoulders.

Being with him like this, making love to him was the best ever, but this time it would be different. The first time for a mating, and she couldn't wait, yet she was trying to make it last long too. Max didn't seem to be in any rush either. He was kissing her leisurely all over, her breasts still covered in the bra, her arms, shoulders, breastbone, as if he adored every bit of her. He reached down to whip off his socks, then she pulled off his shirt the rest of the way and ran her hands over his pecs, flicking her thumbnails in a gentle caress over his nipples.

He slid his hands around her back and then unfastened her bra and pulled it off her shoulders. Leaning down, he kissed each of her breasts, then licked the nipple of one and suckled, and did the same with the other. They were peaked and sensitive to his touch, her pheromones and his going wild with anticipation. Even his nipples were hardened pearls, and his erection was straining at his boxer briefs. A beautiful sight.

She moved her hand over his erection, felt it pulsing with need, and she inserted her thumbs slowly beneath the waistband of his boxer briefs and began pulling them off, glancing down to see his arousal spring free.

He quickly kicked off his boxer briefs the rest of the way, and then he did the same to her with her panties, a slow seduction— sliding his thumbs beneath the waistband and then slipping them down her hips, but instead of letting her kick them off, he slid them all the way down until she climbed free of them.

He lifted her on the bed and she quickly scooted over so he could join her—all the way this time. She was so ready for this after years of not finding the right wolf for her.

He climbed on top of her, keeping his weight off her like a wolf on the prowl, leaning his head down to kiss her mouth. And then he spread her legs with his knee. He swept his hand down her body in an erotic caress until he found the center of her and began to stroke her nubbin. Pleasure and need pooled in that region, her channel moist for his penetration. His strokes were gentle at first, working her up to the zenith of the climax, pleasuring her in a way no one else had ever done, making her needy and desperate for completion.

She ran her hands over his muscled shoulders, loving the feel of his hot skin beneath her fingertips, but he stole every thought filling her head—the sexy smell of him, their musky scent arousing her, his stroking her nub harder, faster, in an attempt to coax a climax out of her. His gaze was on hers, hot-blooded, lust-filled, and she knew he felt the same way about her as she felt about him. The need, the want, the craving for making this permanent between them.

Her breathing hitched, her heart beating as she felt the rising crescendo of the climax before it hit. And then she cried out with exaltation, "Ohmigod, Max." She swore he was the greatest lover of all time. But that was before she even knew how he could make love to her all the way.

His smile was strained. "Are you ready?" he asked, his voice drenched with lust.

"Yes." They were committing to this, no going back.

He eased into her, slowly, stretching her, making her feel the oneness between them, the connection even greater. He started to thrust, slowly at first, building up steam, deepening the penetration, then he began to kiss her again like he needed to touch every inch of her while he made love to her. To show her how much he cared about her.

She was running her hands over his back in long, sweeping caresses, kissing him, tonguing him, showing him she felt the same way about him.

With that one act of penetration, they had made the commitment to be together forever. He continued to thrust, and she ran her heel in gentle caresses over his leg, and then he was coming, pausing, thrusting, pausing again, as if he was trying to hold on, to experience the wonder of it being their first mating, then thrusting again.

This time he came in an explosive rush, heating her insides, his heart and hers beating hard, but he wasn't finished as he continued to pump into her and rub his body against hers now, kissing her like she was the one he loved most of all.

She enjoyed the closeness, the love they had for each other, and she felt she could stay like this in his arms and never part.

He kissed her finally, pulled out of her, and moved off her. Then they cuddled and their relationship had changed again. From one blind date, not even knowing the other was a wolf, to falling in love and mating for life. She couldn't be happier.

All the rest? Figuring out what to do about his place, telling her folks—oh, she needed to do that right away, well, just a lot of things they had to do. But for now, she wanted to bask in the glow of their lovemaking and snuggle with her wolf.

When they finally woke, they made love in the shower, and then once they were dressed, she wanted to call her parents and her sister and brother and let them know she and Max were now mated.

"I'm calling my parents to let them know about us." Once she called her mom, she said, "Hey, Max and I are mated wolves now."

"Honey! She and Max did it!" her mother shouted to her father.

Becky smiled and kissed Max's cheek while he waited to hear how that went over while she put her phone on speaker.

"You didn't bring him here to meet us first," her mother scolded.

Her dad was on the speakerphone then. "You didn't need our approval. We know you made the right decision."

"That's true. We want you to come over for dinner and celebrate the occasion," her mother said. "Tomorrow evening? Can you both get away?"

"We have the time off." Becky realized she needed to tell her boss it was a done deal. Then she wondered how things were going between Pamela and Christopher.

"Okay, come over for dinner then. Have you told your brother and sister yet?" her mom asked.

"Not yet. I need to call them and my boss, and Max needs to let his pack leaders know the good news."

"What goes around, comes around," her mom said to them. "I was telling your dad that the other day. Here we thought we would never get any of you three mated to a wolf. But saving Pamela when she was a girl set the whole thing in motion. It might not have seemed like the right thing to do in the beginning—to some people—but it all worked out in the end."

"I couldn't agree with you more," Max said. "I can't wait to meet all of you." He kissed Becky's cheek.

"We'll see you at six," her mother said. "Oh, and when we can schedule a dinner with Pamela and Christopher"—as Becky had been happy to tell her parents that Christopher was a wolf and Pamela was going to become one of them finally—"we'll have them over as a reunion of sorts."

"I'm sure she'll want to do the same with you," Becky said.

"Welcome to the family, Max," her dad said. "We'll have to get some fishing in with my son, Dale."

"I would like that, sir."

After they congratulated Max and Becky again, they finally ended the call.

"I'll call my pack leaders," Max told Becky.

"Afterward, I'll call my sister and brother and then let Pamela know." She realized now that she didn't want to just talk to the parties she needed to by herself. She needed her mate there so he could hear their congratulations too. The same with him talking to his pack leaders.

Then Max wrapped his arm around her and called Ryan. "I'm putting this on speakerphone."

"What's wrong?" Ryan asked, sounding concerned.

Given what they were talking about with Pamela tonight, Becky understood why Ryan might think something was the matter.

"Nothing's wrong. We're mated—Becky and me, so if any single wolves in the pack had ideas, they can forget it."

Becky chuckled. She hadn't expected Max to say that.

Ryan called to Carol and she joined him on the speakerphone. "They're mated—Max and Becky."

"Oh, that's wonderful. I just knew it would work out for the two of you," Carol said.

Then they explained about what Pamela and Christopher had agreed to do.

"We're so glad about Christopher and Pamela too. We'll have a pack celebration, and everyone will be invited—your family,

Becky, Pamela and Christopher, and of course our pack members. It will be great," Carol said.

Which made Becky think about her family. Would they want to join the pack too?

After they ended the call, she called her sister and brother on a conference call and gave them the happy news.

"We knew it was coming to this," Dale said, "and we're glad for it."

Natalie laughed. "I'm so happy to hear the news. I hope that we'll be seeing a lot of you in the future."

"Now that we have the land to run free on as wolves, you all can come over and join us," Becky said.

"What about the pack in Green Valley? Are you joining it?" Natalie asked.

"Absolutely, and the pack leaders are having a big celebration for us and for Pamela and Christopher, so I'm sure they'll ask you if you want to join the pack too."

"Are there any available bachelors in the pack?" Natalie asked.

Max chimed in then. "Yes, absolutely, and they'll love to meet you."

"What about she-wolves?" Dale asked.

"Yeah, even Rosalind, the pack leader's sister, is available."

Was Max into matchmaking now? Becky hadn't seen Rosalind yet. Max had told her Rosalind had a garden and delivered flowers all over, so Becky hadn't known if she even had a boyfriend.

"We'll see you at dinner tomorrow night at Mom and Dad's," Becky said.

When they all said their goodbyes, she called Pamela last. "Hi, it's Becky. Max and I are mated." She was dying to know if Pamela and Christopher were holding off or if he'd bitten her to turn her.

"Oh, I'm so glad. Christopher is at a business meeting—I know, an emergency night meeting—dealing with some issues I was having. I'll let him know at once. He'll be as thrilled as I am."

"Thanks. If the pack leaders haven't already told you, they'll be having a celebration for you and Christopher and for Max and me with the whole pack."

"I've got an incoming call. That might be them. I look forward to it. Enjoy your day off tomorrow. Your gift from me. And if you need any more time off, just let me know."

"Thanks, Pamela. My parents, Robyn and William, want you to come to dinner one night too, to meet you now that you're all grown up."

Pamela laughed. "I would love that. And when I can have dinner out with your family, I'm paying."

"Did Christopher turn you?"

"Yeah. So you'll need to schedule engagements according to the phases of the moon for me now."

"Yes! Oh, I'm so glad you're one of us," Becky said, Max echoing her sentiment.

"We will do everything to make the transition work as smoothly as it can for you," Max said.

"Thanks, Max, Becky. I knew I could count on the two of you."

Then they ended the call, and they were done with business.

"Do you want to run as wolves?" Becky asked Max.

"Yeah, let's do this." He took her in his arms and hugged and kissed her. "Then we return to make love."

"You read my mind."

Before long, they were running through the dark woods, not on the trail that Becky had made and taken for the three years she'd been here, but they were making their own trails now. *Together.*

The next night, Becky took Max with her to meet her parents and sister. Her mother had put on a lavish feast of roast, carrots, potatoes, broccoli, gravy, and she'd even made a cake. Becky's sister,

Natalie, was smiling big-time at Max, as if she wished she'd had a blind date with the hunky Navy SEAL.

Her brother, Dale, shook his hand and smiled. "We wondered what made you so special when Becky fell so hard for you so quickly."

"We just hit it off," Becky said. "We chased off a cougar together, like the same movies, enjoy playing with each other as wolves. I love helping him with his cases and he's totally accommodating, which is refreshing. I love him with all my heart, and I couldn't imagine not being with him."

"I never thought I would find a she-wolf who can help me solve mystery cases. I love puzzle-solving and I would never have believed my blind date would be helping me to find a missing dog—one of the cases I was working on. Or that she would be checking me out to see if I could handle a case for her boss, though she didn't even realize that was what she was doing."

"No, I was too busy thinking about next dates and where this might lead," Becky said.

"To mated bliss," Max said. "I couldn't be happier that you chose me."

"I feel the same way about you for me."

"So this all came about in truth because Pamela knew Becky's mother was a wolf and had rescued her, and then hired Becky and thought you were a wolf too?" Becky's dad asked as they sat down to the meal.

"Yeah. It was a mystery I had to keep unraveling. The only thing that wasn't a mystery was my attraction to Becky. Once I'd met her, I just couldn't think of anything else. Well, my job, sure, but I was fortunate that my job often entailed spending more time with Becky. I think Pamela planned it that way."

"We gave Becky such a hard time about going on a blind date, even if her boss was the one who had set it up," her sister said.

"Yeah, you should have seen the last blind date I went on. It was not good," her brother said. "So we thought it would turn out the same for Becky."

"Well, you know I went out with your dad on a blind date. Not the kind like you went on. At least with him, I knew he would be a wolf. We had so much fun. We knew that it was fate," Becky's mother said.

"I still don't want to go on another," her brother said. "The problem is that we need to have a dating service for wolves."

"Oh, yeah, now that's something that you should set up," her sister said.

Becky laughed. "Mom, you never told us you went on a blind date with Dad."

"Yeah, it was just something we never thought we would do. After meeting your dad, I ended up rescuing Pamela as a young girl, and after that, your dad and I mated. He thought the world of me for saving the girl. He'd been at my house that day, planning to have lunch. We had the meal cooking in the slow cooker, and he was working on a cake for later when I heard a girl call out that she was 'queen of the ice.' I told your dad I had to go and check it out. He was about to pull the cake out of the oven, but it had to bake just a few more minutes, so he couldn't go with me right away.

"As a wolf, I had watched her before when she'd play on the ice, an only child, no supervision, worried she might fall through the pond during the spring thaw. Running as a wolf was the fastest way for me to get there. When I arrived, she saw me, the ice cracked with a deafening sound to our ears—and she went into the water. I didn't have any time to think. I just reacted. In retrospect, I wouldn't have done anything any differently. In the back of my mind, I knew the danger we were in when I did it, but I figured that she was young enough, and since she had suffered from hypothermia, we could convince her that she hadn't seen what she thought she had. I was trying to run her back to the house, but she was soaking wet, chilled to the bone, and so was I. That's when I howled as a human for your dad to come and help me. He met me three-quarters of the way home and took her from me so I could shift, stay out of sight, and head home and warm myself at the same time."

"Apparently, she knew just what had occurred all along," Becky said, "and in the end, it was lucky for us. She joined our kind and found her mate. And I found mine."

The family agreed.

Max squeezed Becky's hand in agreement. "And I found mine."

She loved him and she was glad he loved her just as much in return.

EPILOGUE

WHEN BECKY AND MAX MET WITH HER PARENTS AND PAMELA and Christopher for dinner at her parents' home, it was a tearful but joyous reunion.

Becky's mom hugged Pamela. "I hadn't mated yet when I rescued you in the pond. You don't know how many times I watched you as a wolf from the woods, making sure you remained safe until you returned home. I could never understand how your parents would allow you to roam through the woods on your own and play on the frozen pond or even go swimming by yourself. So I observed you in case you needed rescuing. Then that one day, I heard you playing, calling out to your imaginary friends, declaring you were 'queen of the ice,' and I had to watch over you. I never expected you to fall through the ice!"

"That was her maternal instinct," her dad said, "before her own children were even conceived. I knew she'd make the perfect mate."

"And the perfect mom," Becky said, her siblings agreeing.

"Did you ever wish you hadn't rescued me because of all the trouble I caused for you?" Pamela asked, giving Becky's dad a hug too.

"No, never. I would never have forgiven myself if I hadn't at least tried to save you." Robyn began serving up the chicken legs and baked potatoes while Becky and her sister and brother began pitching in.

Pamela smiled. "I loved you both for it. Truly. All I could talk about was how much you had meant to me. My parents got sick of hearing of it. Even so, my dad wanted to reward you for saving me.

They made sure my nanny wouldn't allow me out on my own any further, which was a pain, but I still sneaked out when I could, all because I wanted to see the wolf again who had saved me."

"I was there. Watching. But you never went on the pond in winter again."

Pamela smiled. "Nope, I learned my lesson that time."

Everyone was overjoyed to welcome Pamela—and Christopher—to the family, because in Robyn saving her, Pamela had become part of it. Becky realized Pamela was like a big sister to her, and not just her employer any longer.

In the weeks that followed, Becky and Max had set up house at her place, and he had sold his own home to another pack member looking to have a home on the boundary of the pack's property. Pamela had replaced all her former staff with wolves. Her former staff was happy to receive all the money she had given them to start new jobs, and everyone had found new employment because of her praiseworthy accounts of their service—except for two who were happy to retire.

Becky was thrilled that Pamela had found her husband, her mate, and had become part of a wolf family, finally living the dream that had haunted her for so many years. Even Becky's parents and her sister and brother were glad to welcome her into the family after Robyn and William had saved her life so long ago.

But more than anything, Becky was thrilled to have found her own mate—on a blind date, no less.

Max was so thrilled to be working at the new job for Pamela, another fellow wolf, and so thrilled to be part of the bigger family.

Ryan and Carol had wanted to grow their pack in Green Valley. Instead of losing some of their wolves to work on Pamela's staff in Mountain View, they had effectively extended their pack territory to her city. All of them wanted to take part in celebrations with the rest of the pack. That wasn't something Pamela had anticipated, and she was overjoyed to be included in all these new experiences.

Best of all, she was planning her own wolf party to be held at her estate.

═══════════

Max would always be grateful to Pamela for bringing him together with Becky, the love of his life, his mate forever, and the joy they shared. Not a minute went by that he didn't thank his lucky stars for that first blind date that had changed so many lives. And all in a good way.

He loved Becky and she adored him, and now when they went on runs through the woods, they often saw other wolves of her staff, and Pamela and Christopher themselves, running too. The cougar that had chased them that one day? He was out of there for good. The wolves ruled!

Acknowledgments

Thanks to my editor, Deb Werksman, who makes it possible for me to share more of my wolf tales and now even some jaguar shifter tales. To the editorial staff and the cover artists who design such beautiful covers. Thanks to Bonnie Gill, Donna Fournier, and Loretta Grucz Melvin who all helped me brainstorm some issues. And to my fans from all across the world who offer suggestions for titles and which characters they want to see get their happily-ever-afters next, send pictures of hunky men and of wolves and jaguars, and tell me why they've fallen in love with my wolves and jaguars—you continue to be my inspiration!

About the Author

Bestselling and award-winning author Terry Spear has written over sixty paranormal romance novels and four medieval Highland historical romances. *Heart of the Wolf*, her first werewolf romance, was named a 2008 *Publishers Weekly* Best Book of the Year, and her subsequent titles have garnered high praise and hit the *USA Today* bestsellers list. A retired officer of the U.S. Army Reserves, Terry lives in Spring, Texas, where she is working on her next werewolf romance, continuing with her Highland medieval romances, and having fun with her young adult novels. When she's not writing, she's photographing everything that catches her eye, making teddy bears, and playing with her Havanese puppies. For more information, please visit terryspear.com or follow her on Twitter @TerrySpear. She is also on Facebook at facebook.com/terry.spear and on Wordpress at terryspear.wordpress.com.

TRUE WOLF

New York Times and *USA Today* bestselling author Paige Tyler's STAT: Special Threat Assessment Team fight paranormal enemies and fall in love once again.

As STAT agent and wolf shifter Caleb Lynch investigates a case of stolen nuclear weapons, Brielle Fontaine is his hottest lead. Brielle's supernatural abilities are a force to be reckoned with, making her one of STAT's biggest threats and a most useful ally. He'll have to get close to her, but when the team comes under fire from supernatural terrorists, the growing attraction between them could lead to something much more explosive…

"Unputdownable… Whiplash pacing, breathless action, and scintillating romance."
—K.J. Howe, International bestselling author, for *Wolf Under Fire*

For more info about Sourcebooks's books and authors, visit:
sourcebooks.com

WILD COWBOY WOLF

Cowboys by day, wolf shifters by night—don't miss the thrilling
Seven Range Shifters series from acclaimed author Kait Ballenger

Grey wolf warrior Dakota Nguyen has everything she ever wanted, but
when the daily grind gets lonely, her best friend, security technologist
Blaze Carter, always knows how to cheer her up. Lately, she has a feeling
that there might be something more between them. But even as friend-
ship turns to passion, a hidden enemy threatens to destroy the pack and all
that Blaze and Dakota fight so hard to protect. Now, there could be deadly
consequences to acting on their desires…

"Kait Ballenger is a treasure you don't want to miss."
—Gena Showalter, *New York Times* bestselling author

PRETTY LITTLE LION

Sexy, action-packed paranormal romantic suspense—the Third Shift series from award-winning author Suleikha Snyder

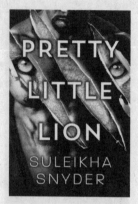

Lion shifter and Third Shift co-founder Elijah Richter is on a mission: seduce arms dealer Mirko Aston's gorgeous girlfriend, use her as an entry point to the organization, and discover what the global terrorist is planning. It should be simple. Then he meets Meghna Saxena-Saunders—influencer, celebutante, ex-wife to a handsome Hollywood hotshot, and a highly trained assassin—and all his plans are blown out of the water.

"Clever, romantic, heroic, and filled with hope for a better future. Suleikha Snyder has crafted an amazing world."
—Alisha Rai, award-winning author, for *Big Bad Wolf*

For more info about Sourcebooks's books and authors, visit:
sourcebooks.com

A MOST UNUSUAL DUKE

A delicious mix of Regency romance and shapeshifting
adventure in the exciting new Shapeshifters of the
Beau Monde series from author Susanna Allen

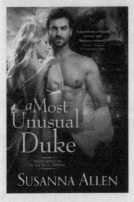

The Prince Regent insists his cousin and fellow bear shifter Arthur
Humphries, the Duke of Osborn, take a mate to ensure the continua-
tion of their species. After all, Arthur is an Alpha, so he must set a good
example. The duke would very much prefer to continue his comfortable
bachelor lifestyle, but just because he will marry Beatrice, the widowed
Marchioness of Castleton, does not mean he will fall in love, right?

**"Sparkling wit, scrumptious chemistry, and
characters who will go straight to your heart!"**
—Grace Burrowes, *New York Times* and *USA Today* bestselling
author

For more info about Sourcebooks's books and authors, visit:
sourcebooks.com

Also by Terry Spear